Losing Lucy

By

Ian McKnight

<u>1997</u>

CHAPTER 1

Heavy rain slanting through the lead grey sky. The few mourners huddled in small groups seeking shelter under umbrellas as they hurry through the leaf-strewn car park towards the chapel. Under the cover of the porch I wait to greet them. Brief hellos. Handshakes and the occasional hug. Conversation difficult at times like this. Taking a last drag at my cigarette and casually flicking it into the neatly-tended shrubbery. Where it catches on a leaf, and is quickly extinguished by the persisting downpour. Duncan ushering the guests into the dimly lit room where the coffin lay. Of polished pine with a small brass plaque, it shows no trace of dust nor fingerprints. She would have approved. Glorious displays of flowers in abundance, fragrant fresh and scentless silk, arranged in large ornate vases everywhere. Shining dark oak and thick plush carpets. Heavy velvet drapes. All these places are furnished alike. The stuff must all come from the same funereal mail-order catalogue. Funeral Parlours R Us. I take my place at the end of the front row, Duncan at my side. Aware that all eyes are on me. Scrutinising my every move, gesture, and expression. A certain protocol has to be followed here. Solemnity rules! Take care to suppress a latent fart. And don't look the vicar in the eye, especially the left one which tends to wander independently of the right. Hope to God Duncan hasn't noticed. If he starts giggling, I'm done for. Please, Duncan, don't say anything to make me laugh. Not now. Memories of an earlier ceremony many years ago when Duncan stood by my side mimicking the clergyman's words with his own litany.

"Daily Bebuggered, we are gaberdine today in the presents on our Lawn..."

Repressing a smile as the vicar begins his toneless address, telling the gathering of how a beautiful, vivacious young woman of 40 had been cruelly torn from the ones who loved her by cancer, how she fought bravely to the end, how she eventually sought comfort in the Lord and accepted Him as her Saviour.

"Bullshit!"

I glance round nervously. No-one has heard. It wouldn't do to upset the faithful. But Lucy had never been a believer. She had cried for God and Jesus only when the pain had been intense and unbearable. I remembered the last few weeks. The long days and nights as she slipped in and out of consciousness. I'd slept in a chair at the bedside longing to take her fragile body in my arms but afraid to do so lest I crushed her skeletal frame. Until the night she'd called to me, holding out her thin pale arms to embrace me for the last time. And I'd hugged her as the life ebbed away. Now her pain was over. Soon she would be only dust and ashes, a scoop-full of which I would take with me in the small discreet urn the funeral parlour had recommended as "very popular these days". I had bought it immediately with the proviso that the small adhesive label underneath which bore the legend "Made in China" should be removed.

At a sign from the vicar, I take a deep breath and rise to my feet. Head high, shoulders back, I walk forward to take my place at the lectern. Clearing my throat to address the gathering of relatives and friends many of whom I swear I've never laid eyes on before. Perhaps they worked with Lucy or came to our wedding. Or maybe they just like funeral services, and the free nosh afterwards. Lucy's Aunt Edna there at the back, wearing the same black dress she wore at our wedding, and the same mournful expression.

"Thank you all for coming. Lucy would be pleased. When we knew she was dying, we discussed many things. Often, we just talked about the things we had done together. But there were also practical matters to consider. One of which was her funeral service. It was Lucy's wish that it should not be a solemn affair. But that those who knew her would come and meet and think and talk about her life, not her death. And that they would afterwards attend a party in her honour, at the White Lion. And, please note. It is to be a party. Not a wake."

Pause for a second or two as the insistent small voice from a child at the back yells 'Mum I need to poo.'

Clearing my throat again, and seeing the vicar cast an anxious glance at the clock, I continue. I want to get this over quickly, but with due regard for decorum and Lucy's wishes.

"Before she died, I promised Lucy I would recite the words of a song at her service. She would have liked me to sing it, but you would all have walked out. It was her favourite, and the words had a special significance for us. Please bear with me. I am finding this a little difficult."

Pausing to wipe away a tear. Clearing the throat once more.

"The first time ever I saw your face...."

Not even having to look at the words I had written down previously, I recite the lyrics perfectly, faultlessly, pausing only to stifle the sobs that threaten to well up into my throat.

"...like the trembling heart of a captive bird..."

Remembering how my own heart had pounded as her wasted body slumped in my arms. Thinking how the days before had raced to their inevitable conclusion, and how those since seemed to be interminable. The letters sent and the responses. The cards and messages of sympathy. The awkward phone calls where neither party knew what to say. Except Duncan, the Imperturbable, who could cope with any manner of slings and arrows of outrageous fortune. And fire back some of his own. He'd simply dispensed with the formalities, offered his sympathy, and then reeled off a string of dirty jokes which left me convulsed with laughter.

"The first time ever I saw your face."

Silence at first. Then applause from Duncan, joined by others, and finally a standing ovation, as I walk wet-eyed back to my place at Duncan's side. His heartfelt words.

"Well done, mate. I'm proud of you. Lucy would have been too."

And then the tears finally come, welling up from deep within and streaming down my cheeks as the vicar presses the button to set the conveyor in motion and the tinny background music from the concealed speakers plays its solemn welcome to the furnace.

When the music's over, turn out the Light.

At the door, shaking hands and accepting hugs from friends and relatives mouthing platitudes, to which I reply,

"See you at the pub."

That was Lucy's idea. It was one of the things we had discussed. Her party. Her "Leaving Do", she called it.

A final few words with the vicar, and a shake of his cold, damp hand. He had refused the invitation to join us at the Lion, believing it was not in keeping with the solemnity of the occasion. Solemnity be damned. Let's get rat-arsed falling-over drunk!

The White Lion is heaving, disco blaring loud enough to wake the dead. Pushing through the crowd towards the bar only to find the awful Eversos barring my way. Our neighbours, Mr and Mrs Everson, a sanctimonious pair with the annoying habit of finishing off each other's sentences. Lucy used to like them. I always thought they were boring and intrusive.

"The service was..."

"Yes. The lyrics to a song. Lucy's favourite. By Roberta Flack."

"I see."

"If you'll please excuse me..."

"Of course. But Ray. Please come around and talk to us. Any time you feel the need. We're always there."

"Thanks, Everso. Please excuse me."

Extricating myself, and making for the bar. Passing faces I don't recognise. Then the grinning face of Lucy's boss, the lecherous Jonathon, his pretensions betrayed by his cheap suit with its shiny arse and beer-soaked elbows.

"Here, Ray. There's a pint for you."

"Thanks."

"Good party, mate. Plenty totty."

"Yes."

"So, what are you going to do now?"

"Have a drink."

"No. I mean, what are you going to do with the rest of your life?"

"Take up masturbation."

"Ha, ha. No, seriously."

"I'm going to take up masturbation."

"Well, I hope you pull it off. Get it? Masturbation. Pull it off."

"Yes, Jonathon. With plenty of practice, and a bit of luck, I hope I can surpass even you and become the World's Biggest Wanker. Thanks for the drink."

"Charming."

When Lucy had first started at the office, he'd flirted with her immediately. It didn't bother her at first. Until one day he patted her bottom and offered her a lift home. She smiled and accepted. And when he stopped in a layby and took out his hard dick, she grabbed it and squeezed as hard as she could, raking his balls with her long fingernails until she drew blood and he begged for mercy. She'd taught him a lesson and he never touched her again. But it didn't stop him harassing the other girls in the office.

Party livening up. Young girls dancing to the disco with its flashing lights and pounding music. Jonathon, a lascivious smile on his face and a dribble of spit at the corner of his mouth, ogling the teenage tits. I'm engaged in light banter with friends and drinking heavily, avoiding the Eversos who are doing their best to catch my eye. Instead turning to Lucy's parents, she wet-eyed while his are becoming distinctly glassy.

"You two OK?"

"Can't say we approve, Ray. But we know it's what Lucy wanted, so I'm going to make damn sure we enjoy it. Come on, Ma. Let's jive!"

"Aye. Come on. Let's show these kids how to dance."

And to the strains of Eddie Cochran's "C'mon Everybody" they jive and bop and twist the night away, Mr. Summer pausing for frequent refreshment of the Scottish Malt variety. They are a devoted couple, who had accepted me, though with initial misgivings, into the warm bosom of their family as Lucy's choice of partner. Over the years they had become accustomed to my eclectic brand of humour and, though not always understanding it, they had tolerated me purely because they, and everybody else, could see how much their daughter loved me, and how I in turn absolutely adored her. I never thought much of them, though. Pretentious and middle-class. I can't believe they're actually dancing and appear to be enjoying themselves when I've just had their only daughter cremated. They're the last people I would expect to see entering into the spirit of things. I was half expecting them to overrule Lucy's wishes and demand ham and cucumber sandwiches cut into neat little triangles with the crust removed, and tea served in the best china.

Still, judging by the amount he's consumed, he won't remember anything about it tomorrow, but I bet Mrs Prim-and-Proper Summer will remind him for the rest of his miserable golf-and bridge-club life.

"Ray?"

"Yeah?"

"You all right?"

"Fine, Duncan. Just thinking, that's all."

"Yeah, I know. Listen, Ray, if ever you need company, or just somebody to talk to, Elaine and I are always there for you. You know that, don't you? Don't ever forget, mate. OK?"

"Cheers, Duncan. Have a drink."

"I'll get 'em. Two bitters over here, pal! Two bitters, eh! That's me and you to a T, innit?"

Duncan was right. He'd been my best mate for over thirty years, and my Best Man. We had shared so many experiences, from early teenage fumblings behind the Mecca dancehall, through drunken escapades and student LSD experiments to the bliss and heartache of marriage and domestic suburban life. Though Duncan was a year my senior, even as teenagers we had been equals. Where Duncan had led me into drugs and drink, I had influenced Duncan's musical and literary tastes. Each had been the catalyst for the other, as our excesses grew wilder. Though now burdened with wife, kids, mortgage and overdraft, Duncan had never changed, nor ever would. The eternal teenager, provider for wife and offspring, Duncan was and always would be a serial philanderer, and my hero. Not that I would ever wish to emulate him; I was too devoted to Lucy for that, and secretly Duncan wished he could have turned out like his best mate.

The beers arrive and we silently toast one another.

"Where's Elaine?"

"Probably powdering her wotsit."

"Cleanest wotsit in the north of England."

"I'll say. I personally inspect it every night to ensure it remains in prize-winning condition. And I can say without fear of contradiction that it passes muster and that the white powder on my tongue is talc and not cocaine. For I felt duty-bound to hold an impromptu inspection in the back of the taxi on the way here. And made him drive twice round the block until the deed was done. Took us ages to disentangle her wrists from the rear seat belts. And the bastard kept the meter running."

The party now in full swing. And what's this? Raucous noises from outside. Profanities and belches. And the doors caving inwards under the weight of a group of revellers from the Irish Club on Hayward Street who may have smelt the free food, and gate-crashed the party. Duncan immediately to the fore, shouting "Rammy!" Mr. Summer to the rear, urging and cajoling all able-bodied guests to repel the boarders, while Mrs Summer darts to the Ladies. The bar staff, on three pounds sixty an hour, summon up all their courage and take refuge in the office, the manager following them, pausing only to take the till drawer with him. I take the opportunity to slide behind the vacant bar to select a bottle of fine Malt for intended use as a missile. Instead pouring myself a large glass as mayhem prevails. Duncan in festive mood shouting "Fuck the Pope" and "Guinness is shit". Punches and glasses thrown. Shouts of "For St. George and the Queen!" and "English bastards!". In the midst of the chaos, a young girl in tears screaming that someone has grabbed her tit. The culprit Jonathon smirking in the corner, not one to miss the chance of a sly grope. The DJ catches the mood and plays 'Saturday night's alright for fighting'. And Duncan leaps on to a table, glass in hand raised aloft and wearing a heavy ashtray of dark green glass as a crown playing Olivier playing Henry V urging dear friends once more into the breach until a huge grimy Irish fist strikes him in the stomach. Whereupon he pours the contents of his pint glass over his assailant's head, accusing him of being a philistine with no respect for a great thespian talent. As the strains of Chumbawamba chanting 'I get knocked down' blare out from the sound system. And finally, the police arrive and cart away the insurgents along with the blood-soaked Duncan and a prone Mr. Summer felled by a stray beer bottle. What a swell party this is! Lucy would surely have disapproved. Probably turning in her urn.

CHAPTER 2

The courthouse of soot-blackened brown stone, full yet cold the next morning, where charges are read and the miscreants bound over to keep an unlikely peace. After which Duncan invites the Irish to join him for a pint at the scene of the previous night's carnage. They decline the offer, but shake his hand all the same, declaring him an honorary Irishman and a crazy bastard. Duncan, well pleased, decides to celebrate his new status by going for a drink anyway, since Elaine would need time on her own to forgive him his momentary lapse into minor misdeed.

Glad of the company, I go along with him and by mid-afternoon we're both drunk. Wandering from pub to pub, we settle in a backstreet watering hole as rain sweeps the dirty streets. The pig-faced, pot-bellied barman eyes us suspiciously, noting the bloodstains on Duncan's shirt collar.

"Cut myself shaving", explains the unshaven Duncan.

Settling into a corner seat, Duncan poring over the juke box selections until his face lights up with delight. Soon "Street fighting man" plays through the speakers and the barman promptly turns down the volume, ignoring Duncan's protestations.

"Can't beat the Stones."

"Agreed. Soothing and relaxing?"

"Indeed. Can't listen to this without thinking about some of the nights out we used to have."

"Me too."

"So, what you going to do?"

"I don't know."

"Elaine and I have to go back home at the weekend. I'm sorry but we've a business to run."

"I know. It's good of you to have come all this way."

"Have you thought of moving back up north?"

"It's crossed my mind."

"Well, think about it. You don't know many people down here. All your old mates are in Yorkshire. Do you good to meet up with some of them again for a night out. Besides, the beer's like piss down here."

"Overpriced, too."

"Indeed."

"I suppose I could go back to Scarsby. The flat hasn't been sold yet. Been on the market for six months and not a single offer."

Each taking a long swig and silently sharing reminiscences. Of times when we were young and at the centre of the universe. Never looking ahead but enjoying the now. Experiencing, savouring and adapting. Life had been a million laughs, and we both smile as we recall those hedonistic days.

"Hey, Ray. Do you remember that night we were drinking in that pub when that gang of teddy boys walked in?"

"Funny. I was just thinking about that."

"Jesus. We could have been killed."

Duncan dissolving in a fit of giggles as I mentally replay the event. As was often the case in those days, we would visit new hostelries regularly on Saturday nights rather than using a 'local'. And one summer evening we'd found ourselves at the bar of a pub on the outskirts of town. Drinking steadily, laughing and joking and eyeing up the local talent. When in walked a gang of five men, in their early thirties, dressed in uniform drape jackets, drainpipe trousers and brothel-creepers. Bootlace ties and greased hair. Enormous quiffs and DA's. Duncan, mouth filled with beer, was unable to contain his mirth at the sight, and drenched the barman with a fine spray of bitter. Teddy boys glaring at the two youths who dared to mock their peacock-proud appearance, each glare producing ever wilder hoots of hysterical laughter from the pair who launched into a nonsensical conversation when the manager asked them to quieten down.

"Tutti Frutti?"

"Bebopalubop!"

"Ramalamadingdong."

"Doowop!"

Approached by a sneering ted, so close his quiff touched Duncan's forehead. I took the glass from my partner's hand and set it on the bar. Landlord quickly on the scene.

"Settle down, lads. Don't start any trouble in here."

"C'mon, George. You know us better than that. We come in every week. Have you ever known us cause any bother? It's these two kids that are the problem."

"Us? We're just out for a laugh and a quiet pint."

"Well, make sure it stays that way. Or you're out!"

"And when you leave, we'll be right behind you."

The final whispered threat from the retreating Lardhead as he rejoined his mates. Who grouped together and discussed tactics, occasionally casting a glance in our direction to reinforce the threat and ensure we didn't slip away unnoticed.

"Shit, Ray! What are we going to do now?"

"Strikes me we're going to take a pasting. Let's get it over with."

We finished our drinks and shouted a loud defiant goodnight to the enemy. Through the back door and across the car park towards the toilet block. A nervous glance over my shoulder confirmed my fears of impending blood and possible fractures.

"Let's face 'em here, Duncan. At least in the open someone might come and break it up before they kill us."

"No. In here. Come on."

Duncan pushing me through the heavy wooden door into the dimly lit Gents. Smell of stale piss and disinfectant. The pair of us pressed tight against the wall behind the door as the enemy burst in. In an instant, Duncan pushed the back-marker hard into his mates, grabbed my arm, switched off the lights and the pair of us shot out of the door, slamming home the steel bolt on the outside. Breathing heavily, hearing shouts and obscenities from within. Duncan shouting defiantly back as we ran across the road and jumped aboard a passing bus. And laughed throughout the journey back to town, grateful for the landlord's habit of bolting and padlocking the toilet block overnight to keep out minor miscreants.

"I wonder if they're still in there?"

"Could be. We'll have to go back someday and see."

"Not on your life!"

"So how about coming back up north? More adventures await."

"Not for me. Those days are over."

"Ray, I know it sounds hard and callous. But you've got to get over Lucy and get on with your life. Or get a new one. It'll take time. But, believe me, it'll happen."

"Maybe. But I'm not ready yet."

"No. Of course not. But you've got to make plans. You've got to look ahead. Lucy wouldn't want you to grieve for the rest of your life."

"I know that. But I've got to come to terms with it all. And it's not easy. Half of my life's been torn away. I... I don't know what I'm going to do. But Lucy did say I should enjoy life after her. It's just, I don't know where to start. It's been a long time since I was free and single."

"Well, you're in luck. I'm just the man to help you. I've been single all my married life. You want another?"

"Please."

A few people wandering in, seeking shelter from the downpour. Shoppers, mainly, and pensioners, two of whom sit at the next table and invite us to join them in a game of dominoes. Duncan unable to resist the challenge, raises the stakes to fifty pence a game. Serious stuff.

"Fives and threes! A man's game. Forget your chess and backgammon. This is it! The ultimate in mental conflict. Cerebral challenge. No room for the faint of heart. Nor the weak in spirit. Double-six down. For four."

"There's eight, then."

"I'll take six."

"And another four."

"Six, again."

"And two."

The battle an hour old, and Duncan and I are each two-fifty down. Duncan leaping to his feet, animated.

"You just pegged three!"

"No, I didn't."

"You did! You pegged three. And only scored two. You're cheating."

"Steady on, lads. It's only a game."

"I don't like cheats!"

"Nobody's cheating, lad. Settle down."

"All right. But I'm watching you."

"One."

"Same one."

"Two."

"No score."

"Similar."

"Three."

"Knocking."

"One."

"No score."

"Two."

"Eight."

Duncan on his feet again, eyes blazing.

"You fuckin' cheat!"

"What's up now, lad?"

"You've already knocked on fives. And then you lay the double."

"You're mistaken, lad."

"Do you think my head buttons up the back, or something? Have I got 'mug' stamped on my forehead?"

"Leave it, lad."

"Leave it, my bollocks!"

Duncan overturning the table. Drink and dominoes everywhere. The barman on the scene, asking us to leave as he dabs at the wet carpet and dries the dominoes on a towel, counting them back into their wooden box. I pick up the scattered coins and drop them into the charity bottle on the bar having first deducted our expenses.

"Jesus, Ray. Look at the state of me now. I'll have to go back to the hotel and change. Then we can continue our musings."

"Not for me, Dunc. I'd better get off home."

"Christ, Ray. You can't leave me now. Elaine will be waiting. I need support. She won't have a go at me if you're there. Come on. Show a little Christian charity. Blessed are the meek and that. And the piss-poor in spirit."

This hastily-booked hotel, which had seen better days. Brick-built in the 70's on the site of an old coaching inn. Reproductions abound in the small reception area, where the receptionist hands Duncan a folded note. From Elaine.

"Duncan,

I have had enough. I've gone home. Give my love to Ray. No doubt you'll be seeing him. Call me tonight. You'd better have a good excuse. You bastard.

Love,

Elaine."

Duncan doing a gleeful little dance in the foyer, watched by a puzzled receptionist.

"What do you think about that? She's gone home and left me, almost all alone in a strange, hostile city. It's no wonder I get into trouble if that's the support I get. She's going through the change, you know. She's had more hot flushes than a curry-house toilet. Let's go up. Help yourself to the mini-bar while I shower and change."

Selecting a small can of beer. Inserting the index finger through the ring-pull, thumb braced opposite for leverage. And pulling, to release foam and a fine spray over the wallpaper. Drain the remainder of the precious liquid and wipe down the wall with a cushion from the cane chair.

Into the hotel bar, where Duncan orders beer and sandwiches. Rare beef with a thin smearing of Dijon mustard, washed down with the watery pint. Duncan spotting two women seated together in a corner.

"Fancy a bit of entertainment tonight, Ray?"

"What sort of entertainment?"

"The sexual sort. A light-hearted romp. Many wicked ways are to be had."

"Not for me, Dunc."

"Come on."

"I'm not ready."

"Part of the rehabilitation process. The juices will flow. I promise."

"No thanks. Besides, I've never been unfaithful to Lucy."

"Ray. You're not being unfaithful. Lucy's gone. Face it. And now she's gone, needs have to be satisfied."

"Comes easy to you, doesn't it? You were unfaithful to Elaine three days after your wedding."

"Who told you that?"

"Lucy. Elaine told her."

"Well, yes. It's true. But it was Elaine's fault. She got sunburnt on our honeymoon and couldn't lie on her back. So, I had to find a substitute. And the Spanish hotel maid was more than adequate. But I didn't know Elaine had found out. She never said anything to me. Anyway, there's no further harm to be done, is there? Might as well be hung for a sheep as a lamb. And tonight, I'm well hung for anything. Play along, Ray, please. Just entertain the tomato-skinner while I exercise the Pink Plunger on her mate."

Joining the ladies at the table, Duncan charming and entertaining, while I sit next to the gap-toothed one, who could indeed skin a tomato through a tennis racket. Nevertheless, not unattractive. Duncan plying them with drinks and risqué patter and inviting them to continue the party in his room. To which they willingly agree. Duncan rubbing his hands in anticipation of rubbing other things.

Raiding the minibar in Duncan's room, as he extracts a small tin from his suitcase and proceeds to roll four huge cigarettes. The tomato skinner throwing up in the bathroom while Duncan kisses and fondles her auburn-haired friend. Pouring vodkas into two glasses, topped up with tonic. Sipping one and offering the other to the pale faced Julie, who politely declines. Gallantly offering to take her home, but she says she'll be all right soon, alcohol sometimes affects her like that, and could she stay. And she sits on the floor next to my chair, watching as Duncan whistles "The Stripper" and Mandy obliges with a raunchy dance routine. Julie's hand on my knee as she watches Duncan struggle out of his clothes, throwing them everywhere. The colour returning rapidly to her cheeks as she begins to breathe heavily. Mandy lying on the bed, hands behind her head, eyes closed, legs apart. Duncan doing a little war dance round the bed, hand to his mouth, going "woo woo woo woo woo", prong pulsating. As Julie leaps to her feet and throws herself on the bed. To bury her face in Mandy's crotch. Licking and sucking, pausing only to tear off her dress and underwear. Duncan circling the bed, erection in hand, prowling, seeking an opening. Which is quickly closed as the girls manoeuvre to perform a sixty-nine. Duncan moving ever closer, spies his chance and slips it in while Julie surfaces for air. And here I am, still seated, drink in hand, desperate to take it out. And plunge it in. Instead finishing my drink and leaving quietly.

CHAPTER 3

The phone ringing. At the unearthly hour of eleven in the morning. Ignoring its persistent call, my head pounding. Eventually dragging myself to the hall to answer.

"Hello?"

"Jesus, Ray. Have I got you out of bed?"

"Yes."

"Sorry, mate. I was just ringing to see if you were OK. Where did you get to last night? You missed one hell of a party. Had to send the night porter for more rubbers. Christ, it was unbelievable! I wish I'd had a camcorder. Could have made a fortune! Jeez, I've had some experiences, but, honest, man, I'm still creaming after this one. Are you OK?"

"Yeah. Duncan. I just felt tired and had a headache, so I went home, that's all."

"Well, listen, Ray. Julie was really keen on you, so I've got her phone number. She wants you to call her. Here, you got a pen? Take this down, 506383, you got that?"

"Yes. I've got it. What about you? You OK? When are you going home?"

"This afternoon, Ray. Got a call in my room this morning. From Elaine. She said if I didn't go back immediately, she'd file for divorce. Well, at least she's still speaking to me. So, two-thirty-seven train. Platform seven. Meet me in the station buffet bar as soon as you can. See you."

Tearing up the piece of paper on which I've scribbled the phone number, and depositing it in the overflowing bin. A long, leisurely warm shower, breakfast of large malt whisky, and a taxi down to the train station. Where Duncan awaits, pacing impatiently.

"Christ, Ray! Where've you been, man?"

"Duncan, I'm sorry. I... I just can't. Well, I just can't go on like this. I'm in mourning for Christ's sake! Lucy's dead, in case you've forgotten. I know she wanted a party when she'd gone, but it can't last forever! And the fact that she's gone doesn't mean she never existed. It doesn't mean I'm free and single and ready to poke anything available. Duncan, we're different now. Things have changed. I love your company, honest. But you have to realise that I need time, on my own, to get over everything."

"Ray. I'm sorry. I understand. I really do! It's just that I tried to take your mind off things. Appeal to the baser instincts, I suppose. And I was wrong. And selfish. Can you forgive me?"

"'Course I can! Come on. Let's have a beer before you go."

Just time for three pints before the train arrives on time. Duncan buying a couple of sausage rolls for the journey, then racing out to the ticket barrier and on to the platform. A heartfelt hug. Genuine tears in Duncan's eyes. Leaning out of the carriage window, shouting, 'don't give up without a fight' and, seeing the red scarves draped round the passengers' necks, screaming 'fuck the United!' as the train pulls slowly away. Leaving behind its diesel fumes and turd on the track.

Say goodbye. It's independence day.

CHAPTER 4

Another sleepless night in the cold unmade bed. Last made by the kind nurse from the hospice after Lucy had been taken to the funeral parlour. She had put on crisp clean sheets. Bending over to flash her long black-seamed legs while tucking in meticulous hospital corners, which I'd crumpled forever during my first night alone of thrashing rolling tossing restlessness. Rising red-eyed and weary with the weak wintry dawn. Splash the face with cold water. Brush the teeth and scrape the tongue of fur. Strong hot coffee in the one remaining clean mug. Sink full of dirty crockery, which will have to be tackled soon. Laundry basket full of dirty clothing, and a separate basket of items to be ironed. Perhaps take on a housekeeper and cleaner. Or shake myself from this self-pitying torpor and just get on with it. I've lived alone before my marriage. Looked after myself then. Cooked, cleaned, washed, ironed. Kept a tidy flat. Marriage had spoiled me. In many ways. Lucy had always accepted, or rather insisted, that it was her role to look after me, and the household. As well as working full-time. And perhaps, one day, becoming a mother too. So much energy, and life. Now ended. Must get a grip. But not today. One more day of mourning. And tomorrow I shall start life anew. Rummage through the wash-basket for the cleanest and least creased of shirts. One here slightly beer-stained, but otherwise acceptable as long as I remember to keep the jacket buttoned. Just rub a little deodorant under the armpits to mask any trace of stale smell. A quick inspection in the mirror. Unshaven but otherwise quite presentable. For a newly-bereaved widower. Shuddering momentarily at the phrase, with which I don't yet feel comfortable but will have to get used to.

Out into the cold morning air, hunching up against the strong breeze blowing in my face. No friendly faces to be seen among these crowds on their way into town. All preoccupied with their own thoughts, too busy to notice my odd socks. One navy, one black, now so conspicuous in daylight.

Presenting myself at the reception desk, from where I am ushered to a seat to wait until the manager is available. Leafing through dog-eared financial journals. Leaflets full of advice on how to invest, interest rates, mortgages and loans. Until finally invited to enter the oak-panelled office with its smiling, welcoming bank manager.

"Mr Light. How nice to see you. May I say how sorry I am to hear of your sad loss. Please accept my deepest sympathy."

"Thank you."

"Well, then. To business. How can I be of service?"

"You've been writing me letters."

"I see. What sort of letters?"

"Letters insisting I come to see you. Reminding me that my account is in the red. Not to write any more cheques. Which the bank will not honour. Usual crap."

"Ah. I see. It's the computers, Mr Light. Nevertheless, they do seem to have highlighted a problem vis-a-vis your cash flow."

"I need an overdraft."

"I see. What sort of figure do you have in mind?"

"I don't know."

"What sort of term are we looking at?"

"I don't know. But probably short term. Until I receive the money from Lucy's insurance and the like. I've had a lot of expenses recently."

"Of course. Let's take a look at the state of your finances."

Keying in details on his computer terminal. Frown of concern.

"Mmm. I see your problem. More money going out than has been coming in. Your wage is no longer being paid in. I take it you are on some sort of compassionate leave at the moment."

"Yes. Indefinitely."

"I see. Well, we can, of course, offer you an overdraft, subject to certain assurances that you will have the wherewithal to repay. Your solicitor, I assume, will be able to provide me with details of your wife's, your late wife's, financial provisions. I take it she has bequeathed you the bulk of her estate?"

"All of it."

"In that case, there should be no problem. The late Mrs Light had a sizeable account at this branch. And when you do receive your bequest, please do not hesitate to contact me for advice on how best to manage this most unfortunate of sources of income."

Rubbing together his dry hands before shaking mine. Which I then wipe unnoticed on my trousers. He gives me the creeps. His hands are like those of a corpse. Thin, white and bony. Not used to touching flesh. Only counting coin and thumbing banknotes. Escorts me to the door and opens it for me. Before disappearing back into his sanctum to balance books, count cash and immerse himself in other people's money.

Go celebrate this forthcoming influx of funds in the nearest hostelry. The doors of which are locked. Checking the watch, which shows five long minutes to opening time. Pretend to inspect the merchandise in this nearby shop window, which, unfortunately, is full of ladies' underwear. Ignore the stares of passers-by and the two young ladies standing giggling by my side.

"I don't think they stock your size, love."

"I think you may be surprised at my size."

"I doubt it, pencil dick."

Charming! Thank God the pub doors are opening. Slide quickly inside. Safe and dry and warm in here. A pleasant fresh-coffee smell. Coal fire burning in the tap room whose smoke-stained walls are covered with horse brasses. Long polished oak bar with its gleaming brass rail. Glasses shining on display. Mock-Victorian decor of the type so beloved by brewery architects and planners. Corporate falseness. But at least traditional hand-pulled cask-conditioned ale. Just waiting to be sampled by an appreciative and discerning drinker. In which category I most definitely place myself. The barman approaching, his crisp white shirt open at the neck and sleeves rolled up to the elbows. Wearing his corporate smile.

"Morning, sir."

"Morning. A pint of bitter, please."

"Certainly, sir. Any bitter in particular?"

"This one, I think."

"Coming up."

"And do you have anything to eat?"

"Yes, sir. We do lunches between twelve and two. All home-made stuff, cooked by the wife. Highly recommended in the local pub guide. As, of course, is the beer. There you are, sir. That's one-eighty, please. Shall I get you a menu?"

"Yes, please."

Poring over the extensive selection. Of soups, starters, steaks, fish and pies. Choice of chips or jacket. Salad or vegetables. Mouth salivating at the prospect. Mustn't make a hasty decision. Better have another pint first. Prepare the stomach for its forthcoming feast. Not good to eat on an empty stomach. A liquid cushion is required to prevent the food from lying too heavily in the pit.

"Another bitter, please. This is an excellent brew. And well kept."

"Thank you, sir. We do our best. Are you ready to order any food yet?"

"Yes. I think I'll have the home-made steak in ale pie, with the golden french fries, and seasonal vegetables."

"Thank you, sir. A sound choice, if I may say so."

"You may."

"In that case, sir, a fine choice. Ha ha."

"Ha ha."

A pleasant barman. A little unusual for a city centre pub. But this one obviously maintains traditional values and standards. A welcome haven among the plethora of over-decorated, over-priced theme pubs. With their garish range of bottled drinks, most of which I've never heard of, but which weren't marketed with the likes of me in mind anyway. Drinks for the young. Wean them off the teat and on to alcopops. So they can run riot among the city streets at night, putting the frighteners on the god-fearing public. Don't want to grow old in a society which gives free rein to these lawless yobs. God knows what it will be like when their ill-conceived offspring reach the age of immaturity. The behaviour of these kids would put even Duncan to shame.

More customers entering now, looking forward to a good lunch to break the monotony of the working day. Shop workers and office staff ordering soft drinks and mineral waters. Lunchtime drinking frowned upon these days in the business world. So different from the days when

Duncan and I would throw back five pints each in our lunch hour, then buy a packet of mints and return to the office suitably refreshed before burying our heads in paperwork. We had both quickly mastered the ability to look incredibly busy without actually doing much. But then it didn't really matter. Efficiency, and the all-consuming drive for profitability came later. Then, it was simply a case of, well, working for a living. Without having to cut the throats of colleagues in the stampede for advancement. There was a peaceful co-existence with one's fellow workers. And promotion came with length of service. Or the untimely death of a superior. Death again! Keeps returning to my thoughts. Push it away to the very back of my musings. There. Back on track. Well, no work to go back to this afternoon, so time to enjoy the drink. Call for another. Keep the throat lubricated to facilitate the intake of the imminent meal.

Served at a small round table on a mat depicting a hunting scene. Clean and polished cutlery wrapped in a green paper napkin. A tray at the side containing condiments, from which a sprinkling of salt is required. Cut through the thick crust, showering the table with tiny fragments of pastry. Brush them on to the carpet while nobody is watching. Dark, thick tasty gravy, and tender meat chunks surrounded by a mountain of chips. Peas and carrots in equal proportion. Turn the fork over to scoop the peas, careful not to let any escape to be trodden into the Axminster by these shiny-shoed business executives. Clear the plate and down the pint. And just order one more to wash it all down. Need courage to face the task waiting at home. But plenty time yet. Check the pocket for cash. Yes, no rush. More pints are required to increase the glow of false well-being.

And once suitably refreshed, I walk out into the cold afternoon air. A weak sun pokes momentarily through the glowering dark clouds but brings no warmth with it and the wind turns my alcohol-reddened face blue.

Into this warm but empty house. Turn the central heating up a couple of degrees and make a mug of tea. No milk, so a small dash of malt will have to suffice. Help defrost the extremities. Root around in this cupboard. Ah, here they are. Refuse bags, black, large. Just the job. Grab a dozen or so, and into the bedroom. Open the wardrobe, take out Lucy's dresses and lay them on the bed. All these for the charity shop. Except this party frock. My favourite. Hers too. I can't bear the thought of anyone else wearing it. Stuff it in a separate bag. For those special things which are to be destroyed. Her underwear. Drawers full of drawers. Some of which I haven't seen before. Somewhat tarty, or as the ads say "exotic". Perhaps she bought them just before she fell ill, and never got around to wearing them. And all these things I bought her for special occasions. But still, five big bags full as her posthumous donation to charity. And a further two bags whose contents I will burn in the back garden later. Next, I need to tackle her personal things. Rummage through her handbags. Odd coins and notes, plastic cards and the necessities for feminine hygiene and grooming. And what's this? I didn't know Lucy had a mobile phone. Hang on to that for now. Switch it on. Check the bathroom cabinets. Make-up, toiletries and the like. All for the dustbin. And that's it. Lucy's life. All neatly bagged up for disposal.

A knock at the front door this late afternoon. The concerned face of Mr Everson.

"Hello, Ray. How are you?"

"Fine."

"Only Mrs Everson and I haven't seen much of you these past few days and wondered how you were and if you needed anything."

"No, thanks. I'm fine."

"Well, we were wondering if you had any washing or cleaning or ironing or anything you would like Mrs E to do."

"No, thanks. Everything's shipshape and under control."

"Well, at times like this, people sometimes let things slip a little. It's nothing to be ashamed of. Quite natural, in fact. And Mrs E would be Everso pleased to help."

"I don't need help, thank you."

"Well, perhaps you would do us the honour of eating with us this evening."

"Thank you. That would be nice."

"Splendid. Come around about six."

"OK."

I haven't the heart to refuse this well-meaning neighbour, and a good hearty and wholesome home-cooked meal would be most welcome. Cooked in someone else's kitchen, with someone else to do the washing-up.

A further rummage in the wash-basket unearths nothing in the way of fairly clean shirts. Try the black bags. Inspecting the garments until I eventually find a crisp white blouse. A reasonable fit and quite fetching. Wear a sweater so as not to expose the flower motif on the breast pocket. There. Perfect. Try the dresses on later, perhaps. Give the Eversos quite a shock. Or perhaps a thrill. Who knows what secrets lie behind their double-glazed door.

Presenting myself at the Eversos at the appointed hour. Handing over the gift of a cheap bottle of supermarket wine, which is received tactfully and then put aside 'for later'. Martinis in the lounge with Mr Everson while Mrs E slaves in the kitchen. Engaging in small talk as tempting aromas waft through. Mahogany-veneered table laid with white linen cloth, fine silver and a chateau-bottled red. Mrs E serving the tempting fare, a chicken concoction in red wine with herbs. And steaming tureens of vegetables and new potatoes nicely sautéed. Followed by a fresh fruit salad and a fine selection from the cheeseboard, coffee and mint chocolate wafers. Brandy and a cigar in the lounge with Mr E, while Mrs E clears away and fills the dishwasher.

Relax and look at the furnishings and decor and knick-knacks where everything is polished and just-so.

"You know, Ray. I'm glad you came around. We've enjoyed your company."

"And I've enjoyed yours, and the wonderful meal. Thanks, Everso..."

"Now I know you think Mrs E and I are a pair of old fuddy-duddies..."

"Yes, actually."

"Well, we are. But I want you to know we were young once. And we knew how to enjoy ourselves. Oh, yes, by Jove, we did. I could tell you some tales, but Mrs E would be Everso embarrassed. The point is, Ray, we're both retired now, but life hasn't always been easy for us. We're comfortable enough, what with my pension from forty years in the Post Office. But we've both come through a great personal tragedy to get to this point. We had a daughter. Lesley. A beautiful girl. Full of life. Intelligent. Loving. Well-mannered. All you could ever wish for in a daughter. We loved her so much.... When she was eighteen, we threw a big party for her and all her friends. They were hundreds of them.... She'd sat her A-levels, and was hoping to go to university.... Then one evening during the summer, she went out for a drink with three friends, in a car - the driver didn't drink - and on the way home a drunk driver crossed on to the wrong side of the road and hit them head-on.... Lesley died instantly. Her friends survived. And so did the driver of the other car... He was fined and banned from driving for a year.... Two days later, Lesley's exam results came through the post. She got three grade A's... She would have gone to university. And probably had a brilliant career. And a wonderful life... But none of her dreams were fulfilled... So, you see. We really do understand what you're going through. There were times when Mrs E and I wondered if we'd ever come through it. But we did... Even though not a day goes by without us thinking about our Lesley. We both feel Everso sorry for you, Ray. But, believe me, life has to go on."

"I'm sorry. I never knew you had a daughter."

"It's our grief, Ray. We don't make a habit of sharing it. But I thought it might help you to know that you're not alone in having lost a loved one. But, you know, that's not the end of the story. When Lesley died, we vowed we wouldn't have another child. Even if we'd been able. So, two weeks after the funeral I went out and bought Mrs E a puppy. A mongrel. Scamp. It was the last thing she wanted. It messed in the house. She pleaded with me to get rid of it, but I refused. And in a very short time, she grew to love the dog, and he became part of the family. He could never take Lesley's place in our hearts, but he filled an emptiness we felt in our lives, and we loved him dearly. He's buried under the sundial in the front garden. He used to love lying on the lawn, the little rogue."

"That's a very moving story, Mr E. Do you perhaps have another small glass of brandy?"

"Of course, Ray. You know, when you moved in next door, Mrs E commented on how much your Lucy resembled our Lesley. Not just in her looks. But in her attitude to life, her sunny disposition, her ready smile. We miss her a lot as well, you know."

"I'm sure you do. And thank you for sharing your feelings with me."

"Not at all, Ray. Any time at all, if you need to talk, please come around. We're glad to help in any way we can."

"Thank you. I will."

Exchanging goodnights at the door. The E's waving until I disappear behind my own front door. Feeling deep sympathy for the old couple, who had borne their grief in private and with dignity. And not drowned themselves in drink and self-pity as I had.

Odd electronic jingle coming from the bedroom. Lucy's mobile playing "The Stripper". Answer it.

"Hello?"

"Lucy there?"

"No."

"When will she be in?"

"She won't."

"She work for you?"

"Not any more."

"Got any other girls?"

"Who is that?"

"Tony."

"You got the wrong number, Tony."

The light over the back door flooding the garden as I pile newspapers, bits of wood and finally Lucy's things in their black bags. Set light to the paper and stand back as it catches. Pop back inside to fill a glass with Malt and return to watch as the flames consume Lucy's clothes. Reminded briefly of the crematorium and its furnace. And Lucy's ashes in the little urn. Poke this fire with a stick. Make sure nothing remains as the breeze lifts blackened bits of paper into the air and the pile is reduced to a glow of embers. Soon to be extinguished. And stand there, sipping whisky until nothing remains but ash. Out of which a gold-coloured button gleams dully from its sooty background. Lucy, still shining.

CHAPTER 5

Awaking early next morning. Vague recollections of a recurring dream. Which didn't make sense. Forget it. It's the drink. Sort the washing into piles and fill the machine. Add powder and fabric conditioner. Select a program and push the button. Easy. Pile up all the dirty crockery and fill the sink with hot suds. Leave them to soak for a while and in the meantime, unleash the vacuum cleaner. Which gives off a burning smell, emits sparks, and falls silent. Unplug the beast and attack it with a screwdriver. Just tighten this loose connection, change the bag and clear out the tubes and orifices with a knitting needle. And Hey Presto! Plug in and switch on, and... Nothing. Write 'take vac for repair' on list of things to do, along with a hundred other items. And must deal with the pile of mail collecting on the hall table. Some of it unopened, but all unanswered. Including the latest one from work.

"Dear Ray,

May we at Barker and Sons Ltd. once again say how distressed we are at your sad loss. We, of course, understand how stressful a time this must be for you, but wonder if you could possibly give us some indication of a date when you might conceivably consider returning to work. Work can be quite cathartic in times like this. It may help to take your mind of your current sadness, and, I have to say, your in-tray is overflowing, and customers are overloading our switchboard with calls of complaint.

I would remind you that you have only been with us for six months, and therefore, according to the rules laid down in our company handbook, you have already exceeded what we would regard as 'permissible' compassionate leave. We live in a competitive society and work in a highly competitive field, where margins are small and there is no room for 'less than 100%" company men. It therefore goes without saying that we are relying upon your speedy return to active duty.

Yours, in sympathy,

James P M P Barker.

PS. The payment we receive from you for rent on your company house by Direct Debit has been dishonoured by your bank. I trust you will have already resolved this problem by the time this letter reaches you. Such small oversights, I know, can sometimes occur when one's thoughts are not firmly focused."

This sounds to me like a thinly-disguised threat of the sack. Barker is not known for his philanthropic nature. He has no interest in people, except where they can assist him in making a profit. I remember young Dan, who started not long after me, in the IT department. An excellent technician, always friendly, helpful and garrulous, Dan had only one problem. He was clinically obese, a fact which he took in his stride and often joked about, relishing in his nickname of 'Desperate'. Barker took a dislike to Dan not because of his size, but because the office chairs tended to buckle under his weight. Whenever he jacked one up to a comfortable height to work at his computer terminal, five seconds later there would be a sharp crack and the seat, with Dan wedged firmly in it, would drop about a foot, creating a shockwave which reverberated round the office. Barker wasted no time in giving him his marching orders, but didn't have the guts to tell him why. He merely had a letter sent to his desk, saying his work was below the standard expected, and his employment was therefore being terminated at the end of that day. The lad was devastated. I stormed in to see Barker. Pleaded with him to give the boy a chance. I even told him he was passing up a golden opportunity to fill a niche market by designing and selling a range of reinforced, indestructible rubber office chairs. But he was adamant, the heartless bastard. So, after work, I took Dan for a drink, and told him if he wanted a reference to give my name and address, rather than Barker's. But he was inconsolable. It was his first job since leaving college. He was bright, and affable, and had dreams of a long and successful career. And Barker's Scrooge-like concern over a couple of broken office chairs had reduced him almost to tears and left his dreams in tatters.

"It's not the fact that I've been sacked that bothers me so much, Ray. It's the fact that I've been sacked for being fat. Not because I'm not good at my job. Just because I'm fat. Jesus! I've put up with taunts about my size all my life. All through school and college. People take the piss, but I don't mind. Really, I don't. But I'm good with computer systems. Came top in my course at college. I know what I'm about. And if he'd just come to me and said something about the broken chairs, I'd have paid for them, out of my wage. I would have worked standing up, for Christ's sake, if he'd just given me the chance. I know I'm fat. But I'm young and strong. And I'm healthy. OK, I like my food and my beer. But I don't smoke. I don't do drugs. My girlfriend is overweight. And we're both happy as we are. And that bastard Barker..."

And I swore then that I'd get even with Barker for the way he'd treated Dan. And now it looks like it's my turn for the chop. Perhaps a pre-emptive reply will give him something to think about, while I plot a fitting revenge.

"Dear James 'Pull My Plonker' Barker,

Thank you for your kind letter showing me the way to righteousness and redemption by making money for your company. It is most gratifying to know that there are still some unfeeling capitalists out there, and nothing would please me more than to grovel before your worthy self, and pick bales of cotton for you and call you 'Massa' and 'Boss' were it not for the fact that my wife has just died. So, kiss my selfish socialist arse.

Sincerely,

Ray Light (of my life)

PS. Your company-owned house is in desperate need of fumigation, as I shit myself upon reading your threatening letter. Please arrange a visit from Rentokil immediately or I will withhold any further monies due. If you fail to comply with this request, I will take my claim to the Small Claims Court, as I only did a small jobby.

PPS. Your recent correspondence has been passed to the upholders of law and order, to the 'Serious Letters Squad'. Beware! You are under surveillance. Keep your nose clean. Wipe it whenever it emerges from beneath a customer's shirt-tail.

PPPS. Please excuse the fact that this envelope does not bear a stamp, but having worked for you for six months, I have run out of lick."

Emptying the washing machine, then shoving the load back in to dry. Not yet domesticated sufficiently to hang it on the line and take it in every ten minutes between showers of winter rain. Besides, keep the neighbours guessing. If I peg out too much underwear, they might get the mistaken impression that I'm soiling it too quickly, and perhaps enjoying life more than is deemed acceptable under the circumstances. Perhaps I was a little hasty in burning Lucy's underwear. Skimpy. Brightly coloured. Sexy. Could have hung it out to give the neighbours something to talk about. Hang her life on the line. And take it back in tomorrow. If it's still there.

The front doorbell ringing. Too insistently to ignore. Whoever it is knows I'm in. Can't be the bailiffs yet, as the friendly local bank manager has arranged my overdraft, at an exorbitant rate. Open the door to the Everso's, who are not alone. Mr E holding a lead, on the other end of which is a dog. Of indeterminate parentage. Panting, tongue almost reaching the ground. And a long, waggy tail which knocks over the empty milk bottles and sends them rolling down the path. Mrs E immediately off in pursuit, collecting them but not daring to put them down within range of this pathetic-looking animal.

"Hello, Ray. Mrs E and I were talking about the conversation we had chez nous. And we agreed we should do something to try to help you through your loss. So, we went down to the RSPCA and found this poor fellow. Desperate for a home. Ray, if he doesn't find one within a week, they will have to put him down. Now call us interfering if you like..."

"You're interfering."

"I know, yes. And you've every right to be annoyed. But we thought this little fellow would be good company for you. Dogs are very therapeutic. They give affection unconditionally. In return for food and human company. Please take him. Give it a try. If it doesn't work for you, I promise we'll take him off your hands. And give him a good home. But we just couldn't leave him in the kennels. To die. He looked so sad. But so desperately keen to please whenever anyone approached his cage. His tongue would come out and his tail start thumping. Until you walked away. Then he would lie down, all curled up in a corner, looking straight at you with those sad, pleading eyes."

"Does he have a name?"

"No. They took him in as a stray. Found him tied to the railings at the kennels. They called him Nigger. On account of his colour. But suggested his new owner find him a new name. On account of political correctness. And the fact that shouting his name in the street at night could cause problems in some areas. Though, thankfully, not on this street."

"Let him off his lead."

Released, the dog runs past me into the house, where he has a good sniff round. Before squatting in the kitchen and dropping a hot sticky plop. Then returning to sit at my heels, tail wagging furiously.

"Ah. Don't worry, Ray. Just marking his territory. They do that."

"If he does it again, I'll mark his territory. With my boot."

Mrs E to the rescue, pushing past to clean up efficiently and without fuss. I crouch in front of the miscreant mongrel about to lay down the law. But instead I'm overwhelmed by the beast in its desire to show affection. Knocked backwards as the animal rears and places two paws on my chest. Then smothers me with great wet sandpaper licks from the long slobbering tongue. Say 'yes I'll take him', in the hope that he'll calm down and show due gratitude and respect for his new master. But instead, the animal becomes so excited that he pees a small pee on my trouser leg.

"Ray. Look. It won't be like this for long. Just till he gets used to you. He's just excited, that's all. As soon as he realises you're his new master, he'll settle down. I promise you."

"Take him back."

"I can't, Ray. He'll be put to sleep. But if you could just take him for a couple of weeks. If you returned him then, they'd try again to rehouse him. Give him a reprieve."

"Two weeks. That's all I'll give him."

"Thanks, Ray. Give it a try. And never forget you're giving him a new lease of life."

"Two weeks. That's all."

"What are you going to call him? I think 'Lucky' would be rather appropriate."

"I think 'Plopper' would be spot-on."

"As you wish. Oh, and try not to let him bark during the night. Mrs E needs her eight hours."

"I'll remember that."

Leading Plopper into the kitchen. Where he sits looking up as his new master fills with water one of the bowls the E's had Everso thoughtfully brought with them. Lapping greedily. Water splashing everywhere. Taking him on a tour of the house, pointing out the places which are out of bounds. Such as the bedroom. And the bathroom. Like a little privacy in there. Do my plops behind the closed door. And not in the middle of the kitchen.

Seated at the table, my new companion laid quietly by my feet. Looking up occasionally, giving a quick flick of the tail, then settling down again with head on paws, one ear slightly cocked. And I remember when I was eleven, I had a mongrel I called Scruff. Who would sit by the garden gate when I went to school, and be there to greet me when I came home. I used to wonder if he sat there all day waiting for me, but mum said after a while he would go inside and mope all day, until he sensed I was on my way home, when he would bark to be let out into the garden. He used to follow me as I did my morning paper round, trotting alongside as I cycled the streets. He never seemed to be more than a few feet away. Until one morning he was delayed by a young Labrador bitch, and ran across the road to catch up with me. Only to be knocked down by a car. I dropped my bike and ran to him as he lay in the middle of the road, twitching, tongue lolling, blood in his mouth. I cradled his head and stroked him, my salt tears soaking his fur. As he whimpered and died.

A kind man came out of his house and covered Scruff with a blanket. He lifted him carefully and put him in a corner of his garden shed. Then parked my bike next to it. He drove me back to the newsagent, where he handed the bag of undelivered papers to Mr Patterson who gave me a sympathetic wave through the shop window. Then he drove me home, just as dad was returning from his night shift. Mum put me to bed. And when I got up at teatime, dad said Scruff's body had been taken care of by the

RSPCA, and I had to thank the kind man the next time I saw him.

It felt strange and lonely without Scruff. When I came home from school I kept hoping and praying he'd be there, waiting at the gate for me. I believed in miracles then. Even though every morning I passed the spot where he was killed, and could still see the bloodstains on the cobbles. And the following Sunday I saw the car which had hit him. In the drive of a house where I was to deliver a heavy batch of Sunday papers. I fed each section one by one through the letter box. And the final one I dropped through one sheet at a time, setting light to the last page and pushing it through well alight.

When Mr Patterson found out, he sacked me, and told dad, who took me round to see the man. And instead of apologising, dad thumped him in the mouth for killing Scruff and driving away without stopping.

A week or so later, a small ball of brown yellow fur was waiting when I came home from school. Expanding and contracting in dad's hands in measured sleepy breathing. And as warm and cuddly as he was, and as affectionate, loyal, obedient and devoted he became, I never loved him as I had Scruff. I brushed him, fed him and exercised him, but that was all. Dad understood and tried to make me see I was taking it out on the dog. It wasn't the pup's fault Scruff had died. He wasn't trying to take Scruff's place. All he wanted was a little love in return for his abundant affection for me. And I told dad I was afraid to love him too much, because of the pain I'd feel when he died. And dad told me 'tis better to have loved and lost than never to have loved at all.

And when dad died less than a year later after an accident at work, I wanted to thump his boss in the mouth. Mum was never the same again. She tried life with a new man, who was kind to me, and helped me with my homework. But mum was never really happy again and took me aside at my eighteenth birthday party to tell me she was leaving him. I remember looking at him across the pub, buying drinks for my mates. Relaxed and happy, he had no idea how mum felt, nor of her intentions. I felt so sorry for him. A good man, who'd never tried to take dad's place, and whom I'd grown to respect. And then mum died, and finally Lucy. And if I could ever meet Tennyson, I'd ask him what the hell he meant when he wrote those lines. What did he know of love and loss?

CHAPTER 6

Walking briskly through the damp air down to the shopping centre with its windswept arcades. Designed and built in the 1970s, most of its shops are now boarded up. A playground and battleground for louts and vandals, and a no-go area for anyone else after dark. Newspapers blowing around, gathering briefly in corners before being whisked into the air by sudden gusts. Distributed free each week to forty thousand households, and read by no-one. Plopper stops to sniff at a page, then raises a leg and marks it for future reference. Dutifully sitting while I wrap his lead round a post, and watching and whining pathetic little sounds as I pop Barker's letter in the post box before disappearing into the supermarket.

Sauntering up and down the wide aisles, selecting tins and packets to drop into this trolley which seems reluctant to go in the direction in which it is pushed. As it constantly veers off to the left, I steer it in the opposite direction to compensate. Until, distracted by a mini-skirted shopper with immeasurably long legs, I lose control and collide with a display. Pyramid of packets collapsing, skidding across the floor in all directions. Assistant manager appearing smartly on the scene to survey the damage. Marshalling troops of underlings who sullenly react to barked orders to clean up and rebuild before the area manager's inspection. Feeling his cold glare on the back of my neck. The subversive dismantler of displays of carefully constructed pyramids of merchandise, I stand waiting alongside until the display is rebuilt, and then casually remove a pack from half way down and walk away as the whole lot collapses again.

Collect Plopper on my way out. He seems pleased to see me. Tail wagging ferociously. Try to pat his head. But every time I do, he moves and lashes my hand with his friendly sandpaper tongue. He's a good boy. Or maybe he realises I've bought him a bag of doggy treats and is acting purely in self-interest. I wonder if dogs do that. Or is it simply a human trait? Animals have some amazing qualities but they haven't yet become as corrupt and self-seeking as we higher primates.

A slight drizzle this late afternoon. Weather improving since the morning's heavy rain had washed the streets clean of their customary pools of blood and vomit, as the tail-wagging Plopper leads me down damp pavements to the small park with its few stunted bare trees. Freed from his leash, Plopper heads straight for the play area, sniffs around and squats by the swings to ease out a tentative turd.

"Excuse me!"

An old man with an equally old terrier approaching. He has a large red-blotched bulbous nose from the end of which a dew-drop hangs ominously.

"Excuse me!"

"Yes?"

"Aren't you going to clean it up?"

"What?"

"Your dog's mess. Aren't you going to clean it up?"

"What am I supposed to do with it?"

"Take it home."

"Thanks, but I've already got plenty at home. You can have it if you want."

"You can't leave it there. It's a health hazard. What about the kids?"

"Kids don't play here any more. Just glue sniffers. So, let them sniff the shit."

"You have to clean it up. It's the law. Here, you can have this bag."

"Listen. If I wanted to walk around carrying a bag full of shit, I'd have a colostomy. Come on, Plopper. Time to go home."

Plopper eyeing the terrier suspiciously, and growling, teeth bared.

"Get that dog away from my David. It's vicious!"

"He's just a pup. Playing."

A yelp from David as Plopper sinks his teeth into the neck of the terrified terrier.

"I'll report you. Keeping a dangerous dog. Allowing it to foul in a public place."

"Shut it! Or I'll set him on you!"

"I'm going. There's nowhere safe for decent folk anymore. But you haven't heard the last of this!"

I feel a little better these days. Plopper gets me out and about. Even if it's only to walk the streets. Perhaps the E's were right. He is good company. Demands very little of me except food, exercise and a little affection. And I'm sleeping better, though not without a regular unpleasant dream. But when I wake up, it's comforting to find someone pleased to see me and to hear the dull thump of his tail on the carpet. He's settled down well and since that first day has had no further accidents in the house. It's reached the point now where I have sufficient confidence in him to allow him a free run of the house. I no longer shut the bedroom door at night. I couldn't stand his pathetic whining at bedtime so we've established a little ritual. He lies on his bed in the hall. Curled up. One eye open. And as soon as I get into bed and turn out the light, he comes softly padding in and lies at the side of the bed to dream his little doggy dreams and occasionally chew a slipper.

A week later, a letter arrives. Hurrying to get to it before Plopper chews it up, I manage to wrench it from his jaws leaving a corner for the pup to savage. From the council, Department of Environmental Health.

"Dear Sir,

Following a complaint from a member of the public, I am writing to inform you that your conduct vis-a-vis your dog, which answers (sometimes) to the name of Plopper, on the evening of last Thursday, the 19th, is totally unacceptable under the terms of the council's recently introduced bye-law regarding dog mess and the correct disposal thereof. Should you be in any doubt as to the wording of this law and the responsibilities it imposes on owners, I have enclosed a pamphlet which should explain fully your legal obligations and the fines which may be imposed as a result of non-compliance. I should also inform you that wardens now patrol the area where the offence occurred, and will not hesitate to take action against your future failure to clean up Plopper's faecal deposits.

You may be interested to know that "poop-scoops", together with a supply of strong deodorised plastic bags are available from this office at the greatly discounted price of only £1.50. That's right! Only £1.50! Get yours while stocks last.

Yours sincerely,

Neville P. Shirtliff. BSc Hons.

(Director of Services, Dept of Environmental Health)"

Refuse to be intimidated by petty officialdom. Rummaging in the drawer for pen and pad, immediate reply in mind as Plopper curls feigning sleep round my one remaining intact slipper. A quick pause for thought, then writing feverishly.

"Dear Mr Shitleft,

Thank you for your kind letter explaining my legal obligations as regards your recently introduced, and not before time, I might add, bye-law. Being a responsible, upright and law-abiding citizen, I am already au fait with the minutiae of the law in question. However, I would like to point out that I doubt that you have any hard evidence that any contravention of the said bye-law occurred on the evening in question, 'hard' being the operative word. If necessary, I am able to produce evidence from a highly respected practitioner of veterinary medicine, a Mr Biswas Turdandasoftun (FRCVS), which will prove quite conclusively that at the time of the alleged incident, Plopper was incapable of producing poop due to a severe case of canine diarrhoea, which as you will surely be aware is impossible to scoop once it meets and becomes embedded in grass-seeded soil. That being the case, I would advise you that I intend to make available to you an answer to this most vexing of problems. I am prepared to offer you at the ridiculously low price of only £3.75 (inc. VAT) my newly-invented Deluxe Eezy-Plop Mini-mess mop and deodorised bucket (UK patent pending) in hard wearing polyurethane, and in a range of striking and attractive colours, specifically designed to deal with this most embarrassing of canine problems. (Soft-finish canine bum-wipes, impregnated with a range of perfumes will also be available soon.)

Assuring you of my best intentions at all times, as the inventor of the Plop-and-Go, a remarkable tool for removing dog shit from the soles of trainers, I remain yours faithfully, Plopper's Loving Owner, and prompt Council Tax payer,

Raymond Light (widower of this parish and general good egg)"

Washed and dressed and out with Plopper down to the post box. Stopping at every lamppost to sign his dribbly autograph. Keep him on a tight rein as he's taken an instant and obvious dislike to the other neighbourhood dogs. At which he barks and snarls. That's my boy! Sometimes I wish I could bark and snarl at their owners. A miserable lot, who treat Plopper and me with distrust and suspicion. I never realised before how cold and unfriendly people are around here. Except the E's, who always have a wave and a smile and a friendly word. And a pat and a biscuit for Plopper. Pull him away from the rear wheel of this parked white van which I've seen around for the past few days with its mysterious occupants. Covert surveillance of some sort. Better keep a close eye on my neighbours. Perhaps the E's are Russian spies. More likely that little shit from the council has posted watch on Plopper's excretory activities. As soon as we've passed, they'll leap out of the van and into action. Weighing measuring sampling and analysing recent turds. A fine way to earn a living. A noble vocation. Tonight, I shall feed Plopper on curry. Spice up their job a little.

A little light rain beginning to fall. The sky a sea of clouds gathering grey. A chill wind whipping up litter. The weatherman said a long spell of unsettled weather is on its way across the Atlantic. Seems fairly settled to me. It's been like this for days. Better turn the central heating up a notch and batten down the hatches for a long cold winter. Buy in plenty of Malt and hibernate in my warm nest with Plopper.

Walking round these fields at the edge of the council estate. In a far corner, a beat-up Transit van parked alongside a half-dozen gleaming caravans. Two ragged young boys pulling metal scraps from the remains of a bonfire while a scrawny mongrel prowls hungrily around. Mr E. told me that travellers turn up here every year, knowing full well that the council will serve an eviction notice, but in the time it takes to enforce they can strip the plumbing from three or four of the empty council houses and be on their way leaving behind a rubbish-strewn site.

Spend a good hour in the fields throwing sticks for Plopper and wandering the streets. And back home trying to rub him dry with an old towel before he escapes my grasp and shakes himself vigorously, showering the walls with muddy spray before settling, steaming, in front of the gas fire. The unpleasant aroma of wet dog pervading the room, but Plopper is unconcerned. Curled up and sleeping, with his nose stuck up his arse. The patch of carpet in front of the fire is already considerably darker than the rest. No doubt Barker will present me with the cleaning bill if ever he sees it. Worry about that when it happens. Just relax and read the paper. Oh, and a glass of Malt, I think, to help the relaxation process.

Plopper licking my hand as I wake suddenly. The newspaper at my feet and an empty glass on the chair arm. What time is it? Christ! Nearly five o'clock. Feel nauseous. Disgusting, rank taste in the mouth. Into the bathroom, Plopper close behind. Splash the sallow face with cold water. Stick out the tongue, which is covered in thick green-yellow fur. Hope I'm not coming down with something nasty. Apart from alcoholism. Clean the teeth and gargle with this peppermint mouthwash which leaves me feeling a little better, but still distinctly subhuman. Need some fresh air and, since Plopper is awake, he needs some exercise. Check the weather; still raining. I wonder if I could just let him out into the back garden. Open the door, but he just stands on the threshold, looking up at me, tail wagging. Looking at things from his point of view, he probably sees it as his responsibility to ensure I get regular exercise. So, who's the master in this house, then?

"OK, come on then. Let me get my coat."

Plopper responding with a bark and a thrash of the tail. And I allow him to drag me through the wet fields once more. A teenager approaching, with an Alsatian dog the size of a pit pony. Plopper freezes, standing stock-still, ears back, tail straight. Put him on his lead, hoping the youth will do the same. But he's obviously congenitally stupid, or mistakenly convinced his beast will obey his every command. The dogs now ten feet apart.

"Shane. Come here, boy."

"Easy, Plopper. Good boy."

Patting Plopper's neck. Ready to unleash him if this monster comes any closer. Give him a fair chance to defend himself. Or run away. The dogs now nose to nose. Now nose to tail. Sniffing each other for traces of fear. Establishing the hierarchy of dominance and submission. Now shoulder to shoulder. Emitting low growls. Hackles rising, teeth bared. Slip his lead off and stand out of harm's way. But if Plopper seems in danger of losing the imminent contest, I am prepared to put in the boot to redress the balance.

Suddenly the violence erupts. Jaws snapping at flesh. The dogs twisting and turning. Ducking and weaving like boxers. No quarter given, nor asked for. Yelps of pain as teeth tear into fur, each dog in turn seeming to have the ascendancy. Until Shane's superior size, weight and strength gradually wear Plopper down. And eventually he's on his back, his belly and throat exposed, panting hard. Shane stands over him, about to deliver the coup de grace. I start to run towards them, hoping to save Plopper by delivering a hefty kick to the ribs of this salivating beast. But Plopper is not finished yet. He has one more trick up his furry sleeve. Twisting his body suddenly. His claws gaining purchase on the wet grass, he launches himself at the Alsatian's underbelly, clamping his jaws savagely round its balls. The Alsatian yells in pain, backing away. But Plopper clings on, determined to extract the maximum amount of sadistic pleasure from outwitting his much larger opponent.

"Get him off! He's killing my Shane."

"It wouldn't have happened if you'd kept him on a lead."

"Your dog started it."

"No, he didn't. He was just defending himself against that horse of yours."

"He's a pedigree German Shepherd."

"How many pedigree German sheep have you got?"

"You what?"

"How many sheep have you got?"

"Sheep? I haven't got any sheep."

"Well, that dog's no use to you then, is it?"

"He's my pet."

"Well, keep him on a lead in future. OK?"

"Just get your dog off."

"Plopper! Plopper!! Leave, boy! Leave! Good boy."

Thankfully, Plopper is in an obedient mood and relaxes his grip. Comes trotting back to sit at my side, tail thumping. Panting heavily, his fur covered in saliva. A few bare patches where clumps have been torn out. The odd trace of blood about his face and neck, but he seems no worse for his encounter. Shane, on the other hand, lies on his side, whimpering, licking his bloody scrotum.

"If I were you, I'd get him to a vet. He'll be no use at herding sheep. He can't even keep his balls in a tight pack. Come on, Plopper. You deserve a nice big juicy bone."

CHAPTER 7

Waking late this morning after a restless night. Hear Plopper barking at the door and growling at the postman. Leap out of bed and race towards the mess of mail strewn around the hall. Just in time to rescue a chewed and damp envelope from the jaws of this slobbering beast. A brown window envelope. From the council. No need to tear it open. The envelope falls apart in my hands to reveal the sticky message within.

"Dear Mr Blight,

I am in receipt of your letter in response to my earlier missive. I may be wrong, but I believe I detect a note of sarcasm in your words. Please do not take lightly the warning you have been issued. On this matter, I have the full backing of the council and the general public, as evidenced by your altercation with the gentleman in the park, who, I have it on good authority, is also a good egg.

Re your comments with regard to the problem of canine diarrhoea, you should be aware that the council is already addressing the issue by proposing an amendment to the wording of the bye-law. Further, our works department is currently testing a number of inventions with which to counteract the diarrhoea disposal problem. Your own invention, however, is not under consideration as the council believe it is over-priced.

Finally, I must repeat my earlier warning to you. Our team of highly trained enforcement officers are currently patrolling your area, and have been issued with descriptions of your good self and your companion, Plopper. So, be warned. Keep your nose, and your shoes, clean.

Yours faithfully,

Nev Shirtliff"

Peruse the rest of the morning's delivery. The usual crap. Junk mail. Save on this. Save on that. Fantastic offers. Never to be repeated. Unless of course you ignore them. In which case an even better fantastic offer, never to be repeated, is made. The rubbish bin fills daily with this stuff. I wish coal fires were still the norm. No shortage of combustible material these days. When I was young, we had to wait until dad had finished reading the paper before we could use it to light the fire. Separate each page. Twist tightly and knot in the middle. Lay them in the grate with kindling on top, then a few coals. Light the edges of the paper then get to work with the bellows. Place a sheet of newspaper over the front of the fireplace and watch as it browns and is gradually sucked inwards, bursting into flame and disappearing up the chimney as the dry wood begins to spark and crackle.

Two envelopes for Lucy. This one an offer of mail order fashion. I doubt they will have anything suitable for her now. Perhaps I'll send for the catalogue anyway, just to see if they do a selection of shrouds in the new winter colours. With matching harps and halos. And this other brown envelope. From the TV licensing people. Reminding Lucy that her licence has expired and has not yet apparently been renewed according to our records. Perhaps I should write back to remind them that dead people don't watch much TV these days. Except, that is, the brain dead, who watch those inane game shows. I shall simply ignore it. It's addressed to Lucy. Not my problem.

Just dash off a reply while seated at this wobbly table, one leg of which Plopper has gnawed almost through.

"Dear Mr Shirtlifter,

Thank you for your letter. Call me paranoid if you will, but I can't help thinking I am being subjected to undue and unnecessary scrutiny by your officers whose van is parked at the end of my street for hours at a stretch, while the occupants drink tea, eat sandwiches and read newspapers. I must point out to you that their habit of discarding litter into the road is most disconcerting, and, I am sure, illegal. Surely the members of your Serious Turd Squad have a duty to comply with litter laws even though their prime concern is the enforcement of poop-scooping.

I would appreciate your comments on this matter.

Yours,

Ray Light (aka the Crap Crusader)

PS. I note your unusual surname. Are you by any chance related to the Suffolk Shirtlifters?

PPS. My shoes are clean."

A quick walk with Plopper for his morning constitutional. Avoid the fields and take him round the allotments and disused railway sidings. Call at the shops for bacon eggs sausages mushrooms and an uncut loaf. Need to keep the cholesterol level high to keep out the cold.

Enjoy this leisurely breakfast with the butter-spread thick wedges of bread. I intend to make a habit of this. A new life should start with a good breakfast, and, surprisingly enough, I actually enjoyed cooking it. Savouring the various aromas. And salivating. If only there was someone to do the washing-up. Well, it can wait for now.

Slide the envelope into the post box, and pop into this public house to escape the drizzle. Order a pint and settle on this wobbly stool at the bar. Clean, warm and friendly hostelry. Smell of hot food wafting from the kitchen. Perhaps partake of some after sufficient liquid ingestion. A grey-haired gent also seated at the bar nodding a greeting, the movement displacing a shower of dandruff from his head.

"Bit damp out."

"Yes. Chilly too."

"It's an overcoat warmer than yesterday though."

"Yes. It is."

"Haven't seen you in here before."

"I haven't seen you in here either."

"I'm in here every day."

"That's probably why. I've never been in here before. I was just passing. Fancied a pint."

"Good choice. Best pint in town this. Knows how to keep a good pint, does Harry. You know the secret of keeping good ale? Temperature control. And hygiene. Harry's cellar is spotless. You could eat your dinner off the floor. Mind you, you'd find it a bit cold. Ha ha."

"Ha ha."

"I was in this game for a while you know."

"Really."

"Yes. After I left the merchant navy. Then I did my back in, and haven't been able to work since."

"Oh."

"Aye. Mind you, I wish I'd stayed on in the navy. That was the life. Seen the world, I have. Had experiences most people can only dream about."

"Really."

"The Far East. That's the place to be. Fleshpots like you wouldn't believe. Catering for all tastes. I could tell you some tales. I certainly could."

"I'm sure you could."

"You couldn't spare a cigarette, could you? Only I've just run out, and I refuse to pay the price of these vending machine packs. You pay full price, and only get about sixteen fags. Extortionate."

"Help yourself."

"Thanks. So, what do you do for a living? Office job, I'd guess, from the look of you."

"Yes."

"Thought so. Clean hands. No callouses. Or visible scars. I'm very observant, I am. I can usually tell a man's trade from little tell-tale signs. Things that most people would miss. A student of human nature, I am. A graduate from the University of Life."

"How interesting."

"You know what's unique about English pubs?"

"What?"

"There's always someone to talk to. It's the only place in the world where you don't have to sit on your own. You can talk to complete strangers. Share a pint. Have a laugh. I like that. I'm enjoying talking to you. You're a good conversationalist."

"Thank you."

"I mean it. I bet you've got some great stories to tell. Had an interesting life. Packed with incident. And sex. Go on, tell me about some of your sexual escapades."

"I wouldn't wish to bore you."

"No chance of that. And you know something else that spoils British pubs?"

"What's that?"

"Kids. They're taking over. With their jukeboxes and fancy drinks and pool tables. I hate fuckin' kids."

"Well, don't fuck 'em."

"Ha ha. That's funny. I'll remember that."

"You know what I think is wrong with British pubs?"

"What's that?"

"They are asylums for the emotionally distressed and the socially inadequate. For sad people who try to give the impression they've led really interesting lives. Had remarkable experiences. When really it's all just a comfort blanket to cover their deficiencies."

"I hadn't thought about that. But yes, I can see your point. There is some validity in what you've said. And I have to admit you do come across some odd people in pubs. Anyway, go on. You were going to tell me about your sex life. Ever had a Thai tart?"

"I'm sorry but I really have to go. Running a bit late for an appointment."

"Oh, well. It was nice talking to you. Call in again some time for a chat."

"Thanks. I will. 'Bye."

Have I become a magnet for the arseholes of this earth? Lucy often complained about the unwelcome attentions of strange men. But in her case, it was understandable. Men couldn't resist trying to chat her up. Normally it amused me; occasionally it annoyed me. But she could deal with it. A pity that women never try to chat me up. Wonder how I'd deal with it now I'm a single man. I'll probably never get the chance to find out, not when I attract sad boring old bastards in pubs.

CHAPTER 8

Saturday morning again. I don't really know why I still look forward to weekends. Every day is the same to me now. Old habits die hard. Retrieve this solitary envelope from behind the door. In its customary soggy state. But I prefer Plopper savaging envelopes than tearing lumps out of other canine acquaintances. Oh, dear. It's from the council. I hope they haven't got wind of his latest savage escapade. Honest, he's not dangerous. Just playful and a touch over-exuberant in his treatment of canine private parts.

"Dear Ray,

I am sorry to hear you have a persecution complex and regret that I must bear the responsibility as it was my decision to deploy the officers at the end of your street. You will be pleased to know they have now been redeployed in another area as a result of your complaint regarding litter. However, please do not regard this move as the granting of carte blanche to Plopper and your good self. Instead, look upon this action as a sign that I have the utmost trust in your law-abiding nature and moral uprightness.

Yours,

Nev

PS I have no relations, sexual or otherwise, in Suffolk."

And by way of reply,

"Dear N,

I am pleased to see that common sense has prevailed in this matter. You can rest assured that as a result of your trust in me I will continue to tread the straight and narrow path to righteousness, for I know if I stray from that path I may end up with mess on my clean shoes. Furthermore, I promise not to pollute the atmosphere by driving a car.

Neither will I raise crops and spray them with organophosphates, nor will I manufacture chemicals and dump effluent by-products in the water-courses. I wish it to be made a matter of public record that I regard you as a man of the highest principles for the sensitive way you have handled this affair. Thank you.

Your friends,

R and P.

PS. If not Suffolk, how about Middlesex?"

Monday morning checking the mail. A letter from the phone company informing me I have been disconnected, due to the fact that my account is long overdue and requests for payment have been ignored, and that, reluctantly, court action will be taken to recover the debt. Lift the handset to check. No sound issuing from this instrument, but that's hardly surprising as the cable bears the unmistakable marks of Plopper's teeth. Must make out a cheque to ward off the threat of debtors' prison. And tear open this envelope containing a bank statement which shows my finances to be in a perilous state. Exercise Plopper, then shower, shave, dress, and a light breakfast of bacon slices enveloped in thick crusty bread. Slip the newspaper cutting into the overcoat pocket and catch the bus into the city centre. This 'no smoking' policy on public transport is most unfair. The buses are allowed to belch their diesel fumes into the atmosphere with impunity, but woe betide the passenger who lights up a fag. Mustn't upset the Clean Air lobby, who would doubtless have a communal asthma attack were I to enjoy my preferred recreational drug of tobacco. It seems I don't have equal rights with the do-gooders. Perhaps I should sue for the effects on my health from passive boredom listening to their claptrap.

Hop off the bus in the centre, and enjoy a smoke as I walk through the precinct towards the address of Jobs R Us, whose advert for vacancies for professional men caught my eye. Present myself at the desk, where a young girl called Alison hands me an eight-page registration form to laboriously fill out. Personal details. Employment history. Qualifications. The usual stuff, which is all on the CV in my pocket. But which they refuse to accept, because it's in the wrong format for input to their database. Ticking various boxes. Writing cryptic and pithy comments here and there. And finally handing it back to Alison, who asks me to take a seat until one of their recruitment consultants can see me. Alison busily keying my application into the database. Tutting and muttering under her breath as her terminal beeps repeatedly and displays error messages. In exasperation, she photocopies the document, and takes it through to a side office, returning to request me to go through to see Mr Cooper.

Rising to greet me, his hand outstretched to shake mine limply.

"Morning Mr... Light."

"Hello, Mr Cooper."

"Call me Gary."

"Not *the* Gary?

"Pardon?"

"Gary Cooper, the film star."

"Never heard of him. Anyway. What can I do for you?"

"I should have thought that was obvious. I haven't come here to buy a bunch of bananas."

"No, of course. You're looking for a job. Right?"

"Right."

"And what sort of thing are you looking for?"

"It's all written down on my registration form."

"OK. Let's have a look through it. When would you be available to start, by the way?"

"Immediately."

"Do you drive?"

"Yes. But I can't."

"What do you mean?"

"The magistrates saw fit to disqualify me. It says so on the form."

"Do you have a car?"

"No. It says so on the form."

"Pity. You could have started tonight if you had transport. I've got two other chaps lined up for the same place, but I need transport to get them there and back. Let me take your phone number, and if I get someone else with a car, I'll give you a ring and he can take all of you."

"I'm not on the phone. It says so on the fucking form."

"Well, take my card. You can ring me. I'm here till about seven. After that you'll get me on my mobile."

"And what is this job?"

"Easy work. Clean modern environment. Work wear provided. And free transport there and back."

"And what exactly is the nature of the work?"

"Vegetables. Grading and packing. Guaranteed forty hours a week, and plenty of overtime. Four-fifteen an hour on nights. Thirteen-week contract. But if you're good, they usually extend it."

"No."

"Sorry?"

"Don't insult me by offering me a job packing vegetables."

"Well, they are looking for intelligent people. People who know their onions. And their carrots, and potatoes."

"Please don't be glib with me. I don't appreciate fatuous remarks."

"OK. No problem. It's not your line. Let's see what else we have. Ah. How about this. Plenty of travel. Some nights away, for which an extra allowance is payable. Plenty overtime. Decent pay. A good, reputable company."

"What's the job?"

"Driver's mate."

"Goodbye Mr Cooper."

"Wait, Mr Light. Come on. Think about it. You need a job, right? Or you wouldn't be here. Look. Let me be honest with you. I need to fill these vacancies to meet my target for the month. Otherwise my commission's well down. And I mean, like, rock bottom. Zero. Zilch. I've got bills to pay as well, you know. Mortgage on the riverside flat, HP on the Beamer. Give me a break. How about it? Just try the job for a week. If you don't like it, fine. No problem. Come back and I'll fix you up with something else."

"If you're really desperate for money, why don't you get in your BMW and drive your lads to the factory so you can all work through the night packing vegetables? Easy work. Clean modern environment. And work wear provided. Why not give it a try, Mr Cooper? Or else try Hollywood. Goodbye."

Walk out through the reception area where Alison is cursing her computer terminal and slamming the mouse against the table. Snatch my registration form from her desk and tear it into little pieces before her wide eyes as redundant executives fill out their registration forms in the forlorn hope that there is a rewarding job somewhere out there. Their hopes will be dashed when they meet Mr Charisma Cooper.

So much for searching for suitable employment. Why couldn't he have offered me a job as a recruitment consultant. When I put my mind to it and really concentrate, I can be a total arsehole. But perhaps they only recruit those to whom acting the arsehole comes naturally. Still, while I'm in town I may as well call into the Jobless Centre, which is just along the road. Pass the security officer on duty in reception and make my way directly to the boards. All arranged in long rows, bearing details of work grouped into various categories. Start at the first row and work my way along. Grab a handful of slips on which to note the reference numbers of those which interest me. And after forty-five minutes of reading and studying details of each and every vacancy, my handful of slips remain blank. Study the faces of fellow job-seekers. Blank, expressionless, soulless. Only there as part of the charade of the job-seekers charter. Call in once a week. Apply for a job you have no chance of getting, then sign on every fortnight and get a giro to pay for a fortnight's supply of beer and fags. And of course, hold a little back each week to cover the subscription to satellite TV. And here I am, smartly dressed in black overcoat, charcoal grey double-breasted suit, white shirt - the front of which I've ironed to the best of my ability - and silk maroon paisley tie. And don't I look a prat! Among the rest of the punters in jeans or tracksuit bottoms, trainers, T-shirts at this time of year, and baseball caps. Many wearing earrings or nose studs. Bearing tattoos, the likes of which, in my opinion, should only be sported by hairy-arsed marines. Bound to make a wonderful first impression if ever they attend a job interview. Probably not yet mastered the art of joined-up writing, and some of them definitely struggling with the nuances of the English language, as I discover from standing by a board near the clerical officers' desks pretending to peruse the vacancies while eavesdropping on the conversation between a harassed member of staff and a would-be giant of industry.

"I want to apply for this. Wot you fink?"

"Just a second, please, Mr Trethick, while I bring the details up on the screen. Here we are. 'Young dynamic people required by national company to train as computer programmers. Minimum of 5 GCSEs required, including maths. No experience required, but must have an interest in computers and be willing to attend college on day-release, for which the company will pay. Salary negotiable.'"

"Sounds ace, know what I mean."

"Well, Mr Trethick. Do you have five GCSEs, including maths?"

"Well, no."

"How many do you have?"

"None."

"None?"

"I got expelled. It wa'n't my fault, know what I mean. A teacher had it in for me. I fink if they'd let me stay I'd have got at least six GCSEs, wiv maffs as well. I were OK at maffs. No problem, know what I mean. Could add and take away and times no bovver."

"But Mr Trethick. They require these qualifications. Without them, you're really wasting your time."

"Yeah, but I fit the rest of the advert, know what I mean?"

"Well, no, actually. Perhaps you could tell me what you mean."

"Well. For a start, I'm young. And, what was it, dynamite?"

"Dynamic."

"Yeah. I'm young and dynamic. I like playing wiv computers. Got some ace games. And always get top scores. My name's on the top players' list on every machine in every arcade in town. Ask anybody. They all know Gaz. A whizz wiv computers. And on top of that, I don't mind going to college as long as they pay. Some of me mates are at college. It's a laugh. Know what I mean?"

"Yes, Mr Trethick. Here's an application form. Fill it out and send it to this address."

"Fanks."

Nice to know the future is in safe hands. Of this spotty embryonic entrepreneur. A real go-getter. For a start, he could go get a decent haircut.

Do a little shopping while I'm in town. Stock up on the items I've allowed to run low. Soap, deodorant, razor blades. Stuff that Lucy bought as a matter of course. The cupboards always well-stocked. In case of World War Three. Feel as if I've been shaving with a butter knife for the past few days. Tearing out the stubble rather than slicing through it. Nothing to beat a clean fresh blade. And a pack of sticking plasters for the inevitable shaky-handed accidental nicks. And better get myself a bottle of shampoo while I remember. Plopper has been eyeing me suspiciously of late since I've resorted to using the stuff Mr E bought for him. Plopper's a clean dog. Doesn't need it as much as I do. And though it smells a little on the pungent side, it keeps me free of fleas.

The rain coming down more persistently now. People sheltering in shop doorways and seeking refuge in the covered shopping arcades which are already populated by groups of bored schoolkids playing truant. Pop into this garish place to sit and have a bite to eat. A fast food joint, its corporate logo reminiscent of the huge whalebone arches I remember seeing in a book as a child. Shiny functional plastic tables and chairs. The decor bright primary colours. Identical to a thousand other places around the country serving up their portion-controlled, chopped and shaped tasteless shit. Spam for the nineties. And behind the counter an acne-scarred highly motivated customer-service-orientated crew member greets me with a monosyllabic grunt. Perhaps I can make his day. Have a little fun.

"Burger and chips, please."

"We don't do chips. Fries."

"Burger and fries, then."

"Regular?"

"No. This is my first time."

"The fries. You want regular fries?"

"How often is regular? Every twenty minutes?"

"The portion. Regular's the portion you get."

"Regular, then."

"Right. You want a shake?"

"No thanks. I prefer to towel myself dry."

"What?"

"Never mind. Just burger and regular fries."

Minced beef sizzling on the griddle. Paper-hatted crew members busily about their tasks. No sign of the captain of this culinary ship. Probably wears a paper hat with a paper peak to distinguish him from the minions.

"There you go. Enjoy."

"What are these?"

"Regular fries. What you ordered."

"Some of them are irregular."

"What?"

"Some of them are slightly longer than the majority. And some are just a tad thicker."

"I can't help that."

"Well, it's not good enough."

"You want to see the team leader?"

"Yes."

"Jane! There's a man here who wants to complain."

"Yes, sir. How may I help?"

"I was merely querying why these so-called regular fries seem to be slightly irregular in shape, size, and, for that matter, colour."

"Regular is the size of the portion, sir."

"I told him that."

"All right, Simon. Get on with your work. As I was saying, sir. Regular refers to the portion. Not the actual size and shape of the fries."

"That's misleading. And extremely confusing. First, he asks me if I'm a regular customer. And by the way if I were would I get better treatment? Then he asks me how regularly I want my meal served. And finally, I get this rubbish."

"What's wrong with it, sir?"

"It looks most unappetizing. A leaf of limp lettuce. Watery relish. Soggy slice of tomato. And what appear to be wood-shavings in this cremated ersatz meat."

"Those are onions, sir."

"I know my onions. And these most definitely are not."

"Would you like another one, sir?"

"I'd prefer my money back so I can go elsewhere and buy some proper food."

"Very well, sir. Here you are."

"Thank you. And, by the way, a friend of mine is about to issue a law suit against your company. As a long-term sufferer of Parkinson's Disease, he objects to your staff asking him if he would like a regular shake. Have a nice day."

CHAPTER 9

And among the midweek mail, the latest missive from my friend at the council.

"My dear R,

I am eternally grateful for your comments which have made my job seem worthwhile at a time of self-doubt. After all, what's a turd, or two, between friends? I propose that we meet to celebrate our mutual understanding. From nine o'clock every Friday night I can be found in the Queen's Arms on Grabhorn Street. You will recognise me immediately. I will be the one not attired in bondage gear.

N.

PS. I have had several relationships of the Middlesex variety."

Must think carefully before penning my reply to this most unexpected of propositions. Into the toilet to tear off a single sheet of this quilted toilet tissue.

"Dear N,

Are you propositioning me?

R."

Let's see what sort of reply this elicits. Perhaps I should have added a PS requesting a contribution towards the postal charges I am incurring in dealing with this loathsome creature.

And by return of post, his succinct reply.

 "My dear R,

Yes!

N."

This time I shall wait a few days before replying. Keep him in suspense. Imagine him sorting through his mail every morning eagerly awaiting my letter. Spoil his day for a while. Make him grumpy with his staff. I wonder what he looks like. Short and bald, maybe, but with immaculate fingernails. A dapper little chap with a silk hanky poking from the breast pocket of his brown herringbone suit.

Out with Plopper on this bright cold evening to wend our way to the cul-de-sac of breeze-block garages for rent. A half-moon providing sufficient light to allow me to pick my way through this minefield of dog crap which Plopper tends to favour for his toilet. Some dark corners allowing him some privacy to raise his tail and lower his buttocks. Kicks his legs backwards in triumph, scuffing up little showers of dust, and does a quick lap of honour. Stops by a clump of grass and tall weed, nose down snuffling and tail wagging.

"Here, Plopper."

No response. Just a more vigorous thrash of the tail. Edge forward cautiously, wary of hidden horrors in the dark grass. Plopper backing away, sits down and makes sad little whining noises. And there, just visible in the deep grass, is a small sparrow. Sitting there, making no effort to escape as I reach down to pick it up. Plopper looking on approvingly as I hold it small and warm in the palm of my hand. Its tiny chest rising and falling in great heaves. Faint flutter of a heartbeat under a broken wing. The trembling heart of a captive bird. And I don't know what to do for the best. Take it home and nurse it in a shoebox until it recovers and is eternally grateful. Teach it to sit on my shoulder while I do Long John Silver impressions at parties. Then fly round the room and on command plop on my enemies. Or lay it carefully back in the grass in the hope that it returns safely to its family before some mangy old cat gets it. And while I'm coming to a decision, the sparrow slowly keels over on to its side and lies there lifeless. Plopper's big eyes reflect my sadness as I lay the stiff little corpse back in the grass and cover it with a leaf of dock.

Time for a quick note to my friend at the council.

"N,

I am sorry to have to disappoint you, but I spend Friday nights in the company of a Master of the Rolls and several civic dignitaries. Should you ever be invited to one of our gatherings, please do not hesitate to approach me. I will be the one not wearing short trousers and schoolboy cap.

R.

PS. I trust Operation Turdwatch is going well."

Another night in another pub. Quite a lively place with people gathered in groups to drink and talk, and laugh. While I sit alone at the bar, nursing a full glass. I prefer it this way: to be alone, but alone in a crowd. In front of me appears the friendly face of the smiling barman.

"You're getting to be quite a regular in here."

"Sorry?"

"I said you're becoming quite a regular."

"Yes, I like it in here. Nice pub."

"Thanks. I'm Andy. What's your name?"

"They call me the Lone Binger. Righter of wrongs. Smoker of cigs. Drinker of drinks. And general all-round good egg. But you can call me Ray, if you so wish."

"Pleased to meet you, Ray."

"Likewise, Andy."

Nice to know there's somewhere I can go to pass the time of day. Where I will be served with civility and not be pestered by some other sad old duffer.

Looking around at the groups of people, when I see at the far end of the bar a familiar face. She's walking towards me on impossibly long, shapely legs.

"Hi. I thought I recognised you. You don't remember me, do you? Julie. We met in a hotel bar. With my friend, Mandy. And your friend. I can't remember his name, but he was a wild one. I remember yours, though. Ray, isn't it? I was hoping you might have called me. I gave your friend my number to pass to you, but he probably forgot."

"Yes."

"So, how are you? You left suddenly, I thought I must have upset you."

"I wasn't feeling very well."

"Me neither. Especially the next morning. I had to phone in sick. Listen. I'm sorry about what happened that night. I mean, I'm not usually like that. I've never done anything like that before. I don't know what came over me. I'm usually quiet and a bit shy. I don't have many friends. That's why I go out with Mandy once a week. Her husband works nights, and we let our hair down a bit. You don't mind me talking to you, do you? Only you always look so sad. Can I buy you a drink? I'm having one."

"I'll get them. What would you like?"

"Ta. Half a lager, please. Mandy's not coming out this week. That's why I'm on my own tonight. She's got a black eye. Her husband beats her up. Accuses her of going with other men. Which she never used to do until he started hitting her. Then she thought she might as well do it if he's going to beat her up anyway. I don't like men like that. Which is why I live on my own. OK, I get lonely, but I'd rather be lonely than live with someone who didn't love me. Do you know what I mean? I know I'm not very attractive, but I've got a nice figure..."

"I think you're rather attractive."

"Thank you. You are nice. I said that to Mandy as soon as I saw you. I was glad she fancied your friend. You've got such nice sad eyes. You're not the type who'd beat a woman up."

"You don't know me."

"I can tell. I've known a lot of men who just want one thing. I nearly got married once, but I couldn't go through with it. So here I am, thirty-six years old, and still single. No, you're different. You could have taken advantage of me when I was drunk. But you didn't. And I respect that. And I'm sure it's not because you're gay or anything. You're not, are you? I'm sorry. I shouldn't have asked that. That's none of my business anyway. Not that it would matter if you were. I mean, we could still be friends. You're so easy to talk to. You're not, though. Are you?"

"What?"

"Gay."

"No."

"Oh, I'm glad. Not that it would have made any difference. But I would like to get to know you better. You've got such sincere eyes. You're not married, are you?"

"My wife's dead. Not long since."

"Oh God. I'm so sorry."

"That's OK."

"I bet you really loved her. I can tell."

"Yes."

"No wonder you look so sad. You poor man. Do you want to talk about her? They say it helps."

"Thank you, but I'd rather not, if you don't mind."

"Of course not. But if you ever want a shoulder to cry on, I could be there for you. I wouldn't mind. Everyone says I'm a good listener. People at work are always telling me their problems. So, do you mind if I give you my phone number again? Just in case. You can call me any time. Pour out your heart. And I'll just listen. And sympathise. I really am ever so sorry about your wife."

"Thank you. You're kind."

"Everybody says that about me. Someone once said, and I wasn't supposed to overhear, but I did, she said I've got a heart of gold. Underneath a face of granite. And that hurt, you know? I mean, I know I'm not beautiful, but I do have other qualities. A girl at work paid £2500 to have her breasts done. And mine are natural, and just as nice. I'm not embarrassing you, am I?"

"No."

"I bet your wife was beautiful."

"Yes."

"See. You're talking about her already. You can relax with me. Say anything you like."

"Thanks, but I really don't want to talk about Lucy just now."

"Lucy. What a beautiful name! Classy. Not like Julie."

"Julie's a nice name. Nothing wrong with that."

"Thank you. You are kind! Now, can I buy you a drink?"

"I'll get them."

"No, I insist. It's not as if we're on a date or anything. If a man asks a lady to go out with him then I think it's only right that he should pay. But this is different. We're just two friends having a drink together. So, I should pay my way."

"If that's how you feel. Could I have a small Malt whisky?"

"Ooh, I like that. That's classy. Not just a whisky. A Malt whisky! You've got very discerning taste. I like that in a man. Well, I can't let you think I'm common, drinking lager. I only drink it when I'm a bit short of money."

"Then let me pay. What would you like?"

"Well, thank you. If you insist, I'll have a vodka and lime. With just a dash of ice. And a slice. Of lime, if they have it. Will you excuse me, please, for a minute? While I go to the Ladies."

"Of course."

Act the gentleman and stand up while Julie shuffles from her bar stool and wiggles her way to the Ladies on those legs of unlikely length. Nice arse, too. Wonder if Duncan had poked her. Dismiss any doubt immediately. Of course, he had! Duncan had poked every woman he'd ever met. Except Lucy. He'd confided in me on my stag night, that although he had urges in that direction, he regarded Lucy as out of bounds, off limits. And untouchable to anyone but my good and worthy self. And he would defend her honour with his life, if necessary. Though he knew it wouldn't be. She was perfectly capable of defending her own. And it was obvious to anybody she had the hots only for me. Drunk, towards the end of the night, he'd called her Lucy Lockedfanny. To whom only I had the great rusty key. And proposed that we go together to the local whorehouse in order that I could get it oiled. So that it would slide in easily and open the sacred lock....

"I'm sorry. Have I been long?"

"Sorry?"

"You look miles away. I thought you'd forgotten all about me."

"No. I was just deep in thought."

"That's OK, Ray. I don't mind. It'll take a lot of getting over. If you want me to leave you alone with your thoughts, it's all right. I don't mind. I do understand."

"No. Don't go. I'm enjoying your company. But I don't want to talk. Just listen. Tell me all about yourself."

"There's not a lot to tell, really. I'm the youngest of five. Three brothers and a sister. Born on a council estate. Tried really hard at school, but left at sixteen without any qualifications. Engaged and pregnant at seventeen. He didn't want it, so I had an abortion, and now I'm sterile. I left home after that, and moved here, and got a job as a junior in the accounts department at an insurance company. Did well, and now I'm a supervisor at the call centre. Not bad for someone with no qualifications! I've been with them for eighteen years now, and I've got my own flat. My own personal, private space. It's my retreat. I've had it for seven years, and in all that time, I've never invited anybody back there. Would you believe that? It's not that I'm ashamed of it, or anything. It's just that it's mine, and it doesn't belong to anybody else. Once I'm in there, with the door locked behind me, I'm in my own world. I can do what I want. Nobody owns me. Nobody can tell me what to do. If I want to walk round naked, I can, provided all the curtains are closed, of course. It's my refuge. My home! And I love it, It's just that it's so... lonely, sometimes."

Chivalrously offering a handkerchief to my sniffling companion. Who mumbles a muffled thank you, blows her nose and wipes her eyes before offering back the soiled linen. Which I decline.

"So, Ray. What are your plans for tonight? Meeting your friends?"

"I don't have any friends here. We only moved down here a few months ago, from Yorkshire. All our friends are up there."

"Don't you have anybody you can talk to?"

"Plopper."

"Sorry?"

"I've got Plopper. A little mongrel dog with a Rottweiler complex. Some neighbours bought him for me after Lucy died. I didn't want him, but he's sort of become attached to me. I can't keep him, though. I don't have time to devote to him. I'll have to go back to work soon. If I've still got a job to go to, that is. They keep sending me letters."

"How long have you been off?

"Nearly six weeks."

"You poor man."

"I don't want your pity."

"I know. I'm sorry. It's just that it's so difficult not to feel sorry for you. Life's really kicked you in the balls, hasn't it? If you'll excuse the expression."

"I think that's a fair reflection of the events of the past few months, yes."

"And you've spent all this time on your own? It's not good for you."

"Why not? I happen to enjoy my own company. I can tell myself a joke and laugh uncontrollably."

"Are you looking after yourself? Are you eating properly?"

"Yes. Most of it goes into my mouth. And I chew each mouthful fifty times. Or until it's been masticated to a soft mushy pulp. Whichever is first."

"It seems to me that most of your food comes in liquid form these days."

"Ah. This is the ultimate in convenience food. Requires little in the way of preparation. And is most satisfying."

"Let me buy you something to eat."

"No thanks. I'm fine."

"Well, I'm hungry. At least keep me company while I get something to eat."

And so, to the small cosy Italian restaurant, with its red and green paper tablecloths and attentive waiters, who take our coats and usher us to a corner table with a posy of flowers and a candle in a Chianti bottle. And hover while we ponder over the menu before finally opting for pizzas to be washed down with a carafe of house red. Which we drink and have replenished by the time the food arrives. Oven-hot pizza, with a sprinkling of soot for authenticity. Cutting a slice and pronouncing it the best pizza I've had since the last one. Lightening up, and forgetting for the time being that life has kicked me in the balls, I become all smiles, engaging my new and pleasant companion in light-hearted conversation. Feeling oddly at ease with her. Though determined to keep her at arm's length, I feel drawn to her warm-hearted nature and venture to tell her so. She returns a shy smile and blushes a little.

The night has turned considerably colder, but Julie declines the offer of a taxi home as her flat is only a few minutes' walk away.

"Ray. Thank you. I've really enjoyed myself this evening."

"So have I."

"I'm glad."

"Me too. Goodnight, Julie."

"Ray, walk me home, please. The streets are not safe for a woman on her own at this time of night."

"I'm hardly in any condition to walk anywhere."

"Please, Ray. It's not far. Take my arm. Oops, you are drunk. I didn't realise you were that bad."

"It's the fresh air. It's not good for someone who's spent all day in a bar. I'm all right. Just hang on to you and get you home."

"And what about you?"

"I shall sleep where I fall."

"Nonsense. You'll come back with me and have some coffee."

Linking arms, we stagger along as I sing quietly. Julie supporting my weight. Leaning me against the door, holding me upright with one elbow on my chest as she rummages in her handbag for her keys. Which she fumbles and drops. Bending over to pick them up, she releases her hold on me, and I slide down the door and sit on the ground, a broad smile on my face. Julie picks up the keys and unlocks the door which swings open under my weight as I fall back, my head hitting the doormat and raising little clouds of dust. Rolling over, raising myself on all fours, and crawling after her into the lounge, collapsing into an armchair. Julie hangs up her coat and disappears into the kitchen, returning minutes later with two mugs of coffee.

"Here, Ray. Drink this."

"Thanks."

"You're welcome. Now how do you feel?"

"Tired. Otherwise fine. Except rather slightly drunk."

"You can stay here tonight if you like."

"Thanks. But I don't like sleeping in chairs. Gives me backache."

"You can sleep in my bed. I'd like that."

"Will you take advantage of my drunken condition to ravish me?"

"If you like."

"I do believe I would like."

"Well, then. Come through when you've finished your coffee. Bathroom's through there. Bedroom's the door next to it. I'll be waiting."

Wash my hands and face and private parts which may later become more public in the sink in this tiny cluttered bathroom. Full of women's things. Tights hanging over the towel rail. Underwear drying on a line over the bath. Brightly coloured, sexy garments, not unlike Lucy's. Clean the teeth using Julie's toothbrush. And a dab of the deodorant here, and here, and just a little under here. Hoping she'll excuse the familiarity.

A light from the bedside lamp shedding a warm glow around the bedroom. Sparsely furnished, but tidy. Decorated in shades of warm peach and pale green. Julie smiling at me from the double bed, arms held out in welcome. Undress hurriedly and slide under the duvet as Julie shifts sideways towards me, kissing hungrily, all teeth and tongue. Her hand moving from my neck, down my body, until it reaches its goal. Rubbing me slowly and gently, rhythmically, while covering my face with passionate kisses. My hands on her slim shapely body, feeling the hard, erect nipples, the flat belly with its hairy bush. Into which I will shortly be pushing up my shoot. Julie making little appreciative noises as a finger explores her moist warm opening, her excitement increasing as my thumb brushes her clitoris. Rubbing harder and faster on my pole, which suddenly erupts, spewing out wave upon wave of hot sticky fluid over her hand, as she reaches her own climax, stiffening, her back arched as she pushes her body forward against mine.

"Shit. I'm sorry. I'm so sorry. I guess I got carried away."

"It's all right, Ray. Honest. It's my fault. I should have stopped when I knew you were coming. There's tissues on the bedside table. Pass me one, please."

"Here."

"Thanks."

"Is one enough?"

"Probably not. There's a lot."

"It's been a long time."

"You must have needed it."

"I guess so."

"Well, now you can relax, and we'll do it slowly. I'll get you up for it again, and then, if you don't mind, would you do me how I like it?"

"How's that?"

"Doggy-style."

"Oh, shit. I've got to go."

Leaping out of bed, grabbing clothes from all corners of the room and dressing hurriedly, wrestling to tuck a half erection into the underpants. Julie naked in front of me trying to pull it out again.

"Ray, please don't go. Please stay. I'm sorry if I've upset you. Please come back to bed. I want it so much."

"I have to go home. I'm sorry. It's nothing you've done. Or said."

"Why can't you stay?"

"It's Plopper. He's been locked in the house since about three o'clock. I need to take him out. And feed him. And clean up the shit he'll no doubt have dumped behind the door. And repair furniture, fixtures and fittings on which he exercises his teeth. I'm sorry."

"Will you see me again? Call me?"

"Of course. If you wish."

"Please. Take my phone number, and address."

"Thanks. Got to go."

Kissing her on the cheek, while she cups my balls gently in her warm hand, and gives them a little squeeze goodnight.

Discomfort from an over-full bladder. Should have relieved it before leaving Julie's. Never mind. Next left, and head for the toilets in the park, careful to keep away from the swings where piles of dog muck await the unsuspecting pedestrian. Into the Gents to read the graffiti as I splash the badly stained stainless steel. Crude drawings of monstrous anatomical parts, telephone numbers, and boastful descriptions of past couplings. A sullen-looking youth lurking in the corner stall, pretending to splash.

"Suck you off for a tenner, mate."

"What?"

"I said I'll suck you off for a tenner. Phil's the name, fellatio's the game. That's my motto. Come on, man. How about it? OK, then, a fiver. As long as you're quick. Only I'm expecting a regular any time now. What about it? I'm good. Satisfaction guaranteed, or your money back."

"Do I get my deposit back?"

"What?"

"If I'm not satisfied, do I get my semen back?"

"What you on about? Nutter! Fuck off. How am I supposed to make a living with weirdos like you about?"

"You're the weirdo."

"Pervert!"

Squaring up to the youth and grabbing him by the throat. His face an inch away from mine as a middle-aged man enters.

"Oh, I'm sorry. I'll come back in ten minutes, shall I?"

"No. Wait, Frank. The gentleman is just leaving."

"He can stay and watch if he likes. I don't mind. I'll pay extra."

"Forget it. I'm off."

"Sorry about that, Frank. You get all sorts of weirdos in here. The usual, is it?"

Legging it across the park. Short cut across the flower beds and over a low wall on which I catch my foot, stumble and fall crashing to the pavement, pain shooting through my fingers. Struggle to my feet and examine my hand under the sodium street light. Some swelling and discoloration round the base of the fingers, which are stiff and throbbing. As my other member had earlier been, until Julie's hand had brought a premature end to proceedings.

Almost home now, passing the row of rented garages, the end one of which has been newly sprayed by a graffiti artist. In bright yellow, green, blue and black, it now bears the legend 'You don't need a weatherman to know which way the wind blows.' And alongside it, a stylised representation of a huge clenched fist with the index finger protruding in red, black and white, with the autograph 'Mac the Finger' printed below. Freshly sprayed, the faint smell of cellulose still in the air. And he's right. I know that the wind at the moment is freezing my balls off. Finally, at my front door. Fumbling with the keys, and making reassuring little noises in response to the distressed yelps from within. As the door opens, Plopper races past me and on to the Eversons' front lawn. And by the sundial which marks Scamp's grave, he deposits a copious crap, before returning, tail wagging, to his neglectful master. Stepping inside, switching on the hall light to illuminate the scene, which, thankfully, is free of doggy accident areas. Inspecting the house, and breathing a sigh of relief as Plopper tours proudly with me, showing me here and there, tail thumping furiously. Putting down fresh water, and opening a tin of fish-smelling dog meat, which Plopper devours in a matter of seconds, before lapping up most of the water, the rest splashing over a wide area.

"Good boy, Plopper. Good boy. I'm sorry."

Plopper at my heels as I wash and inspect the injured hand in the bathroom. Swollen and sore, but still able to pour myself a Malt, I slump in the chair, Plopper laid in front of me, head on paws, tail swishing every time he catches his master's eye. Before falling asleep to dream his doggy dreams. Of fields, and sticks, and cute lady dogs. And trees and lampposts and interesting smells. Of marrowbones and dog biscuits. Eyes rolling, tongue out, twitching in his sleep. And making little growling noises at imaginary enemies. As my nightmare returns with its recurring theme.

Walking into this strange cold room. Fluorescent-lit. A table opposite, and behind it a chair, upon which sits a man in uniform. A long red scar curves from his right temple to the corner of his mouth, which breaks into a thin smile.

"What do you want?"

"I've come to sign the papers."

"What papers?"

"The papers for my release."

"First you have to satisfy the conditions."

"What conditions?"

"The conditions which will determine whether you are fit for release."

"What are they?"

"First. Did you love your wife?"

"Of course!"

"Then why did you let her die?"

"She had cancer. Of the bowel."

"Answer the question! Why did you let her die?"

"There was nothing we could do. It was incurable."

"You tried all available treatment?"

"Yes."

"Did you try all available treatment?"

"Yes! I told you."

"Are you sure?"

"Yes. No. She refused a colostomy."

"Might that have cured her?"

"No."

"How do you know if you didn't try?"

"The doctors said it was too widespread. The possibility of it having any beneficial effect was almost infinitesimal."

"Wasn't it worth a try?"

"We both agreed. It was a joint decision!"

"Scruff died. Your parents died. Lucy died. Why is it that everybody you have loved has died?"

"I don't know."

"Dismissed!"

CHAPTER 10

Waking in a cold sweat. The Stripper's tinny tune sounding muffled from the drawer. And when I answer, there is a pause and then a click as it goes dead. A regular occurrence these days. Switch it off and throw it in the bin. My brain reeling with the guilt for all the deaths. Sobbing in the chair. Plopper comes over and curls up at my feet. Then reaches up to lick my aching fingers. Into the bathroom to wash the throbbing digits. Examining them again. Rather purple-black round the base and somewhat stiff, but not broken. Tape them up for a day or two as a precaution.

Look out of the window to see Mr E shovelling the brown stuff from his lawn. Wonder if he'll suspect Plopper. Go out and say hello. Act naturally and try not to look guilty. Hope Plopper doesn't give the game away by committing a repeat indiscretion while I speak to Mr E.

"Morning, Mr E."

"Oh. Good morning, Ray. How are you this morning?"

"Just fine."

"What happened to your hand?"

"I slipped while walking Plopper. Nothing serious."

"Would you believe this? Somebody's let their dog go to the toilet on my lawn."

"There are some irresponsible owners about. Just don't care."

"Mmm. Listen, Ray. I've been thinking. If you're having problems. You know... getting relief... if you understand my drift."

"No."

"Ray. I know you've lost your wife. But you still have, well, urges. Of a sexual nature."

"Oh. I see. Well, yes."

"There's a woman I use. Lives quite close by. Very clean and discreet. Been going to her for years. Since Mrs E lost interest in that respect. I could get you an introduction if you like."

"Thanks. I'll think about it."

"You do that. And not a word to Mrs E."

"Of course not."

Horny old goat! Who'd have thought it. Still, perhaps it's not such a bad idea. Lucy said I'd not to live a monastic life. Share my body, and my heart. Except I don't think I've enough heart left to share.

Walking Plopper on this cold morning. Just a touch here and there of frost. Through the streets, across the field and past the sprawling comprehensive school. Idle daydreams of my own school days, when life was full of girls, football, cigarettes and illicit alcohol. To be taken regularly, and in equal measure. Where every misadventure had its risk, and therefore its irresistible appeal. The cricket pavilion on the edge of the sports field, a plain, squat concrete building, so unlike the elaborate wooden Victorian structure of my old school. Where one day, Duncan and I, patrolling our domain as school prefects, had chanced upon a fifth-former and a girl from the nearby Grammar about to engage in sexual shenanigans. Duncan demanding an immediate halt to proceedings, and fining the boy five cigarettes in exchange for not reporting him to the headmaster. The girl lying on the grass, knickers down, parts exposed, proved too much temptation, and a bargain was quickly struck whereby Duncan would complete the act to their mutual satisfaction at a negotiated rate of three cigarettes. The remaining two of which we smoked afterwards as Duncan lectured on how everything has its price, but that price is not absolute and the key to business success lies in spotting opportunities and negotiating favourable deals. Which Duncan had done ever since. And when Yvette, the French mistress, arrived, he opened a book, taking bets from fellow pupils on which member of staff would be the first to screw her. Raking in piles of pennies on the English master at seven to two, and the geography teacher at four to one, he finally announced the winner to be an outsider - the games mistress, whom he assured everybody he had seen through the gym window, locked in a passionate embrace, hand up her skirt, with Yvette. And although he'd concocted the story, it later took on a measure of probability, as Yvette was sent back to France in disgrace after tales of sexual activities with young girls to whom she gave private tuition. Thereafter, the gym mistress, who cycled to school, became known as the "dike on a bike".

Circumventing the estate, past the boarded-up off-licence and general store, its stone frontage still blackened from the fire which caused its closure some years back. Mr E had once told me about it; how the retiring owners had sold it to a young Asian family in the '70s. How despite initial local opposition and mistrust they'd built a thriving business and won over the locals through their courteous service and extended opening hours. How the two sons had taken over the business and improved trade and profits. Until the rise of a new generation of racist thugs made their presence and intentions known through their systematic persecution of the family. Graffiti at first, then escalating to scratching the paintwork of their car, then kicking the headlamps in, and smashing the windscreen. Then attacks on the shop. Windows broken during the night. Slogans daubed on the windows. Paint and excrement plastered over the door. Piss through the letter box. Physical assaults, culminating in the attack on the father by a group wielding baseball bats. And, finally, while he was still recovering in hospital, an arson attack which burnt out the shop and accommodation above, though the family, mercifully, escaped. Three youths were arrested, but not charged. The two sons, however, started up another business with the insurance money. Renting units on the industrial estate, they'd begun manufacturing electronic components for the computer industry. They were now millionaires, with a purpose-built high-tech factory, where, unsurprisingly, they employed only Asians apart from a few token whites on the shop floor to appease the race relations do-gooders. Good for them. And Mr E told me there was one thing above all he admired in Asians. Not their capacity for working long hours. Not their ability to close ranks and look after their own. Not their single-minded pursuit of success. None of these. What Mr E most admired was their ability to grow thick luxuriant moustaches.

I'm beginning to quite enjoy these regular outings with Plopper. Bring some semblance of routine to a life which has lost its order. Faithful and obedient friend. Stay, Plopper. Sit, Plopper. Very well, then. Ignore me and do whatever you like, Plopper. Meet other people with their dogs. Like this woman with her old mongrel. Snappy, snarling, ill-tempered bitch. Lip permanently curled. Teeth bared. Nasty piece of work. Shouldn't be allowed out without a muzzle. However, her dog is a good-natured beast and plays and frolics happily with Plopper. Pity the miserable old sow doesn't share some of the traits of her canine companion. On the other hand, the thought of her sticking her nose up Plopper's backside is most off-putting. Still, I suppose I ought to show some friendliness towards a fellow human being, though any connection between this old trout and the rest of the human race is decidedly tenuous.

"Morning. Rather cold, isn't it?"

"Would you kindly get that mangy hound of yours away from my Bess!"

"They're all right. Playing quite happily."

"Call him away. I don't want Bess to catch anything from him."

"What exactly are you implying?"

"Well, look at him! When was he last bathed and groomed? He could be full of fleas. Or worse. Has he had all his injections?"

"Yes. Well, nearly all."

"What do you mean, nearly all?"

"Well, he hasn't had his rabies jab. But, you see, if I take him for it, the vet will inquire why he needs it. And when I tell him I found the dog as a stray in France and smuggled him back through the Tunnel, they'll take him away from me and put him in quarantine. And he might not even have rabies. I know he froths at the mouth now and again, but that could be caused by anything. Doesn't have to be rabies, does it. He may have eaten a small animal which has disagreed with his digestive system. Could be anything. I mean, he bit me a few days ago, and I feel OK. Just thirsty, that's all."

"My God! Bess! Come here at once! You! What's your name? I shall report you."

"Monsieur L'Escargot."

"Wait while I write this down. Mr Les Cargo. And what's your address, Mr Cargo?"

"1, Aortic Valve Avenue, Upper Thorax."

"Whereabouts is that?"

"Near the heart. So, it's a long way away from you."

"I'm inclined to believe you've deliberately given me a false name and address. However, I shall not waste my time with you. You're obviously a scoundrel. Now take your horrid dog and go away."

"I suppose a blow-job is out of the question?"

"How dare you!"

"You sad old bat! Why don't you open your legs and let a little joy into your life?"

"Well, really! You horrible man. I shall report this to the police. Obscene language and sexual assault! Are you trying to pick me up?"

"Don't flatter yourself, lady. I'd rather pick up a leper's turd. So, wind your stringy little neck in, and go home. Come on, Plopper."

Plopper immediately to my side in a rare show of solidarity with his master, walking alongside me as we leave Lady Snooty aghast in the middle of the field. Good boy, Plopper. Let that be a lesson to you, son. Stay away from those who think they are a cut above you. They're always out to give you grief for infringing upon their pathetic existence. Sad, really. I suppose the old dear must have got quite a shock when the colonies gained independence and she no longer had black slaves to order around. Now takes out her spite on the general public. Then goes home to sit in her conservatory. With her G and T. And husband named Reginald. And together they sit for hours bemoaning the lack of moral standards and manners of the working, or rather, unemployed, classes, and compose long rambling letters to the Times. Well, Plopper. We don't care, do we. We still have our morals and standards of behaviour to uphold. Even if they are somewhat dissolute these days.

Alan called at the house this afternoon, bearing a letter from Mr Barker.

"Hello, Ray. How are you?"

"OK."

"I'm sorry to have to disturb you at home. Mr Barker sent me. He's written to you a few times and tried to phone you. But got no replies. Except, of course, for that letter you sent, which his secretary photocopied and passed round the office. God, I wish I dare say things like that to him. Anyway, he sent me round to give you this letter."

"What's it about?"

"I don't know. It's sealed. But he wanted to make sure you received it, which is why he sent me to deliver it by hand."

"Do you want to come in?"

"No. Thanks, Ray. I haven't time. I'm having to do this in my lunch hour. Got to get back. And here's a card from your friends at the office. We sort of guess you won't be coming back."

"Thanks."

"All the best, Ray. See you."

"'Bye."

Opening the card. Signed with best wishes by all the staff at the office, except of course the boss, whose personal message was contained in the sealed envelope. Throw it on the pile with the rest of the unread or unanswered mail. But perhaps better take a quick peek at it first. Perhaps old man Barker's feeling sorry for me and offering me a rise. Tearing the envelope open and extracting the cheap company stationery. To read news of further misfortune.

"Dear Mr Light,

Because of your reluctance to respond to my repeated communications, and inability to negotiate a timely return to your duties, I have no alternative but to terminate your employment with Barker and Co. (Rubber Goods UK) Ltd., with immediate effect.

Under Paragraph 2(a), section 1 of your terms and conditions of employment, which document you signed upon joining the company, you are entitled to no further payment, having already more than exhausted your entitlement. Your dismissal is in accordance with the rules laid down in the aforementioned document, in the section entitled 'Grounds for Dismissal', Section 2 - Unauthorized or Excessive Absence. I do not need to quote verse and chapter to you; the company lawyers have assured me I have more than sufficient grounds for dispensing with your expertise in the high-powered world of designer rubber goods.

Further, since the accommodation you are currently occupying is provided by the company at a below-market-level rent, it is subject to your employment by the said company. (Please refer to Section 5 of your tenancy agreement.) You will, therefore, vacate the premises, leaving the fixtures and fittings and overall decoration in 'good order' (see Section 9), within 28 (twenty-eight) days of receipt of this notice of eviction (see Section 14), which was delivered by hand on November 15th of this year of falling market share.

Finally, may I thank you for the hard work and sound ideas you contributed to the company before your sad loss. I am magnanimous enough to ignore your scurrilous earlier communication, attributing it simply to a momentary aberration. However, my lawyers have retained a copy in their files.

Yours, most sincerely,

James Percival Muncaster Pope Barker (MD

PS. It has come to my attention that you are keeping a canine companion in the aforementioned company-provided accommodation. This, too, is contrary to the terms of your tenancy (see Section 12). Whilst I must insist that the dog be removed from the premises with immediate effect, I appreciate that this may take a day or two to arrange. Might I suggest, therefore, that, in order to minimise any damage to furnishings, you purchase a Barker 'Woof-woof canine coat and galoshes set' in hard-wearing Rubbasoft (TM and Patent Pending), catalogue number WW4307M. As a final gesture of goodwill, you may purchase this at our company shop at the exceptional price of £17.99 (normal RRP £23.99) which is giving you a 'staff' allowance of 25% off, as a special thank you for your service with us.

JPMPB."

Can't take this lying down. A final salvo across the bows of the bumptious boss is required.

"Dear James Plumb My Posterior Backwards (Mouldy Dick),

Thank you for your kind letter enquiring about my health. It will come as no surprise to you that I have been declared insane. The psychiatrists found it totally unnecessary to put me through the usual exhaustive tests; once they established the fact that I had accepted an offer to work for you, that was sufficient grounds to confine me to the 'soft room', where they play me nice music all day. They say I am making progress, and one day may be allowed to walk in the park with the company of a mere two armed guards and my strait-jacket. My therapy at the moment is concentrated on dispelling my desires to kill you, and on dissipating the loathing I feel for you and your fucking shitty company. Oops, sorry about that. The medication seems to be wearing off. They say I'll be on medication for the rest of my life, and once I'm freed as part of the 'Neglect, sorry, Care in the community' program, I won't be a danger to anyone - as long as I remember to take my medication. This worries me slightly, as my memory is not too good these days. Sometimes, I can't even remember what I've just said. This worries me slightly, as my memory is not too good these days. Sometimes I can't even remember what I've just said. Sorry, where was I? Oh, yes, in the padded cell. They puree my food, you know, in case I find any hard bits with which to facilitate my escape. And so far, they've been successful in thwarting my plans. I tried to tunnel my way out using a spade made out of mashed swede, but they caught me within two yards of the perimeter fence. A shame, really. I was coming to pay my respects. Don't worry about the house. Plopper is looking after it for me. Poor sod, he hasn't been fed for ages. Do, please, call round to see him. He too is a freemason, and would be delighted to see you with your trouser leg rolled up.

Yours, in extreme psychosis,

Ray.

PS. Any chance of sending me a cake containing a file and spade made of hard-wearing Rubbasoft (TM and Patent Pending) in order that I can break out of here and come around to your house and beat you to a pulp with a rubber marsupial? You hard-hearted, miserable illegitimate issue of a festering twat. Sorry, where was I? Oh, yes. Thank you for your kind letter enquiring about my health.

PPS. Plopper, too, is a persistent and annoying Barker. Are you by any chance related?"

Pop this into the post box. No stamp. But marked 'for the personal attention of Mr Barker, MD, from his mere minion of an (ex) employee, the Upright and Dishonourable Mr R Light, BSE.' A time of crisis, this. Need to rally the troops. Except there aren't any. Ring Julie. Tipping out the pockets in this piss-smelling phone booth, small change rolling in all directions. And finally, her voice.

"Julie, it's Ray."

"Hi. I'm sorry I'm not able to take your call just now. But if you leave your name and number, I'll get back to you as soon as I can. Please speak clearly after the tone. Beeeeeep."

"Fuck answerphones! Julie. I'm sorry. I just needed to talk. I'll call you later. 'Bye."

"Ray, It's Julie. Don't hang up. I'm here. Sorry, I was in the shower. How are you? Are you OK? What's wrong?"

"Oh, Julie. Hi. I'm sorry to bother you. I didn't know whether you were at work or not. I just phoned on the off chance that you might be in."

"Well, I am. So, what's up?"

"Why aren't you at work?"

"I rang in sick."

"And are you sick?"

"No. I just felt low after you left so abruptly."

"I'm sorry. I had to go."

"I know. And was Plopper OK? Had he done his worst?"

"He was fine. Everything was fine. Till I got up today."

"Ray, what's happened?"

"I've lost my job. And my home."

"Aw. Ray. You poor man! What are you going to do? Listen, if it's any help, you can come and stay with me. It's no problem. If it will help you out. No strings, Ray. Honest. Bring Plopper, too. You're welcome."

"Julie, thanks, but I couldn't. I mean, we hardly know each other."

"So why are you turning to me?"

"Because...There's no-one else. Because I like you. And because I think you like me."

"Well, thanks, Ray. Thanks for making me feel so wonderful. You want to drink at the Last Chance Saloon. Well, that makes me feel so good."

"That sounds like a line from a Western."

"It probably is. I've spent a lot of my life alone, watching old films on TV."

"Julie. I'm sorry. Please can I see you?"

"Of course, you can. Do you want to come around?"

"Have you eaten yet?"

"No."

"Well, let's go out. I'll pick you up about eight. And Julie..."

"Yes."

"Thank you. And put on your red dress, baby. 'Cos we're going out tonight. Put on your high-heeled sneakers... and I can't remember the rest."

"Ray, are you drunk?"

"No. I'm just trying to sound deliriously happy. When in fact, it would not be too far from the truth to say I'm just a smidgeon pissed off."

"OK, Ray. See you about eight. 'Bye."

"'Bye."

Hanging up. Should have phoned Duncan. Don't know why I'm dragging Julie into this. None of her business, really. And unwise to see her too often in case she gets the mistaken impression that I can't stay away. Oh, Lucy! None of this would have happened if you were still with me.

Take Plopper for a long run. Throwing a stick and watching him bound happily after it. But instead of retrieving he lies down and reduces it to matchwood, before returning pleading for another. Sad eyes in such a happy face. Wonder if he knows his master is to be evicted. Wonder if he cares, as long as he has someone to love, someone to feed him, stroke him. And throw sticks for him. If only human relationships were as simple. Perhaps if Mr Barker had dropped a stick at my feet, I may have thrown it for him to fetch. When I'd feel more inclined to beat him around the head with it. No. He's not the type to be a stick-fetcher. He's a thrower, who expects everybody else to fetch, and jump through hoops at his command. Well, goodbye Mr Barker. I don't expect ever to see you again. Unless it's in court.

'Ray Light. You are charged with being disrespectful towards your former boss and his rubber empire. How do you plead?'

'Extremely guilty, your honour. But I would ask that the jury take into account certain mitigating circumstances.'

'Such as?'

'He's a bastard, your honour. He won't fetch sticks. And imports cheap Taiwanese inflatable rubber dolls, whose orifices chafe one's willy. And they're prone to punctures.'

'They go down on you?'

'Only the deluxe models, your honour.'

Manage a small smile at that one. Nothing wrong with old jokes. Duncan would approve. Plopper lying panting, slivers of timber visible between his jaws. Time to go home, Plopper. Dinner time. Then, while I'm out, and you're on sentry duty, you can have a quiet nap with the house all to yourself. Just don't eat any more of the furniture, there's a good boy.

A shit, shower and shave. Heaping Plopper's bowl full of evil-smelling tinned meat, mixed with biscuit. Good boy. Scoff the lot, and keep control of your bowels until I return.

Which may be quite a while if Julie still has the hots. Taxi at the door. 'Bye, Plopper. Be good. Or else hide the incriminating evidence before I get back.'

Julie waiting as the taxi draws up at her door. Turns out the lights, locks up and sits next to me in the back, as I instruct the driver to take us to 'L'Etoile', a cosy French restaurant where I'd often dined with Lucy. Both silent in the back of the taxi, for the whole of the fifteen-minute drive to this quiet place, a favourite rendezvous for cheating husbands with their expense-account whores. Where Lucy loved to play the game of guessing who were the genuine married couples, and who were enjoying illicit flings. She had tried to point out the subtle little differences in the way that real lovers touched, and looked at each other, without having to glance over their shoulders to see who may be watching. How furtive liaisons were betrayed by over-attentiveness, and unease, on the part of one or other, or both, of the players. How the meal itself was unimportant, and merely gastronomic foreplay, a part of the courtship ritual. Wining and dining a woman, and expecting something in return. And however much she pointed out the various nuances of expression and subtleties of behaviour, I remained blithely unaware. All I wanted to do was gaze into the hazel eyes of this gorgeous wife, listen to the sound of her voice, and enjoy the occasional soft touch of her hand on mine as she leaned forward to make a point.

"Ray? We're here. Do you want me to pay the taxi?"

"Er, no. Of course not. Sorry."

"You're miles away again."

"I'm sorry."

"That's OK. I'm getting used to it."

Small but comfortable and welcoming restaurant. A whiff of garlic in the air as we peruse the menu. Accordion music wheezing softly in the background. Trying to tempt

Julie into tasting the escargots, without success. Ordering twelve for myself instead. And a large rare steak, while she settles for a peppered sirloin.

Eating in silence. I can't help glancing round to see if the other diners are watching us.

"Ray, you're making me nervous. You'd better tell me all that's happened."

"I had a letter delivered this afternoon. By hand. From work. I've been sacked. For unauthorised absence. And since the house came with the job, I've been given twenty-eight days to move out. Apart from that, not much has happened, really."

"What about your hand?"

"Oh, just bruising. I fell over a wall on my way home last night."

Telling her the story of my encounter in the park and the cottage industry in the toilets. Joining her in laughter as I embellish the tale. Genuine laughter. Julie wiping away small tears. Reaching across the table to touch gently the back of my hand, which I turn over to clasp hers. And raise it to my lips to plant a soft kiss.

"Julie, thank you."

"For what?"

"Being here for me."

"I'm always available for a free meal. And enjoyable company."

"I've a confession to make."

"Go on."

"When I rang you this afternoon. I did it because I couldn't think of anyone else to turn to. And when you made me aware that you were aware of that fact, I felt awfully guilty. I almost called you back to cancel. But then I would have felt even more guilty for turning down your warm-hearted offer of a shoulder to cry on. And in the end, I'm glad I came."

"Me too."

"Julie, why haven't you ever married?"

"I suppose the easy answer is I've never met the right man. I did once meet a man I thought I could be happy with. And we got serious and talked about marriage. But then I told him I was sterile. And he ended it. He wanted kids, you see. So, it seems I can't find anyone who has the same expectations about married life that I have. And I keep on meeting emotional cripples. Oh, Ray. I'm sorry. I didn't mean to imply. I mean, you've been through a hard time, that's all. You'll come out of it. Oh, I'm sorry. I've upset you. That's another reason I've never married. I keep saying the wrong thing, without thinking."

"Don't worry. I'm not in the least offended. But it's the first time anybody's made me realise that I'm an emotional cripple. Lucy was my crutch. And God kicked it away and sent me sprawling on the ground. For people to piss on."

"I meant what I said earlier."

"What was that?"

"When I said you and Plopper could move in with me. Until you get sorted out. No strings, honest. Come and go as you please. It will be a bit cramped, but we'll manage."

"Thanks, Julie. But no. I wouldn't dream of invading your private space."

"You already have."

"I don't wish to impose on your generosity."

"I don't mind. At least think about it."

"I have. I'm moving back to Yorkshire. We still have a house there. It hasn't sold yet."

"Take me with you."

"I can't. I intend to move on again. I'm only going back until the house is sold. Then...who knows?"

"Marry me, Ray."

"What?"

"I'm sorry. I shouldn't have said that. Forget I ever said it. There I go again. Opening my big mouth without thinking."

"It's nice of you to ask. But I can't."

"I know. I just couldn't help blurting it out. I'm glad you said no really. I'm just being impulsive again."

"I'm glad you see it that way."

"Can we still be friends?"

"Of course."

"When are you leaving?"

"I don't know. But soon. As soon as I can get things organised."

"Will I see you again before you go?"

"If you wish."

"I wish."

"OK, then. But no sad farewells. I want us to part as friends. No tears. No regrets."

"I'll do my best. Will you come home with me tonight?"

"For a nightcap?"

"I've a couple of bottles of red wine. But I had something else in mind."

"I'm not sure it's a good idea."

"Why not?"

"Because I'd feel like I was using you."

"So, use me. As long as I can use you too."

"No commitment, Julie."

"None. Just good old-fashioned sex."

"I do believe I am tempted."

"You should always give in to temptation."

"No. I prefer to fight against it. And then eventually give in."

"Don't fight too hard."

"I won't. Just a little. Just a token gesture of resistance."

"Well, here's a token gesture. To break down your resistance."

Her hand under the table. Reaching across and gently rubbing my member, which stands to show its appreciation.

"Careful, Julie. Remember what happened the last time you rubbed the magic lamp."

"The genie appeared. And threw up all over my hand."

"Next time, he may grant you a wish. So, use it wisely. And leave the rubbing till later. Or his cork may prematurely pop. And spoil the party again."

"I'm sorry. I find it difficult to keep my hands off you."

"Julie, you're not alone. Since Lucy died, I've found it difficult to keep my hands off myself."

"You'll go blind."

"Then I'll masturbate in braille. Down at the Blind Institute. Where no-one can see me coming."

And in the taxi, she takes my hand and places it under the hem of her short dress. Encouraging me to explore further. Which I do, to discover a distinct lack of fabric covering the pubic region. She grins her toothy grin.

"I took them off in the restaurant."

"How considerate. Kept the flies away from my gateau."

"You say some awful things. I'll make you pay later."

"American Express?"

"No chance! You'll pay with your body."

"I hope you won't short-change me."

Taxi driver listening, and watching in his mirror. Sorry to disappoint, pal. But this one is private, and will take place behind locked doors. So just concentrate on your driving! Removing my fingers from Julie and sticking two up at the driver, who mutters obscenities. Fine. No tip for you, Mr Taxi Driver. Except keep your eyes on the road. And don't ogle the passengers with due care and attention. Tell your mates about it, and then go home and wank yourself stupid while your fat ugly wife snores alongside you.

Here's the door against which I slumped not too long ago. Must steel myself for the promises within. Gasping for air now. Should have taken a deep breath before Julie wrapped her long lascivious tongue round my tonsils. Feelings of guilt about what is bound to happen being eroded by the swelling down below. Never mind letting the heart rule the head. Or vice versa. Just let the todger take control. Once it gets a full head of steam, it needs to be vented. Thar she blows! Or will soon enough unless I manage to release the grip of this siren. For what I am about to receive, God, I am truly thankful. And definitely up for it. Forgive me, Lucy, for I know damn well what I am about to do.

Gently pulling away and allowing her to lead me by the hand to the bedroom. Where she switches on a single bedside lamp which casts a glow of warm peach round the room. Removing her coat and hanging it in the cheap melamine self-assembly wardrobe. Turning her back, and looking at me over her shoulder. Move across the room to obey the unspoken command and slide down the zip of her dress. Pause to kiss her bare shoulder and wait for the sigh of appreciation before venturing further. Thus encouraged, pull down the zip to its limit. And place a hand inside the dress on her buttocks. Feel the silk of her underwear. A familiar sensation which has never failed to arouse the member. Push my hand inside the elastic waistband and cup the warm flesh of her arse. Slide a finger up and down the crack, until she turns around and steps out of her dress. Warm touch of my hand down her goose-bumped arm. Fingers entwine as she pulls me to her lips. Arms round my neck, then my collar. Loosening my tie. Unbuttoning the shirt all the way down and pulling it free of my trousers. Where her hand lingers at the front just enough to send a further supply of blood coursing through the erection. Hurrying now. Helping me out of my jacket. Which is abandoned over a chair, along with the shirt and tie. Feel the trouser zip being lowered and the belt loosened and the trousers unfastened till they drop to my ankles. Oh God! I hope she doesn't notice the odd socks, one black, the other dark grey. But what does that matter? Besides, I do believe she is staring at a spot somewhat higher than my ankles. Slide out of the underpants while she removes her underwear. Take a few moments to admire her beautiful body.

"You're staring. Ray."

"I'm sorry. I was just admiring."

"And do you like what you see?"

"Very much."

"Then come to bed."

Taking her in my arms and kissing her with genuine longing. I'm sorry, Lucy. Please forgive me. You know I wouldn't do this if you were still with me. But I need this as much as I want it. Push her gently back on the bed. Feel no resistance as I slide into her warm wetness. Her breath in my ear. Warm, heavy and sweet. Gyrating her arse in response to my thrusts. Both breathing heavily as we reach a rapid hot and sticky conclusion and relax entwined in each other's arms.

"I feel like a cigarette."

"A few moments ago, you felt like a cigar! A great huge long fat cigar! I don't know how I managed to take it all. Can you get it up again?"

"Not yet! Give me time to get my breath back."

"OK. You've got ten minutes. Then you're due for the second performance."

"In that case, do you mind if I have a smoke?"

"I'd rather you didn't in the bedroom if you don't mind. Have a fag in the lounge. And while you're there, would you mind opening a bottle of wine? It's in the kitchen. The glasses are in the end cupboard, next to the fridge."

"I won't be long."

"Make sure you're not. Or I'll come looking for you."

Hope the todger's up to this. It's been a while since it's been put to the test. God, don't let me down now! I don't want to disappoint this woman who's been so good to me. Lucy, I don't know whether you can read my thoughts, but I'm sorry if I seem to be enjoying all this. But the fact is, I am enjoying it. Immensely. Julie makes me feel good. I've enjoyed her company. And sex is good. I don't want to compare it with making love to you. It's different. But enjoyable just the same. And please God, make the old fella big and strong again in ten minutes time. I can't walk back into the bedroom with this limp sorry-looking thing. I need to be able to carry a bottle of wine in one hand, and two glasses in the other, and still push the door open with the proud projection. It seems odd that, though sex with Lucy was wonderful, for the last few years once always seemed to be enough to satisfy us both. But right now, I get the impression that Julie could go all night. And I desperately hope I don't disappoint her. Please God, just this once. An erection! An erection! My kingdom for an erection!

Dock the fag, pick up the bottle and glasses and shyly push open the bedroom door with my elbow. And here's a sight to stir the loins! She's lying there. In a red satin basque. Stockings and suspenders. Looking like a high-class whore.

"Don't be shy. Come in. And close your mouth."

"I'm sorry. I didn't expect...."

"What do you think?"

"I... I approve."

"Oh good. I was wondering. I thought you might think I looked a tart or something. But all I want to do is seduce you. And turn you on. I'm sorry. I bet you think I look real cheap."

"Not at all, Julie. I like it. And I think it's having the desired effect."

"Come and sit down. And let's have a drink. There's no rush, is there?"

"No. But I can't stay the night. I'm sorry. But I can't leave Plopper."

"That's OK, Ray. Just give me one more hour. I'll make it worth it."

"It's already been worth it."

"Well, there's more. But this time I'm going to make love to you."

"Be gentle with me."

"No chance."

"You'll spill the wine."

"Then put it down."

"You'll spill something else if you fondle it like that."

"I promise you this time I won't spill a drop."

"It's getting hard."

"Mmm."

"Will you suck it a little?"

"Mmm."

"That's nice."

"Mmm."

"I like that.

"Mmm."

"Gently, please."

"Mmmm."

"Slowly, now."

"Mmmm."

Watching her head bob up and down. Feel the gentle steady pressure on my tool, which has grown again to monstrous proportions. Close my eyes and imagine it's Lucy. It feels much the same. Only the cheap perfume dispels the fantasy. Lucy would never wear anything as cloying.

"Julie, slow down now."

"Mmm."

"Julie, stop now. I'll come."

"Mmmm."

"Julie, I'm coming."

"Mmmmm."

"Julie. Stop. Let me put it in."

"Mmmmmmmm."

"Ohhh. Ohhhhh. Ohhhhhhh. Oh, Julie. Ohhhh. Julie. Ohhhhh."

"Mmmmmm."

"Ohhh, Julie. Thank you. Wow!"

"Did you enjoy that?"

"Mmmmm. Wonderful."

"I need a rest now. My jaw aches. Pass me the wine, please."

"Here."

"Thanks."

"What's it taste like?"

"What?"

"Semen."

"Salty."

"Like swallowing oysters?"

"Don't know. Never had any."

"Oh."

"It's not unpleasant. Just hard to describe. Like thick sticky salty cough mixture, I suppose. But like drinking the whole bottle in one go."

"That's not very romantic."

"Romance is not on the agenda. Only sex. Remember?"

"Yes."

"Do you think you can get it up again?"

"I doubt it. I'll try."

"Would you like to watch me masturbate? Some men find it turns them on."

"Yes."

"Lie there and watch."

Her mouth enveloping her index finger, which then traces a moist path down her body to her bush. Rubbing gently against her clit. Back and forth. Side to side. Then slow circular movements. And every now and again two fingers dipping deep into her as her face reddens. The pace of her breathing increasing as her rubbing becomes more frantic. Head back, eyes closed, gritting her teeth and expelling air in a faint whistle through the gaps between her molars. Her other hand moving rapidly from one tit to the other, rubbing and tweaking the nipples so that both remain erect. Reminds me of a plate-spinning act. And then she stiffens and moans like a wounded animal. And it's all over. A broad smile on her face as she offers her fingers to my lips. Open my mouth to suck them. My way of returning her earlier oral favour. As the todger begins to stir again. Signs of life again at last, though still some inches short of an erection. Notice she's staring at it. Willing it to rise and point proudly at her bush. But it just twitches a little and remains flat against my belly. Perhaps if I play with it a little I could get it hard. But I don't want Julie to think I'm a wanker. Besides, I expect she'd prefer to give it the kiss of life again. I hope so. I find there's nothing quite as intimate as oral sex. And it's never failed to arouse me in the past. I hope she can read my thoughts. I don't really want to ask her for a blow-job again. I'd rather she volunteered.

"Did you enjoy the show?"

"Yes. Very much."

"I didn't fake it, you know. That was a real orgasm. I always come when I masturbate. Practice, I suppose."

"Me too."

"You can, if you want. I mean, only if you want to. I've never watched a man masturbate since I was about twelve. Me and another girl used to go to his house at lunchtimes and watch him. He gave us money and sweets. He never touched us. He just liked someone to watch him. Sad really."

"I'm sorry I don't have any sweets."

"Silly! I'll watch you for nothing. Honest, I'd like to. But only if you want to."

"I'd rather you did it for me. You have such a soft touch."

"Do you think he'll respond?"

"I really don't know. But I'm praying."

"Me too."

Soft warm breath on my belly. Her hand tenderly cupping my balls. Lips closing round my length. The familiar rhythmic movement of her head. Her tongue caressing the wobbly stalk as she coaxes a reluctant erection. Manoeuvring now, her mouth still clamped round the throbbing flesh. Turning, her knees now beside my head. Her inner thighs rubbing my ears as she lowers herself over my mouth. Take a deep breath and slide the tongue into the slippery hole. Serious danger of suffocation unless I bring her to orgasm quickly. My nose buried in the crack of her arse as I kiss the pink. God forbid she should fart! Let my tongue play round her clit. Lap the juices. Feel her thighs tighten and her buttocks clench. Able to suck in fresh air as she clambers off. Astride me in a flash. Holding me and guiding me in. And bearing down to take the full but slightly wobbly length. Riding like fury. Pounding up and down as it slips out. And she quickly puts it back in and takes up the rhythm again. Now shorter and slower strokes. Now longer. Now faster. Now slower again. Using me for her pleasure and satisfaction like she would a dildo. As I lie still. Scared to disturb her erotic trance. Feel the blood pounding in my ears. Pulsing in time with her gyrations as she comes once more with her feral moan. And grinds to a shuddering quaking halt, her sweating body draped over me. Her mouth to my ear, whispering a quiet thank you. And I lie there silently, her body on top of me, wondering if this is how a woman must feel when she submits to a man's desires without really wanting to. A sense of duty. Or thanks for taking me out and buying me a meal. No love. No great desire. But a reciprocal arrangement whereby we satisfy each other's needs. With Lucy, when we made love it was only when we both wanted to. Which, thankfully, was quite often. And when one of us came, that was only half time. And the game wasn't over until we were both satisfied. But we were so compatible sexually. Our appetites were similar, as was our stamina. But Christ! This woman could shag me into a premature grave.

"Julie, that was wonderful. But I'll have to go soon."

"Haven't we got time to do it again?"

"I'm sorry, but no. Besides, I couldn't possibly."

"I bet you could."

"No. Honestly. I surrender. I'm beaten. And I shall walk home with my tail, or what's left of it, between my legs."

"I'd rather have it between mine."

"There'll be another time. After I convalesce. And have my heart checked out."

"The only thing wrong with your heart is you won't let anyone into it. I'm sorry. I shouldn't have said that."

"No. But you're right."

"I'm sorry, Ray."

"So am I."

"Will you ring me?"

"Yes, I promise."

"I believe you. Normally I don't when a man says that. But I know you will."

"Yes, I will."

"And by the way, do you know you were wearing odd socks tonight?"

"No. Oh God! I wasn't, was I?"

"Yes. I noticed straight away. But I didn't like to say anything. It's part of your charm."

"It's not charm, Julie. It's neglect and carelessness. Lucy would never have let me out of the house like that."

"I don't mind what you wear, Ray. I'm not Lucy."

CHAPTER 11

Approaching home. Strange. There are lights on in the living room. Intruders? Or mere forgetfulness? Approach with caution. Front door thankfully locked. Turn the key, depress the handle. And step gingerly inside. No greeting from Plopper, but a familiar face emerging from the kitchen.

"Hello, Mr Everson. What are you doing here? What's going on?"

"I'm sorry, Ray. You've been burgled."

"Burgled?"

"Yes, Ray. The noise woke up Mrs E. And she sent me to investigate. They forced the back door, Ray. And created quite a mess. I haven't touched anything. The police are on their way. And I took the liberty of phoning someone to secure the back door as a temporary measure. I hope you don't mind."

"No. No, of course not. Thank you. Where's Plopper?"

"He's with Mrs E. He's still shaking, poor chap. Made a lot of noise and probably put up quite a fight. And he's limping. I think they must have kicked him. I'll keep him tonight and take him to the vet in the morning if you like. You'll need time to sort things out. In the meantime, you'll need to make a list of the things that are missing."

Wandering from room to room, surveying the damage. Drawers and cupboards emptied, their contents strewn on the floor. Small amount of money taken. And a silver carriage clock. Video gone. And Lucy's things. Two watches, both presents from me. The gold one with the heart-shaped face. Her favourite, a gift on our fifth anniversary. The one she only wore on special occasions. Brooches, earrings and necklaces, and a gold pendant inscribed L.L. For Lucy Light. Or Loves Life. Or Lost Love.

And her rings. Dress rings. An eternity ring of sparkling diamond and ruby. And her treasured engagement and wedding rings. All of which I'd carefully laid out on the dressing table, ready to pack up and send to her parents. An open invitation to burglars, gratefully accepted.

At least they've left the Malt. Pour a large glass while awaiting the police. Write a list of all the articles missing. A van driving slowly by, then stopping, reversing and pulling up outside. The emergency joiner, who secures the back door with stout timber, and measures up for a new frame. Leaving a quote for the proposed replacement, and a bill for £75 for the fifteen minutes of temporary repair work. Burglary is lucrative business for some, while a cause of great misery for others. He's probably delighted to live in this criminal-infested city which I can't wait to get away from.

The police unsympathetic, but efficient. Going about their business in a matter-of-fact way. Seen it all before. Purely routine. Arrange for a dusting for fingerprints, remarking sarcastically that the place could do with a dusting anyway. Giving me a crime number for my insurance claim, and a leaflet about a victim support group. Then off into the night in their relentless pursuit of villains, such as street vomiters and drivers with insufficient tread on their tyres.

And the following morning, digging through a pile of documents which Lucy had filed away. Looking for the household contents insurance. Here they are. All bound together, with 'Insurance Docs.' written on the front in black marker pen. The ever-organised Lucy. Thumb through them for a phone number and write it on the back of an envelope, along with the policy number and crime number. Empty the jar of silver for the phone, and take a stroll to the box at the end of the road. Seems strange not to have Plopper at my heels, but perhaps it's better that he spends some time with the E's. Who are to be his new master and mistress, though none of them know it just yet.

Have to find a way of breaking the news gently. Ah, good! The phone box has survived another night without being vandalised. Dial the number, and a response almost immediately. Sure I recognise the voice.

"I'd like to make a claim on my contents insurance, please."

"Ray? Is that you?"

"Yes."

"It's Julie. Why are you ringing me at work?"

"I guess I couldn't wait to speak to you again."

"That's nice."

"Yes. But unfortunately, it's not entirely the truth. Though I am glad to be talking to you again."

"Did you enjoy yourself last night?"

"Immensely. That is, until I got home. Which is why I wish to make a claim."

"Ray, I'm sorry. I thought you were joking. I thought it was just an excuse to speak to me. Because the manager often listens in on calls to make sure they're not personal. And to check on our professionalism and courteous and helpful manner."

"Julie, I rate you 100% in that respect. You may tell your boss I say so."

"So, how may I help you, sir?"

"I've been burgled. I wish to claim on my household insurance."

"Do you have a policy number, sir?"

"Yes. It's CW4/307991032-6."

"And you are Mr Light?"

"Yes."

"Your address, please, sir?"

"52, Maple Avenue."

"Thank you, sir. Please hold a moment while I check your policy details."

"OK."

"Right, Mr Light. Oh, it's OK now, Ray. I heard the click in my headphones. It means the boss has stopped listening in, so we can talk."

"Julie. Some bastards broke into my house last night while I was with you, and stole all Lucy's jewellery."

"Oh, Ray. I'm so sorry. I seem to be bringing you some awfully bad luck."

"It's not your fault. I left Plopper on guard. And he failed miserably in his duties. Poor little bugger. At least he was there, and did his best."

"Ray, I'll send you a claim form in the post tonight. Unless you'd prefer me to take one home, and if you come around this evening, I'll help you fill it out. They can be quite tricky, you know."

"What time shall I come?"

"Any time after six-thirty. I'll make you a meal if you like. I owe you."

"That would be nice. Thank you."

"I'll see you tonight."

"Bye."

This is becoming a hard habit to break. Must try to concentrate on the business in hand this evening. Keep the trousers zipped up. But must find a way to repay the assistance and the meal. Perhaps a bottle of wine will suffice, but I very much doubt it. Best be prepared, and ask Mr E if he'll look after Plopper overnight. Then I may get a free breakfast too.

And Julie entertains me and keeps my spirits up with a bottle of Malt she's bought specially. Helps me with the claim form before dessert in the bedroom. My just deserts. And we sleep in each other's arms. Till I awake in the early hours needing a pee and can't get my arm from beneath her neck without waking her. And having to pay the penalty of a quick one.

Breakfast of coffee and toast served in bed on a plastic tray. Julie showering and dressing while I crunch the toast from the tray on my lap. Breakfast in bed is best eaten alone. The presence of a warm female body alongside often causes tremors under the duvet which threaten to tip up the tray if not properly balanced on the end of the tool.

Slip silently out of bed and tiptoe across to the wardrobe inside the door of which is a long mirror. Admire my naked torso. Becoming a little flabby round the midriff but nothing to worry about. Write it off as the inevitable consequence of a rapid descent into middle age. That way I feel no guilt about going to seed. Still look quite attractive in a worn sort of way. A little gaunt about the cheeks and puffy round the eyes which are red-rimmed and tired-looking. That's only to be expected. I think I'm bearing up quite well, considering. Maybe Julie is right. Perhaps I should move in with her and look for a job. Take life as it comes. See how it goes. But I wonder how long it will be before she tires of me and my annoying little habits. Which I'm sure I must have. I'll give it some thought over a quiet drink later.

"Admiring your body?"

Julie sneaking back in, dressed and ready for work. Catching me unawares. Naked and defenceless.

"No. I..er. Well, yes."

"You don't have to. I admired it for you last night. Gave you the MOT. And you passed. You're in good shape. And everything's in working order. You could do with a little exercise to get rid of the paunch though."

"I'll walk the dog."

"That's not enough. You need to do sit-ups and the like. You should join a gym. Work out a bit."

"I'm not vain enough to pose around in a gym. And I don't want men looking at my body. They may have unnatural inclinations."

"You might meet new friends. You need to socialise more. Meet people. Take up new interests. Anyway, get some clothes on before I ravish you. I'll be late for work if you don't get a move on."

Walk down to the bus stop with her. A quick shy peck on the cheek before she boards and waves as the bus pulls away. Take a leisurely walk home. Have a shave and a long soak in the bath and ponder my future. If I am to have one.

CHAPTER 12

Cold bright Sunday morning. Up early to exercise Plopper. Remove the sticking plaster from the fingers. Flex them. Just a little stiff. But much more inflamed after I spend fifteen minutes scrubbing them hard with a nailbrush to remove the marks left by the plaster. Then a hearty breakfast. Growing accustomed to the routine now. Walk the dog. Shower and shave. Breakfast. Wash up. Dry and clear away. Tidy the house. Maybe dust a little. Push the vacuum around. Then take a stroll. Down to the Cenotaph this morning, to watch the parade of old soldiers come together to honour their fallen comrades. Marching proudly, chests out, bedecked with ribbons and medals. Some being pushed in wheelchairs. Others hobbling along on artificial limbs. Doing the Military One-Step. The marching band at the rear. Blaring bugles and booming big drum. And the machine gun rat-a-tat of other timpani.

Gathering round the monument to lay their wreaths, salute and pay their respects. A dignified occasion for these brave survivors who repelled the might of Hitler's forces. Only to fall prey in their old age to marauding gangs of lawless youths who look upon them as easy victims.

Right on time as I walk down this shady lane, remembering Mr E's directions. The green wooden gate on the left at the end. Number 69. Rather appropriate. Walk past. Turn down the alley. Double back, and use the rear entrance. If you'll pardon the expression. Knock quietly on the door. Answered immediately by a smartly-dressed woman. In her mid-forties, I would imagine. Respectable-looking, with a trim figure. And a warm smile.

"You must be Ray."

"Yes."

"Come in, love."

Tidy house. Tastefully furnished and decorated. Some nice objets d'art, and antiques.

"I don't normally accept new clients. But Mr E persuaded me otherwise. He's such a nice gentleman. One of my best customers. All my gentlemen come on recommendation. If you know what I mean. So, what would you like?"

"Mr E recommended the erotic massage."

"An excellent choice for your first visit. Of many, I hope. Please follow me."

Mounting the stairs behind her. Looking up at her slim legs in the short, but not tarty, skirt. Believe I caught a glimpse of stocking-top. A sight to gladden the heart. Into this room, with its low leather bench. Scent of massage oils. She leaves me to undress and lie on my stomach on the cold leather. A small towel to cover my modesty. Relax and await her return. As she enters, dressed in a white overall. Buttons down the front, of which the top two are undone. Nice display of firm cleavage. Wonder if a fondle is extra. In fact, since no prices have been agreed upon, I wonder if I've taken on more than I can afford. Still, perhaps she'll accept my flexible friend. The credit card, that is.

Relax as she applies the aromatic oils. Firm but gentle hands soothing away the stresses of life. Almost falling asleep under the hypnotic spell of her soft voice as her hands trace over my shoulders and down my back. Removing the towel and slipping an oily hand between my buttocks. Continuing down. Stroking the backs of my legs with calm, unhurried movements.

At her bidding, turn over on to my back, first replacing the towel. Under which her fingers sweep in oily rhythmic movements. As the towel rises on its concealed tentpole. She undoes two more buttons, so that her large dark and hard nipples peep into view as she moves. Hands moving away now. Rubbing my chest. Though the tent remains erect. Now down to the feet. Massaging slowly between the toes, as I stifle a giggle. Now the shins and knees. Then the thighs. For an unbearable age, until finally her hands slip once again beneath the towel and begin to oil the stem. Casting the towel aside, modesty forgotten, as her hand slides up and down the slippery pole. As she leans over and plants a kiss on the end just as a little wet pearl escapes. All her buttons now undone, revealing her firm body naked except for white suspender belt and shimmering stockings. A quizzical smile on her face as she looks straight into my eyes, her right hand gradually increasing its tempo. As I reach the point of no return. And erupt in a huge Krakatoa, the white-hot lava spewing out from deep within. Running over her fingers and cooling as it streams down my belly. Twitching and jerking as she milks the very last drop. Before handing me a man-size tissue, and fastening her buttons, watching as I mop up.

"Thank you. You're very good."

"Thank you. I know. All my gentlemen tell me. Do you know, they're all so very different. And each one requires slightly different handling. Once I get to know what you really like, then you'll find the pleasure even more enhanced. But you mustn't be ashamed to tell me. Otherwise you'll never attain the real heights of sexual ecstasy. Now would you like anything else?"

"Not for the moment, thank you. Though I think I may pay you a further visit."

"By all means. I'll give you my number. When you call, you'll get the answerphone. Leave a message, stating the preferred date and time. Use your call-sign, which is Sunshine. For Ray, you see. Give me a number I can reach you on, and if I don't ring back within an hour, then your booking is confirmed. Oh, and it also helps if you can indicate the type of service you require, or how long you wish to book. So that I can arrange my appointments. And ensure I have the materials at hand to fulfil your desires. I had one gentleman who liked seasonal fruits pushed up his bottom. And he gave me very little notice, so we both ended up peeling satsumas and cutting the segments in half before we could commence his treatment. So, give me as much notice as you can. To avoid disappointment. Though I rarely disappoint. I always have some trick up my sleeve. Oh, and don't worry. I'm very discreet. If I do have to phone you to cancel, all I'll say is 'This is Valerie calling from Sunshine Windows and Conservatories. Would you be interested in any of our services?' If you're free to talk, then do so. If not just say no and put the phone down. If you do that, your appointment is cancelled and you'll have to ring to re-book. Is that OK?"

"Yes, that's fine. Now, may I have the bill, please?"

"Don't sound so formal, love. Call me Val. Look upon me as a friend. A sexual therapist. Not a prostitute. I'm here to help you. Not make you feel furtive and guilty. Unless of course that's what you want."

"No. That's not what I want. Right, Val. What do I owe you, love? For your tender administrations?"

"Is fifteen all right?"

"Fine."

"All services are open to negotiation. Because I enjoy some more than others. I also enjoy some clients more than others. So always enquire about my special offers. And don't be shy. I can cater for all tastes. I even have a friend available to make up threesomes, if you require."

God! That's everyman's dream. And I'm free to pursue it. So why do I find it so easy and natural to say no?

"Thank you. But no."

"Well, whatever. Thanks, Ray. It's been a real pleasure pleasing you. Honest. I mean that. Please come again, so to speak."

"Thank you, Val. I will. With a list of demands which will stretch your imagination, if not your delectable body."

"I shall look forward to that. 'Bye, love."

"Thank you for having me."

"Thank you for coming."

"'Bye."

Feeling refreshed and relaxed as I walk home. Can't beat therapy. Never mind bereavement counselling! A good shag, or similar relief, is the answer. Whistling a merry air as I push open my gate. Mr E at his window sees me. And winks.

Calling in this city centre pub early in the evening. Need a livener or two to get me through the last few days I will ever spend in this god-awful city of thugs, thieves, rogues and vandals. What sort of place is this? Full of youths swigging lager from the bottle. Loud jukebox. Pool table and fruit machines. This may be a mistake. I feel a little out of place here, and somewhat uncomfortable. Squeeze my way to the bar, past a scruffy youth with 'No Fear' tattooed on his forehead. Where it should really say 'No Brains'.

"Pint of hand-pulled bitter, please."

"We don't do hand-pulled. No call for it in here."

"So, what have you got?"

"Bitter? Keg. Special or Premium."

"What's the difference?"

"Ten pence a pint."

"A pint of the cheaper, please."

"Pint of special. That's one-sixty-five, mate. You've just missed Happy Hour."

"Looks like it."

Stand quietly at the end of the bar, away from the morose mob. Two youths seated at a table, glancing over in my direction and whispering. Pretend not to notice. Stay calm, though somehow, I sense trouble. One of them approaching, wearing the obligatory baseball cap. Never seen a game of baseball in his life. Perhaps I'll try to start a new fashion trend, and walk round wearing cricket pads. But better deal with this situation first. The youth now stood next to me, placing a carrier bag on the bar. Notice his left hand is swollen, red and purple, with puncture wounds clearly visible. Heart beginning to pound a little faster.

"You interested in any cheap presents for the wife?"

"I might be. What happened to your hand?"

"You a copper?"

"Me? No, lad. On the dole. Same as you, probably."

"S'right. Me, I've never worked since I got expelled from school. No intention of, either."

"So, what happened to your hand?"

"Fuckin' dog bit me."

"Did you report it?"

"Don't be fuckin' stupid! Call it an occupational 'azard. Well, are you interested?"

"What have you got?"

"Some nice rings and fings. Jewellery. Watches, an' that. Some nice stuff."

"Show me."

"Not 'ere. Follow me into the toilets."

And in the gents, he empties out the contents of the carrier bag on to the piss-stained tiled floor.

"What do you fink?"

"What I really want is a video recorder."

"Got one at 'ome, mate. Fifty quid to you."

Slamming the slimy bastard back against the wall, and letting fly with a fist to his mouth, which explodes red. Another one to the unprotected stomach, then one to the nose, which splits across the bridge and sends him reeling backwards, his head hitting the wall. Unconscious, bleeding heavily from nose and mouth, but still breathing. But, to be honest, I don't really care. Go through his pockets. A tenner, and some loose. Put Lucy's jewellery in my pocket, and thank god for the loud music, which seems to have drowned out any noise from in here. A quick wash of the hands to remove the blood, then out through the door, turn right, and, keeping the head down, through the lounge and out on to the street. Walk at a brisk pace, don't run, and remain calm. Easy to say, but difficult to do when one has just committed an act of criminal assault, causing actual bodily harm. With total justification. Just walk on, trying to look inconspicuous, which shouldn't be too difficult. I've been a nobody all my life. Down to the bus station, where a number 14 awaits. Climb aboard, ride for a couple of miles, then get off and walk home the remaining four miles. Take a meandering route. One difficult for the police dogs to follow. Don't kid yourself, Ray. The police are not going to mount a manhunt for an incident as trivial as this. Almost an everyday occurrence in this festering sore of a city. Breathe a little easier. Hands sore. Knuckles swollen, and bearing the imprints of teeth. Now starting to shiver with fear. Take it easy! I'm moving on in a couple of days. They won't find me. Relax. I did the right thing. Even if it was totally alien to my nature and upbringing. It was justified, your Honour. Guilty, but acting out of character, due to the shock of finding my dead wife's personal effects for sale by some spotty, deadbeat youth.

Safe at home once more. Plopper at my side seems none the worse for his ordeal. I wonder if he knows that justice has been done. Peep through the curtains. All clear. No SWAT team waiting for us to emerge. No bullhorn message piercing the calm damp evening. Let's go, Plopper.

Pale slice of lemon moon lighting these dark streets. All quiet. But keep to the shadows and the back streets all the same. Down past the row of garages, where once again Mac has been at work with his cryptic comments. Colourfully emblazoned across the doors of two adjacent garages are the words 'Twenty years of schooling and they put you on the day shift', accompanied by the pictographic signature. Admire the artwork while Plopper performs his ritual leg-raising manoeuvres. Before squatting in an overgrown corner for a sly shit. And at last it comes to me. The origin of Mac the Finger's messages, and his pseudonym. Bob Dylan's lyrics! Obviously, the artist is a man of great taste and sensibility. Like myself. Which reminds me. I'm in a bit of a quandary. I've just made an insurance claim for Lucy's jewellery. If I ring them up and say I've got it back, will they tell the police? And if I tell the police, will they inquire as to the circumstances in which I recovered the items? And if I keep it quiet, and the young lout reports the fact that he's been assaulted and robbed, will he be able to give a sufficiently accurate description to lead the scuffers to my door? And what if he admits he only stole a small amount of cash, rather than the £150 I claimed? Perhaps the best bet is to scan the papers for the next few days for news of any assaults in public houses. And in the meantime, pack up and prepare to leave. In which case I'll have to give Julie a forwarding address to where the cheque can be sent. Whatever I do, I can still be traced. Oh, Lucy. If you were still here, these crazy things wouldn't be happening to me.

CHAPTER 13

There, Plopper. Come on, boy. Eat all this nice dinner. So you'll grow up big and strong. And able to fight off future burglars. A knock at the door. God, I hope it's not the police. Insurance fraud, robbery with violence, assault, handling stolen goods. Pretend I haven't heard. They may go away. Christ! A face peering in through the kitchen window. Seen me crouched down behind the table. Better let him in. Can't be the police; they always arrive in pairs.

"Mr Light?"

"Yes."

"My name's Boot. Kevin Boot. I tried to ring you but your phone doesn't appear to be working."

"It's been disconnected."

"That would account for it, then. I hope you don't mind my calling upon you unannounced. But would you mind awfully showing me round the house?"

"I certainly will not."

"Oh. Is it inconvenient? Only I don't have a lot of time. I have to drive back to Leicester tonight. And discuss with my wife whether to accept the job. And I can't really do that without first seeing the accommodation."

"What job? What accommodation?"

"Oh, didn't I mention it? I've been offered the position of Head of Production (Exotic and Erotic) by Mr Barker. Your old job, I believe. He's made me a very generous offer, if the accommodation is up to the expected standard, that is. He's very impressed by my ideas for new production methods, is our Mr Barker. I'm an ideas man, you see. A lateral thinker."

"Me too. And I'm inclined to think I should knock you laterally for this intrusion. Even though you are the incumbent Head of Production (Quixotic and Neurotic)."

"Hey. There's no need to take that attitude. In business there are winners and losers. And I'm a winner. Mr Barker said if I had any problems with you I should ring him and he'd send his security people round to assist in an accompanied viewing."

"There's a phone box at the end of the road."

"No need. I have my mobile."

"Very well. Have a look round."

"Thank you. I told Mr Barker you'd see reason."

"All I see is the futility of further resistance. I don't want you and the heavies breaking the door down at midnight and beating me into submission with Barker's rubber penguins."

"Penguins! Great idea! I hadn't thought of that. Old man Barker will love it. You could have had a bright future with the company. If you could learn to control your aberrant and abhorrent behaviour."

Sit in the kitchen with Plopper as this loathsome man wanders round. Hope he takes the job. He and Mr Barker were made for each other. Ruthless, self-opinionated, ambitious bastards. The sound of doors opening and closing, and tut-tutting from various rooms. The toilet flushing. Hope I left a big brown one for him. Then his frowning return.

"Mmm. Satisfactory, I suppose. But hardly ideal. The lounge needs decorating badly."

"It's been decorated badly. I did it."

"Ha ha. You know what I mean. It's certainly not to Mrs Boot's taste. Still, Mr Barker has offered a generous relocation budget, which should allow us to have it done professionally. When are you having the door repaired?"

"I'm not."

"I'm afraid you must. It's in your tenancy agreement."

"Mr Barker has cancelled my tenancy agreement. Let him claim on the buildings insurance. Buildings damage is his problem, not mine."

"I think you'll find it is your responsibility."

"Tough."

"Well, if that's your attitude. I shall report this to Mr B. I must say, I'm not at all surprised he decided to dispense with your services."

"Get out."

"I haven't finished."

"You have. Now get out. Or I'll set Plopper on you. Snap your spindly legs in two with a single crunch of his jaws."

"OK. I'm leaving. But rest assured your comments have been noted, and will not help should you require a future reference from the company."

"Bollocks to the company. And to you, Boot. To boot."

"Goodbye, Mr Light."

"Piss off, Boot."

Hard to believe that it was only early this year that Lucy and I had come down to spend a few days looking at the area prior to my accepting Mr Barker's kind offer of a job. Though the decision made itself since I was out of work, we still wanted to reassure ourselves we were moving somewhere we'd be happy. And in those mild few days in February we'd stayed at a small hotel, courtesy of the company. We'd dined out, shopped, and toured the area.

And pronounced it satisfactory. And after we moved everything was fine. We settled quickly. Lucy got an office job. And we were happy. Until she started to become unwell and was referred to the hospital. Where they broke the devastating news which tore our world apart, and triggered my descent into sadness, badness and madness.

And as the summer came to an end, and Lucy became bedridden, the city seemed to undergo a metamorphosis. Where initially it had seemed a pleasant and lively city, with its well-tended parks and maze of suburban walkways tree-lined with apple, cherry and sometimes plum, it all suddenly took on a different hue with the early onset of autumn. The greenery fell from the trees, turned brown and decayed to black. The cultivated park lawns became strewn with litter, the detritus of the take-away society. And the concrete and brick city began to reveal its hidden truths. Shop assistants became sullen and unhelpful. Gangs of youths gathered on street corners, imposing their threatening presence on respectable neighbourhoods. Drunks, beggars, pimps and prostitutes hassled residents day and night as the city's underbelly was exposed to harsh daylight. Yet the city had not changed. It's just that we never opened our eyes and looked. 'Seek and ye shall find'. And what I've found, I don't like one bit. Be relieved to return to the quiet charm of Scarsby. Altogether more civilised. Where even the muggers say 'please', and 'thank you'.

Mr E's face at the window, and an unusually broad grin. Gesture to him to enter.

"Hello, Ray. Sorry to bother you."

"No problem, Mr E. What can I do for you?"

"It's what you did for somebody else which intrigues me."

"Sorry, I'm not with you."

"I've just had a phone call. From Valerie. Our mutual friend. She asked me to ask you to go see her at seven prompt this evening. Apparently, she has a, ahem, proposition to put to you. Sounds jolly interesting! You must have made quite an impression on her. Or perhaps in her. You will go, won't you? She's found an hour in her busy schedule specially to see you."

"Yes, I'll go."

"Jolly good! Perhaps I'll get the gory details later?"

"I doubt it, Mr E. Discretion. Remember?"

"Quite so. Well, enjoy yourself, you lucky devil."

"I will."

Wonder what that's all about. No harm in going along to find out. Pass a pleasant hour or so. Shave and have a long relaxing bath. Need to be in good shape for the evening's workout. A brisk walk with Plopper to get the circulation moving. Ensure the heart pumps blood to the required parts. Past the row of garages to admire Mac the Finger's latest handiwork. In multicoloured letters, 'Take the rag away from your face. Now ain't the time for your tears.'

On the stroke of seven, knocking softly on the back door of number 69. Dressed in my best charcoal grey pin-stripe, clean white shirt newly ironed, and highly-polished black Oxfords. Cut quite a dash, if I say so myself.

"Hi, Ray. Come in. Come through to the lounge."

"Thank you."

"My! You do look smart. Exactly what I had in mind. Would you like a drink?"

"Do you have a Malt?"

"Of course. Several. Any preference?"

"Any Highland. As long as it's large."

"Try this. This one's my personal favourite."

"Mmm. Glen Ord, if I'm not mistaken. A fine choice."

"Full marks, Ray. A man of good taste. Discerning."

"Thank you."

"And do you have a particular taste in women?"

"Yes."

"And what type would that be?"

"She didn't belong to any type. She just was. The most perfect creature I have ever met."

"Of course. I'm sorry, Ray. Your late wife. Mr E told me about her. Poor man. You must have been devastated."

"Yes."

"But you still desire women? You came to me."

"Yes, I did. But not so much out of desire. Need is probably a more accurate description."

"Excellent!"

"I'm sorry. I didn't mean to offend you."

"On the contrary, Ray, dear. I think you're exactly what I'm looking for."

"What do you mean?"

"Ray, this may surprise you. But I have a number of female clients. Not lesbians. But women who come to me for sexual relief. It may surprise you to know that there are no reputable establishments in this city to cater for women's needs. So, they come to me. And obviously, I lack the necessary equipment to fully satisfy them. Yes, they can have an erotic massage, oral sex, toys, vibrators. But one vital element is missing. Would you like a top-up?"

"Please."

"There. So, Ray, I was wondering if you would be prepared to work for me. Hours to suit. Cash in hand. Though I would, of course, retain a percentage for use of the premises. But you could make good money. Fifty to seventy-five, for an hour's work. Would you be interested?"

"I don't think so."

"Ray. I know you've lost your job. You must have bills to pay. How about giving it a try? What have you got to lose?"

"My self-respect."

"Balls, Ray! Complete and utter bollocks! Look. I need you. I have a lady who is crying out for the services of someone like you. She's a very respectable and very attractive woman. And very generous, too. Her husband is much older than she, and devotes all his time to his business. Ray, she badly needs a man!"

"What exactly would I need to do?"

"That's more like it, Ray. She likes a massage. Full body. As erotic as possible. She has her own special vibrator. Then she requires oral sex, followed by penetration. Ray, you'll enjoy it! Believe me. And if you don't, then don't do it again. There'll be no hard feelings. And I'd be extremely grateful if you could help me out. Just this once."

"OK."

"Thanks, Ray. Have you ever given a massage before?"

"No."

"Well, then. Let's have a training session. You can practice on me. I'll tell you exactly what to do. And remember. The customer is always right. It is your duty to ensure the highest level of customer service is maintained."

"OK, boss."

"Ray. For the purpose of this training session, I am not the boss. I am a customer. Who requires pleasing."

"So, how should I address you?"

"For this training session, or perhaps we should call it an aptitude test, you should call me Val. But it's important that you establish at the outset how your client wishes to be treated. Some don't like to use their real names. So, ask them to tell you exactly what they want. Then it's up to you to deliver the goods. Come on upstairs. Let's get started."

Val undressing while I wash my hands and inspect the various bottles of oils, some lightly perfumed; others more heavily scented. Pick up a large gold-plated vibrator whose head rotates at varying angles and different speeds. Feel the weight of it. Val lying face down on the leather bench.

"I'm ready, Ray."

"Where would you like me to start?"

"The shoulders. You should avoid intimate contact until the client makes it clear she's ready. Start with the shoulders. Oil your hands. And make sure they're warm. Pick any oil you like, for now. But when you're with a client, use whatever she requests. So, you'll have to familiarise yourself with the full range. But time is money, Ray. Let's get started."

Select a bottle at random. Pour the sweet-smelling slightly viscous liquid onto a palm. Rub the hands together and approach the naked Valerie. Banish all thoughts of impropriety for now. Remind myself this is business.

Applying the oil to the neck and shoulders. Following instructions to the letter. Slightly lighter with the touch just here. And apply a little more pressure there. Slow circular sweeps moving down towards the buttocks, which I'm inclined to give a playful slap, but resist the temptation. Upon request, apply more oil. Work the thumbs gently into the crease of the arse. Down the backs of the legs and upwards again. Beware the genitals. Contact allowed only when the client expressly asks. Or indicates by her body language. Which is exactly what Val is doing at the moment. Turning over and spreading wide her long legs.... And afterwards enjoying a glass or two. Relaxing in the lounge. Val showered and lounging in a towelling bathrobe, before dressing in more erotic attire for her next client.

"So, have I passed the interview?"

"No problem, Ray. You're a natural."

CHAPTER 14

On familiar territory here, so let Plopper off his lead for his lamppost-sniffing, leg-raising rituals. Follow obediently at his heels. Stop to light a fag, as he looks back impatiently, imploring me with those huge brown eyes and metronome tail to get a move on. Trail a few yards behind as he criss-crosses the pavement, twitching nose low to the ground. Make a good bloodhound, if ever the police were ever seeking a desperate criminal poodle bitch. Fresh artwork on the garage doors. 'Are birds free from the chains of the skyway?'. And further along, 'The pumps don't work 'cos the vandals took the handles.' A frenzy of recent activity from Mac the Finger. Let him know I appreciate the source of his references. Nobody about. Leave him a message and await a response. Extract the aerosol can from deep within the pocket and give it a good shake. Spray in crude letters, 'There are no Kings inside the Gates of Eden.' And sign it 'Louie the King.' Stand back and admire the artwork of running paint. Never make an artist, but at least it's legible. The teacher at school once said I am to art what Genghis Khan was to civilisation and made the class laugh. But I was proud to be associated with someone who made his mark on history. Seems I was destined for greatness yet to be.

For three days now, I've refrained from any manner of sexual activity. Ate well, kept off the drink. All in preparation for this important evening. The start of a new career, perhaps. What would Duncan give to be in my shoes? Hair cut, and suit dry-cleaned. Nails cut short, and manicured. I feel quite the ponce.

Slip out into the dark and make my way to number 69. Butterflies in my stomach. Not unusual for the first day in a new job. Wonder how best to describe my occupation on my tax return. Male prostitute? Gigolo? Rent boy? Or perhaps masseur? I think personal trainer has a nice ring to it. No connotations of immorality.

Ushered into the lounge, where my client is already waiting. My god! I recognise her! Shit! Christine, Mr Barker's second wife! The trophy blonde, for whom he ditched his first wife after almost thirty years. I saw her once in his office, but we were never introduced. I don't think she knows me. Val performing the introductions.

"Christine, I'd like you to meet Ray. Ray, this is Christine."

"How do you do."

"Hello. Have we met before? Your face is familiar."

"I don't think so. I would be unlikely to forget such a beautiful woman."

"How charming. Our room is ready. Shall we go up?"

"As you wish."

Follow her up the staircase. Nice legs. Firm buttocks. Smartly dressed in an expensive powder-blue suit. Make-up perfect. Hair just so. Would have passed for a bimbo, if only she had a little more intelligence. Close the door behind me as she turns to face me. Her confident smile, a testament to expensive dentistry, changes to a lascivious smirk.

"These are the rules. You will refer to me as 'M'Lady'. I will call you 'Raymond'. You are here to do my bidding. Is that clear?"

"Perfectly, M'Lady."

"Good. You will now wait outside while I undress. I will call you when I am ready."

"Yes, M'Lady."

Crouching down behind the door, an eye to the keyhole. A sudden tap on the shoulder. Valerie. A finger to her lips. Takes my hand and leads me quietly to the adjacent room. From where we watch Christine through a two-way mirror.

"I shall be monitoring your performance. Be good!"

Returning next door upon Christine's command. Laid face down. Naked.

"You may massage me, Raymond. The jasmine, I think."

"Yes, M'Lady."

Following Val's instructions. Circular, sweeping movements down M'Lady's shoulders and back. Run an oily finger slowly and teasingly down M'Lady's spine, stopping at M'Lady's cheeks. Massage M'Lady's legs, the feet first, then moving enticingly upwards in response to her soft appreciative sighs. Gently rub oil into the thin barely-visible scars underneath M'Lady's cosmetically-enhanced buttocks, pressing the thumbs into her inner thighs as her moans increase.

"I'll turn over now, Raymond."

"As you wish, M'Lady."

Well, what do you know? Bright flame-red curly hair here. The burning bush. Are there no natural blondes left in this world? Concentrate first on M'Lady's shoulders, then her flat stomach. More oil required for these firm but full breasts. Large erect nipples the size of door-stops. Now the smooth waxed legs. And finally, M'Lady's fanny. Tease her with a gentle finger on the clitoris as she arches her back for a second or two before relaxing again, breathing heavily.

"Raymond. Get the vibrator. The gold one. It's on the table."

"Certainly, M'Lady. And how would you like it?"

"Right up to the mark."

Give it to her. Up to the mark, and just a little further as she writhes on the bench. Turn the control to 'full speed ahead'. And prepare to board on command.

"Get undressed, Raymond. I want to see Sergeant Sausage on parade and stood to attention immediately!"

"Yes. M'Lady. With or without?"

"Without. I like my sausage skinless."

Tear my clothes off and pull her roughly to the edge of the bench, her legs dangling over the end, spread wide. And standing up, plunge it straight in. To shrieks of delight from M'Lady as she reached an earthquaking orgasm. Pull out, turn her over, and impale her again. Ride her hard until I come grinding to my own shuddering juddering halt. And withdraw to leave her splayed face down on the bench, breathing hard, a trace of fluid trickling down her leg. After which, she says a quiet thank you and kisses my cheek. I dress and clean down the bench with disinfectant spray while she takes a quick shower, and returns, looking as immaculate as she did when she first arrived.

"Here's a hundred pounds for your services, Ray. And it's all for you. I've already paid the old slapper you work for. Of course, there would be more for you if you were to come to my house when I need you. Please come around on Friday afternoon."

"I can't. I have an appointment."

"Cancel it!"

"It's important. I need to find out if it's getting any better."

"Find out if what's getting better?"

"My gonorrhoea."

"Oh, my god! You have VD?"

"Yes."

"Oh god! Oh, my god! Why the hell did you have sex with me?"

"Your orders, M'Lady."

"Cut the M'Lady crap. You bastard! You fucking bastard!"

"Yes, M'Lady."

"And you're a lousy lover. You and your tiny dick."

"M'Lady, if you require something to fit snugly, I suggest you try a prize-winning giant marrow. Only once previously have I come across such a twat. And funnily enough, his name was Barker too."

"You know my husband?"

"As a soon-to-be-evicted ex-employee, yes."

"You'll be hearing from my lawyer."

"I don't doubt it. And shall look forward to it. I'm sure I can make my evidence stand up in court. Exhibit A. Sergeant Sausage. The tabloids will love it."

Pushing past me. Running down the stairs and straight out of the front door. Never to return. Valerie walks in, wearing nothing but a huge smile.

"Ray, I could kill you for losing me a good customer. But her, I can do without. Stuck-up, patronising tart. Fancy calling me an old slapper. The cheek of it. Fancy a drink?"

"Please. And I'm sorry. I guess I won't be working for you after all."

"Don't apologise. It was worth it for the look on her face when you said you had VD. You were joking, weren't you?"

"Yes."

"Then why the hell did you do it?"

And over a drink I relate the whole story of how her husband had sacked me and was about to evict me. And how I just couldn't resist the opportunity to take my revenge. Afterwards, we sit together on the plush sofa, watching the video recording she'd made from the adjacent room.

"I'll never be able to keep a straight face next time her husband comes around."

"You mean, old man Barker comes here?"

"Every week. Writes me a cheque on the company account."

"And what services does he require?"

"I can't tell you that, Ray. Client confidentiality."

"Go on. I promise I won't tell a soul."

"Promise?"

"Promise. I'm leaving this fair city. Neither you, nor Mrs Barker, nor her cuckolded husband will ever see or hear from me again."

"Well. He comes in and bosses me about like I was one of his employees. Then he orders me to fetch him a coke and a raspberry jam sandwich. And when I come back he's changed his clothes. He's dressed as a schoolboy! Short trousers, cap, satchel, rolled-down socks, the lot! And he drops his short trousers. And instead of underwear, he's got this rubber pouch-thing on. With the end of his willy just poking out. And he says his tortoise is poorly, and will I stroke it and kiss it and make it come out of its shell. And he sits on the bench, eating his sandwich and sipping his coke while I give him a blow-job."

Then before I leave, she gives me a quick one, on the house. She says it's her night off. And this is pleasure, not business.

Well pleased with my evening's work as I follow Plopper on his meandering journey through the dark night streets.

As we approach the garages, he stops dead, ears pricked. Increase my stride to catch up with him and grab his collar.

"Easy, Plopper. What's up, son?"

Plopper emitting a low growl, his gaze fixed firmly on the furthermost garage, where in the dim light from the cloud-obscured moon, I can just make out a figure. Dressed in dark clothes. Working feverishly. His hands tightly wrapped round something cylindrical, which he's shaking furiously like some demented wanker. Totally engrossed in his work, as I sneak up close.

"Mac the Finger, I presume."

Startled. Dropping the aerosol in mid-spray. Turning towards me.

"Shit! Oh, Christ, Ray! Look what you made me do!"

"Sorry, Jonathon. So, this is how you spend your time when you're not panting after young girls."

"Oh, Jesus, Ray! Don't report me. It's an innocent outlet for my artistic talent. That's all. I'm just practising. For the day when I feel I have the confidence to create something really special. Something which will make the whole city take note."

"Such as?"

"I can't tell you. But it'll be big. I promise."

"I didn't know you were a Dylan fan. I always thought you were a tosser."

"I suppose I am. Everyone's called me a tosser since I was at school. But I've always looked upon myself as different, that's all. I go my own way. Do what I want to do. I was a rebel in the sixties, you know that? Got expelled from school for having long hair and smoking pot. But Dylan was my idol, and still is. Which is why I'm intrigued to find a fellow devotee in the area, who's left me a message."

"That was me."

"You?"

"Yes."

"You're into Dylan?"

"Yes."

"Christ! Sorry, Ray. You just never seemed the type. I mean, I've only met you a couple of times. But you always seemed so aloof. And stiff. And formal. You never struck me as the type who could appreciate real music."

"It seems we both underestimated each other."

"Fancy a beer?"

"Fancy a whisky?"

"Yeah. Why not."

So, we walk back to my house, led by the amiable Plopper who has taken to Jonathon now he realises he's with me. Pour the man a large malt, and offer apologies for the fact that the albums have been boxed and taped up securely and the HiFi packed away in sturdy cases. Jonathon loquacious after the first mouthful of malt, pronouncing knowledgeably on every aspect of Dylan's life and work. The conversation animated until the small hours until he goes silent, and says sorry.

"What for, Jonathon?"

"For Lucy. I'm so sorry she's gone. And you've lost her. But I'm sorry I've lost her too. Not because I fancied her. Because I did. Who wouldn't? But because she was so special in the office. She always had a smile. And a really bright...attitude. I'm not sure if I'm doing her justice. It's just that the whole place seemed to light up the moment she breezed in. Christ, Ray. We all miss her. You must be devastated."

"Yes. I am."

"So am I. And I was only her boss. I admit, yes, I tried it on with her. But it was obvious she was devoted to you, and I never stood a chance."

"Jonathon, you wouldn't have been able to handle her even if she'd given you the chance."

"You're right, Ray. You and I are totally different. Only our musical tastes overlap. Artistically, you're a flop, Louie the King."

"And what makes you so special, Mac the Finger?"

"I'm going to make a statement, Louie. That's going to get me in the newspapers. Even anonymously. It doesn't matter. Just as long as I get my fifteen minutes of fame."

"In that case, Mac, I shall look out for it."

Shaking his hand at the door and saying our goodbyes. Watch him stagger off into the distance. Back to his empty flat. To dream his dreams of fame. Even if they are only fifteen minutes' worth.

CHAPTER 15

A bright and early start on this final morning. Just odds and sods to pack, and a few toiletries to throw into the suitcase. Half an hour's work and then I can leave forever this miserable city. But not before I've used the last of the toilet roll. Leave nothing for Boot. Except perhaps an unflushed turd.

Said goodbye to Julie this morning. She came around last night to help with the packing and to take down the curtains. Mr E called to see if he could be of any assistance, and when he saw Julie in the house, he just smiled and winked at me. I shall miss him, and Mrs E. I only wish I'd taken the trouble to get to know them before Lucy died. My early impressions of them were totally wrong and completely unjustified. They're a really nice couple. Hope Boot doesn't give them any problems, or they'll have to send Plopper round to sort him out.

When I explained to them the situation, they immediately offered to take Plopper in and give him a good home, and he seems quite settled with them. They give him lots of love and exercise, and he responds with affection aplenty. And the odd accident on the Axminster. He still watches through the window for me, though, and sometimes when I come home he's sat patiently on my doorstep waiting for me. He thinks I'm leaving him because he's done something wrong, and is desperate to make amends. He even brings the squeaky toys the E's bought for him and drops them at my feet. His peace offering. His way of saying sorry. He's just like me in that respect. All too ready to accept guilt. When Lucy's death really wasn't my fault. Lucy knows that, and I don't need to take her squeaky toys to atone. But I do need someone to tell me I'm not to blame. To lift the weight from my tired shoulders. To give me absolution. Perhaps I should never have rejected the offer of bereavement counselling, but I felt they would try to intrude upon my private grief, and take it away with them. When all I wanted to do was wear it on my sleeve.

Last night was my final night with Julie, and she made love with tenderness and passion. Afterwards, we opened a bottle of champagne, and toasted each other's future. And I kissed the tears from her face. And she told me she'd come to a decision. She'd been saving up for a good holiday, but instead intended to use the money on dental surgery to improve her chances of capturing the right man. And when we parted this morning, she handed me a card which said 'Thank you for being my friend'. Inside it she had written, 'Ray. No strings. No commitment. But I'm always here if you want me. Thank you for brightening up my dull life. Be happy. Love, Julie'.

When I get to Scarsby I will send her some flowers, and a 'thank you' note. Now all that remains is to lock up and hand the keys to Mr E, who has kindly offered to supervise the removal while I head north on the train. One last look round at this place which was our last home together. Lucy's little touches made it a home. The fresh flowers. Her eye for interior design and colour co-ordination. Which stamped her individuality on one of fifty-odd identically-built houses on the street.

Pick up the suitcase and leave. Mr and Mrs E and Plopper waiting at the gate. Plopper advancing immediately, tail swishing. Drops a squeaky bright yellow ball at my feet, sits and holds up his left paw. His sad eyes watching as I stroke his head. Catching my tears on his long tongue.

"Bye, Plopper. Be good."

Shaking Mr E's hand warmly. And a hug for Mrs E, who hands me a bag of sandwiches for the journey.

"Thank you both. Thanks for everything. You've been so kind. I'll miss you."

"You have to go, Ray. You have a life to live. Here is your past. Leave your ghosts here, and start again. You're still a young man. Don't let the past drag you down. You still have a future. Lucy would want you to have a future. Goodbye, Ray. And good luck."

The taxi right on cue. Turn around to wave a final goodbye as it drives off. To see Mrs E dabbing her eyes with a handkerchief, as Mr E chases Plopper who is haring up the road after us, thankfully giving up the chase before Mr E has a heart attack. And Plopper sits in the middle of the road. To bark his final farewell.

The train clickety-clicking north with its few passengers. Opening the bag of goodies to find along with the sandwiches two cans of beer and a little note which reads, 'A gift from Plopper and family'. Brings a lump to my throat. Open a can and silently toast the E's. And Plopper. I'll never forget my last sight of him. But I know he'll be well cared for. He'll forget me long before I forget him. And Julie? I hope she forgets me quickly, and finds someone who appreciates her. I know I've let her down, but she knew from the start that we had no future together. But nevertheless, I'll readily accept the guilt for spoiling a doomed relationship. And as the train gathers speed as it reaches the outskirts of the city I look out of the window and see. Wiping away the condensation until the view is clear. There, high on the plain wall of pre-stressed concrete of the Olympic-sized municipal swimming pool facing the railway. In the familiar artwork, the words 'You'd better start swimming or you'll sink like a stone."

Allow myself a smile. Watching the scaffolding being hastily erected as a graffiti removal specialist arrives. But not before the local TV news station camera crews have got their footage. I hope Jonathon enjoys his pseudonymic fame. It just shows that you can be a tosser yet still be a talented tosser. Hope for me yet.

Finally approaching Scarsby, after changing trains twice. Slowing down, as the green fields disappear from the window view to be replaced by the industrial estate and the scrap yards. Until the train eventually grinds to a brake-screeching halt at Platform Two.

Alighting in the damp November salt air and lugging the heavy suitcase down to the Estate Agents. Bright well-lit premises. Swivelling stands offering well-proportioned family accommodation at remarkably affordable prices. Flats, bungalows, terraces, detached executive residences. All described in the most glowing of terms. Yet still unsold month after month. Approach the counter where a pretty young girl beams a well-prepared smile.

"Good afternoon, sir. May I help you?"

"Yes. I'd like the keys to 43, Laburnum Grove, please."

"I'm sorry, sir. That one's accompanied viewing. Would you like me to arrange a viewing?"

"No. I'd like the keys. I wish to move in."

"Ha ha, sir. I'm sorry. You can't do that until you buy the property. Would you like to make an offer?"

"If I must. I offer fifty pence. And the vendor accepts. There. Are you now satisfied?"

"Sir. I'm afraid the property is priced at £45,000 or nearest. Now if you'd like to view, and then perhaps offer something approaching the asking price..."

"I do not wish to view. I wish to occupy. Is the manager in?"

"I'm sorry, sir. He's out at the moment. With a client. Would you like details of any other properties?"

"No. I have a removal van arriving first thing in the morning. And I need the keys to 43, Laburnum Grove."

"But, sir. I have no record of any offers to buy that property."

"I do not wish to buy it. I own it. I wish to take it off the market and move back in. My name is Light. Ray Light. If you look closely at the file, you will see I am, indeed, the owner. Here is my passport. It bears my name, and a not too unflattering likeness. Now, please may I have the keys?"

"Oh! Er, I'm sorry, Mr Light. Er. The manager must have them. They're not here. Can you come back in the morning?"

"You have two sets of keys. One of them must be here."

"I'm sorry, Mr Light. We don't appear to have them. It will all be sorted out first thing in the morning. I promise. Why don't you book in to one of the town's many splendid guest houses and call back in the morning? We'll have this minor problem sorted out by then. I assure you."

Something fishy going on here. But no point in arguing with this young girl. Best to take her advice and find a hotel for the night. However, since it's still early, I'll take a walk by the house and make sure it hasn't been demolished to make way for a new by-pass. Or something equally ridiculous.

Instruct the taxi driver to stop at the end of the Grove. From where I can see lights from number 43. Walk the rest of the way. Loud, thumping music. Becoming louder as I approach. And hammer on the door till my knuckles bleed. As do my eardrums with the noise. Eventually the door is opened by a sleepy-eyed teenager.

"Look. If you're from the Department of Environmental Health, they've already been once today and issued us a notice. So, piss off. OK?"

"Who are you?"

"I live here."

"Yes. But who are you?"

"Look. What's it got to do with you? I live here. So, piss off."

"Who's given you permission to live here?"

"Not that it's any of your business. But my girlfriend, who's an Estate Agent, rents it. OK?"

"This house is not for rent. I own it. Now get out."

"Fuck you!"

The door slammed in my face. No answer to my persistent knocking, but net curtains twitching around the estate as the neighbours record the scene. What short memories these people have. I used to be their neighbour only a few months ago. But now, when I turn in their direction, the net curtains twitch shut. Welcome home, Ray.

CHAPTER 16

And walking slowly along these streets lined with guest houses, most of which have vacancies. Comparing the prices and the general state of disrepair of most of them. Finally finding one which looks inviting enough. Double glazed and exterior freshly painted. Ring the bell by the glass-panelled door and wait. Hear a noise from within. A figure coming slowly down the dimly-lit stairs. Sorting through a bunch of keys on a long chain. Fumbling for the correct one with shaking hands. Trying several in the lock before selecting one which fits. The face of a thin woman, so thin her bones appeared to be on the outside, with grey hair and complexion to match, appearing round the opening door.

"Yes?"

"Do you have a room for the night?"

"Yes."

"May I come in and see it?"

"Yes. Come in."

"Thank you."

Follow the woman's unsteady steps up two flights of stairs and along a corridor to room 6. Small but warm. Washbasin, soap and towel in the corner. Tea-making facilities. A small cheap self-assembly wardrobe which looked like it assembled itself. No human would take the blame for that. And the bed with the ubiquitous rubber sheet. Toilet and shower just down the hall.

"This will do fine. I'll take it."

"OK. Do you mind paying in advance?"

"Not at all."

"Twelve pounds, please. Breakfast from seven-thirty till nine."

And she presses the keys into my hand and is gone. Watching her from my bedroom window as she hurries across the street to the off-licence and emerges almost immediately with a bottle of gin. A quick wash and change of clothes and out for some sustenance as I feel little desire to spend the evening in the company of my less than charming landlady, who, I think, will be smashed out of her frail exoskeleton by the time she serves dinner.

Patrol the streets of this seaside town now all but empty of holidaymakers. A strong cold wind whistling in from the sea. The town almost shut down for the winter. Lights going off in the shops and offices as people hurry home. A long string of lightbulbs stretching the length of this seafront road. Sequence of colours interrupted at regular intervals by the void of a dead bulb. The neon glow from the burger restaurant and the pizza house opposite compete for custom with their garish display. Large billboards advertising local shows and events long passed. The distant voice of a bingo caller from an almost deserted amusement arcade. The Spa closed for the winter for renovation. Expected to reopen in the spring, if sufficient lottery funding is forthcoming. And at the end of the road a restaurant we used to frequent. Opens at seven. Another hour and a half. No alternative but to slip into a nearby hostelry. And at the entrance, a door to the left for the lounge, and to the right for the tap room. The lounge, I think. A better class of customer in a lounge bar. Wrong. In this case, there are no customers of any class. But then, neither are there any in the tap room. On the point of leaving when a head appears round the gantry.

"Evening, sir. Oh, hello, Ray. What are you doing here?"

"Hello, Billy. I could ask you the same thing."

"Been here a couple of months now. The Ship closed down. Manager did a runner. Cashed up one Sunday night and left with the week's takings. The brewery got the stock-takers in and found some anomalies, sacked all the staff, and shut the place. They've put it on the market now. Hoping some out-of-towner will buy it expecting to make a good living from it. Except they won't. Not in this town. Dying on its feet, it is. Anyway, I thought you moved down south."

"Just back for a short visit. Some business to sort out."

"Isn't the missus with you?"

"No, Billy. She died. A couple of months ago. Cancer."

"Oh. I'm sorry, Ray."

"Me too. Anyway, are you serving drink in this alehouse or not?"

"What would you like?"

"I'll have a bitter, please."

"Ermm. Dodgy, Ray. I wouldn't recommend it. The landlord's been filtering slops into it this afternoon. Stick to the Guinness if I were you. He drinks Guinness, so he never interferes with it."

"Guinness, then."

"Pint?"

"Please, Billy."

The dark liquid pouring slowly foaming and settling to its creamy white head. Worth waiting for. Wipe the condensation from the cold glass, and drink deeply. Imbibe some Irish courage for tomorrow's confrontation. From this stout brewed in London.

"So, what are your plans for tonight, Ray?"

"Well, at the moment I'm just looking for somewhere to eat. Then a few quiet pints, and back to the B and B for the night. For some reason I can't get the keys to the flat until the morning."

"The King's down the road do a decent bar meal. I can recommend them. Under new management. Nice enough couple. So, nip down there for a meal, then come back here for a drink with me. We've got Happy Hour from seven till nine."

"That's two hours."

"Don't be pedantic, Ray. Bitter one-twenty a pint."

"How about Guinness?"

"One-fifty. And doubles of spirits one-fifty."

"Now you're talking! I'll see you in a while."

"See you, Ray."

So down to the King's. Had a bit of a face lift. New carpet, curtains and upholstery. And a fresh lick of paint. Pity they couldn't have had the customers renovated at the same time. Same old faces, plus a few the previous landlord had barred. A pleasant face behind the bar, which is certainly an improvement from the harridan who formerly ruled herein.

"Evening, sir."

"Evening. A pint of bitter, please. And are you serving meals?"

"Yes, love. Till nine. Shall I get you a menu?"

"No need. Do you do steaks?"

"Yes, love. Sirloin or rump?"

"Rump, please. With chips and salad."

"Right, love. And how would you like your steak? Medium?"

"I'd prefer large. And slightly bloody."

"I'll see what we can do, love. We're not one of these brewery chains where everything is portion-controlled right down to the number of peas you get. You want a large steak, that's what you'll get."

"Thank you. How much is that, please?"

"I'll just take for the beer, if that's OK. We'll agree a price for the steak when we find out what we've got. If that's all right with you."

"If the steak is good enough, and big enough, you may charge me whatever you like."

"Take a seat, love. Be about twenty minutes."

"Fine. Thank you."

Sit here quietly in this corner. Stomach rumbling like a distant thunderstorm. Smell of searing beef wafting through from the kitchen. And after fifteen minutes it arrives. On a large oval platter. A large thick cow slice sizzling in its bloody juice. Chips alongside, stacked haphazardly. And fresh-looking crisp salad.

"Here you are, love. That's twenty-six ounces uncooked. My Jack, the landlord, says if you clear your plate, you can have a pint on the house."

"And how much is the meal?"

"Is fourteen-fifty all right?"

"If it tastes as good as it looks, fifteen for cash."

"It's a deal."

Slice into the succulent flesh and taste the tender meat. Mouth watering at the prospect of devouring the rest. The hell with manners and etiquette! Attack the beast. Scoop up portions of salad, potato and cow. And shovel it in.

Ignore the small crowd gathering to witness the spectacle of this one-sided gladiatorial contest of man versus animal. In which I most definitely hold the upper hand. No dead beast will get the better of me. Suppress a small burp after crunching through the raw sliced onion, and finally lay down the stainless steel on the empty plate. To a ripple of applause from the appreciative audience. Stand up and take a theatrical bow. As Jack delivers a foaming pint of bitter, whispering, "Come and eat here anytime. You'll be good for trade."

Reluctantly take my leave with the promise to return, and make my way back to the Horse. Where Billy is still alone.

"Hello, Ray. Enjoy your meal?"

"Very nice. Just what I needed, thanks. Guinness, please."

"Two minutes to go yet."

"What do you mean?"

"Happy Hour. Prices don't come into effect until the clock on the till shows seven."

"So, pour it now, and I'll pay for it at seven."

"Fair enough. Pint of Guinness coming up."

"This Happy Hour certainly pulls in the punters, Billy."

"Give it a chance, Ray. The Lion has Happy Hour from five-thirty to six-thirty. So, by my reckoning, about two dozen customers will be in within the next five minutes. And at five past nine, the lot of them will be gone up to the Bull to catch their Happy Hour. That's the way it works. Better to sell a few gallons at a small profit than sell none at all."

Drinkers coming in now. Singly and in groups. Several the worse for wear already. Make a mental note to avoid the Bull after nine at night. Customers singing, shouting and arguing. This Happy Hour is a misnomer. Attracts the drunks, the depressives, the obstreperous. Who think they are getting a bargain. When really all they're doing is getting more ale for their unemployment benefit. Whereas when Duncan and I drink, every hour in every bar is Happy Hour.

And on cue, shortly after nine, the pub empties, except for a half-dozen old boys playing dominoes. Do my good deed for the day and collect the empties for Billy. Stack them in the glass-washer. Then take the tin bucket and empty and clean the overflowing ashtrays. Wipe down the tables and replace the torn and soggy beermats with fresh ones. Damage limitation exercise. Just in case some respectable customers come in. Attempt to give the impression this is a clean, pleasant and well-run pub, with an atmosphere of conviviality. Rather than a staging post for thieves, knaves and drunks on benefit.

"Thanks for your help, Ray."

"No problem."

"Are you having another?"

"Please. I'm not yet ready to face the Exoskeleton."

"Sorry?"

"Never mind. Another Guinness, Billy."

And at closing time, helping Billy clear up, which didn't take long, before saying goodnight and weaving my way along deserted streets back to Rosanalan House. Open the wrought iron gate slowly, cursing its squeaking hinges. Push the key quietly in the lock, turn it and push the door open. The house silent as a monastery for deaf mutes. Make my way slowly and carefully up the dimly-lit stairs, cringing at every creak of loose board. And safe in my room, undress, wash, dress again, creep along the corridor for a pee and return to undress and climb into bed.

A soft tapping on the door. Ignore it. Lie here in the dark feigning sleep or death, breathing quietly. The familiar jangle of keys being inserted in the lock. Slip out of bed into the underpants. Quiet. Hold my breath. Should have had garlic on my steak. Could have breathed it round the door frame to protect me from unholy nocturnal visitors. Of which I am sure this is one. The mortice lock sliding back as the correct key is inserted. The door yawing open with a groan. And in the doorway, there appears a nightdress-clad skeleton, clutching a half-empty bottle of gin. Press myself against the wall, as the opening door casts light into the gloom and exposes my frightened frame. To the obvious delight of the bottle-waving crone.

"Hello, love. I'm sorry to bother you. I just thought you might fancy a nightcap."

"No. No thank you."

"Well, perhaps you'd just like to talk for a while."

"No. I'm very tired. I've had a long day, and I need some rest."

"If it's relaxation you want, I'm the woman for you. I can send you to sleep with a smile on your face."

"No, thank you. Would you please leave."

"Don't worry, love. My husband, Alan, works nights. We won't be disturbed."

"I believe you're already disturbed."

"Me? No, love. I just believe in looking after my guests. Don't worry if you're hard up, there's no extra charge. It's all part of the service."

"I don't require any further service, thank you. I just want to sleep."

"Oh, I love the way you talk. You're a real gentleman. We don't get many in here. Mostly fishing trips. Groups of men here for the weekend. Drinking, fishing and shagging. That's what they come for. But you're different. Classy, aren't you? Like your sex with a bit of style. Well, I used to be classy till I came here. All the girls in Chapeltown knew me as the classy whore. If they had any punters with a bit of style, they sent them to me. I had a flat. I didn't do it in cars or in dark alleys. I took my gentlemen to bed. And looked after them. And they came back time after time. Till I met Alan. He took me away from it all. Treated me like a lady. Promised me a new life. A new start. And this is it. A shitty guest house in Scarsby. And Alan goes to work every night. Hoping a fishing party books in. Hoping they'll shag me, so we can pay the bills. And then finally, when I get a gentleman in, and turn on the charm, and put it on a plate, he's not interested."

"I'm gay."

"Oh, Jesus! Just my fucking luck! Business on the slide and when I finally get a guest, he's a fucking queer. Well, goodnight, mister. And don't invite any boys in for the night. I'll be downstairs watching the door."

A sigh of relief as she exits. Listen to her lurching down the staircase bemoaning her ill-luck. And I thank god for homosexuals, whose inclinations have saved me from a probable charge of womanslaughter. I could almost sing. If I was glad to be gay.

Manhandle the dressing table across the room and wedge it tight at the back of the door. Note the square of exposed carpet much lighter and cleaner than the rest. And the thick layer of dust along the skirting board revealed for the first time in months. Lie back and close my eyes, hoping sleep will rescue me from this nightmare harpie.

Faint noises from the room above. Murmur of voices talking in whispers. Then the rhythmic creak of bedsprings. Small flecks of plaster dropping from the ceiling and settling on the bed like dandruff. The bare ceiling lightbulb dancing and jerking. As I slumber safely.

And breakfast next morning brought by the jovial Alan home from work. Sizzling bacon rashers, sausage, fried egg and tomatoes. Served up on a stone-cold plate. Apologies for his wife's nocturnal soliciting. Old habits die hard. And refunds two quid off the bill, hoping I'll stay again sometime.

CHAPTER 17

Hand in the keys and make straight for the estate agents, which is thankfully empty of customers.

"Oh, Mr Light. I'm glad you've come so early. To sort out our little problem. The boss isn't in yet. So we can talk."

"Would you kindly explain what's going on?"

"Yes. I'm sorry. Darren, that's my boyfriend. Well, we're engaged. His parents threw him out. And he'd nowhere to go. So, I let him sleep at your house. Just a temporary arrangement. Until I can save the deposit to rent our own flat."

"How long has this temporary arrangement been going on?"

"About four weeks. But it's OK. Nobody's been to view the house. The market's quiet at this time of year."

"I want him out immediately."

"The best we can do is the weekend, I'm afraid."

"Not good enough. Does your boss know about this?"

"Oh God, no! I'd lose my job if he found out."

"Tough."

"Please, Mr Light. Don't tell him. We'll be out on Saturday morning. I promise. We've a new property on the market. They move out on Friday. So, we can move in there for a while. Darren needs an address so he can get his Giro. And he can't get a job if he's homeless."

"So, what do you expect me to do in the meantime?"

"Oh. You can move your things back in. You can have the back bedroom. We don't mind."

"Well, that is kind of you."

"It's the best I can do. I promise we'll be out on Saturday. Unless, of course, you tell the boss. In which case you'll have to get an eviction order against us."

"And what if I just go around and tear Darren's head from his shoulders and stuff it up his arse?"

"I'd be careful if I were you. Darren knows some pretty nasty types. He's been inside. All we're asking is a few days. To get sorted, that's all."

"Very well. Saturday. Or I bring in some nasty types of my own."

"Thanks, Mr Light. You won't regret it."

"And I wish to take the property off your books with immediate effect."

"Certainly, sir. We'll bill you for the administration charge. Here's your key."

"Thank you."

Phone the removal firm and ask them to keep the load in storage for a week. Don't want Darren to feel too much at home, watching my TV from the comfort of my soft leather settee.

Up the path to number 43. Turn the key and let myself in. The house strangely quiet. Faint smell of cannabis. Empty takeaway cartons littering the carpet. Check round. Rubbish strewn everywhere. A thick layer of dust on the windowsills. Overflowing ashtray by the kitchen sink. Black bin liner in the corner overflowing and stinking, a trickle of brown green goo forming a sticky puddle on the floor beneath a split in the plastic. Tiptoe as quietly as I can up the creaking staircase. Check the bathroom. Black ring round the bath. Newspapers and a porn magazine by the toilet. Faint sound of snoring from behind the door of the front bedroom. Peep round to find Darren and a young blonde girl asleep naked beneath a puke- and wank-stained duvet. The back bedroom mercifully empty and relatively clean. Dump the suitcase here for the moment and nip down to the kitchen to see if I can find the makings of a cup of coffee.

Open the cupboards. Mostly bare. A couple of clean plates here, and a mug. Brown-stained but useable. A bottle of tomato ketchup, most of it dried thick and dark round the cap. And a jar of coffee powder, half full. A bag of sugar alongside, full of lumps and small brown patches. No fridge, so further hunting necessary for signs of milk. Ah! Down here, half a carton. Not fresh, but doesn't smell too bad. Rinse a spoon under the tap and dry it on my shirt tail. A drop of water in the kettle. Just switch it on. And that's another thing. I had the electricity switched off when we moved out. And turned the water off. And the gas. But they're all working now. I hope my uninvited guests are paying the bills.

A noise behind me. Turning in surprise to see Darren clad only in underpants, a hammer in his hand.

"Oh, it's you back again. How did you get in?"

"Your girlfriend gave me back my key."

"Right. Sorry. When I heard noises, I thought you were an intruder."

"That's a bit rich coming from you."

"OK. So, what do you want? Has Jude sorted it with you?"

"Jude?"

"My girlfriend. At the estate agents."

"Yes. You're moving on Saturday."

"That alright with you?"

"It will have to be."

"Cheers, mate. Help yourself to a coffee."

"I intend to. And could you tell me who had the gas and electricity reconnected?"

"I did."

"In your name?"

"No. I can't get an account. I owe them money, see. They've had me disconnected before. So, I used your name. We needed the heating, man. You can't expect us to do without at this time of year. This is a cold house, man. You could catch TB or something, living here."

"And have you paid the bills?"

"We haven't had any. Yet. But we'll make a contribution. I swear. On my life."

"Which is worth precious little. How many more people are living here?"

"Only me and Jude."

"So, who's upstairs?"

"Nobody."

"That nobody has an extremely hairy dark bush. And snores like a horse."

"Oh. That's Angie. She's a friend. Just visiting."

"Does Jude know about her?"

"Christ, man. No. And don't even think of telling her. If we split up, I'll have nowhere to go. So, I'll have to stay here till you evict me. Legally. Through the courts. Takes time."

"It doesn't take time to wring your miserable little scrawny neck."

"Easy, man. Look. We'll be out on Saturday, if that's what Jude promised. Just don't hassle us, OK. It's counter-productive. Hey, the kettle's boiled. Make me one while you're at it. Milk and three sugars, please."

"Sorry, there are no clean cups."

"That's OK. Use the red mug on the window sill. That's mine."

"Don't push your luck! I think I'm being tolerant enough. Don't expect me to wait on you as well."

"Suit yourself. Live alone, do you?"

"Yes."

"This is a big house for just one person. Ever thought of taking in lodgers?"

"Definitely not."

"Just a thought. Could help with the bills."

"I don't need help. I can manage."

"I don't suppose you could lend me a tenner. Just till my giro comes."

"No."

"No problem. Just thought I'd ask. Just trying to be friendly. Seeing as you're sharing a house with us."

"I am not sharing a house with you. I am merely allowing you to stay under my roof until Saturday. When, provided you move out, I will forget you ever existed. But if you don't move out, you will wish you never had existed."

"Point taken. Look, we won't cause you any problems. Just come and go as you please. You won't even know we're here most of the time. And look. As a gesture of my goodwill, you can go up and shag Angie if you like. She's so stoned, she won't even notice."

"No, thank you."

"Well, the offer's there. I get a lot of visitors. If you see any you fancy, just give me the nod, and I'll fix you up. OK?"

"I'm not interested in your girlfriends."

"Oh, I see. Well, I know some men who will perform, providing you pay well."

"You're asking for a slap."

"Just trying to suss you out, that's all."

"Don't. My life is none of your business. And the sooner you're out of it the better."

"Suit yourself. So, when's all your stuff arrive?"

"Not until you've left."

"Shame. We could use some home comforts."

"Get your own."

"Well, mate. It's been nice talking to you. I'll have to go. Some unfinished business upstairs. So, don't let me keep you. See you."

Don't feel comfortable here. Get my belongings and book into a B & B for the rest of the week. Call back on Friday to ensure they're keeping their end of the bargain.

Helpful girl at the Tourist Information office recommends a comfortable hotel and phones to make my booking. Head straight there and sign in. Then collapse on the wide well-sprung bed and catch up on some kip.

Rising late in the afternoon to stroll aimlessly along the deserted rain-lashed beach. Huge rollers breaking as the tide rushes in. Fishing boats racing towards the sanctuary of the harbour. And I return to the warm sanctuary of the hotel bar.

CHAPTER 18

Music and loud voices coming from the house. A group of teenagers hanging round the gate, swilling beer out of cans. Push my way through and enter. The house full as a party is in full flow. Couples in the kitchen and on the stairs in various stages of copulatory progress, some of the unions looking a shade unnatural. Takes all sorts.

Jude approaching, in a short blue dress.

"Hi! Come to join the party?"

"I've come to safeguard my property. But I guess it's a little late for that."

"Everything's fine, Mr Light. We're still leaving in the morning. But it's Darren's birthday, so he invited a few friends round for a drink. I hope you don't mind."

"Whether I mind or not wouldn't make any difference, would it?"

"Well, I guess not. Here, have a beer."

"Thanks. I'll keep out of your way. Shut myself in the bedroom and pretend none of this is happening."

Clamber over couples cavorting on the stairs, past the bathroom from which emanates the sound of vomiting. Safe in the back bedroom just vacated by two girls, arms entwined, giggling. Sit on the floor with my back against the door. Prepared to fight off all invaders. Tease open the ring-pull, and glug the beer. Should have brought more, but daren't leave this room in case I can't get back in. Still, always prepared. I have a bottle of Malt in the suitcase for emergency use only. It's going to be a long night, and I daren't sleep.

A tapping on the door. Ignore it. Then a voice.

"Mr Light. Are you in there? It's Jude. Can I come in and talk to you? Please?"

Open the door slightly to a tearful mascara-smeared Jude.

"Come in."

"Thanks, Mr Light. I need to cool off for a minute."

"What's the matter?"

"Darren. He's ignoring me. And chatting up some blonde girl with big tits."

"Angie. She's not a natural blonde."

"Whatever. He really takes me for granted, you know,"

"Then, why put up with him?"

"I love him, I suppose."

"I very much doubt that."

"Yeah. Me too. I'd like to get my own back for the way he treats me."

"So, why don't you? There are plenty young men downstairs."

"I'd rather do it with someone he really hates. Do you mind if I take my dress off? It's so warm."

"I'd rather you didn't."

"Don't you think I'm attractive?"

"Yes."

"Well, then. Let's do it."

"Let's not."

"Come on. Well, how about if I do this for you, then?"

Slipping the thin straps of her dress from her shoulders to expose her bare breasts. A good size on this slim girl. Nice weight to them. Firm and full, with no signs of sagging yet.

Sinking to her knees in front of me as her hands explore my trousers. Lean against the door in case anyone tries to enter. Trousers unfastened and dropped to the ankles. Underpants rapidly follow. Thank God they're clean, and the socks are a matching pair for a change. She's very good for such a young girl. Gentle, and unhurried. A most enjoyable experience. Which, I think, will not last very long. Noise outside, and a fierce hammering on the door. The dreadful Darren. Put my full weight to the door while ensuring I don't disengage from the offered orifice.

"Jude! Jude! You in there? I want to talk to you."

Careful, girl! Remember what your mother taught you, and don't speak with your mouth full. Though I don't mind one bit if you play with your food.

"Jude! Come on out!"

"There's nobody in here except me and two naked young boys. Now go away! They're over the age of consent. And as a practicing homosexual, I demand the right to practice in private."

"Sorry, man. I'm looking for Jude. You seen her?"

"No."

"OK. Sorry to disturb you, you old queen. Remind me never to turn my back on you. Turd-burglar!"

What wonderful relief a good orgasm is! There can be no finer feeling in the universe. Forget troubles, worries. Forget everything. And just enjoy the moment of release. I wonder if that's what Heaven is like. One never-ending orgasm. If it is, Lucy will be having a whale of a time.

"Did you enjoy that?"

"Yes. Very much. Thank you."

"My pleasure. Thank you for coming."

"Thank you for having me."

"Can I sleep with you tonight?"

"I've no intention of sleeping."

"Me neither."

"No, I mean I've no bed, or blankets. Or anything. I just want to stay awake to ensure Darren and his mates don't wreck the house. And that he leaves first thing in the morning. Before the man comes to change the locks."

"You mean you're going to throw us out? After what I've just done for you?"

"Yes. That was our agreement."

"I'll tell Darren you raped me."

"Darren won't be listening. That blonde girl's thighs will be covering his ears by now."

"I'll kill her!"

"Please yourself. But don't do it in my house."

"I'll tell Darren what you've done to me."

"Tell him what you like. I've had about enough of this. Just enjoy your party. Don't break or steal anything. And get out in the morning. Otherwise, I may have to violate the conditions of my probation."

"What are you on probation for?"

"I have been released on licence. From a hospital for the criminally insane. I do bad things."

"Such as what?"

"Well, the last time I was at a party, I took exception to a particular record the DJ played. And hacked off his hands with a machete. When someone tried to pull me back, I bit his ear off. And swallowed it."

"I don't believe you."

"I can't help it. One minute I'm so calm and normal. And the next, I'm psychotic. But the medication has helped enormously. Keeps things under control. Thing is, I can't remember where I put my tablets. They're not in my case. God! Can you hear that music? I hate it! The rhythm does weird things to my brain's alpha waves, they told me. Upsets the chemical balance. But I'm fine with the pills. Wonder where they are. If Darren's stolen them, I'll cut off his head and eat it. You've got nice breasts. I could boil them in a pan with some cabbage. And a slice or two of your kidney."

"Jesus! You're weird! Please may I go?"

"Certainly. And would you kindly ask them to turn down the music just a little. While I search for my pills. Perhaps I left them in the kitchen. I'll come down and have a look. I must say, I am a little peckish. Perhaps I could find some tasty morsel to tempt my palate."

"No! You stay up here. And look for your pills. I'll get the music turned down. Don't worry. Just relax. Everything's cool. OK?"

"OK."

A minute after she left, the music suddenly falls silent. Then the sound of people leaving. Peace at last. A soft tap on the bedroom door.

"Mr Light, sir. It's Darren. Everything's OK, man. Everyone's gone. There's just me and Jude. Listen. We're going to bed now. We're going to sleep behind the door. And I've got a hammer. So, don't you try anything. I'm not frightened of you, man."

"Turn the music down, Darren, it's making my head ache."

"The music's off. Finished. Just you concentrate on finding your pills. They must be in there somewhere. Everything's cool, OK?"

"If you say so, doctor."

"Jeez. That's right Mr Light. You're safe. No-one's going to hurt you. The nasty music's gone. All those nasty people have gone. You're OK. Just find your pills, and get some rest. OK?"

"OK, doctor. Goodnight."

"Goodnight, Mr Light."

And early in the morning, peeping out from an upstairs window, I watch them leave. Two supermarket trolleys laden with their worldly goods in plastic bags. Squeaking and rattling their way down the uneven street. Descend the stairs at a pace. To survey the damage. Which, thankfully, is minimal. A note left by the sink.

"Dear Mr Light,

Thank you for your hospitality. We've left now and won't be bothering you again. We cleaned and tidied as best we could. We were both up early. We couldn't sleep. Please see a doctor. We hope you get better soon.

Jude and Darren."

No sign of their key. Well, I shall just have to sit tight until the man arrives today to fit the new locks. Should be here soon. Then, once the place is secure, I can venture out for a bit of shopping. Buy cleaning materials, bleach and the like. Wipe away all traces of uninvited guests. I shall spend a few hours this evening cleaning up. Then first thing tomorrow, it's down to the DIY store for paint. Give the place a bit of a face-lift before the furniture comes. Then, in the next few weeks, I shall tackle the lot, room by room.

Put it back on the market at a reasonable price, and hope to sell it fully furnished. Even leave the TV on. Tuned to their favourite soap.

CHAPTER 19

A walk down towards the town on this unseasonally pleasant afternoon when a man leaps out of a bus shelter, barring my way. Oh God! A tramp. Smell him from here. Long matted grey hair and beard. Greasy stinking clothes. Down on his luck. If he ever had any.

"Excuse me, boss. Could you kindly spare me the price of a cup of tea?"

"How much is it?"

"Just a quid, sir."

"A pound! For a cup of tea?"

"Yes, sir. It's the tourist trade, sir. Drives the prices up. So the likes of me requires financial assistance from members of the general public just to scrape by."

"Here."

"God bless you, sir. Er, I don't suppose you could spare another quid, could you? For a cheese and pickle sandwich. I don't like to ask. But I haven't eaten for three days. And man cannot live by tea alone."

"How do I know you won't spend it on drink?"

"You have my word as a gentleman, boss. I have been a total abstainer for... some days now."

"Here. Here's a tenner. Get drunk."

"Thank you, boss. You're a real gent. You'll get your reward in heaven. And any time you're passing, call in. Don't bother to knock. The door of my bus shelter is always open to you. Come in, sit down and share a crust."

Walk away from the grimy smiling face. Watch him from a safe distance cross the road to the off-licence. And emerge a minute later with a carrier bag loaded with liquid comestibles, but no tea. Or cheese and pickle sandwich. Carry on down to the harbour. Smell of fish and ozone. Seagulls feasting on discarded scraps of burger. And dive bombing shoppers. Showers of white plop splattering dark winter coats.

Returning home in the early evening, laden with two bags of shopping and a pizza I've just collected on the way. A commotion at the bus shelter. Walk past on the opposite side of the road and take a sly peek. A small crowd, and ambulance and police in attendance. Leading away the tramp, unsteady on his feet, blood trickling from his head. Mouthing obscenities at all and sundry. And pointing an accusing finger in my direction, shouting.

"That's him! That's the bastard who gave me ten pounds to buy cider and sherry. When all I wanted was a cup of tea and a sandwich. A man of his upbringing and obvious intelligence should know better than to give a tenner to the likes of me. I shall sue you, sir, for wilful negligence. With a large amount in damages for pain and suffering. And dry-cleaning bills. For I have just pissed myself."

Watching as they lead him into the back of the ambulance which pulls away. Only to be replaced immediately by a council wagon, whose occupants set about cleaning up and hosing down the bus shelter. Must be more wary in future. Take care with one's spontaneous acts of charitable kindness. Which leave one open to potential law-suits. Don't offer a cigarette to anyone, lest they sue for damage to health.

Hurry back to the house before my good reputation is sullied further. Dump the shopping in the kitchen. And forget the cleaning. I'll do that tomorrow, instead of painting, about which I've had a change of heart. I'll try to sell it as it is, but at a lower price. After all, the first thing anyone does on moving into a new house is redecorate anyway. As long as it's clean, it will do.

Sit on the carpet in this bare living room and attack the pizza before it goes cold. Then, I think, it's time to show my face again at the pub which used to be our local.

Through the open double doors of this pub officially called the Anchor, but known locally by its rhyming nickname. Turn left through the half-glazed door into the smoke-filled tap room, which should have been heaving with bodies at this time of the evening. But is now strangely quiet. A strange face behind the bar. A short plump middle-aged woman in a black leather mini skirt. Painted, bitten fingernails. Huge earrings dangling from beneath frizzy-permed hair. Tight lime green top overflowing with cleavage. A face as severe as the north one of the Eiger. The personality of a crash-test dummy. And a smile which says I'm game if you fancy. I return a look which says not on your life, and order a pint which pours flat and warm, and possesses a sour taste.

"Excuse me, love."

"Yes, dear?"

"I'm sorry, but I think this beer may be ever so slightly off."

"Why? What's wrong with it?"

"It's warm. And just the slightest bit sour."

"It's probably something you've eaten, dear. Pickled onions, or something. Nobody else has complained."

"I'd like you to change it, please."

"Very well. But I can assure you there's nothing wrong with it. My Stan knows his business in the cellar. Won an award, he did."

"What for? Discovering a new strain of botulism?"

"Cellarman of the year. At our last pub. In Ripon."

"You mean this is now your pub?"

"Yes, dear. Didn't you read the name over the door? And see the sign 'Under new management'?"

"No. I didn't. I expected Terry, or May, to be behind the bar as usual."

"They went a month ago, dear. Left the place in a mess, too. Cellar was filthy. But my Stan soon sorted it out."

"And did all the customers leave with them?"

"Some did. And some we barred. We want to attract a better class of customer from the riff-raff who used to come in here. Businessman. People like yourself."

"I'm not a businessman. I'm unemployed."

"Oh. Well, I'm sure it won't be for long. A smart, good-looking gentleman like you. A cut above some of the scum who used to drink in here. It's all changed now, dear. For the better. We have happy hour every night from seven till eight. A disco on Saturday night, and Karaoke on Sundays."

"Disco? What time does it start?"

"In about an hour, dear. You've come just at the right time. Chance to get a seat at the bar before the place is packed out. It's seventies night tonight. You'll enjoy it."

"I won't be staying, thank you. Keep your pint! Let the Cellarman of the Year drink it. He deserves it. Good night."

"Good night to you, too. And piss off, and don't come back. You're barred, Tosser!"

What has happened to the world? When the havens of rest from stormy waters are taken over by harridans such as the one I've just encountered. Is all hope gone? All I ask is a good pint, a friendly atmosphere, and a crack with the staff and customers. I remember when every pub in the town was full to overflowing on Saturday nights, without the need for gimmicks such as discos, and karaoke and the like. And now they use these attractions to divert attention from the fact that they haven't the personality to pull in customers, nor the skills in the art of innkeeping to maintain a loyal trade. Cellarman of the Year, my arse! I wouldn't trust the unseen, but much-heralded, Stan to look after a salt cellar!

Walk a half mile up the road to the next hostelry. The Swan. A place we never liked and rarely frequented. But it has to be a vast improvement on the dump from which I've just been barred. Hear the noise as I approach the doors. Jukebox music, the buzz of conversation, and laughter. Welcome signs of life on this lonely planet.

Inside a few people I know by sight. Nod hello and settle in a corner to enjoy a drink. Or two. But mindful of the fact that tomorrow I must give the house a good clean before my worldly goods are delivered on Monday so a raging hangover is to be avoided. Unless, of course, I decide to clean some other time. In which case I might just persuade myself to get cabbaged tonight.

CHAPTER 20

Up early on this Monday morning. A crispness about the air. Winter definitely about to set in. Shower and eat a hearty, greasy breakfast. Watching impatiently through the window for the removal van. Which arrives on time, manned by two pot-bellied giants in grubby overalls. Seemingly in a hurry. Stand back and direct traffic. Settee and easy chairs in here, please. Dining suite in there. All packed boxes into their designated rooms, for unpacking later. Each box thoughtfully labelled by Julie, their contents and destination written on each one in bold black felt-tip. Along with instructions such as 'This way up' and 'Fragile'. Which notes of caution seem lost on the removal men, who treat every box as if it were indestructible. And within less than an hour, they are finished, and present the bill, which I pay without complaint simply for the pleasure of ridding the house of their sweating, heaving bodies and stale-beer breath. And as I unpack the boxes, I'm surprised to find everything intact, which is more a testament to Julie's careful packing than the attention of the removal men.

Everything in its place now. Fridge cooling down nicely. Go on a spending spree tomorrow and fill it up. So I'm not tempted to eat, and drink, out every night. Must get a grip on the excessive expenditure, before the bank manager writes again. Empty out the black bag containing the dirty laundry, and pile it into the washing machine. Add the powder and conditioner and select the program. And press the switch. Upon which, nothing happens. Oh, well. A minor setback. No need to get annoyed. Get someone to come and fix it. And in the meantime, unload the machine and pile everything back into the black bag and pop down to the laundrette.

No-one on duty at the empty laundrette, so read carefully the instructions on the machine. How much is a ten-pound load? A bagful? Never mind. Shove the lot in. Fill this compartment with the powder from the machine. Which will be cheap stuff, so put plenty in. Insert the required coins and hear the comforting whirr of the motor and slosh-slosh of water. Sit on the bench opposite and watch the clothes tumble. Something slightly amiss here. A tide of soapy water escaping from the bottom of the machine and lapping gently towards me. And as the washer speeds up, foam seeps out of the back. Fight my way towards the machine which is by now hardly visible, jets of foam shooting into the air and a sea of bubbles spreading the length of the room. Press the buttons. Pull frantically on the door handle. But can't find any way to stop the monster. Which begins to spin. Gyrating wildly and colliding with its neighbours. Groaning, banging, and issuing more torrents of foamy water. Nothing else for it. Urgent action required before I drown beneath a sea of suds. Grab the fire extinguisher and take careful aim. Slam it hard against the door handle. Which snaps off with a sharp crack. The door swings open under the pressure, and spews out soapy water and articles of clothing. Which I retrieve and throw into the bag. Until I'm happy I've got most of it. Abandon ship. Leave the rest to its watery fate. And paddle out of here. With a black bag over my shoulder, which weighs a ton. And leaves a trail of dripping water all the way back to the house.

Fill the bath with clean water and dump the contents of the bag. Rinse out as much as possible. Wring out each item, and arrange haphazardly over the clothes horse to dry. And note for future reference that laundrettes are out of bounds.

CHAPTER 21

And my first Christmas alone. Up early this morning. To open the present I bought myself yesterday. No surprise, a bottle of Malt. Pour a wee dram, and wish myself a Merry Christmas.

I've made some concessions to the spirit of Christmas by draping a length of red and gold tinsel round the antique pine mirror which hangs over the fireplace. And below it, the two cards I received. Arranged as ornamentally as it's possible to arrange a mere two cards. One at each end of the mantelpiece. A card from the E's and Plopper. A nice Victorian Christmas scene of choirboys singing in a snow-covered landscape. A vendor of hot chestnuts in the background adding a nice touch to the atmosphere. Written inside, in Mr E's spiky handwriting, 'Best wishes from both of us, and a big sloppy kiss from Plopper, who's settled down nicely'. And this other card from Julie. A rude one. Which some would find offensive, but which made me laugh when I opened it. Bearing the brief message 'Thinking of you. Love, Julie.'

Only two cards. When we always used to get scores. Nothing this year from Mr and Mrs Summer. Haven't heard a word from them since I received a polite note informing me the items of Lucy's jewellery I sent had arrived safely. Perhaps now Lucy's gone, they're showing what they felt about me all along. Not good enough for their daughter. Cast out from the bosom of their middle-class family. Probably cut my likeness from all the photos so Lucy's smiling image alone appears, untainted by my leering visage alongside. Well, stuff 'em! Snobbish, smug, pretentious prats. Though I do feel a little guilty about not sending any cards myself. I shall write to Julie, and to the E's after Christmas. Blame the postal service for the non-delivery of the seasonal greetings I neglected to issue.

Get cracking! Peel the spuds and put them in a pan of water. Prepare the carrots and sprouts. Thick slices of turkey breast bought from the local butcher. Ready to serve. Just take out of the fridge and slap them on the plate along with a little stuffing. A nice piece of Stilton and crackers to follow the shop-bought trifle. And a bottle of port, and one of brandy to finish off. But first a hearty breakfast, and tidy up the house a little to pass the time until noon. Then down to the pub for the odd pint of Christmas cheer. This will be the first time in many, many years that I've been out for a pint on Christmas Day. Our ritual was always the same. We always spent the day together at home, without visitors. That was how we liked it. But now, I need to get out. Be in company on this day of all days.

Walking down the road as the town hall clock chimes twelve. A light flurry of snow falling from the lead-grey sky. The first time in several years that flakes of snow have fallen on this day in this town. Adds to the seasonal atmosphere. Everybody hates rain, but loves to see the snow settle. Then everyone curses when it lingers, melting and freezing, causing chaos on pavements and roads.

Past the town hall with its huge light-bedecked tree, a gift from its twin town somewhere unpronounceable in Norway. Some of the bulbs already broken by vandals, and others, within reach, unscrewed and stolen. And here a hastily boarded-up shop window, an early victim of Christmas revelry. And an 'out of service' notice on this post box the contents of which some jolly prankster has set alight. The glorious crowning achievement of some sad life. A story to tell his grandchildren with pride.

And into the pub, already full of faces I recognise. A genial atmosphere. All friends, being merry together, while their wives stay at home and prepare the dinner. Or perhaps conduct their extra-marital affairs, safe in the knowledge that their coitus will remain uninterrupted while the pubs are open.

And by three-thirty, I've had enough, perhaps more than enough. Time to leave. Give the publican some peace.

Time to relax with his family for the rest of the day. The pub closed tonight, as are most in this town these days. Out onto the pavement. Snow falling steadily. Two or three inches now. More where the wind has blown it into rippled drifts against walls. And instead of turning for home, walk in the opposite direction, towards the harbour. The town quiet, save for the odd group of revellers staggering home for dinner.

Lean on the harbour wall for a few minutes. The wind blowing in from the sea. Snowflakes landing on my face, collecting on my hair and eyebrows. Glistening and melting. Light up a cigarette and stroll north along the deserted promenade, treading the virgin snow. Past the rows of shops and kiosks selling novelties, gifts and fast food, all shuttered up for the winter. Desolation Row-on-Sea. Finally turn left along this street of hotels and guest houses, many still displaying vacancies. Take a right down this narrow side street which leads to the park, at the other end of which I live. Dark now, and away from the street lamps, and it's an overcoat colder than it was an hour ago when I left the pub. Glad I left the central heating on for a cosy welcome. Think I'll have a shower to warm up when I get in. Or perhaps a brandy will do the trick. Noises in the dark distance. Shouting, singing and obscenities. Seem to be coming in my direction. And yes, here they come, emerging from the darkness, towards me. Three teenagers, the worse for drink, but persevering. Each swigging from a can. Keep my head down, and avoid eye contact. Move off the path and give them a wide berth. I sense trouble, as they change direction and set on a collision course to intercept me. Stay calm, Ray.

"'Scuse me, mate. You got a fag?"

"Sorry. I don't smoke."

Stupid answer, Ray. Since I just happen to have a lighted cigarette clearly visible in my hand.

"Really. Just keeping that for a mate, are you?"

"It's my last one. I'm giving up."

"Oh, well. With the money you're going to save, maybe you could give us a fiver to get some cigs, then."

"I have no money. I spent it all at the pub."

The three of them close up. Menacing. The ringleader who's doing the talking is directly in front, his cohorts to my left and right, mocking, jeering. Wonder if I can make a run for it. Are they armed, and dangerous? Or is it all a bit of bravado? Let's find out.

"You picked the wrong man, lads."

"Yeah? I don't think so, do you? I mean, right, there's three of us. And one of you. So, that tells me you're outnumbered, yeah? Right, dad? So, give us your money, OK?"

"I don't think so."

"You don't think so? Well. Tell you what. Either you give us your money. Or we kick the fuck out of you and take it anyway. Your choice, dad."

"Be warned. I have a black belt in the marital arts."

"Get this! Marital arts! Martial, you mean. Martial arts."

"I know what I mean. And I mean I can fuck you lot without pausing for breath."

Use the element of surprise. Launch a swinging right hook into the face of the youth on my left, knocking him onto his back in the snow, his baseball cap landing some distance away. Dark spots of blood forming an arc on the white ground. But the force of the blow pulls me off balance and before I can recover, a boot hits me in the stomach, expelling the air from my body. Gasping and winded. Sinking to my knees in the snow. Look up just in time to see a second kick coming straight for my face. Manage to duck a little. But take a stinging blow to the cheek. And another to the ribs. Struggling to my feet as I absorb another kick to the side of the head. And one full in the face. And now I'm back on the ground. Boots raining in from all directions. Curl up into the foetal position. Try to protect the vital organs. And pray. Raised voices in the distance. The cavalry.

Shouts of 'bastards' as the youths run off. Raise my head to see my saviours, a man and woman out for a walk with the dog. Both bending down to take a close look at me. I can't focus. My face a mask of blood and snot. Pain coming in waves. Allow my head to fall back into the cold snow. Numb the pain. And through one open eye, watch as the drops of blood form dark pools in the whiteness. Relax the body. Try to breathe through the pain. Conscious of the soothing voice telling me the ambulance is on its way. Fumble in the pocket for the pack of cigarettes. Remove one and put it to my lips. But there's no feeling there and it falls into the snow. And the last thing I remember is, I wet my pants.

CHAPTER 22

Waking next morning in the hospital bed. Able to open one eye and squint at the nurse studying my chart.

"Good morning. Mr Light, is it?"

"Yes."

"Thought it might be. That was the name we found on an envelope in your pocket. The police went around to your house, but couldn't get an answer."

"No. I live alone."

"Well, Mr Light. Do you remember what happened?"

"Vaguely. Set upon by some youths. I guess I lost."

"You did. But you were lucky. It seems someone came along and frightened them off. It could have been a lot worse. As far as we can tell, you've no fractures. Thank God for modern fashion."

"I don't follow."

"Trainers, Mr Light. You took quite a kicking. But trainers don't do as much damage as bovver boots, or winkle-pickers, for instance. What are you laughing at?"

"I haven't been kicked by anyone wearing winkle-pickers for about thirty years."

"Well, I've been a nurse that long. And I remember what damage they can do. I've seen somebody's eyeball crushed without the socket being damaged..."

"Are my eyes OK? Only I can't open my left one."

"It should be fine. Once the swelling goes down, and the stitches are removed."

"Stitches? God! How many? Where?"

"Five above your left eye. Three in your lip. Three inside your cheek. Like I say, you've been lucky. Comparatively speaking, of course. I mean you were unlucky to have been attacked in the first place. Now try to rest. And lie still. You're on a drip. In your arm. So, don't disturb it. Doctor McAllister will be round to see you shortly. Oh, and the police will be coming back to talk to you this afternoon."

"Nurse. How do I look?"

"Like a man who's been beaten up. Bruised and battered."

"Any permanent damage? Visible scars?"

"You'll have a scar over your eye which will fade in time till it's hardly noticeable. And your lower lip will be fuller than it used to be. But don't worry. You're still an attractive man. And your lips will still be kissable."

"Do I take that as a proposition?"

"Ha, ha. No, Mr Light. I'm only interested in your health. Sorry to disappoint you."

Lean back on these pillows and look around at my fellow patients in this Unit of Intensive Neglect. The bandages and plaster casts. Victims of accidents and festive excess. I feel no pain, only a general numbness and aching in the limbs. Run my tongue round the inside of my mouth and over my lips. Feel the roughness of stitches, but nothing more. Like after a visit to the dentist. You can bite your lip and only have the vaguest sensation that your teeth are gripping something. Then you try to drink something. And it dribbles down the side of your mouth and down your chin. A drooling idiot, with a permanent piano string of spit dangling from your mouth.

Try to make sense of what's happened. When I was the same age as those lads, I would never have dreamed of picking on an innocent, outnumbered victim. For vicarious gratification. When I was young, fights were the result of provocation by rival groups. And had some sort of, well, justification, I suppose. If someone gave you a slap, it was normally because you'd done, or said, something to deserve it. But it's all changed now. You hear of pensioners being beaten up and robbed of small change. It's become tribal. Kick a grandad, and increase your social status within your peer group. But never have the bottle to do it on your own. Make sure you've got mates with you to ensure you've got numerical superiority. I hope you young bastards feel good about it. How you kicked a middle-aged drunk. I hope you can boast about it to your friends. Without having to tell them how you ran away when two other people arrived on the scene. And the lad I hit. I wonder if I managed to break his nose. And if I did, will he boast that it happened in the heat of battle? And wear it flattened in the middle of his face like a badge of courage? Close my one seeing eye and try to sleep.

Waking some time later feeling pain throbbing through my body. Aching ribs. The clock on the opposite wall shows 3.15. Though what day, I'm not too sure. But Christmas is over anyhow for me at least. Turn the head slowly to look around. Visitors at every bed bar mine. Bedside lockers piled high with fruit, flowers and cards, while mine is bare except for a jug of water and a cardboard bedpan.

"Mr Light?"

A young policewoman at the bedside.

"Yes."

"Do you feel well enough to answer a few questions?"

"As long as they're not too difficult."

"I'd like you to tell me everything you can remember about what happened to you yesterday."

"Yesterday?"

"When you were attacked."

"Yes, sorry. Was it only yesterday?

"Yes. Christmas day."

"Yes. Well, I'd been to the pub for a couple of drinks. Lunchtime. The Swan..."

"What time did you leave?"

"About three-thirty. Then I went for a walk. Down to the harbour and along the promenade. Then down Wentworth Street and through the park. That's where three young lads decided to have some football practice with my head."

"Three youths. Can you describe them?"

"Sixteen. Maybe seventeen. Baseball caps. Dark jackets. Jeans. Trainers. Shirts hanging out."

"That doesn't exactly narrow it down. Would you recognise them if you saw them again?"

"I don't know. I'm not sure. Perhaps."

"Why did they attack you?"

"One of them asked me for a cigarette. I refused. He then demanded money. Then they set on me. Then someone - a man and a woman - came along and they ran off. Then I woke up in here."

"Did you hit any of them?"

"I managed to throw one punch. Which connected."

"In self-defence?"

"Yes."

"Are you sure you didn't start the fight by punching one of the lads?"

"Of course not. I feared for my life."

"Well, sir. I ought to tell you that we picked up three youths yesterday. They roughly fitted the descriptions given by the couple who came to your aid. One of them had blood on his shirt and a broken nose. According to him and his mates, they were walking through the park when they were attacked without provocation by a madman, and were merely defending themselves when the couple arrived on the scene."

"That's absurd."

"The trouble is proving it. It's their word against yours. We have witnesses who saw them kicking you, but they're claiming self-defence. And the one you hit could possibly prosecute you for attacking him and breaking his nose."

"I wish I'd broken his neck."

"OK, sir. When you get out of hospital, I'd like you to come down to the station to make a statement. And you should perhaps discuss with your solicitor whether you wish to proceed with a prosecution."

"Forget it."

"Tell me. Wouldn't it have been easier just to have given them a few cigarettes?"

"I don't give in to urban terrorism."

"You've paid rather a heavy price for your principles."

"Without my principles, I wouldn't have much left. Some things are worth fighting for. Like law and order."

"Then it seems like we're both fighting a losing battle."

"Perhaps. But I shall continue. Will you?"

"To be honest, and please don't tell anyone this, sometimes I don't know. Sometimes I think it's all a waste of time. Even when we're lucky enough to catch criminals, it's very rare they get the sentence they deserve. They can be back on the streets the next day, taunting us. Between you and me, even if you successfully prosecuted the lads who attacked you, it wouldn't do much good. They'd probably get community service. And they'd get even with you eventually. So, in my opinion you did the right thing by punching one of them. And if you don't press charges, they'll probably leave you alone. And the one with the broken nose will certainly rue the day he crossed your path. But then again, who knows?"

"You mean he may be a trainee psychopath. And seek revenge."

"It's possible. All I'm saying is, if you're out alone at night, keep to well-lit areas. Cross the road if you feel threatened by anyone approaching you. And be prepared to run away. And this is all off the record."

"Of course."

"I see so many victims of unprovoked attacks. Pensioners. Children. The disabled. And drunks. Always those who are vulnerable. And when, occasionally, I hear of some thug dying of a drug overdose, or some kids dying after crashing a stolen car, then I feel that perhaps there is some justice in this world. I'm sorry. I shouldn't be talking like this to you. Please don't repeat what I've said to anybody. If it got back to the station I'd be in serious trouble."

"I promise I won't say a word. As long as you promise not to report me for deliberately breaking that kid's nose for having the audacity to demand I give him a fag."

"It's a deal."

"Thank you, constable. I'm sorry, I didn't catch your name."

"Williams. Sarah."

"Well, thank you again, Sarah Williams. And I would love to thank you again by buying you a drink when I'm discharged and you are off duty."

"Well that's nice of you. But my husband wouldn't approve. Still, I'm glad you're obviously feeling better. So. it seems none of the kicks landed in the vital area."

"Happily, no. I even managed an erection when the nurse brought me a bedpan. So, I do believe the todger is, thankfully, undamaged."

"I'm glad."

"Why are you glad, Sarah? You're married. So, the state of my todger is, to you, immaterial."

"Yes, that's true. But who knows what the future holds. I may get divorced, and since I have your name and address on file, I might just look you up to make discreet enquiries about the condition of your todger."

"I'm always available to help the police with their enquiries."

"Thank you, Mr Light. Take care."

"Ray."

"Take care, Ray."

"Thank you, WPC Sarah. 'Bye."

"'Bye."

And the doctor calls to see me later in the day. Pleased with my progress and says I may go home the next day. Nurses bringing my tablets and helping me slurp my soup and mop the dribble from my chin. And in the evening a young Chinese trainee nurse comes and pulls the curtains round the bed. Pulls down the sheets, removes my hospital-issue pyjamas, and gives me a bed-bath. Signs of life down there. All is well. Perhaps when the scars heal they will add character to my face. Make me look rugged rather than disfigured.

And allowed to go home after breakfast. Dressing slowly and painfully. My trousers, overcoat and shoes caked with dried mud. Bloodstained shirt. Check the pockets. Not enough for a taxi. Stop at the nurses' station on the way out to thank them, collect my prescription for painkillers and enquire about buses. And a kind nurse going off duty offers me a lift home.

Squeeze slowly and painfully into the passenger seat of this tiny old hatchback. Signs of rust and neglect, but, she said, reliable. Negotiating the morning traffic, driving carefully and smoothly so as not to cause further pain to my bruised and aching body. Light fall of swirling snowflakes kissing the windscreen, melting, tracing thin rivulets down the glass. And being brushed aside by the intermittent swipe of the rubber wipers. The nurse puffing away at a fag as an icy wind whistles through the open window. 'Roll down the windows and let the wind blow back your hair'. Well, this isn't exactly Thunder Road, and driving through Scarsby in the depths of winter probably never crossed Springsteen's mind when he wrote it. But a town full of losers this certainly is.

Refusing the kind offer of further assistance into the house and giving assurances I'm fine, I can look after myself, thank you. Lean against the door and wave as she drives away, then hobble into this cold house. Turn up the dial on the thermostat and hear the reassuring roar of the boiler as the heating clicks on. Find a clean glass and open the bottle. Pour a small measure of the water of life. Swill it round the mouth and feel the pain from the stitched wounds. And carefully and agonisingly ascend the stairs to undress and climb gingerly into the unmade bed.

A full twenty-four hours before I stir, awoken by the pounding of rain against the grimy panes. No remaining trace of seasonal snow. Only the incessant drumming of this downpour. Great black anvil clouds scudding their way across the afternoon sky, propelled by a stiff north-easterly. Passing cars raising spray as the rain smacks the streets and races away along the gutter and down the unblocked drains to replenish the sea.

Lurch into the bathroom on unsteady legs. Inspect the face and body. Purplish-black bruises turning various shades of yellow. Swelling of the face beginning to subside but tender and painful to the touch. Swallow two of these painkillers. Wash and dress in clean clothes. Leave the muddy things where they lie abandoned on the bedroom carpet for now. Slowly down the stairs and into the kitchen. Inspect the contents of the fridge. The turkey slices still on their plate smell rank. Likewise, the milk. The pans of vegetables standing ready on the cooker. Empty the water down the sink and throw the spoiled Christmas feast into the bin. Cut off a wedge of ripe Stilton and allow it to melt in the mouth. Pull the cork from the bottle of port and pour a glass. And light, with difficulty, a cigarette which hangs limply between my swollen lips. Suck air noisily through the corner of my distorted mouth and inhale a little of the smoke. Wish myself a belated Merry Christmas. Peace and goodwill to most men. Piece of good willy to all deserving women.

And as the late afternoon skies turn dark, the rain stops and the strong wind blows away the clouds to reveal a full bright moon rising out of the sea. The wind lulling now to a slight breeze. The temperature dropping rapidly. Black ice forming on the roads and pavements causing scores of minor accidents. A busy night ahead for the emergency services. But I shall play no part in it. The state of the pavements forces me to remain housebound at this most joyous time of year.

The next morning dawning cold and clear. White frost on those roofs upon which the sun has yet to shine. Pavements still treacherous, but negotiable with care as I shuffle along to the corner shop for provisions. A loaf, dozen eggs, two litres of milk, assorted packets of soup and yoghurts. Things which don't require chewing. And next door, the off-licence, for a bottle of malt. All I can carry in one trip, but sufficient sustenance for a few days.

Lunch of scrambled eggs with buttered bread from which I've removed the crust. Yoghurt to follow. In the evening I shall have soup into which I can dunk pieces of bread. And tomorrow, by way of variety, I shall have soup for lunch, and scrambled eggs in the evening.

CHAPTER 23

The final day of this eventful year breaking cold and frosty. A smattering of overnight snow has settled and frozen hard on the untreated pavements. Watch the reflection on the bedroom wall of the rotating amber light on the council gritting wagon. Swing my legs out of bed and slowly shift my full weight on to my feet to test their reaction. The pain is tolerable now. More a constant ache, and the stiffness in my limbs is easing somewhat. The end of the road to recovery not too far away now, and I think today I will test my strength by walking down to the nearest pub. Should really have had the phone reconnected. Could have rung for a taxi. But no matter. If I can make it the half-mile, I can gather sufficient strength to make it home again. Providing of course I don't encounter any young louts.

The walk was worth it. Sympathy from staff and customers. Told to sit down and get comfortable. Just shout when I want anything. Drinks brought to my table by the solicitous barmaid. When my face eventually becomes free of stitches and bruising, I shall return and thank her, buy her a drink. Find out how the land lies. And whether she'll allow me to thank her in the way I have in mind once the swollen testicles have returned to their normal size.

Back home well refreshed before dark. Kept to the main road. No short cuts where danger may lurk. Another plate of scrambled eggs. Pile the plate, pan, and knife and fork in the sink on top of the rest. My New Year's resolution will be to do the washing-up. Grab the bottle and a glass and retire to the lounge. Settle in the comfy armchair, the one by which Plopper used to lie all curled up, his nose up his backside. I wonder if he misses me like I miss him. I doubt it. He'll be spoiled to death by the E's. Probably forgotten all about me by now. I hope so, really. I wouldn't want him to pine for his missing master. No, he'll be happy enough all right. Perhaps now and again when he's walking past the house which used to be his home, he'll stop for a second and remember. Then he'll cock his leg and pee on

Boot's gatepost, and walk on, tail wagging, Mr E struggling to keep pace with him.

Switch on the HiFi, tune to CD and load the cartridge. Take the remote back to the chair and press play. Ah, Springsteen! Atlantic City. Memories of Leeds in 1985 when Lucy and I joined tens of thousands of others in Roundhay Park on a hot July Sunday afternoon. Stewards at the gates stopping people taking in cans or bottles of alcohol. We were prepared. Lucy carried a two-litre plastic bottle of coke and smiled as they allowed her to take it through. They were unaware that the contents were fifty per cent coke, fifty per cent vodka. So, we sat on the hill and enjoyed the event, taking in the emotion and energy of the performance and the adulation of the worshipping fans, occasionally sharing our drink with others in exchange for the odd joint. And each track that plays brings back a particular memory of a certain place, a certain time. When early in our marriage we would open a bottle of wine, put some music on and make love on the lounge carpet. Or when out driving together with the radio on or a cassette playing, suddenly feeling the mutual urge to pull off the road for impromptu intercourse. And the tunes which were playing at those times remain indelibly imprinted on my mind. And every time I hear any of them, the memories come flooding back.

And as the seconds and minutes and hours tick by, my thoughts return to the events of this unhappy year. Our move to a new life down south courtesy of Barker's job offer. Lucy's enthusiasm in transforming the dowdy nineteen-thirties house into a comfortable welcoming home. The day she came home early from work feeling ill. The tests. The treatment. And the inevitable conclusion. This is the first New Year's Eve I've ever spent alone. Desperate for a knock on the door. WPC Sarah making further enquiries. A worried nurse to check on my progress. Anybody is welcome tonight. Even thugs, come to ransack the house. As long as they keep me company for a short while. Raucous noises outside from passing revellers. The whole world going somewhere. To pubs or parties. To church even. Too slippery outside for me to attempt to get to the phone box. Besides, I've drunk so much I doubt I can stand. And who would I call? Julie? But I would expect her to be out partying. And if she was at home alone, would a call from me cheer her up or depress her further? And as the town hall clock chimes twelve, the empty glass slips from my hand and bounces on the carpet. My eyelids close, and sleep comes quickly and mercifully.

And on the second day of this new year venturing out for a little shopping. Feeling much stronger now and steadier on my feet. No longer taking the painkillers as they interfere too much with my drinking habits. And the pain is now merely a dull ache, and the stiffness in my limbs wears off after a little exercise. And hop on the bus to the hospital for the removal of these stitches which are becoming itchy and uncomfortable.

Given a clean bill of health, so it's down to the pub to celebrate. Call in to see Billy, only to be informed he's left. So along to the King's where I'm immediately recognised as the man with the huge appetite. Only now it's not so huge on account of the damage to my mouth. So, I settle for a large bowl of homemade vegetable soup and a soft roll for dunking therein. Chat to the hospitable hosts and spend a most pleasant afternoon.

And on arriving home I write a long letter to the E's, telling them everything is fine and thanks for their card and I hope they received mine which I posted ages ago. Making no mention of my recent trouble. Remain positive and upbeat about the future. And I start to write to Julie. But don't know what to say. And in the end, I give up and tear up what I've written.

But I promise myself I'll make the effort and sit down and really think carefully about what I want to say. And write a carefully worded letter which will give her hope. But not too much. Platonic in tone, but erotic and lustful in essence.

And in the following days I make regular visits to the King's on the pretext of exercising my limbs, until my mouth feels sufficiently well to tackle a small fillet of steak. And it tastes so exquisite! Succulent. Tender. Juicy. Mouthwateringly so. And at this point, I know I am well and truly recovered from my ordeal and celebrate with several pints. However, I make sure I'm safely home behind my bolted door before it gets dark.

And in the evenings, I've taken to watching sport on TV again. Watch every game of football I can. Now I don't have to fight Lucy for the remote control, I'm at liberty to resurrect my passion for football. And I can safely say without fear of contradiction that in the last few weeks I've watched more football than in the past fifteen years. Lucy hated it so much that in the end I stopped even asking if she minded if I watched a game. And just gave it up. In a successful, happy marriage, sacrifices have to be made. But for the life of me, I can't remember Lucy making any. Perhaps her sacrifice was in marrying me. She tamed me. Made me respectable. With a decent career. And a nice comfortable home. Cut down my drinking. Reformed my sloppy habits. And now I'm reverting to the man I used to be. And letting her down. She would be alarmed at the amount of alcohol I consume. But if she were here, I wouldn't drink so much anyway. Because when I'd had a few drinks she refused to make love to me. Made me wait until I was panting with desire. Prepared to give up anything. Then she'd relent and we'd make wonderful passionate love. Was it worth it?

CHAPTER 24

Seated in the King's one late January afternoon. Enjoying a pint after lunch of home-made steak pie chips and peas. Reading the newly published local weekly newspaper. And on the front page a large picture of a pensioner who had been mugged a couple of days earlier. His tired and worn face battered and bruised. Punched and kicked. By three youths. Who demanded cigarettes and then money. And when he refused, they beat him up and stole his wallet. Unable to give a detailed description of his attackers as his eyesight is poor. But one of them had a broken nose. He remembered that. If he'd been forty years younger, he'd have given him a black eye and a sound beating. Served in North Africa in the war. Mentioned in despatches. And now living on his pension, which he'd just drawn from the post office, and which they'd stolen.

Finish my pint and walk down to the offices where the newspaper is edited. Through the door to the reception desk. Ask to see the editor. Who is presently in a meeting. Ask the girl if she will kindly pass these fifty pounds to the editor to forward to the victim, to help make up for his financial loss. Asked to wait a moment while she contacts the sub-editor. A large jolly woman who comes through immediately to shake my hand and beckon me into her office.

"I believe you'd like to make a donation to the pensioner who was mugged."

"Yes. I'd like to send him fifty pounds. Could you arrange that, please?"

"Certainly. Could I have your name, sir?"

"I wish to remain anonymous."

"Fine. But I can't help noticing that you appear to have suffered some recent facial injuries. Is there any possible connection here? Sympathy, perhaps? Have you been a victim of a similar attack?"

"Please don't look for a story here. Yes. I was attacked. At Christmas. And I believe by the same youths. But I didn't suffer any financial loss. And I'd like to make a token contribution to help this poor old sod. That's all there is to it."

"Would you mind if we took your photograph?"

"I certainly would. I don't relish the prospect of a repeat attack."

"Would you mind if we ran a story without giving your name?"

"If you wish."

"So, tell me what happened."

And after I leave, I call at the police station and ask to speak to WPC Williams. Who is off duty. But a note is left for her to call on me regarding the attack on my person, and this latest development.

Sarah comes around early in the evening and I make her a cup of tea before coming to the point.

"I'd like to bring charges against the lads who beat me up."

"Has this change of mind anything to do with the story in the paper?"

"The old man. Yes."

"Well, to put you in the picture. We've already picked the lads up. They're in custody at the moment. And we've got a confession from the youngest, which implicates the other two. We intend to charge them on one count of robbery with violence with regard to the attack on the pensioner. In return for not pressing charges on a number of other related incidents. We're hoping their solicitor will accept this. Save a lot of time, trouble and money."

"And if they accept?"

"Like I say. We won't pursue the other cases. Such as yours, where they claim self-defence. Makes things complicated. But if we get one charge to stick, we'll settle for that. Give them a taste of life on remand. Before they get bailed. And eventually community service."

"Sounds like they get the better of the deal."

"The way it works, Ray. Besides, you look none the worse for your ordeal. Best let it drop."

"I will. On condition that you allow me to take you out for a drink."

"Sorry. I don't make deals."

"You intend to make a deal with violent young louts."

"That's not down to me personally. The decision of a higher authority."

"Then ask your higher authority if I may take you for a drink."

"My husband wouldn't approve."

"Don't tell him."

"Some other time, Ray. Maybe."

"Is that a definite maybe? Or a perhaps maybe?"

"I'll think about it. Thanks for the tea. I'll have to go. Take care of yourself."

"I will. And I'll wait patiently for your knock on my door in the early hours."

"The only time I knock on someone's door in the early hours is to convey bad news. Or make an arrest."

"In that case, I shan't wait patiently. I shall wait impatiently."

"Bye, Ray."

"Bye, WPC Sarah."

As I drink my first coffee of the day and savour my first fag, I like to watch the groups of kids passing the house on their meandering route to school. Most of them eating their breakfast of crisps and sweets on the way and dropping the wrappers casually in the street. Hardly a uniform between them. A scruffy lot, shirts out, tieless, scuffed shoes or trainers. And I remember my first day at the big school, when I turned up with my highly-polished shoes and brand-new blazer from which mum had picked every speck of fluff. And at break-time a group of older boys had grabbed my cap and were tossing it between them while I tried in vain to retrieve it. Until a tall fair-haired boy stepped forward and told them to stop and give my cap back. Whereupon, one of them flung it up on the roof of the bike shed and received a bloody nose from the fair-haired boy. In the tussle that ensued, I was knocked to the ground, while the fair-haired boy set about my four tormentors, until a teacher arrived and escorted us all to the headmaster's office. He refused to listen to any explanations or excuses, and put all six of us on detention. The others were made to write out five hundred times "If I have the desire to fight, then I must sign up to fight for my country." Whereas I was given the task of transcribing the results from the school sports days of the last ten years into a large ledger. And I noticed that every year Victor Ludorum was mentioned. And I thought what a great athlete he must have been, and pictured him as a tall, handsome sixth-former with a retinue of admirers, and bet that no-one had ever dared pinch his cap. And the fair-haired boy came over to me and said his name was Duncan and gave me his school cap which he said he never wore and if he told his parents he'd lost it they wouldn't say anything. I told him my name was Raymond Light and thanked him. And he said, ever so nonchalantly,

"No problem, Flash. Nobody at this school will bother you again. If anybody picks on you, just tell them you're Duncan's friend and they'll leave you alone. I'm the cock of this school."

And it wasn't until years later that he told me the full story. On his own very first day at the school, three older boys had picked on him and roughed him up, stealing his dinner money. Instead of reporting the incident, he waited after school and followed the trio until they split up. He then went after the smallest and gave him a black eye. The following day, he again suffered a beating from the three. And after school, exacted his revenge by following the second of the trio, hitting him repeatedly in the face until he cried. And on the third day after the trio had given him a good kicking behind the science block, he was so bruised and sore that he skipped classes for the afternoon, instead nursing his wounds in the toilets. Then he followed the ringleader, a stocky, cocky lad. Ducking up alleys, over fences and through gardens, he managed to get ahead of his adversary, and as he strolled, whistling, around a corner, Duncan smacked him full in the face with a heavy length of stout timber. His nose exploded and blood spread over his face. As the huge grin spread over Duncan's. And they never bothered him again, nor did anyone else as the word got around. That Duncan the Dastardly showed no fear. Nor any mercy. Except to the weak and oppressed.

CHAPTER 25

This house is beginning to get me down. No matter how high I turn up the heating, there's still a coldness about the place, as if Lucy's ghost has followed me back here. I still have her ashes and her memory to comfort me. But her physical warmth is missing, and her spiritual presence is sometimes chilling. This recent letter from the estate agent, however, is cheering. A potential buyer has expressed interest and wishes to make a derisory offer of forty thousand, which I am nevertheless inclined to accept. But this afternoon a young couple are coming to view, so it's out with the polish and duster. Vacuum the carpets and spray liberally the air-freshener to neutralise the stale smoke smell.

And on this Monday afternoon, at two o'clock, they arrive, look round and pronounce it ideal. And I make them a coffee and answer their questions. They are engaged and looking to buy their first home together. Full of excitement. Pleading with me not to accept any offers until they've been to the building society to discuss a mortgage, and I agree to give them until the weekend.

And a knock on the door on Wednesday evening. Which I open to find the young couple, previously so happy, but now looking distraught.

"Hello, Mr Light. We're sorry to disturb you. Can we come in to talk about the house?"

"Come in."

Show them into the living room with its feature fireplace and a host of original Victorian features carefully restored to their original glory. And allow them to sit on this lovingly neglected High Street store settee with its carefully broken spring and casually cigarette-burned upholstery. Make them coffee into two lovingly cracked and stained mugs. And listen to their proposal, tendered by a young, fresh-faced and somewhat nervous Gary.

"Mr Light, I'll come straight to the point..."

"Call me Ray."

"Ray. I'll come straight to the point..."

"Please do."

"I will. You see. The point is...well...the building society are prepared to lend us forty thousand. And... well..."

"Well?"

"Well. That's it, really. That's what we'd like to offer."

"I've already been offered forty. And turned it down."

"That's what we expected you to say. So..."

He turns to look at Ruth for confirmation. And she takes his hand and nods a yes.

"Well, we've got an extra two thousand saved up. We've saved it for our wedding and honeymoon. But, I guess, the house is more important. Particularly, with the baby coming along. So, we can offer forty-two. Is that enough?"

"You're pregnant?"

"Yes. Three months. And we really wanted to get married before she's born..."

"Before he's born!"

"OK, Gary. Before he's born. Gary desperately wants a boy. But, whatever. The child needs a home. And we're really keen on this one. Will you accept forty-two, Mr Light?"

"Under these circumstances, no. Most definitely not!"

"Oh well. I'm sorry we've wasted your time."

"Look at it this way. If I accepted your offer, you would have a house. And nothing more. No money in the bank. And soon another mouth to feed and only one wage coming in. And unable to afford your wedding. And what about furniture? Do you have any?"

"Some. But not much. We were hoping you might leave the curtains. We don't have any curtains. Just a bed, really. And mum's old cooker, and table and chairs."

"Well. There you are! What sort of start is that for your life together?"

"We'll manage."

"You mean, you'll struggle!"

"So, we'll struggle."

"And that's precisely why I won't take your forty-two thousand. But what I will do is accept your initial offer of forty grand, and as a wedding present, I'll leave you all the furniture. Cooker, washing machine, fridge, curtains. The lot. All in. No extra charge. Is it a deal?"

"It's a deal, Mr Light. Ray. Thank you. You are serious?"

"Certainly. You had better get things moving before I change my mind."

"We will! Thank you. The sooner we get this in writing the better."

"You have my word as a gentleman. But not a scholar."

"Goodbye, Mr Light. Ray. Thanks once again."

"My pleasure. Goodbye."

Feel relaxed and pleased with myself now I've done this good deed. Help tip the balance of my Karma in a more positive direction before I shuffle off. A small step towards my god, whoever he may be. Celebrate with a glass of malt which is allowed as I have not yet quite achieved sainthood, whatever this young couple may believe.

Tomorrow morning, I shall phone the solicitor, and instruct the estate agents accordingly. But first I shall allow myself the liberty of a small celebration, and I'm sure Lucy would have been proud of me. I remember when, not so long ago, I was one small half of a happy couple. And it was wonderful. Gary and Ruth will, I hope, share the same experience. And baby makes three.

A letter from Duncan this morning, which I read over my coffee and burnt toast.

"Dear Ray,

I have news of the utmost importance for you. Dramatic developments. Enormous events, following a calamitous coupling. I'm coming over to see you on Thursday. Meet me at the railway station, 2.15pm, platform four. I hope this reaches you. Otherwise, if you're not there, I'll be combing the bars until I find you.

You'll easily recognise me. I'll be wearing a great big smile.

See you,

Duncan, the Disburdened."

Waiting on the platform this chilly afternoon as the carriages pull to a halt. And off steps Duncan, beaming. Refusing to divulge details until his tongue is sufficiently lubricated. Through the car park, and into the Travellers', where we settle with pints of bitter.

"So, Duncan. What's the big story?"

"Unbelievable things have happened. Major upheavals on life's otherwise smooth path."

"Go on."

"What's happened to your face?"

"I was in a fight. And took the silver medal."

"You OK?"

"Yes. Fully healed. Now, come on. Let's hear the news."

"Elaine's left me. Well, thrown me out to be more accurate. Things came to a head when she found a pair of panties, slightly soiled, and not hers, in the glove compartment of the car. The result of a recent dalliance. Coming on top of the fact that she's developed an embarrassing little rash on her powdered fanny, for which she is blaming me, she's decided to dissolve our long partnership. Business as well as matrimonial. I would be ruined if it weren't for the most amazing stroke of fortune. A few weeks ago, I replied to an ad in the Sunday Times. An American woman, 50-ish, but surgically enhanced, wished to meet an Englishman of discerning taste and impeccable manners with a view to a long-term relationship and life on a ranch in Colorado. We met. I, of course, charmed and bedded her. And we fly to the USA on Monday. Imagine, Ray! The USA! Home of the brave. Land of the free. The New World! The Big Adventure. I've spent my life waiting for."

"What's the catch?"

"No catch, boy. No catch. OK, Sherry's already buried two husbands. Under a mountain of litigation. But they've both come out of it with pots of dosh."

"How long do you think it'll be before she finds out what you're really like?"

"Doesn't matter. As long as we tie the matrimonial knot first. Ray, she's absolutely enamoured with me. Best thing since peanut butter. And pecan pie. She's captivated by my breeding, my charm, my manners. And of course, my prize-winning dong."

"Duncan, you have no breeding. Nor manners. Charm, yes."

"A pretence I can keep up indefinitely. Just remember to be surreptitious when picking the bogeys, and not to wipe them where they can be found later and used as evidence against me."

"Well, I hope it works out for you."

"It will. So, what's happening with you?"

"I've had an offer on the flat. All being well, the sale should be completed in a couple of months."

"Where are you going?"

"Don't know."

"I need an address. So I can write to invite you over to be my estate manager."

"Write care of my solicitor. He'll be able to contact me."

"So be it. More drink is required, I believe. Toast the traveller. On his long journey to the promised land. Where men are men. And women are rich. And absolutely begging to tickle my tool. Seize the day! And fondle the silicon-enhanced."

"Good luck to you, Duncan. Looks like you've landed on your feet again."

"I hope I'll soon land on my back. With a rich and nubile on top. But what about you? Do you have a regular sheath for your meaty weapon?"

"Not at the moment. I'm halibut."

"You mean celibate."

"Quite! No fish in the sea for me. My wiggly worm bait isn't exactly dragging them in."

"Well, if ever you're in desperate need of an empty, I'm sure you'll find Elaine most accommodating."

"Come on, Duncan. You know I wouldn't dream of it."

"Don't worry about offending me. She's a free woman. Doesn't matter to me if the Pope podges her. Oh, I forgot to mention. I bumped into Predator One the other day. She asked me to send her best wishes."

"Really."

"Yes. She seemed genuine enough. She'd heard about Lucy. Probably from Elaine. They still keep in touch, every now and again."

"And how is she?"

"Seems well enough. Three kids now. But no man at the moment. A part time job, and a council flat. What more could she want?"

"After three marriages, she should have been able to put a little aside."

"Not her way. As you well know. Money is for spending. Particularly when it's someone else's. Which is one reason she's had three husbands."

"But not the main reason."

"Well, no."

"There is the small matter of her voracious sexual appetite and propensity for extra-marital relationships with all and sundry. Hence the appropriate nickname."

"Yes, there is that."

"And is she still at it?"

"I would imagine so. I try to keep my distance. And Elaine says it's none of my business."

"She's quite right. It's nobody's business but her own."

Predator One. The woman I'd met shortly after Duncan married Elaine. She'd worked with Elaine, and Duncan, in one of his moments of weakness, had poked her. To her credit, she never told Elaine, but Duncan would have nothing further to do with her. However, she'd then latched on to me. And fearing, I suppose, that my life would be lonely without Duncan's constant company, I started to see her regularly. The sex was great, and I was quite content just to go with the flow, or rather the whirlpool, into which she literally sucked me. Shortly after we married, rumours began to circulate. I took little notice until it became apparent there was more than a little truth to them. And when I confronted her about her numerous affairs, she admitted them all. But said she'd give them all up. It was me she loved. They were just sex. And sex with me was the best. Which was quite a compliment, considering she'd sampled half the population of Yorkshire. And of course, it didn't stop there. She was a serial adulterer. A female version of Duncan. Except without the charm. Just a great body and an all-consuming appetite for sex. For two years we stayed together. God knows why. Until one day I'd finally had enough and walked out, filing for a 'quickie' divorce. And since she was fond of quickies, it went through unopposed. But not until she'd taken half of everything I'd worked for. For a while afterwards I kept women at a safe distance. Emotionally, that is. I still dated, and slept with a number of women. But the moment any relationship showed the slightest sign of becoming serious, I finished it. Then one night, in a pub, I met Lucy. I was on a stag night, and she was with a few friends. We talked for a few minutes, and I asked her out. To my surprise she said yes. And the following evening, I turned up ten minutes early at our proposed rendezvous, more in hope than expectation, and there she was, already waiting. We hit it off immediately. She was so easy to talk to. And though I made it quite clear from the outset that I wasn't looking for a serious relationship, within a couple of months I proposed, and she accepted. And never once did

I regret it. I only wish we'd met ten years earlier. Or more. I wish we'd been together forever. And wish it could have remained so. Forever.

"Predator One, eh. Thank god you eventually got rid of her."

"Anybody can make a mistake, Duncan. Put it down to experience."

"Aye. What an experience."

"It wasn't all bad. The early days were fine."

"Well, she's available. Why don't you go see her?"

"Not bloody likely! Why don't you go see her?"

"It crossed my mind, Ray. But she's not my type. I like to do the chasing. It's the challenge. The thrill of the hunt. And I need the practice as I strive to achieve my black belt. In the marital arts. So, what's this town like for action?"

"Quiet, Duncan. Especially at this time of year."

"So, what's say we liven it up a little?"

"How long are you staying?"

"Overnight, if that's OK with you. I'll doss on your floor. Unless, of course, I meet someone who offers me alternative accommodation. We can have one last wild night before I go back to tie up a few loose ends. And then jet off into the great wide open."

"I'm not in the mood for a riot."

"Nor am I."

"Duncan. Every time we go out, there's a riot. And then you leave and I have to face the music."

"That's not fair, Ray. I just seem to attract trouble. Through no fault of my own. I promise tonight. Best behaviour. Scout's honour. OK?"

"You were never a scout!"

"No. But I once fondled an Akela behind the snooker club. And she granted me honorary membership. Said I was a fine upstanding member. Pity they don't do a badge for it."

"Let's get something to eat. It's going to be a long night."

And so it turns out. Duncan insists we eat at a licensed restaurant, where we dine on steaks, washed down by house red, with Drambuie to follow. And all through the meal he chatters excitedly about his new life in the States. How he intends to stay with Sherry long enough for her to set him up in business. Then commit some indiscretion which will lead to divorce and a generous financial settlement. And thereafter, from the contacts he's made, he'll find another eligible divorcee, woo her, bed her, wed her. And begin the cycle anew. And I can't help but be impressed by his eternal optimism. By the way he makes things happen. Rather than let them happen to him. And any setback is just treated as a spur to goad him on to something else. Maybe something totally different. But he never stays down for long. He is absolutely irrepressible. Yet I, who shared so many experiences with him over the years, am totally unable to get over the loss of Lucy. And find that life is just a path I follow. Not knowing, nor caring much, where it might lead. And when I come to a fork in the path, I have no idea which way to go. I don't even seem able to make a logical decision. I just take the path that seems the easier. And it's usually the one that runs downhill.

"So, Ray. What next?"

"What do you fancy?"

"Show me the sights."

"There are no sights. This is Scarsby! This is a town which had its heyday in the industrial revolution. When the railway brought holidaymakers in their thousands from the West Riding. To bathe in the clean water. And take the sea air. Well, the clean water's gone. And the sea air stinks of diesel. The Winter Gardens are closed. Not just for the winter. Permanently. The pier collapsed years ago. And won't be rebuilt unless a grant is obtained from the Lottery. And the donkeys have all died. This is the Great British seaside experience, Duncan. Nobody comes here any more. Even the whores have closed their legs and shut up shop."

"I used to come here as a boy. Dad used to bring me to go out on the boats. Fishing. I hated it. I was always sick before we'd left the harbour. I remember once. There was this huge fat guy sat at the back of the boat. I guess they made him sit at the back so it wouldn't capsize. And when I was sick, he laughed. And called me a nancy boy. And when we were fishing, my line kept on getting tangled with his. And he shouted and cursed and called me names. And I think my dad was frightened of him. Because he kept telling me to ignore him. But on the way back towards the harbour, I saw all the seagulls following the boat as the skipper gutted the catch, and threw all the entrails overboard. And because I'd been sick, I hadn't eaten any of the sandwiches mum had put up for me. So, I stood at the front of the boat and broke them up into small pieces. And tossed them into the air above the boat to attract the gulls. And I soon got used to the speed of the boat and the prevailing wind so that I knew exactly what trajectory was required. And I maintained a constant supply of titbits for the gulls all the way back to the harbour. As they flocked above the stern of the boat. And as they flocked and wheeled and turned and swooped, and fought over the scraps, they shat. All over that fat bastard. And dad had a great big smile on his face, and couldn't wait to tell mum when we got home."

"So, Duncan. Where would you like to go?"

"Show me the good pubs."

"No chance. I may wish to use them again."

"So, show me the bad ones. The dives."

"No problem. There are plenty. None of them worth a second visit."

"Just the ticket. Let's get ourselves laid. Lead on."

And so, we tour the town's least salubrious establishments. Drinking, laughing and joking like in the old days. Duncan, as always, on the lookout for opportunities for sexual exercise. In his pursuit of excellence in matters coital. Engaging in conversation with any female who takes his eye, regardless of the fact that many are already in male company.

And into this small, friendly quiet pub. The old-fashioned type. With real ale, and a real fire in the tap room. Casting a warm glow over the domino players. No loud juke box; just light and low background muzak. And as we're talking, I notice a man at the far end of the bar staring at us. Tubby, short and balding. Staring straight at me, and smiling. Doesn't look like a trouble-maker, psychopath, or gay even. But you never can tell. Ignore him and turn away to watch this exciting game of dominoes. Where, at a penny a point, tension is running high. And out of the corner of an eye, I see him approaching. Best face him, in case he's armed and dangerous. Enough is enough. I don't need anybody else to stab me in the back.

"Ray! It's Ray, isn't it?"

"Yes."

"And you. I know you. But I can't for the life of me put a name to you."

"Duncan."

"Duncan! That's right. Yes, for Christ's sake. Smelly Kelly!"

"I beg your pardon!"

"You don't remember me, do you?"

"No."

"Maurice. Maurice Lancer. We were in the same class at school."

"So it is! Morris Dancer. Or was it Bengal Lancer we used to call you? I forget."

"Whatever. You two have hardly changed. I knew you as soon as you walked in! So how are you both doing? Fancy meeting you in a pub way out here after all these years. And the two of you still together. Flash and Smelly. What a small world!"

"Yes. You've changed though, Bengal."

"Yeah. Filled out a bit."

"No, I mean, your trousers are longer than they used to be. And your head is somewhat threadbare."

"Still the same old jokers, eh. So, what are you doing here?"

"Having a quiet drink."

"No, I mean, what are you doing in Scarsby?"

"I live here. Duncan's visiting."

"You live here? Christ, so do I! How long have you lived here?"

"Not long."

"We moved a couple of months ago. Nice place. Hey. Why don't you let me show you round? Make a night of it. I know some great pubs. Where the action is."

"Thanks. But no. We're just out for a quiet drink."

"You two! Out for a quiet drink? That'll be the day! You were hell-raisers even at school."

"We've matured."

"So. You two married?"

"No."

"No."

"Free and single, eh. Well, how about it? Why don't we do the town? Pick up some fanny?"

"No thanks. Not tonight. Won't your wife be expecting you?"

"Well, yes. But not for a while yet. Hey, why don't you two come back to meet her? She'll be thrilled to bits to see you after all these years."

"Do we know her?"

"'Course you do! Felicity Hodgson was her maiden name. You remember her!"

"I'll say! Fun-fair Felicity! The best white-knuckle ride in town. She left school early. She was pregnant."

"That's right. We had a daughter."

"What do you mean, we?"

"Our daughter. Sam."

"It wasn't yours. At least a dozen of the fifth form had equal claims."

"Say what you like. As far as we're concerned, Sam was our love-child. We married as soon as I finished my A levels."

"Well then. Congratulations, Bengal."

"Thanks. Let's have a drink to celebrate. Will one of you two get them in? I've only got a fifty-pound note. And they won't accept it here. I'll get them in when we move on."

"We've no intentions of moving on."

"Oh, come on, Flash. You wouldn't begrudge buying me a pint for old time's sake."

"Actually, I would."

"Still the joker, eh. Come on then, Kelly. Get them in."

"No."

"What's the matter with you two? You'd turn your back on an old school friend?"

"You were never a friend. You were short. Fat. Pimply. Obnoxious. A swot. A tell-tale. And you only shagged Felicity when you cadged a quid off me to take her to the pictures. And came back to school the next day boasting to everyone who'd listen about what you had been up to. But you never offered to pay back the quid. You miserable prat."

"Hey. I'm sorry. It must have slipped my mind. An oversight. Here. Here's your quid. Take it."

"A quid's no good after all these years. With inflation. Buy a round and we'll call it even."

"I just told you. I've only got a fifty. And they won't accept it."

"I'll change it for you."

"Er. No. Look, it's OK. I'll just nip home and get some smaller notes. I just live up the road. I'll be straight back. Just hang on for fifteen minutes. And listen, Flash. Just in case something urgent has come up at home, and I can't get back, give me your address and phone number. And I'll call you. And we'll go out for a good night."

"It's 603252. 18, Echidna Street. Got that?

"Yeah. Thanks, Flash. I'll look you up. Cheers, Kelly. I'll see you."

"See you."

"Do you remember him, Dunc?"

"Yeah. A prize prat."

"Funny. That's exactly how I remember him."

"I shagged his wife."

"Me too."

"Yeah, but I shagged her after she married him. Seven hours after to be exact."

"You didn't! Not on his wedding night?"

"I most certainly did. I just happened to be in the pub where they had the reception. I think you had flu at the time. Anyway, I was there, he was drunk, she was hot. So, I couldn't disappoint her on her wedding night, could I? So, I jump-started her married life for her."

"You're a first-class bastard."

"Thank you. That's the highest honour that's ever been bestowed on me. But I do deserve it, I must admit. But to be honest, I expected the Order of the Garter. Because I took hers as a souvenir that night. Kept it for years. In fact, I almost persuaded Elaine to wear it under her wedding dress. But she insisted on something borrowed, rather than stolen. Anyway, what's the chance of meeting up with some willing totty tonight."

"Not good. Unless you want to risk a trip to the bars and clubs down the front."

"And does that mean potential trouble?"

"Possibly."

"Then let's do it."

"Later maybe. I need a decent drink first. The nearer you get to the harbour, the more water they put in the beer."

"All part of the natural cycle, I suppose. Draw water from the harbour. Put it in the beer. And piss it straight back into the sea."

The talk naturally moving on to sex, Duncan's specialist subject.

"You know what my ambition is, Ray?"

"To give the keynote speech at the annual convention of the Gay Pride movement?"

"No, but that's an idea. I could have fun with that. Stand up and declare that the natural resting-place for the penis is the vagina, and that ladies should spend their lives in the pursuit of the todger. And I'll fight any man who thinks otherwise. And be happy to take to my bed a group of lesbians and show them the error of their ways, free of charge."

"That's not a very liberal attitude."

"Liberal, my arse. Hellfire and damnation to these sexual deviants! Abominations!"

"As I recall, you derived not a little pleasure from watching a couple of ladies engaged in lesbian activities in your hotel room not so long ago."

"Yes, but before they left I'd put them back firmly on the straight and narrow. Showed them the path to redemption with my phallus."

"I can vouch for that."

"You can?"

"I can. I got to know the tomato-skinner quite well a short time after."

"Did you now?"

"I did."

"And did she show any unnatural inclinations?"

"None at all. As the friction burns on my willy will confirm."

"There you are then. Another convert to heterosexuality."

"She wasn't a lesbian. It was a temporary aberration caused by smoking strange substances you rolled into cigarettes."

"Ah, yes! Wonderful stuff. Frees the inhibitions and sets the libido soaring."

"It made Julie throw up."

"Merely an unfortunate side effect. But it made her horny as a rhino."

"Where did you get it?"

"Morocco, last summer. I tried it in a brothel. And ended up blowing the entire holiday budget in a single night. Told Elaine I'd been mugged and had to wire home for more money. Anyway, before we came home, I bought some. Hid it in my shoes as we went through customs. Wore my sweatiest socks so the sniffer dogs wouldn't detect anything."

"Any left?"

"Indeed. I have some in my pocket. But not to be used unless we get into some serious female company. Otherwise there's the danger you may feel so randy you could shag a spring-loaded letter box."

"You were going to tell me about your ambition."

"I was."

"So?"

"I wish to take to my bed the entire female chorus line of Riverdance. And shag each and every one of them to a total standstill. Put an end to all their ridiculous jigging about."

"A most laudable ambition."

"Indeed. What about you?"

"My ambition is to climb to the top of Blackpool Tower and toss myself off. Then walk back down and take a bow in front of the huge semen-splashed crowd."

"Highly commendable."

"And after that I intend to start up a Campaign for Real Uncle Dereks. CRUD for short."

"And its aim?"

"Self-explanatory. When I was a boy, every family had an uncle Derek. Or a Bert. Or a Cecil or Cyril or Cedric. And an auntie Gladys, or Hilda or Doris. Where have they all gone? They've been replaced by people called Dean and Darren and Wayne. And Sharon and Tracy and the like. All these kindly old relatives have gone. They've been body-snatched. And in their place, we've got these gum-chewing, card-scratching pods."

"I had an Uncle Percy and an Aunt Gwen."

"Exactly!"

"He smelt of mothballs. And she smelt of lavender water."

"But that was better than having an Aunt Kylie."

"Far better. I never had lustful thoughts about Aunt Gwen."

"So, what do you want to do this evening?"

"Trash this town."

"Too late, Duncan. It's already trashed."

"Shame. You know, this is the sort of place where I could settle. Be a big fish here."

"There are no big fish left in this pond, Dunc. The sharks ate them all. There are only small fry left. Two-bob millionaires. Small people with big dreams."

"I do not come into that category. I'm a larger than life person with above average sized dreams. So, what say we go down to one of the clubs on the front and have fun with the bouncers? Test the limit of their professional courtesy and phlegmatic nature."

"Neanderthals, Duncan. They act only on instinct. Haven't yet evolved any higher cortical functions. Best not rattle their cage."

"Neanderthals don't live in cages, Ray."

"So, we've discovered a new branch on the evolutionary tree. The missing link. Scarsby man. Skilled in the use of tools. Especially the baseball bat."

"So, let's have a quiet tour of quiet pubs."

"No problem. They're nearly all quiet this time of year."

Wandering from pub to pub, Duncan with one eye ever open to any opportunity for sexual liaison. Chatting up the ladies everywhere, and having to move on frequently whenever jealous husbands or boyfriends appear. Duncan on his best behaviour, avoiding confrontation. Not daring to risk any misdemeanour for which he might be arrested and miss his flight to the New World. About which he talks incessantly. In between reminiscing about the times we'd had together as teenagers at the local discos, where if we didn't pull, we'd drink ourselves stupid.

And after the pubs close we meander back to the house, laden with beer and whisky. Duncan pausing in an alleyway to splash the wall. Steam rising in the cold night air. Then sitting at the kitchen table until daylight, cold and grey, heralds Duncan's new dawn.

Breakfast of bacon sandwiches and mugs of strong coffee. Pounding headaches kept at bay with glasses of malt. Hangovers are for later. Saunter together down to the railway station to await Duncan's train, which arrives on time. Exchange farewells, handshakes and hugs, and wave him out of sight. And bend forward to retch violently on the platform.

And home and straight to bed where sleep comes quickly if fitfully.

And for a while, life returns to its dull normality. I miss Duncan. He has the ability to conjure up cheer wherever he goes. In fact, I miss him probably more than I miss Lucy. Which is odd. Since for the past fifteen years I've been with Lucy every day, and probably met up with Duncan no more than a few dozen times. Lucy tolerated him. But thought he was a bad influence on me. And preferred to go out in a foursome, with Elaine, rather than allow us out on our own. In case he led me astray. And the only occasions when I came home drunk and happy were when Duncan and I had been out together. Like old times. But it was clear that Lucy disapproved. She was always cold and distant towards me for a few days, until it was deemed I'd done my penance. Still, it was a price worth paying.

CHAPTER 26

Mail this morning. A fat envelope from the solicitor. Contract to be signed. Buyers wish to complete in fourteen days. And this other air mail letter in Duncan's spidery hand. Tearing it open for his news.

"Dear Ray,

Disaster has struck. Of the highest magnitude. My hopes and dreams in tatters. My home, home on the range will soon be but a memory. Sherry took umbrage with the fact that I, shame on me, have been shagging her ex-Miss Denver daughter. The girl's husband, Wyatt the Third, Junior, was none too pleased about it either and a fierce argument ensued during which I referred to him as the Turd, a splash-in-the-pan, and broke his nose. I explained to no avail that in the land of opportunities one must grasp them. Which I did, both of them, fondling them with alarming regularity. It must be the Colorado air. Does things to the libido. The bottom line as they so quaintly like to put it over here is that she ordered me to leave, not just the ranch, but the goddamn country. But before I did, I wiped bogies on her curtains, and in the globe of the world in which she kept an array of liquor, I took a sly shit. That should break the ice at her next social gathering, don't you think? I desperately need somewhere to stay. Can you put me up for a few days until I find my feet or a rich lonely widow? Arriving Monday morning, about nine, at Heathrow. If you can help, leave me a message at the Pan-Am desk.

Yours,

Duncan the Desperate."

Send him the following telegram.

"Duncan. Stop. Come to Scarsby. Stop. You're welcome to stay. Stop. Ray. Stop."

Leave the legal documents in abeyance until Duncan arrives. Can always claim they got delayed in the post. A quick clean round, push the vacuum a little. Dust and polish here and there and a spray of this fragrant stuff. Open some windows to release the stale smoke air. And let in the traffic's diesel fumes.

Monday evening, waiting at the train station for the connection from Hull. On time and almost empty, except for the beaming Duncan, who drags me into the buffet bar.

"Good to see you, Ray. Do you know it's quicker to get from the US to London than from London to Scarsby? Three trains for Christ's sake! I need a drink."

"So, I gather your stay in America was not wholly successful?"

"Put it down to experience. Which it certainly was. And, get this, Sherry gave me five grand as a parting gift, to cover my expenses, and loss of earnings and everything else I claimed to have suffered. And, of course for the pleasure she derived from the long dong. But the best news of all. I start a new job next Monday. What do you think of that?"

"Tell me more."

"I got into conversation with a guy sat next to me on the plane. Turned out he's a property developer. By the time we landed, I'd convinced him I was the best salesman ever to have walked the earth. And he practically begged me to accept the job. Selling timeshare, in Tenerife."

"Jesus."

"Indeed. So, Duncan the Irrepressible flies off again at the weekend. To charm the tourist totty. Into parting with pesetas. A new life in the sun. A new start. Amidst the temptations of tanned flesh. So, pal. What say we party for a week? Starting now?"

"Let's do it."

"That's the spirit. Let me dump this bag at your place. And inside, we should find your present."

A quick stop at the house, where Duncan showers and changes and stows his luggage, whilst I send for pizzas and open a bottle of wine. And Duncan fishes out of his bag my present. A brown aromatic lump, neatly and tightly foil-wrapped.

"So, this is the famous Moroccan."

"It is. It is. Help yourself, Ray. Tonight is the night for an excess of excesses. Tonight, for all his sins and debauched habits, Saint Duncan will be stoned in public."

"So, what's the Moroccan for 'This is real hot shit'?"

"It's spelt 'squiggle squiggle dot, squiggle dot, dot, dot squiggly dot' and pronounced with a wide-eyed grin."

"Well, squiggle dot, Dunc."

"Squiggle dot, Ray."

Then on to the pubs and clubs of this seaside town. Duncan loud and brash, flashing the wad of notes and buying drinks for the ladies. Turning on the charm and the patter. The prodigal son. Seeking his fatted calf among the herds of middle-aged women out for a drink after bingo. Gathering around him an entourage of admirers and freeloaders, who giggle and guffaw at his innuendo-laden repartee, and willingly accept the offers of free drink, and tentatively puff on his limitless supply of roll-ups.

"He's a one, your mate."

"Pardon?"

Turning in the direction of the voice. Which belongs to a slim redhead, petite and pretty, with an engaging smile and sparkling eyes. Hair done in a 'bob' cut. But none too professionally. More like a two-bob cut. Keep these uncharitable thoughts to myself. Let's not spoil Duncan's party.

"I said he's a right one, your mate."

"Yes. He certainly is. I'm sorry, do I know you?"

"Probably never noticed me. But I've seen you before. Shopping with your wife. Not for a while though. You wouldn't recognise me. Without makeup and my hair hidden under a cap. I work on the deli counter at the supermarket. Don't you shop there any more?"

"No. I hardly shop at all these days. We moved away."

"And now you're back?"

"Yes."

"Wife not with you tonight?"

"She died."

"Oh, I'm sorry. I… I don't know what to say now. And I'm not usually lost for words. It's just that that's the last thing I expected you to say. I mean, when two men are out on the town on their own and you ask where their wives are, you expect them to come up with some lame excuse such as 'she's staying in to watch a film on TV' or something like that. You just don't expect such an unexpected answer like that."

"Expect the unexpected."

"Sorry?"

"Expect the unexpected. It's one of Duncan's mottos. Says it helps him prepare for life's tribulations."

"I see. You're not like him though. I can tell."

"What do you mean?"

"Well. I can see you're enjoying yourself. But you're quite happy just to go with the flow. You're not in control of your life. It's just passing you by. Whereas your mate, Duncan, is in charge of his destiny."

"Till it bites him in the arse."

"You don't really do that disgusting thing, do you?"

"What disgusting thing?"

"Like your mate said."

"And what's that?"

"I don't like to repeat it. I don't like saying things like that."

"In that case I can't answer your question."

"How can I put it. Without sounding...indelicate."

"Try."

"Well... You don't really... you know... leave things... in women's handbags."

"What sort of things?"

"Oh, dear. This is difficult. Sort of... disgusting... things. Human... things."

"Are you perhaps accusing me of shitting in people's handbags?"

"Well, yes. Not accusing, no. It's just something your mate said. You don't do that, do you?"

"I most certainly do not."

"That's a relief. I mean, I knew it couldn't be true. It's so disgusting."

"It's one of Duncan's more endearing little habits."

"You're kidding."

"He likes to leave little mementoes whenever a relationship breaks down. But don't worry. At the moment he's in a very strong onanistic relationship. And he doesn't have a handbag. So, you're quite safe."

"Good. But I shan't let go of my handbag."

"Stay close. I will ensure it remains undefiled. Now, would you like a drink?"

"I shouldn't really. I've had lots already. But go on then. Lager, please."

More customers flocking in as the Karaoke starts up. A thin middle-aged man with long grey hair lank beneath a grease-stained cowboy hat sings a few country and western songs in a strangulated nasal voice. Off-key but impassioned. Songs of unrequited love and failing crops. Obviously little joy in his life, but no excuse for inflicting his pain on a pub full of revellers. Who boo him off the stage and demand more jollity. Duncan taking the microphone to give a comic rendering of an old Karaoke favourite, changing the lyrics to include references to outsize sexual organs. Referring, of course, to his own. Receiving a standing ovation. And an offer of later liaison with a frisky blue-rinsed pensioner. Duncan seeking a new venue starts a conga round the pub. Revellers joining the line as it snakes round the tables and out into the street. Duncan holding up traffic as the line crosses the road heading towards the harbour. Twenty yards further back, I dance gaily along, the redhead behind with one hand round my waist and the other on my bottom. Whispering in my ear.

"I like being near the harbour. I love the smell."

"Of seamen?"

"Depends how you spell it."

"I've been fishing once. And I can't spell."

"I fancy it tonight. Let's nip back to my place."

Disengaging from the dancers as they meander down the middle of the road before Duncan gives a hand signal to turn left and leads the way through the doors of the nearest pub.

The redheaded Jackie pulling me into a shop doorway. Kissing me and slipping a warm hand down the front of my trousers. Encouraged by the instant response, she unzips me, hitches up her short skirt and drops her knickers, and guides me in. Banging her hard against the shop door, and reaching a rapid climax. Jackie, off-balance with one leg round my waist, moans and throws back her head. Which strikes hard against the door frame and sets off the wailing burglar alarm as she slumps unconscious to the ground.

"Oh shit. God. Please don't be dead. Wake up. Please wake up."

Slapping her face gently until she gives a soft groan and opens her eyes.

"Wow. Did I pass out? That was some orgasm. Jesus! I can still hear bells ringing. And it feels like you've blown the top of my head off."

"We'd better move. Let me take you home."

"Good idea. I could use some more of that."

"I'm sorry. I'll have to leave you. Must get back to Duncan. Make sure he's OK"

"You bastard! You can't just leave me like this!"

"I'll ring you."

"You don't know my number."

"Well, I'll come and see you at work."

"Promise?"

"Promise."

"Well, when you do, I'll slip you a bit of free sausage. In exchange for the bit you slipped me."

"That wasn't a bit. That was all of it."

"No offence. But I'm used to my husband. Who is a bit bigger. But you use yours better. Make the most of what you've got."

Bundling her into a taxi at the rank. Which she refuses to allow to drive off until she's given me a kiss, tongue deep down the throat, and had another quick fondle in my trousers. A fiver for the driver. With instructions to take her home before her tongue tears out my tonsils and her vice-like grip crushes my testicles. Must find Duncan. Walking back past the doorway where a police car now awaits the shopkeeper's arrival. Cross the road and try to look inconspicuous.

"Excuse me, sir."

Oh, God. They know! Brazen it out. Act the innocent.

"Yes, officer. May I be of assistance?"

"Would you kindly check your person, sir. And rearrange your clothing so as not to give offence to the good ladies of this town. Nor encouragement to the bad ones."

"Yes, officer. I'm so sorry. It seems my zip is faulty. I'm just going home to change."

"Make sure you do. The magistrates round here take a very dim view of the indecent exposure of private parts in public parts."

"Thank you, officer. Goodnight."

"Goodnight to you, sir."

Securely zipped and out of sight of the police. Heartbeat returning to normal. Pick up Duncan's trail by calling at the watering hole in whose direction the snake was last seen heading. Opening the door to a scene of carnage. Broken furniture. Overturned tables and chairs. Floor awash with beer. Landlady dispensing first aid to distressed customers. Sound of a police siren becoming louder as it approaches. Keep the nerve. Walk straight through the lounge and out of the back door. Legging it up the narrow alley to a safe distance. Then straight home to await the return of Duncan, architect of this anarchy.

Pour myself a large malt, and sit in the dark, safe from the sirens heading in the direction   of the town centre. Soon a loud knocking on the door, which opens to reveal the beaming Duncan.

"Christ's sake, let me in. Quick, and lock the door. Leave the lights out. And pour a drink for my faint heart. Which has pumped furiously while I ran all the way from town. Jesus! The seaside was never this much fun when I was little. I would seriously consider coming to live here. Were it not for the fact that I'd get arrested."

"Tell me about it. Or I shall drink this fine malt alone."

"Where did you get to? Seems we lost you somewhere along the line."

"Your tale first. Starting at the pub at the end of the High Street."

"Ha ha, yes. A fine establishment. Filled with happy souls. Well. We snaked our way through the lounge and up to the bar. Where I ordered drinks for all the thirsty conga dancers. Many of whom were drinking them as fast as the staff could pour them. The bill came to over seventy-odd quid. But since they were holding a charity fundraiser for an unfortunate young soul born without lower limbs, I, having first-hand and regular experience of being legless, offered the landlady an extra fifty notes if she'd get her tits out and dance round the pool table. Which she did to tumultuous applause. However, devilment then got the better of me, and I produced a mere ten pound note and some small change, stating that unfortunately I'd left my wallet at home. And would she kindly put it on my slate. Or at least allow me to do the washing up. At this juncture a few of the regulars threatened to give me a sound thrashing unless I paid up. But my new-found friends came to the rescue. And thrashed them instead. In the melee, I managed to tweak the landlady's left nipple before we danced on to the next port of call. Waving a wad, I suggested we call for burgers, for which I would gladly pay as a token of my appreciation for their assistance. But not before we'd danced round the harbour. Where unfortunately some of the assembly either fell or jumped or were pushed into the water. Not having time to wait for wet and bedraggled stragglers, we danced into the burger franchise where I ordered twenty-seven burger-and-fries. I excused myself from the queue at the counter to visit the gents. But when I saw the fire exit door at the end of the corridor, I couldn't resist the temptation. So, I left them waiting for their food, without paying, and ran back here. A fine night's entertainment, I believe. Ranking high in the charts of my all-time Great Nights Out. And you?"

"Against my will, I was dragged away from all the fun and had to endure the most unwelcome advances of an attractive purveyor of polony and handler of exotic sausage. Who coerced me into a knee-trembler in a shop doorway."

"You prat. And all I got was a feel of some old woman's blue-veined sagging tit."

"However, when I banged her, she banged her head and set off the burglar alarm. So, our coitus was somewhat interruptus-ed. With the result that I was almost arrested for walking the streets with my willy on display.

"Ray, that is wonderful news. I do believe you are again tasting the sweet excesses of debauchery for which we were once renowned. Let's drink to that. And drink to it again. And again, and again. Until not a drop remains. Cheers! To my partner in perversion!"

Fill a glass for Duncan with this smooth malt. Which he downs in one. Pushing the glass towards me for instant refill. The wide grin on his happy face. Never down. Never sad for long. And from his pocket he produces a small foil packet, the grin spreading wide across his alcohol-flushed face.

"Saved some for you. A nightcap. Or, in the case of the Moroccans, a night fez."

"Tell me, Duncan. Do you miss Elaine?"

"Elaine who?"

"Elaine your wi... Your soon-to-be ex-wife."

"No. Not a bit. Elaine is the past. The past has happened. And can't be changed. However much anyone may wish things may have been different. What's done is done. And cannot be undone. So, I can look back on the past with some fond memories. But it is done. Finished. Even the words I've just spoken are already in the past. And can't be un-spoken. So, there is no point in hanging on to the past. Nor even the present. Because the present too is only transitory. What you have to do is live for the future. Because the future, by definition, is yet to come. And who knows what it will bring? So, you must embrace the future and all its intriguing possibilities. Because, while you draw breath, the future will provide new challenges, opportunities, and the potential for damn good lays. Don't think about the last. Simply look forward to the next."

"I'm losing Lucy."

"No, Ray. You've lost Lucy. Face it, man."

"When I packed to move back here, I got rid of a lot of Lucy's things. Personal things. Clothes, and the like. But for some reason, I never threw away her toothbrush. And this morning, when I saw the two toothbrushes in the bathroom, I couldn't remember which was mine, and which was Lucy's. I stood there in front of the mirror. For an age.

Trying to remember. Trying to apply some logic. Was mine the blue? Or the red? Blue for a boy? But blue was Lucy's favourite colour. Or, then again, did she just pick two contrasting colours at random? Knowing that order prevailed in the household, and that the position of the toothbrushes in the rack would ensure that the correct one was always used."

"So, what did you do?"

"Used the red one."

"Wise choice."

"In what way?"

"You made a decision. Alone. One that was obviously important to you."

"But was it the right decision?"

"Yes. Because if you chose correctly, you used your own toothbrush. And if you chose incorrectly, you're telling Lucy that you still feel a part of her, and she's still sharing her life with you. By sharing her toothbrush."

"You can sound really profound at times. When you're talking absolute bullshit."

"I know. Part of my charm. Listen, Ray. It doesn't make any difference which toothbrush you use. Lucy has no need for hers. Look upon it as something she's left behind for you. Use it. And think of her. And never forget, she's part of your past. The most important thing in your life so far, without a doubt. But past. Don't ever forget her. Don't ever forget the love she gave you. And you gave her. Always hold on to her memory. But let her go. If you can't do that, then you have no future."

"Then I have no future."

"Is it the guilt?"

"Yes."

"But why? There was nothing else you could do."

"We could have fought harder. Another operation, maybe. Anything to buy some time."

"Time for you? Or for Lucy? Lucy didn't want any more time. Or pain. She wanted the suffering to end. And for you to carry on without her. She wanted you to be free of her pain. She was adamant in refusing further futile treatment. She accepted her life was over. But yours isn't. Ray. You have absolutely no reason to feel guilty. If anyone has, then it's God."

"I don't believe in God."

"Well, Jesus, then. Who perhaps wanted her for a sunbeam. So instead of taking someone who deserved to die, he chose the one who would make the best sunbeam. Come on, Ray. Give it up."

"Give what up?"

"Your martyrdom. Your elevation to sainthood. You're torturing yourself over this."

"I can't help it."

"So, go down to the market square in the morning and invite people to stone you to death. Or flagellate yourself with barbed wire in front of the Town Hall. Tell the whole world you're a martyr. Saint Raymond of Scarsby, Bringer of Relief to Lusting Women. You're becoming pathetic, you know that? Look. Stop trying to make yourself into one of the great tragic figures of western history. What's happened to you is sad. But not tragic. You had fifteen good years with Lucy. And a happy life before her. Think of all the sad bastards out there. The ones who never found the love you did. Think of me, for example."

"You?"

"Yes. Me. OK, so I married. Got two grown up kids. But I never had love like you had. I had a home, a family. Status. A decent income. The trappings of success. Affection. Sex. But never love. Why do you think I go around screwing whoever I can? Because I'm still searching. That's why. Searching for what you found. You never realised how much I envied you. While I tried to cling on to a sense of stability, you had it all. And now you've got the nerve to wallow in self-pity. And you're driving yourself insane with guilt. Well, give it up, Ray. Enough is enough. Lucy suffered. And you've suffered. But don't make your friends suffer. It's time for you to get a life. Or join a monastery."

"I think the loneliness is making me mentally ill."

"So? At least schizophrenics have someone to talk to. Come on. It's time for you to get a life. And just remember, you had one before Lucy, so there's no reason you can't go on without her. And that's what she'd want. She's hate to see you in this state. Come on, man. Get a grip."

Duncan becoming heavy-lidded and tired, but serious and sincere. Banging a fist on the table and calling for silence.

"Will the accused please stand. Raymond Light, you stand before this court and in the eyes of God having been accused by yourself of complicity in the sad and untimely death of Lucy Light, your late wife. After carefully considering all the evidence, and in the absence of a jury, I, as your peer, am now able to give my verdict. Raymond Light, I find you not guilty. You are free to leave this court and live your life without blemish to your character. Case dismissed."

"Thank you, your honour."

"Now, more drink?"

"Last one."

"A toast, then. To Lucy."

"Lucy."

And later, the nightmare again.

Walking into this strange cold room. Fluorescent-lit. A table opposite, and behind it a chair, upon which sits a man in uniform. A long red scar curves from his right temple to the corner of his mouth, which breaks into a thin smile.

"What do you want?"

"I've come to sign the papers."

"What papers?"

"The papers for my release."

"First you have to satisfy the conditions."

"What conditions?"

"The conditions which will determine whether you are fit for release."

"What are they?"

"First. Did you love your wife?"

"Of course!"

"Then why did you let her die?"

"She had cancer. Of the bowel."

"Answer the question! Why did you let her die?"

"There was nothing we could do. It was incurable."

"You tried all available treatment?"

"Yes."

"Did you try all available treatment?"

"Yes! I told you."

"Are you sure?"

"Yes. No. She refused a colostomy."

"Might that have cured her?"

"No."

"How do you know if you didn't try?"

"The doctors said it was too widespread. The possibility of its having any beneficial effect was almost infinitesimal."

"Wasn't it worth a try?"

"We both agreed. It was a joint decision!"

"And what about the other deaths?"

"OK, so I shouldn't have let Scruff out on the streets without a lead. But I was only young. It was a long time ago."

"I call as witness Lucy Light."

Lucy appearing at my side. Feeling the warm touch as she takes my hand. The sound of her soft warm voice.

"It was a joint decision, though Ray pleaded with me to have the operation. I'd had enough pain. And so had Ray. He's not to blame."

"And the others?"

"He's not to blame. He's only guilty of loving too much."

"Here are the papers for your release. Dismissed."

CHAPTER 27

Waking, head pounding around next noon. The bottle empty. On the table a note.

"Ray,

Sorry, I couldn't say goodbye. I left early to catch the first bus out of town as I fear remaining here may be bad for my health. And my liberty. I'm going down to London to sample its delights until my flight to the sun. One day, I shall return. You can bank on it. I guess I said some nasty things last night, and I apologise. But think about it, and you may find the odd grain of truth. I hope you do. The world needs the likes of you and me to keep it on its path to its inevitable destruction. In the meantime, look after yourself. I believe your rehabilitation is almost complete. And if love is your drug, then sex is your antidote. Though not yet available on the NHS, it can still be obtained at a reasonable price. And if you decide you've had enough of women, get yourself a hairy-arsed bricklayer. And one last word of advice. Take at least one good shit every day, for the bowels are the gateway to the soul, and the gateway must not be obstructed.

My highest regards,

Duncan the Dissolute and Debauched."

Sadness at his departure. Without the chance to say goodbye. And thank you. To the man with the indomitable spirit. And the mad Moroccan smoking substance.

And mid-afternoon, popping out for provisions and a replenishment of malt. Disguised in dark glasses, which attract undue attention on this sunless winter day. Buying a paper to confirm my suspicions of the front-page news.

"SVENGALI OF SCARSBY"

Hurrying home to digest this in safety and comfort, along with the malt. Must cut this out and mail it to Duncan. To pin on his cell wall. If ever they catch him.

"The town's emergency forces were called into action last night to deal with a number of separate but, police believe, related incidents, with damage to property running into thousands of pounds. They include:

The wrecking of a town centre public house

Injuries to several innocent customers

A pub landlady being sexually molested

A con-trick depriving charity of a large amount of money

Three innocent bystanders thrown into the icy waters of the harbour by a marauding group of hooligans

Chaos in a burger restaurant when the supposed ringleader ordered fifty meals and disappeared without paying

The alleged rape of a supermarket counter assistant

Numerous outbreaks of fighting and vandalism culminating in a pitched battle on the seafront between the police and a line of drunken conga dancers.

A publican's false teeth being forcibly removed from his mouth and deposited in the Crustacean Tank of a popular high-class harbourside restaurant.

Human faeces in a pub's charity collection bottle.

Police are keen to locate a mystery man, described by an eye-witness as a 'Pied Piper' who allegedly orchestrated the chaos, leading naive and innocent revellers into problem situations with which, fuelled by drink for which he sometimes paid and sometimes conned out of the town's honest and trusting publicans, they felt compelled to act as he ordered. This 'Rasputin-like' character is described as being in his mid to late forties with mad staring eyes and a vicious smile. Police believe he may have had an accomplice, a pervert, who may have been responsible for the crimes of sexual or scatological nature. Members of the public are requested to contact the police with any information regarding the identities of the two fugitives, who are believed to be armed and dangerous."

Then, below, an interview with a pub landlady, Mrs Armytage, of the North Star.

"'At around 9.45 a large group of drunks came dancing through the doors and making a nuisance of themselves. My husband Ronnie, an ex-footballer who had trials with Leeds and almost once represented his country at schoolboy level, asked them to behave and managed to defuse a number of difficult situations, but he was simply overwhelmed by the numbers, losing his false teeth in the process, and in the end, I had to call the police. By the time they eventually arrived, the group had moved on and we were left to clear up the damage. It was then I noticed that somebody had defecated in a large whisky bottle which sits on the bar for charity. I can't believe anyone could do such a thing. I mean, it's only got a narrow neck, and nobody saw it happen. We had to empty the bottle into the sink and disinfect the money. This incident has shaken my faith in human nature. And on top of that, someone mixed something nasty into Ronnie's pipe tobacco, and when he lit up at the end of the night, he experienced the most awful stomach cramps and diarrhoea.'

The collection raised £31.79 in aid of Rwandan refugees. Mr Armytage's false teeth were later recovered from the lobster tank and safely returned to him."

And underneath, a report on the wonderful display of indoor plants at the Horticultural Society's annual show at the Town Hall which attracted a total attendance of almost a hundred. Ten percent up on last year's figure. Full report and pictures on pages seven eight nine and ten. A short article in the inside pages showing the residents of Scarsby in a better light. Anonymous donations totalling almost two hundred pounds received by a pensioner who was the victim of a recent brutal assault. A picture of the smiling war veteran, now fully recovered. The culprits brought to book. Episode closed.

And early in the evening the police arrive at my door. Two officers. And one of them is WPC Williams. Must be careful not to make reference to our non-relationship in the presence of this other officer.

"Good evening, sir. I'm PC Jones and this is WPC Williams.

"Yes. We've met before."

"Really."

"Yes. WPC Williams interviewed me in hospital at Christmas."

"That's right, Alan. He was attacked by the same lads who set on the old man. I filed the report."

"Well, sir. We'd like to ask you some questions regarding your whereabouts last night between the hours of 20.30 and 23.30."

"Yes, officer. I went out for a couple of drinks and came home early. I was back here by about ten o'clock."

"A man fitting your description was seen in the High Street by one of our officers. In a state of partial undress."

"Yes. Unfortunately, that was me. I explained to the good officer that my zip was faulty and promised to go straight home. Which I did."

"We believe you spent some part of the evening in the company of a man calling himself Duncan."

"That's true. But I don't know him."

"Witnesses have stated you seemed close friends."

"Would that we were. The truth is, I met him in the public conveniences near the war memorial. And offered him a bed for the night. However, during the course of the evening, we were separated and I haven't seen him since."

"Do you make a habit of this sort of thing?"

"What sort of thing?"

"Offering strange men a bed for the night."

"Frequently. I am a practising homosexual, obviously over the age of consent. And what I choose to do in the privacy of my own home is my business. And is not, thank God, illegal these days."

"Are you saying you have no interest in women?"

"None whatsoever. Abhorrent creatures! No, I prefer the intimate company of men. Especially those in uniform."

"I've no reason to doubt him, Alan. I've seen Mr Light around town on a number of occasions. But never in the company of a woman. And it would explain why he was attacked for no apparent reason. A possible case of queer bashing."

"Mmmm. Well, sir. We won't take up any more of your time. It appears we've been misinformed. But we have to follow up every lead. We're sorry to have troubled you."

"Not at all. Good night."

"Good night, sir."

"Oh, and by the way. I'm not sure his name is Duncan. When we met he introduced himself as Harry. He may have used the name Duncan to disguise his real identity."

"Thank you, sir."

Pour a malt to calm the nerves. And beg forgiveness for telling porkies. And thank God that WPC Sarah seems to have a soft spot for me. But she didn't lie. Just a little economical with the actualité. The only reason she hasn't seen me out in female company is that she's so far refused to submit to my obvious charms. At least she's got me off the hook. Say three Hail Mary's. And a Hail WPC Sarah. Worth it if it keeps Duncan in the clear until he's safely out of the country. And causing chaos elsewhere. Wonder what the Spanish is for 'Svengali'. El something or other, no doubt. Sign this contract of property sale and pop it in the post to the solicitor first thing in the morning. Request a speedy exchange and completion. Otherwise have him charged with soliciting.

CHAPTER 28

Two long weeks now since Duncan's flight to freedom. The chaos he caused in the town largely forgotten, the local newspaper instead carrying stories of sex and corruption and extravagant spending of taxpayers' money by the local council. And the exciting news that a second-rate 60's rock group is making another comeback and will be performing in the town during their forthcoming nationwide tour of third-rate venues.

No further visits from the police, which is good news. And no further visits from WPC Sarah, which is not. Still, I'm sure I'll get over it. Though kinky games with handcuffs will long remain an unfulfilled fantasy.

Waving goodbye to the Mini-van containing all my worldly goods except for the contents of a holdall. All personal little items, bound for safe storage, with instructions for its disposal expressed in my recently amended will. A collection of vinyl albums, and CDs for Duncan. Some mementoes of Lucy for her parents. Along with albums of photographs, the pictorial record of our life together. The complete collection, save one, which I carry with me at all times. All monies, including the residue from the sale of the flat, and the payout from life insurances, to be divided equally between the E's and Plopper, and Julie. With the other third share to be banked on Duncan's behalf pending his eventual return. And a fiver to old man Barker to buy lettuce for his poorly tortoise. And just this morning I'd received a letter from my itinerant mentor.

"Dear Ray,

I hope this catches you before you move out, which is why I've written my address on the envelope. If it's returned, I'll know you've moved on to who knows where.

I send you greetings from this sunny land, and, sincerely, wish you were here. I have only experienced limited success so far on the selling front, so I work in a bar four evenings a week. This pays the rent on a small apartment which is no more than adequate. But since I sleep most nights in sumptuous hotel rooms as a guest of various luscious women, there is no problem. Great news! I have already been made an honorary member of the 18-30 club - for those well enough endowed within that range in centimetres - and as a result there is a long queue of nubiles waiting for their turn to slide the slippery pole down to the depths of my depravity. Some even insist on paying for the privilege, for Christ's sake, and wine and dine me to excess. If this continues, I swear I shall die a happy man. Come and join me! There is enough to go round. That is, if I ever need to take time off for treatment with penicillin. Should I ever return to Yorkshire, I have a new business venture in mind. I plan to start up a Pratagram service, where people will invite me to birthday parties and the like, so that I can insult the host and spill beer down his wife's dress before throwing up in the middle of a pub and making a general nuisance of myself. A professional party saboteur. What do you think? Is there a market for such a service? If not, I'm sure I could generate one. How does 'RentaTwat' sound to you?

Your ally in adversity,

Duncan the Disreputable Designer of Disaster, and Dalliances Dangerous."

I have to smile at his optimism. I wish I possessed that same quality. The ability to turn adversity into advantage. To make something out of nothing. And when we're out together, I'm happy just to bathe in his reflected glory. If he ever writes a book I am determined to take a leaf out of it. But perhaps there's only room in this world for one Duncan. And I'm glad he's my friend. Respond with a quick note.

"Dear Duncan,

Your letter arrived on the day I left Scarsby. I am pleased for your happiness. Long may you continue to play the conquistador in the Spaniards' own backyard. I regret I have no intentions of joining you at present. A man's got to do what a man's got to do. I never had chance to say goodbye before you left. So, goodbye, and thank you. One day you must write a book. So that future generations can learn from the Master that, however many times life kicks you in the bollocks, they nevertheless continue to function with increased vigour. I have enclosed the local newspaper's account of your recent exploits, which seem likely to double the number of holidaymakers this season since you put this sleepy resort on the national map. And if you return, I will gladly join you in your venture. But only if you call the company 'Twats R Us'.

Take care,

Ray, the Resigned yet Remarkable in his own quiet unassuming way, and Regularly Rat-arsed."

Turn off the gas and water, and flick the switch for the electric. Meters read and cheques in the post. All accounts settled. Leave no bad debts behind. Lock the door for the final time, and drop the keys in at the Estate Agents. In a few days the incoming couple will breathe new life into this house. A slow walk to the railway station, lugging the heavy holdall. Taking in the sights and sounds and smells of this seaside town for the final time. Wave goodbye to the friendly local butcher, from whom Lucy would regularly purchase T-bone steaks and other bovine goodies. To feed my insatiable appetite. For life and love. 'Sold' notices being pasted in empty shop windows as leases are taken up in preparation for the tourist season. A mood of optimism about the town as it awaits the influx of holidaymakers and day-trippers which will keep it alive for another year and sustain it through its winter hibernation, from which Duncan's brief sojourn only temporarily roused it. Passing the street market from where I can hear the familiar sound of Irish music emanating from what Lucy used to call the Diddley-Dee stall. Our home town for a few happy years before I lost my job and we made the ill-fated trip down south. Leaving Scarsby now without regret, and never to return. Purchase a ticket at the kiosk and repair to the buffet bar to await the arrival and departure of my train. Sustenance for the journey. A ham sandwich and a pint. And time for another, and then a third pint. Hope there's a toilet on the train. Otherwise have to stick it out of the window when we go through a long tunnel.

Alighting at Hull. Through the barrier and out to the taxi rank. A short drive down to the docks to wait for my boat. When I was very young, grandad George had promised me a little fishy on a little dishy when it came in. I wonder if there will be a presentation ceremony at the quayside, where I will be handed a small mackerel on a silver platter. Allow myself a little smile at the thought. But more likely I'll be detained at customs and have my baggage searched. Look at my reflection in the taxi window. Haven't shaved for three days. Do I look like a desperado? A dangerous internationally-wanted criminal? Or just someone who doesn't care too much about his appearance any more? Delve into the overcoat pocket and fish out the passport, with its eight years old photograph. I've aged, and more than eight years. They used to say you shouldn't smile for your passport photo. But I couldn't help it. Lucy had put her hand through the curtain on the booth and had been tickling my ribs when the light flashed. She always told me off for looking too serious whenever my photo was taken, and the final print in the sequence of four was unusable for passport purposes as she had her finger up my nose. Still, my passport likeness bears a slight resemblance to its bearer. And these days, customs clearance is a mere formality. Duncan and I once went on a school holiday to Germany. And on our return, out of the whole group of twenty-eight pupils and teachers, only one of us was stopped by the customs officers. Duncan. Who was made to open his suitcase on the table. And among the dirty socks and underpants they discovered two bottles of Schnapps, a thousand cigarettes and sixty-two cigarette lighters. Gifts for his large family, was his futile explanation as they confiscated everything which he wasn't entitled to bring back. They even asked him if he had an import licence. To which he replied, no, but could I have one, please, and smiled his most charming of smiles. After a long delay, and intervention and personal assurances from the teachers, they let him through, and even allowed him to keep one of the lighters, one which didn't work. But Duncan was far from downhearted. For, taped to various parts of his body, under his one size too large school uniform, he had a further twenty-seven lighters, which he later sold for a sum more than sufficient to offset his outlay and so turned in a healthy profit on the enterprise.

The taxi drawing to a halt. Pay the man, and walk down towards Departures. Check in, clear customs and walk along the ramp to board this huge ferry. Show my ticket to this pleasant smiling lady who gives me directions to my cabin, wishing me a pleasant trip. Perhaps it would be more pleasant if she were to join me in my cabin. But that would be impossible. The cabin is smaller than the average toilet. God help me if I get an erection. I won't be able to turn around in here. Still, at least I will be able to get some sleep if I adopt the foetal position. And if they turn off the engines which rumble and throb directly beneath in the bowels of the ship, and which create a harmonious vibration in the tumbler by the small sink. Nothing else for it. As soon as they hoist the mainsail, I shall repair to one of the many bars for the duration of the twelve-hour voyage. Only to leave my seat when meals are served.

Disembarking at this massive port of Rotterdam, from where a bus will take me to the train station for the journey onwards to Amsterdam. So, this is Holland. The land of windmills, clogs and Dutch caps. Where a young boy once stuck his finger in a dyke, and she gave a shriek of unexpected delight.

Lucy and I came here some years ago for a long weekend. Stayed in a homely hotel down by the Rijksmuseum. Wandered the streets on a sultry August evening and found ourselves in the red-light district. Coerced with little reluctance into watching a live sex show. But sat towards the rear of the theatre, in the non-participants' seats. Left the action to a group of sweaty, fat German businessmen who came in late and sat at the front. And helped one of the acts perform her routine with an unpeeled banana.

Out through the Centraal Station onto the wide concourse, where a hippy guitar-strumming busker is singing Mr Tambourine Man in a soft voice. Eyes closed, uncaring, singing seemingly for his own pleasure as people bustle past, ignoring him. Toss some coins into his open guitar case, whereupon he grins and says 'Thanks, man.' Walk on down Damrak, and continue downhill, checking the side streets for the one I'm seeking. Finally, a left here, and a few doors along, and this is it. The European Headquarters of the Beauty of Light Foundation. Open the door and enter the brightly-lit reception area, where a young lady in a long flowing white robe sits smiling behind a desk.

"Good morning, sir. How may I help you?"

"My name is Ray Light. I booked a place on your seminar."

"Just one moment, Mr Light. Ah, yes, here it is. Would you take a seat, please? Someone will be with you shortly."

"Thank you."

Sit in this comfortable chair and leaf idly through a magazine while the receptionist phones a message regarding my arrival. And after a few minutes, a door to my left opens and through it walks the most stunning creature I have ever laid eyes on. A young girl, maybe twenty, perhaps slightly younger. With golden straight hair down to her waist. Clear deep blue eyes. No make-up nor jewellery. And what seemed to be a slim, perfect figure beneath her long white robe. And a flashing, warm, welcoming smile.

"Mr Light. I am so pleased you chose to attend. You are most welcome. Come, follow me. I will show you to your room and explain what your three-day seminar will consist of. And, of course, I will answer any questions you may wish to ask. Come. My name is Astra. Please take my hand."

Up the narrow stairs, following this beautiful girl, my eyes fixed firmly on her bum as it sways from side to side in front of me. Three whole flights following this hypnotic metronomic motion. The spell eventually broken when she stops at a door, and motions me to enter. A small, but bright room. All white. With a single bed with white sheets, a wardrobe, chair and small desk. And an en-suite toilet and shower. No phone, TV, or radio. Astra follows me in, and closes the door quietly behind her.

"Mr Light, I hope you will be comfortable here. You have answered our advertisement, so you know a little about our aims already. But I will explain the rules once again. You have booked to stay for three days. During these three days, you must not leave the building. We provide bed, breakfast, a light lunch and your evening meal. You will be woken at six-thirty, to be ready for body-cleansing therapy at seven. This will last for two hours, until breakfast. After breakfast, you will be bathed and massaged. You will then spend two hours in the Room of Stillness, where you must sit without speaking. You are allowed only to communicate silently with your inner thoughts. You are encouraged to analyse your problems and seek the strength to discuss them in group therapy after lunch. Following group therapy, you will spend the rest of the afternoon in the company of your allocated corporeal companion for meditation. Your evening meal is served at six-thirty in the evening, after which you will join our soul-cleansing therapy group, until ten. You are then free to retire to bed, if you so desire. But we strongly recommend that you stay with our discussion group until midnight. If you do so, I am sure you will find your stay here most worthwhile. For that is when our Enlightened

Leader joins us for scriptural interpretation. Because we wish to cleanse your body and soul, we must insist that you bring into our house no newspapers, mobile phones, books, nor any form of communication with the outside world. Now, Mr Light. Do you have any questions?"

"No."

"Good. Please, Mr Light. Please take part in every activity which is offered. Open your mind. Brush away your preconceptions, and let The Light shine on you and illuminate your life. Participate and learn. I guarantee that after three days you will be reborn a different person. Will you approach the experience with an open mind?"

"Yes."

"Good. Now will you please take off your clothes and put on your robe. Don't be shy."

"I'm sorry, but I believe I may have an erection."

"That is not an unnatural experience, Mr Light. While we cleanse your body, you will doubtless have numerous erections. But be assured that the needs of the body, as well as the soul, are catered for here."

Christ, I wish she hadn't said that! Grown another inch already. Down, boy. Behave while I turn my back and slip out of my clothes and into this white gown. Which now protrudes embarrassingly at the front.

"Hebe will be with you shortly. She is to be your corporeal companion, and confidante. You may open up your heart to her, and tell her anything. Unburden yourself of all your fears and guilt, safe in the knowledge that she will never impart that information to anyone else. Now please give me your cigarettes."

"I'm sorry. I can't go without a smoke for three days."

"Cigarettes are provided, Mr Light. And smoking is allowed in your room and in certain other designated areas. But you may only smoke the brand we provide. They are herbal, and free of toxins. You will find them quite pleasant, and they will satisfy your craving for nicotine. There is a pack in your bedside cabinet. Please ask when you require more. Ah, here is Hebe."

A young girl has slipped silently into the room. Beautiful, slim, golden-haired, and with the same beatific smile as the other blonde. Though I believe I can detect a hint of lasciviousness about the eyes. And this erection refuses to wilt, particularly when I notice Hebe staring straight at it. As the first blonde leaves, Hebe takes my hand and sits beside me on the bed.

"Mr Light. You are nervous and tense. Please do not be. I am here to help you relax. I will stay with you until lunch, when you will meet some of the other guests. Please, come and shower with me. I must cleanse your body. Come."

Slipping off her robe to reveal her exquisite body. Small firm breasts with hard erect nipples. And a natural blonde too. Follow her into the shower where warm water cascades over our bodies as she washes me all over. Lathering the erection with gentle hands. Then hands me the soap, encouraging me to explore her body. Locked together in a tight soapy watery embrace, she kisses me passionately. And then breaks away to fetch thick fluffy white towels with which to dry each other. And inevitably on to the bed, where we make love with a passion and intensity I thought I'd never experience again. And cuddled together afterwards, smoking the herbal cigarettes and drinking a glass of slightly viscous red wine with a strange bitter-sweet aftertaste. And feeling oddly light-headed. And euphoric. More so than the usual feeling of post-orgasmic well-being. And I tell Hebe all my troubles and woes.

Then down to lunch in the spacious and brightly-lit dining room. A dozen or so other guests, mostly male, already eating. Only one of whom looks up and greets me with a polite nod. Sit in the empty seat next to him. And fill my glass to the brim from the carafe of wine. Upon which he casts me a worried glance. Introducing himself as Charles, and as we shake hands he presses a piece of paper into my palm, and smiles after looking round to ensure nobody has noticed. Push the note into my robe pocket to read when alone. My light lunch arrives; a bowl of soup followed by a cold meat salad, and more wine. And when everyone has eaten, the herbal cigarettes are passed round.

Following the group into this large brightly lit room. Slip the note from my pocket and read it while nobody is watching. 'Beware the indians. Some of them are chiefs.' Maybe Charles is a nutter. Must ask him what he means. Easy chairs arranged in a semicircle, with one chair facing the rest. Already occupied by a dark-haired woman with clipboard in hand. Sit and relax in the chair next to Charles. Smoking is permitted in here, so light up a herbal to calm the nerves.

"Good afternoon, everybody. We have a new guest with us today. Ray Light. Mr Light, perhaps you would be kind enough to tell us all why you're here."

"Well, I came for three days of rest and tranquillity, as your adverts promised."

"And what exactly are you running away from?"

"Nothing. I just needed a break."

"Everyone who comes here is hiding from something. Something which must be brought out into the open so that you can be cleansed. Do not be ashamed. Nor afraid. Tell us."

"Well, my wife died. And I felt I was losing control. I need to take stock of my situation before I can decide what to do with my life."

"And in which direction would you like your life to proceed?"

"I haven't decided."

"Then perhaps we will be able to help you decide. Any comments, anybody?"

Silence for a while. Looking round at these people, most of whom are staring at their feet. Catch the eye of a fat red-faced man who returns my glance, asking hesitantly and with embarrassment.

"Mr Light. Do you have any homosexual inclinations?"

"No. Most certainly not!"

"Oh."

The fat man looking somewhat disappointed. Lowering his gaze. Seize the initiative, and try to get someone else to talk. So I can sit and listen and relax. And enjoy this feeling of calmness which is suffusing my body. Look down at the backs of my hands. See the hairs waving back and forth like a field of corn in a whispering summer breeze. Watch my fingernails grow. My tongue feels dry and bloated. Force it to move and listen to myself speak. This doesn't sound like me. Too high-pitched, as I ask the obese gentleman.

"Are you a fat puff?"

"Yes."

"And do you have designs on my body?"

"Yes."

"Come anywhere near me and I'll break your fat neck!"

"Mr Light! This is a place of harmony and peace!"

"Yes, I'm sorry. I feel a little queer. I... I mean, strange."

And then the giggles start. I can't help it. I get this uncontrollable urge to laugh, and however hard I try to suppress it, I still emit this strangulated high-pitched giggle. And soon the whole room follows suit with the exception of the dark-haired woman who tries desperately to call the meeting to order. In the end, she gives up and presses a button by the side of her chair. The door opens and a tray of drinks is brought in and passed round. I feel so happy and carefree, I take two glasses and light up another cigarette. And watch the dark-haired woman make a note on the pad on her clipboard. And in what seems like seconds, the lights glow ever brighter, so I have to shade my eyes to see the other guests, who, strangely, don't seem to be affected. But the lights are hurting my eyes, piercing my brain. They glow, and fade. Glow and fade. Emitting an ever louder hum. My hands! My fingers are glowing! Luminescent. Holding them up to the light, I can see right through them. The bones, cartilage and tendons. Stripped of flesh. Like viewing X-rays. And then the bones dissolve in the intensity of the light and I'm staring at the stumps of my wrists. And as I watch, my forearms slowly wilt, like warm plasticine. And drop off at the elbows, falling to the floor. I watch as they slither across the floor and out through the door. I try to shout for help. But all I can do is laugh. Out of control. As my body heaves and shakes from the vibration of this humming pulsating light. Which turns its focus now on my brain. Feel my head pounding, the blood boiling. Pain in the temples, from where thick purple veins erupt. My nose bleeding. Lick my upper lip and taste the salt warm life leaving me. And the pounding goes on and on, building to a crescendo in my head. And then the lights go out.

CHAPTER 29

"Mr Light. Mr Light! Wake up, Mr Light."

"Where am I?"

"You're in the hospital, Mr Light. At the Foundation."

"Foundation?"

"The Beauty of Light Foundation, Mr Light. In Amsterdam. Remember?"

"Yes. Why am I in the hospital?"

"Mr Light. You've had a mental breakdown. I'm sorry to put it so bluntly. But here we believe in confronting the truth, and using it to enlighten our lives. So that we're prepared for when our time comes."

"I need to see a doctor."

"You are being treated by a doctor, Mr Light. Our Enlightened Leader is a doctor of medicine, with a private practice in Switzerland. He has already examined you and prescribed your treatment."

"How long will I be here?"

"A few days, probably. Then you should be well enough to rejoin the group."

"I do not wish to rejoin the group. I want to leave and go back to England."

"I'm afraid that's not possible at the moment. We would be failing in our humanitarian duty if we allowed you to go before we are certain you pose no threat to your own life, or to the lives of others."

"I... I don't understand."

"Mr Light. You came here because your doctor in England diagnosed you as a paranoid schizophrenic. You must remember that."

"No."

"You're trying to block it out. The sooner you come to terms with it, and accept it as the truth, the sooner we can help you control it and live with it."

"This is nonsense. I don't believe it. I just passed out, that's all."

"Mr Light. You lost control. You tried to strangle one of our guests. And attacked a member of staff. And you didn't pass out. You went into an epileptic fit. And this was three days ago."

"No."

"Yes. Mr Light. Accept it. Then we can begin to cure you."

"May I have a cigarette?"

"Of course. Let me loosen your straps."

Christ! I'm strapped to the bed. Like some loony. But at least that means I've still got limbs to strap. When I recall dreaming they'd melted away. And some of it is coming back to me. Watching my hands melt. The lights. The noise. Am I mad? Have I had a breakdown? I feel strange, and tense. What the fuck has happened to me? I came here to relax. I'm certain I did. I can't recall being on the verge of a breakdown. Is that how it works? One minute sane. Then the next the marbles are lost and spilling across the floor. Jesus! God help me get a grip. Accept this lighted cigarette and inhale deeply. Ah. Calm down now. You're in good hands. Relax. Deep breaths. Think nice thoughts.

Shackled once again to this hospital bed. For my own protection so that I don't cause myself injury while thrashing about in the throes of another seizure. Which is unlikely to happen as they've thoughtfully given me a powerful sedative in the concoction of pills they've poured down my throat. Relax now, and drift off to sleep. Soon be well again. Take my place in society as a responsible and upright citizen. Safe in the hands of these good people. God knows what would have happened if I'd had this breakdown while living alone. Came here just in time.

Drifting now in and out of sleep. And in comes an attractive nurse, who smiles and pulls back the sheets to expose my nakedness. Fingers and tongue coaxing my penis to erection. Close my eyes and enjoy the sensation, unsure whether it's real or another hallucination. Enjoy it all the same as I'm teased towards impending orgasm. And as the climax arrives, open my eyes to see the bald pate of the fat puff. His mouth enveloping my deflating penis, milking me of the last drops of fluid. Unable to move. Snap my eyes shut to block out the scene and lapse again into sleep.

Awake again I don't know how much later to find the nurse washing my naked body. She smiles.

"How do you feel, Mr Light?"

"I... I don't know. I've had a nightmare. I think."

"What about?"

"I can't quite remember."

"Dreams are often indications of unconscious desires."

"Not in this case."

God, I hope not. I hope to God it was only a nightmare. But there's no way of telling delusion from reality. Never had any hint of latent tendencies in that direction previously. Must have been a dream. I must be really seriously disturbed if I'm having dreams like that. Not sure if I dare go to sleep again, but I feel so drowsy, I can barely keep my eyes open.

And waking again later, though how much later it's difficult to judge. No clock in this room. Nor any windows. And my shackles are gone. Ease myself out of bed, and don the robe. Desperately need a pee. Try the door. It's locked. No sign of a buzzer that I can see. Nothing else for it. Hitch up the robe and pee in the sink. Christ! Look at the colour! Bright yellow. And a strong smell. Like a tom cat. Run plenty water. Rinse it all away. But the smell persists. A pack of cigs in the robe pocket. Light one up. The smell of smoke should help disguise this rank smell of piss. Inhale deeply. Wow. Feel dizzy again. Like walking the deck of a ship pitching and rolling in heavy seas. Sit on the edge of the bed for a while. Better leave the fags alone for now. Until we enter calmer waters and I get my balance back. The sound of a key turning in the lock, and the nurse entering.

"Ah, Mr Light. You're up and about. How do you feel?"

"Dizzy. Otherwise fine."

"Would you like to join the other guests for dinner?"

"Yes. I'm starving. How long have I been here?"

"Three days."

"Three days?"

"Yes. The doctor says you are now fit to rejoin the group, and return to your own room. But you must continue to take your medication."

"And what medication is that?"

"It's just something to control your seizures. And keep you calm."

"Very well."

"I'll give you an injection tonight. About ten. That should ensure you get a good night's sleep."

"I've done nothing but sleep."

"Rest is a great healer, Mr Light. Come. Follow me."

Along corridors, up and down steps, through doors, and finally reaching the dining room. An empty chair next to Charles, who nods. Sit there, well out of reach of the fat puff, who smiles. Glare back at the dirty, perverted bastard. And feel a hand on my thigh. Move my hand under the table to grip this unwelcome fondler and break all his fingers. But the hand opens, to press a note into mine, and moves quickly away. Shove the note in the pocket.

And after my medication has been administered and the nurse has left, I unfold the note and read another cryptic message.

'Stop smoking. Drink as little wine as possible. You are NOT ILL. Room 19, 11pm tonight. Please come.'

Feeling tired, so I'm inclined to give it a miss. But I'm intrigued. Quietly open the door and peek out into the empty corridor. Follow the numbers on the doors to the staircase. Up one flight, through the door and along another corridor. 17, 18, and here it is. Number 19. Knock quietly. Charles opens the door, grabs my arm and pulls me inside, whispering.

"I'm glad you've come."

"What's all this about, Charles? Chiefs and indians. Stop smoking. Not ill."

"Listen, Ray. You must leave. If you don't go soon, you never will."

"What do you mean? I'll be leaving as soon as they say I'm well enough."

"You're not ill."

"Of course, I'm ill! I've had a breakdown, for Christ's sake."

"They brought it on. With their drugs."

"They? Who?"

"The people who run this so-called Foundation. It's a front. They get people like you to enrol for their three-day courses. Then they drug you. Bring on a seizure. Then keep you sedated while they empty your bank account. I've seen it before, Ray. It's happened to me. And now all my money's gone, I can't leave."

"But if all your money's gone, why would they want to keep you here any longer?"

"They make you work to pay for your keep. The attractive women hand out leaflets in the streets, with promises of sex to lure people in. The not-so-beautiful have to go on the game. And the men clean the booths in the peep-shows, or make up the orders for the porn video business. Listen, Ray. You have to believe this. Stay awake. The cigarettes they issue. The wine. Even the food. All doped. Sedatives, hallucinogens, uppers, downers. All sorts. A real cocktail which turns you psychotic. Then after a spell in the 'hospital', the dosage is changed to keep you under control."

"So why haven't you left?"

"A month ago, I came to Amsterdam. I'd been stealing money from my employer, and falsifying the accounts for a while. Only small amounts. But I knew one day they'd find out. So, I took fifty grand, got on the ferry, and came over here. I just felt I had to make a run for it. I couldn't bear the thought of being caught and going to prison. And I was approached by one of the girls on the street, and she persuaded me to come here. Well, I thought it would be the perfect place to lie low for a few days while I decided what to do. And the next thing I know, I'm having sex with beautiful women, feeling high as a kite, and telling everyone in the therapy group that I've stolen fifty grand. The next thing I know, I'm having a breakdown, and while I'm convalescing, these bastards are bleeding my bank account. So now I can't leave. I've no money to go anywhere else. And I can't go home or I'll be arrested."

"And you say this has happened to the others in the group?"

"Yes. But there are only five others. The rest are not indians. They're chiefs. They're staff, Ray. Not guests. And the one you called the fat puff, he's the biggest chief of the lot. He's the Enlightened One."

"I'm sorry, Charles. I can't believe all this. You're as paranoid as I am."

"You'll see soon enough, I'm afraid. But then it'll be too late. As soon as your money's gone, there'll be no more sex with these beautiful girls. And you'll be moved out of your room and into a dorm. I'm being moved into one tomorrow. Look, if you don't believe me, at least keep your wits about you. Leave off the fags, and the wine. And somehow try to get the injections stopped. You'll see much more clearly what's going on."

"Thanks for the advice."

"Good luck."

"Goodnight."

And quietly back to my room to think about this crazy situation I'm in. I'm ill, but I'm not ill. My body is being cleansed, but pumped full of drugs to make me compliant to their suggestions. Keep my wits about me. If only I could stay awake long enough to concentrate.

And waking in the morning, still confused. Pour myself a glass of this wine, then change my mind and pour it down the sink. Rinse away any tell-tale signs. Light up a cigarette and leave it to burn away in the ashtray. Light another and do the same. Then down to breakfast and follow the day's routine. A massage. But, I note, no offer of sex afterwards. Perhaps I'm considered too ill. Sit quietly through the therapy sessions, pretending to be in a stupor. Until, in the early evening, I am escorted down to the office. A middle-aged woman I haven't seen before welcomes me, but without warmth or charm.

"Sit down, please, Mr Light. I'll get straight to the point. We're experiencing some difficulties with your bank, Mr Light. Our requests for payment are being refused."

"I've already paid for the course."

"Mr Light. Your three-day course has already finished. And there is the cost of your ongoing treatment to consider."

"I see. So how much do I owe you?"

"The outstanding amount is two thousand pounds. And rising daily."

"But there is three thousand in my bank account."

"Not so, Mr Light. That amount has already been withdrawn to cover the treatment you've had."

"Well, I'm sorry. But there is no more."

"When you came here, you said you had a large amount of money. Left to you by your late wife. Plus, the proceeds from the sale of your house."

"I don't remember telling you that."

"But it is true?"

"Yes. The money is in the building society."

"Then you must arrange to have it transferred. To cover the cost of your ongoing treatment."

"Of course. I'll see to it tomorrow. That is, if you'll allow me out to the bank."

"Two of our staff will accompany you. To ensure your safety."

"Fine. Thank you."

Christ! They've gone through three grand already. I can't remember signing any direct debit authorisation or anything. But I must have done. Perhaps Charles is right. These bastards are going to bleed me dry. Skip the evening session and retire to my room to think. Check the wardrobe. Good. My clothes are still here, and a couple of hundred quid in the lining of my jacket, accessible through a small hole in the inside breast pocket. But my credit card and passport are missing. Nip up to room 19, and knock quietly. Thankfully, he's in.

"Come in, Ray."

"I believe you, Charles. I've got to get out."

"You must go tonight. Wait until about two-thirty. The night staff sleep in the house next door. Once they've locked up and put the alarms on, you're OK for an hour or so, until one of them comes around for a quick inspection."

"Are all the exits locked and alarmed?"

"Yes."

"Then how the hell do I get out?"

"I'll help you. Till then, I suggest we join the group until ten, and act normally. Well, as normally as this place will allow. Here. Have one of these."

"No thanks, Charles. No cigarettes. Your advice."

"These are safe. Well, OK, so you might get cancer. But they're real tobacco. None of their pharmaceutical additives. I nicked them from the office a few days ago."

"You sure?"

"Sure."

"Thanks."

Inhale. And savour the taste. And flavour. Funny, but when I was a teenager. I'd go to almost any lengths to get a smoke of illegal substances. But a legal smoke. Well, this is heaven. Take a couple for later. And as soon as I'm free of this place, I shall treat myself to a pack of my favourite brand. And smoke them one after the other. And marvel at how healthy I feel with a racking cough and breath which smells like a camel's arse.

"And Ray. Don't feel too bad about the blow-job."

"What blow-job?"

"The fat puff. Don't worry. We've all been through it. And hoped it was a nightmare. But I'm sorry to say, Ray, it happened. And it's happened to all of us. And there's more, and worse, to come. Unless you get out of here."

"I will."

Joining the group, followed five minutes later by Charles. Sit lazily through it, careful not to offer any opinions nor objections to the drivel being voiced. Just act drugged and ill, and at ten, retire to my room, accompanied by a nurse to administer my injection.

"Pull up your robe and bend over, please, Mr Light."

"I'm sorry. My arse is so sore from the injections I can't sleep properly. Can I possibly have my medication orally?"

"I'll see. Get ready for bed. I'll be back shortly."

"And I believe I'm overdue a body-cleansing session."

"We'll see."

Some chance of that. It's like Charles said. The sex is an inducement, which stops once they've got access to your account.

"OK, Mr Light, you may take these instead of your injection."

Three blue and yellow pills. In a small plastic beaker. Pour a glass of water to swill them down. Throw them into the mouth, and manoeuvre them under the tongue. Drink the water, throw the head back, and gulp. The nurse seems satisfied. Slide under the sheets and wait for her to leave. But I failed to anticipate this next development, as the nurse begins to strap my ankles and wrists to the bedposts. Think, man. Think.

"Not tonight, darling, thank you. Kinky sex is not appropriate for a man in my state of health."

"This is for your own safety, Mr Light. In case you have a seizure."

"But I thought the pills were supposed to prevent my having a seizure."

"Yes. They are."

"Well, then. Leave the shackles off. They cut into me and stop me from sleeping. Besides, I've drunk a lot of your fine wine tonight, and if you tie me down, I'll piss the bed. Please allow me a little dignity."

"How much wine have you had?"

"I've drunk the whole carafe."

"Very well. I'll leave the shackles off. I'll bring you another carafe in case you feel thirsty during the night. Now, try to sleep."

Leap out of bed as soon as she's gone. Spit the pills down the toilet, and flush them away. They've already begun to dissolve in my mouth. Taste the bitter sweetness. Fill a glass with tap water, and gulp it down. Hope to God they haven't tampered with the mains supply. Flush the toilet again as I hear the nurse return. And stagger back towards the bed, and collapse on it, eyes closed, mouth open. She seems satisfied, and leaves the carafe of wine at the bedside. Should be labelled 'For emergency use only. To be taken only when you've decided to devote your life and your money to making some fat old puff very rich.' And after the nurse leaves, leap out of bed and into the toilet. Fingers down the throat. Retch away. Make sure that none of these pills can have their intended effect. Drink another glass of water, and retch again. And again, until my throat is sore. And finally sit on the bed and light up one of Charles's cigs.

Enjoy the harsh but familiar catch at the back of my raw throat. Savour the nicotine, which never tasted so good. All I need now is a good bottle of malt. Put that right at the top of my mental shopping list. Smoke right down to the filter. And then to work. Feel drowsy, yet energetic. I know what has to be done, yet the body resists. Be strong, Ray. One day you'll wish to tell this story. Drag the holdall out from under the bed and dust it off. Open the zip, and neatly fold the contents of the wardrobe into it. Take everything which is mine. And zip up. Pull off this ridiculous quasi-religious robe, and shove it down the pan. And dress like a human being once again. Another glass of water, and Charles's last cigarette. And wait.

Eventually a quiet rap on the door. Let Charles in. Converse in whispers, then make our way down to the office. Which, naturally, is locked. No problem. Charles puts his shoulder against it and bursts it open. Switches on the light, and says, 'Hurry.'

The desk is locked. But a few well-aimed kicks force the top drawer. Nothing of interest in there, so remove it, which gives access to the second drawer. Keys! Throw the whole bunch to Charles, while I continue to explore the contents of the desk. In this drawer, a file. A list of names and addresses. Previous victims? Take it anyway. May be useful.

"Ray, I've got it. The key to the rear fire door."

"Open it. I'm off."

"No, wait. You owe me a favour."

"Fuck you."

"Ray! Your passport. Credit cards. You need them."

"Right."

Ransack these filing cabinets until I find a file marked 'Light, R'. Retrieve my passport, and bank card. Ready to go when Charles holds me back.

"Ray. You've got to see this."

Charles has opened every lock and door with his bunch of keys. Ushers me into a back room off the office. Pull the light cord to find a filing system. Filling the whole far wall from floor to ceiling. A series of wooden shelves, divided into pigeon holes. And on an old pine desk in a corner, another list of names and addresses. Alongside each name a cryptic note of preferred reading and viewing material. Examine the pigeon holes. Pictures of every sexual deviation known to man, woman and beast. Take a closer look at these. Bingo! Photographs of the fat man, naked and slobbering. Engaging in the most disgusting sexual practices with naked young boys. Grab a handful and stuff them in a large envelope from the pile in the drawer. Enclose the mailing list, and a business card and promotional literature for the Foundation. Seal it and write 'Chief of police, Amsterdam' in bold letters on the front. Slip this damning evidence into the nearest post box when I get out. And good old Charles has opened the safe and is gleefully counting out money. Hands me a wad of guilders. A quick calculation. About two grand. That will do nicely.

"OK, Charles. Time to go. You coming with me?"

"No. But I'll create a diversion for you. When we open the door, the alarm will ring. So, you have to move fast. Turn left, and left at the end. A couple of hundred yards down, there's a taxi rank. Don't go to the railway station. Get straight out of town. As far as you can. When they come down, they'll see me wandering in the street, throwing money and photographs in the air. Collecting this lot should keep them occupied for a while. And by the time they've sorted everything out and done a head count, you should be miles away. Good luck."

"Thanks, Charles. And good luck to you."

Unlock the back door and pull it open to the immediate sound of the alarm siren. Turn left and race to the end of the street. A quick look over my shoulder to see Charles standing naked in the middle of the empty street. Throwing bank notes and incriminating photographs into the air and laughing maniacally.

Down the street and into a waiting cab. Den Haag, please. And step on it. Stop briefly at a street corner on the outskirts. Pop the envelope in this red box. And relax in the back seat as the taxi speeds through the cold night. And a change of mind. No point in staying in Holland any longer than necessary, particularly as I may be implicated in the theft of an amount of money. Though, arguably, it was stolen from me in the first place. Instruct the driver to head straight for Rotterdam and the first ferry home. Negotiate the price for the journey, including a sizeable tip, on the understanding that, if questioned, the driver will say he took me to the airport. An agreeable man, he even changes a note for me so that I can get some cigarettes from a vending machine. And when I get back in the taxi, I sit in front with him, and supply him with cigarettes as he drives. And tells me some of the rumours he's heard of the Foundation. Run by an evil fat man, who controls many of the city's prostitutes and sex shops. I tell him of the envelope and its contents, and he seems pleased that the police will have the evidence to close down the Foundation and put the Fat One in prison for a very long time. And finally arriving in Rotterdam, he drops me at a cafe which is open for breakfast, and gives me the address of a hotel where I can rest up for the day until the ferry sails. He shakes my hand and wishes me luck.

And in this backstreet hotel I shave off the moustache and hope I don't have any problems at passport control. Lie on the bed to rest for a while, then venture out for lunch. Keep to the back streets. And wear dark sunglasses on this dark sunless day. A few hours to kill. Trawl round the shops and market and eat in a quiet bistro. Indulge my passion for continental meats and cheeses. And choose a bottle of wine whose contents have not been tampered with. Savour the freedom as long as it lasts.

CHAPTER 30

Check out of the hotel in the rain and into the waiting taxi to the ferry terminal. Purchase a ticket and through passport control without a problem. All aboard and cast off into the dark North Sea. Stow my baggage in the cramped cabin and make my way to the bar. A large Malt. My hands shaking as I down it, and call for another. And unwind as passengers throng around, mercifully paying me little attention. And after a five-course dinner, I'm back in the bar where I feel I belong. Drinking alone and looking as unsociable as I can, ignoring any glances I get from fellow passengers. Don't encourage conversation nor seek company. I feel in control on my own, which is a strange thing to say considering the problems I've had since Lucy's death.

"That's another fine mess I've got myself into."

"I beg your pardon?"

A buxom, auburn-haired lady, smartly dressed, at my side, a quizzical expression on her face.

"I'm sorry. I was talking to myself."

"Travelling alone?"

"Yes."

"Then please come and join my sister and myself."

"Thanks, but I'm not very good company. I've been ill."

"All the more reason not to sit drinking on your own. Come on, my sister's waiting. My name's Eve. That's my twin sister Brenda over there."

Pointing in the direction of a tall lady with similarly luxuriant auburn hair. Big busted and matronly, but smiling and welcoming. Join them at their table. Introduce myself and sit between them on the well-padded comfortable bench seat. Engage in small talk but give nothing away. I won't feel completely safe until I'm back on home ground. Brenda's manicured hand resting lightly on my knee as she leans forward to ask her sister to get more drinks. Refusing my offer to get them as I simply must stay and talk to her. And when her sister has gone, she asks me if I have a cabin. A gleam in her eye as I say yes. And yes, I am a naughty man, and yes, you may come to my cabin for some fun and games, and no, not a word to your sister. Eve returning with a tray of drinks. And when Brenda goes to the Ladies, Eve asks me if I'll spend the night with her.

"I'm sorry. I can't."

"Why ever not? Not gay, are you?"

"No."

"Well, then. Don't you find me just a little bit attractive?"

"Well, yes. Of course. But..."

"But what?"

"I can't."

"I'll pay you."

"It's not a matter of money. I... I have other arrangements."

"Brenda! It's Brenda, isn't it? That little shit. She knew I was sizing you up. And she's propositioned you, hasn't she?"

"Well. Er."

"I knew it. We agreed. The next one was mine. She had George on the way over. This is most unfair. And I'm a better lay. She's a selfish lover. I'm not. I give as good as I take."

Brenda returning to the table. Her smile fading as she sees the glowering Eve. She sits down, pressed close against me, her hand on my thigh. Eve hissing and spitting venom.

"You bitch! Cocksucker! Slack-fannied whore!"

"It's not my fault if Ray chooses to spend the night with me. You shouldn't be so shy with men. You missed your chance. And Ray's not interested in you, you old tart."

"Saggy-jugged slapper!"

"Easy, ladies! Calm down for Christ's sake. Don't cause a scene. People are staring. Sort it out between yourselves. I'm going to sit at the bar for some peace. Goodnight, ladies."

Ordering another large Malt. Can't even indulge in some civilised copulation without inciting sibling rivalry. Leave them squabbling at the table.

"Ray. Excuse me. I've come to apologise. Please forgive our behaviour."

"Of course."

"Thank you. We've reached a decision. Or, rather, a compromise. If you're interested. We'd like to share you."

"Share?"

"Yes. A threesome. We've never done it before. But why not? I'm sure we'll all find it an extremely erotic experience. Cabin 344b. Come down in ten minutes. We'll be ready for you."

Order another drink. To fortify the body for the imminent copulatory Clash of the Titians. And make my way down stairs and along corridors. Deep within the bowels of this vessel. Feel the rumbling throb of the engines beneath. And the throbbing within the trousers as I reach the door of cabin 344b, and knock gently. Eve's head appears and she yanks me inside the roomy double cabin with its equally roomy double bed. On which reposes Brenda, naked. Eve is wearing a pale blue pyjama top, unbuttoned. And nothing else.

"I hope you don't mind, but we tossed a coin. And Brenda gets first go. Let's get your things off."

Eve tearing at my clothes, throwing them on to a chair.

"Good God, Brenda! Look at the size of that! Leave some for me."

Eve's hand on my erection, leading me to the bed where Brenda is now sitting on the edge, mouth open. Eve supervising the docking manoeuvre, stroking my balls as Brenda leaves lipstick rings, like tide-marks, on my length. Then quickly on to all fours, smiling at me through her legs. I mount the bed and Brenda in a flash. Eve kissing me, then her sister, her hand trailing between Brenda's legs, rubbing her clit and my stalk at the same time. Brenda meeting my thrusts, breathing hard. Eve plucking at her nipples until she climaxes and collapses onto her stomach as I slide out. Eve on her back now, pulling me towards her, guiding me easily in. Brenda's hands on my buttocks, not trying to spur me on but drag me away. Grabbing my scrotum in a desperate attempt to pull me off. As Eve grips my length and tries to do the same. My genitals the rope in this tribal tug-of-war as the sisters fight for the spoils. A backhander from Brenda draws blood from the nose of a startled Eve. Who responds by launching a swinging right fist smack to her sister's mouth.

"Bitch!"

"Twat!"

Brenda grabbing Eve roughly by the tits. Pulling her forward to deliver a head-butt to the bridge of her once-dainty nose. Blood splattering the sheets. Howls of pain and fury as bejewelled and manicured fingers tear at each other's tearful eyes.

Slide unnoticed off the bed and into the trousers. Pick up the rest of my clothes and bundle them into my jacket. Stow it safely under my arm and edge towards the door. Carefully turn the handle, open the door and run. Away from these savage sisters. Leave them to do it for themselves.

Bemused expressions on the faces of fellow passengers as I make my way back to the safety of my cabin and bolt the door behind me. Stand with my back against the door, breathing heavily. Drop the trousers and inspect the genitals in the small mirror above the corner washbasin. Some redness, but thankfully no scratches nor lasting damage. Slide into the narrow bunk bed. And sleep. To a dream of being pursued by Amazons who wanted not my head on a pole. But just my pole.

Skipping breakfast, lying in my bunk until I feel the engines slow and slam into reverse. Wash and dress, and wait until we dock before I leave this haven.

The engines now silent, I step gingerly through the door into the corridor. A queue ahead waiting to disembark. No sign of the titian twins. Join the queue, seeking safety in numbers. And shuffle along until I'm on the quayside. Walk briskly and confidently through passport control and the unattended green customs lane. And out again into the cold damp morning air to join the queue at the taxi rank. When a shout of my name brings panic and causes my pulse to race.

"Ray! There you are. We've been looking all over for you. We didn't see you at breakfast."

"Er. No. I overslept."

The twins. Both wearing dark glasses. And heavily made-up to hide the bruises. A headscarf covering Eve's red hair. Or what's left of it. Clumps probably all over their cabin. Riven out by Brenda's gold-ringed fingers.

"Can we offer you a lift?"

"No. Thanks. I'm waiting for a taxi."

"You'll be ages in this queue. Are you going into Hull?"

"Yes. To the station."

"We go right past it. Come on. We'll take you."

"Thank you. But I don't mind waiting. I'm not in any hurry."

"Don't be afraid. Brenda and I have settled our differences. You'll be quite safe with us. I promise. Come on. We insist."

"Very well."

Across the car park to this long black limousine beside which the ladies come to a halt. Brenda digging a coin from her handbag and spinning it in the air.

"Call."

"Tails!"

"It's heads. You lose. You drive."

"Bollocks! Best of three?"

"No! Besides, it's only fair. I had to drive on the way here. When you sat in the back with that young hitch-hiker. Who said he was a virgin. But not for long. I was watching you in the mirror, you naughty cow. I heard him say thank you, and how much do I owe you, and you said if you really want to pay me, then lick this. A nice young boy, with a dick like a stallion. You should have seen her, Ray. For days after she walked like John Wayne and complained of a sore fanny. Serves her right. Well, it's my turn now. So here. Take these. You drive, I ride."

"Can I just get a quick feel of him before you start?"

"No! Drive. And keep your eyes on the road."

Tossing the keys to Eve, who mumbles obscenities under her breath and climbs into the driver's seat while Brenda bundles me into the back with her. The limo moving smoothly away as Eve shifts effortlessly through the gears and on to the main thoroughfare. Adjusting the rear-view mirror for a clear view of the back seats of soft black leather.

"Keep your eyes on the road, Eve, dear."

Brenda laughing. Unzipping my trousers and feeling within for signs of life. Suitably encouraged, unfastening my belt and waist button, a huge smile on her swollen lips. Dragging my trousers down, hitching up her skirt, and straddling me, one hand beneath her to ease me in.

Catch sight of Eve's dark glasses, her eyes doubtless watching every move through her mirror.

Riding into Hull, feeling every bump in the road. Brenda taking up a steady rhythm, staring over my shoulder out of the rear window. Waving at a following van driver, who almost misses his turning, veering left at the last moment. Horns blaring as vehicles brake suddenly. As Brenda rides on unperturbed until my own horn blasts its final trumpet and the battery runs flat, and she climbs off, a trace of sweat on her bruised upper lip.

"There. Now that's what I call a ride into town. Are you sure you want dropping off at the station? Only, I think, Eve is ever so jealous."

"The station will be fine. Thank you."

Eve staring at me through her dark glasses. Avert my eyes and look out of the window. To see a wagon driver alongside giving me the thumbs up and pointing at my wilting manhood. Smile back and give him a coy wave. And pull up my trousers before he broadcasts a running commentary on his CB radio. Imagining the convoy of voyeur wagons accompanying us into the city centre. Horns blowing all round. The sisters would be in their element. And both would be bald, bruised, bloody and battered by the end of the day.

CHAPTER 31

Train from Hull to Leeds, then on to this city where I was born. From the station I can see the towering office block. The UK headquarters of the company which employed me for many years. If there was a defining moment in my life, apart from meeting Lucy, it was, I think, the day I was asked to report to the Operations' Director's office where I was informed in a peremptory manner that, due to restructuring, my services were no longer required. And given a generous pay-off cheque and advice on how to claim benefit.

Check in at this grand old hotel which once stood proudly at the entrance to the railway station but now nestles among office blocks built when the rail terminus was re-sited and the area redeveloped. Faded pictures in the foyer evoking a bygone age of the great days of steam. Shown to my room by a young boy in grubby uniform, who struggles under the weight of my holdall. Tip him some coins and receive grudging thanks. Feel jaded and listless, probably due as much to the pharmacological abuse I was made to endure as lack of sleep and copulatory exertions. Shave and shower, then out onto the streets. First stop, the building society. Change these guilders into real money, and withdraw another wad. Present my passbook at the counter and explain the nature of the required transaction to the bespectacled, corporate-clothed teller.

"Do you have any other form of identification, Mr Light?"

Push my passport under the glass. Watch as she examines the old photograph.

"Well, it does bear more than a passing resemblance to you. But the moustache?"

"I shaved it off. Would you like me to wait here until it grows back?"

Sarcasm has no effect on these people.

"Could you tell me your date of birth, please?"

"It's on the passport."

"Yes. I know. I'm merely following the security rules. To ensure you are who you say you are."

"I am who I say I am. I should know."

"Could you tell me your wife's maiden name?"

"No."

"And why not?"

"I don't have a wife. She died."

"Well, your late wife's maiden name then, sir."

"Lucy the Angel of Summer."

"Pardon?"

"Lucy Angela Summer. A beautiful evocative name, don't you think?"

"Mmm. This is rather a large amount, Mr Light. I'll have to get authorisation. Would you wait a moment, please?"

And she disappears, leaving me at the counter to grow a moustache as the queue lengthens behind me. Returning, she asks if I'd kindly go through to the manager's office to see Mr Cartwright. Greeted with a warm vigorous handshake by this affable young money manipulator. Shows me into his sumptuous office, all oak-panelled and leather-furnished. No doubt financed from the unpaid interest on dormant accounts.

"I'm very pleased to meet you, Mr Light. Back in your home city, I believe."

"How do you know that?"

"Computer files, Mr Light. The wonder of the modern age. Facts at fingertips. Or rather at the click of a mouse. I know, in fact, a great deal about you."

"In that case, perhaps you could inform your staff of my identity in order that I can withdraw my money from my account."

"Due diligence, Mr Light. Or may I call you Raymond?"

"You may call me Mr Light. No familiarity until I get my money."

"Of course. You look, if you don't mind my saying so, a little under the weather today."

"I've been ill."

"Nothing serious, I hope."

"Gulf War Syndrome."

"Served in the Gulf, did you?"

"No. Gulf War Syndrome by Proxy. I watched it on the news. It had a dreadful effect on me. I'm pursuing damages through the courts. Now, about my money."

"Of course. But I hope you won't fail to be impressed by the fact that we do have certain checks and controls in place to ensure that no-one but your good self has access to your not unsubstantial funds. I mean, what if someone stole your passbook and forged your signature? You would be somewhat dismayed if money was withdrawn by anyone but yourself."

"There is obviously no possibility of that happening unless such a person has access to my entire life history. And knows my inside leg measurement. And that sort of information is, I suspect, readily available on your computer system."

"Well, yes. But the system is quite secure. I assure you. It's all password protected."

"What is your wife's name?"

"Rachel. Why do you ask?"

"Because your password is L-E-H-C-A-R, or the name of one of your children, or your date of birth. Probably backwards."

"What makes you think that?"

"Because people who work in building societies don't have the imagination to come up with anything unpredictable."

"Well anyway, Mr Light. I'm quite happy to allow you to make this withdrawal in cash. But I would like to offer you some free advice regarding your money."

"Go on."

"Well, you have a large amount in this instant access deposit account."

"Instant access is, I think, a misnomer."

"And you have a bank current account which is empty, for whatever reason."

"I was robbed. By someone who managed to circumvent the system's inbuilt checks and controls."

"And you seem to have no other equity."

"So?"

"Well, it doesn't make financial sense to keep all your eggs, so to speak, in one basket. You should really be thinking of investing a lump sum in a long-term plan."

"Why?"

"Well, for when you retire."

"I've already retired."

"Nonsense. You're too young and fit and healthy to wish to retire."

"Do your computer files show any evidence of recent regular income?"

"Well, no. But if you invested, say sixty thousand, you would have a nice little nest-egg when you're sixty-five. Just let me work out some projections for you. Based on given rates of growth."

"Don't bother. I have no intention of living until I'm sixty-five."

"Ah. I understand your distress, Mr Light. I know you have recently lost your wife. And may I say how sorry I am."

"You may."

"But if you were to invest the bulk of this capital now, and get a little job to keep you going, you could live very comfortably in your old age."

"I had a little job. And didn't like it. And I wish to live very comfortably now, thank you."

"But Mr Light. As custodian of your funds, I would be failing in my duty if I didn't give you the best possible advice. I see myself as the captain of a ship. And my account-holders as passengers. It is my duty to steer a safe course through stormy financial waters, and deliver my passengers, and their nest eggs, to their chosen port of call."

"Well, Captain Fartright. It seems you have a mutineer on board. And if I don't get what I demand, I will scuttle your ship. And you will go down with it. Do I make myself clear?"

"How would you like the cash, Mr Light?"

Comforting bulge of the wad in the inside pocket. There's nothing to beat standing one's ground against a smug arsehole who knows what's good for you. And whose ego needs deflating now and again to remind him that there are real people outside the confines of his plush office. Real people, with real opinions. Not case studies. Or role-play participants.

And take a walk around these city streets, which are vaguely familiar though so much has changed. The old Victorian office blocks of blackened stone have been sandblasted, though their eaves are still streaked with starling shit. And out of the city centre, it's uphill all the way whichever direction you take. Every now and again a flash as a shaft of weak sunlight bursts through the clouds and reflects off the dome of the mosque. Built on the site of a demolished Methodist chapel. A range of pungent smells from the diverse ethnic restaurants concentrated in this quarter and mixing with the foul stench from a burst sewer somewhere close by. The area rather quiet at the moment, but after dark it will come to life as the whores hit the streets and the kerb-crawling drivers pursue their chosen sordid ritual. The mosque will be calling the faithful to prayer, while, on the pavement opposite, the tarts call the unfaithful to their dubious pleasure.

Leaving these litter strewn streets behind as I amble through this municipal park with its graffiti-covered toilet block, now boarded up. When I was six I'd come to the funfair with my parents and gone in there for a pee. And an old man had watched me and raised his eyebrows and asked me if I'd like to see his snake. And I said yes. And he undid his trousers and said touch it and watch it grow as my dad walked in and thumped him, and called him some words I'd never heard before but which I guessed were bad because he said if he ever heard me repeat them he'd thump me too.

Out through these ornate gates once resplendent in green and gold but now rust brown. Wide streets now, tree-lined and clean. Large detached houses with polished cars outside. Here and there an old Victorian lamppost in a well-tended garden. Mock-Victorian conservatories adding space to already huge homes. The sweet smell of affluence in the air, a welcome contrast to the earlier rank odour of effluence.

Into this florist's shop. Two bunches of sweet-smelling and colourful blooms. I neither know nor care what variety. As long as they're fresh and pretty. Take them just down the road and through this imposing arched entrance of blackened stone. Into this place of peace and rest. The borders well-tended. Smell of newly cut grass. Follow the main track downhill, then branch off left by the ornate gothic mausoleum, the monument of a late local industrialist. And two small headstones side by side. Mum and dad. Thankfully undesecrated and free of graffiti unlike some of the others. Pick up the empty crisp packets and discarded can of lighter fuel. A general tidy-up. And place the flowers in the two empty receptacles. Never had much of an eye for flower arranging. Lucy's job. But a reasonable enough effort, bringing a touch of colour and brightness to the scene. Rest in peace, you two. And don't worry. I'm OK.

And further down, set back from the road is the church where we were wed. Stop and read the notices at the gate. Banns, coffee mornings, youth club, and a poster showing a thermometer charting the progress of the roof restoration fund. Still some way off its target. Walk down the path to the open door. The first time I've entered a church since that happy day. Cold and dim inside, but peaceful and welcoming, with freshly cut flowers on the table by the entrance. Standing in the aisle, eyes closed. Remembering that day when the church was full of friends and relatives witnessing the beginning of our life together. The collection box for the restoration fund bears a notice 'Please give generously'. Sad to see that the box has to be secured to the table with a stout padlock and chain. Sign of the times. Extract a twenty from the wad in the jacket pocket, fold it and push it down through the narrow slot. And behold the miracle! As a shaft of sunlight escapes the clouds and, fractured by the ornate stained-glass window, casts a kaleidoscopic pattern on the ground before me, picking out the names of the departed on the slabs of stone. Watch the motes of dust play and dance in the light. And one of these sunbeams is Lucy. A magical moment. The sound of a throat clearing breaking the spell. Turning to face a smiling ageing vicar.

"Good morning. Can I help you?"

"Good morning. I'm sorry... I just walked in... I've been here before. I was married here. A long time ago."

"You are welcome. The door to God's house is always open."

"I'm not a believer."

"Few people are these days. I spend as much time tending to the secular problems of my parishioners as I do their spiritual needs. Your wife?"

"Dead."

"I am sorry. Recently?"

"A few months."

"And now you're revisiting your past. Clinging to your happy memories."

"Yes."

"That's understandable. But you mustn't grieve forever. You must move on. Cherish your memories. But you can't live in the past."

"The church does!"

"Indeed. We try to keep up with the times. Try to convince people that Our Saviour is alive."

"And is he?"

"I believe so. I wouldn't have followed this vocation if ever I'd thought otherwise. But there are so many people who think religion has had its day. And look what's happened. The world today is not the place it was when I grew up."

"Don't live in the past, reverend."

"Ha, ha. Touché."

"I feel guilty, reverend."

"About what?"

"My wife."

"How did she die?"

"Cancer."

"So why the guilt?"

"I couldn't feel her pain. Only mine. I know that towards the end she was in such agony. And suffered pain that the drugs just couldn't relieve. And I kept thinking what's going to happen to me. How will I cope? Why did she have to die and leave me to go on without her?"

"Will you pray with me?"

"I wouldn't know how."

"It's easy. You don't even need to kneel. You can bow your head if you wish. Close your eyes if you wish. Put your hands together, if you wish. Or put them in your pockets. It really doesn't matter."

"OK."

Stand next to this kind old man with the warm soothing voice. My hands clasped, head bowed in silence, listening to his quiet words.

"Oh Lord, I beseech thee. Look down with mercy upon this young man who has known such grief. Be with him in his hour of need, and give him the strength to bear his cross. Light his darkness and show him the way. Amen."

"Amen."

"Don't let your sorrow cloud your judgment. I know you are a good man. Not a saint, but neither are you an irredeemable sinner. You may have given up on God, but, believe me, He hasn't given up on you."

"Thank you, reverend."

"Goodbye, young man."

"Goodbye."

I'm not sure what to make of all this. Still, it's nice to know that God's on my side. And if He is alive, and watching over me, perhaps He could lend a hand the next time I'm outnumbered in a fight. Hurl a few lightning bolts, and plagues of locusts at my assailants. Just enough to distract them while I get in a few good blows.

Taking the bus on the circular route, and alighting close to the area where I was born in a tiny back-to-back terrace house with gas lighting and open fire. Demolished some thirty years ago to be replaced by high-rise flats, which were in turn torn down to make way for these two-storey modern townhouses, continuing the cycle of decay and regeneration. These new homes all identical, distinguishable only by the brass numbers on their homogeneous doors. A satellite dish mounted high up on each house front, beaming mind-numbing game-shows to the masses. Fuelling their dreams that consumer goods, holidays and cash prizes are theirs for the taking by phoning in the obvious answer to a simple multiple-choice question. Cheap starter homes for the disadvantaged in society, whose living expenses are provided by the taxpayer, and for whom life is hard, with only their beer and cigs and satellite TV to sustain them. And down past

Patterson's newsagents, now an Asian mini-market; the fish shop next door a Chinese takeaway. Dad will be turning in his grave. His xenophobic instincts were aroused at the sight of the first West Indian bus conductor, whom, when drunk, he would accuse of taking jobs from British citizens. And the conductor, his hair like Velcro which attracted every speck of white fluff, would just flash a wide smile and produce his British passport. God knows what dad would have made of today's multicultural society.

And this is the street where Scruff met his untidy and untimely death. Traffic calming measures recently introduced. Road bumps and chicanes to keep the speeding drivers on their toes. Follow the route of my one-time paper round. New housing schemes here and there. Sheltered flats for the ageing population. Warden-controlled and with entry systems to deter opportunist thieves who would without guilt or remorse smash in some old man's face to steal a tenner. A violent society, overrun by the lawless. A few still strive to maintain a vestige of civilisation, tending gardens and keeping their homes in good order, as the last wisps of smoke

drift through their windows from the skeleton of a burnt-out car on the waste ground opposite.

Head back towards the city centre down this main thoroughfare. Past the cinema where we would eagerly queue every Saturday morning to watch Flash Gordon save the Universe. Where are you now, Flash? And the cinema which closed down to become a bingo hall is now a carpet warehouse. Handwritten signs outside advertising closing down bargains. Further along, the car showroom. Now used cars, but once the main dealer in luxury limos. I used to press my nose against the gleaming plate glass and marvel at the shiny Mercedes, and the salesmen in their expensive suits. And I promised myself that one day I'd own one. I never did get my Merc, but at least I had the privilege to ride in one, and wear an expensive suit. For our wedding. Did full justice to the occasion. So long ago, yet still fresh in my mind. A cold, rainy morning. And as we left the church, the sun came out briefly while the photographs were taken. And then the rain set in again for the rest of the day. But nothing could have spoiled our day, not even the brief uninvited appearance at the reception of Predator One. Whom Duncan took quietly aside and persuaded to leave without causing a fuss. I later discovered he'd given her twenty quid to go away and get drunk somewhere else. Turning left down a side road, and here it is. Now painted in different corporate colours, the local brewery having been long since bought out by one of the brewing giants, it nonetheless looks much the same. The old double doors open and inviting to the weary traveller. Who am I to resist? Dimly lit inside but warm. A group of schoolboys drinking quietly in a corner, as we used to do all those years ago. Long school lunchtimes spent here with a couple of pints and a dish of warming pie and peas. And sometimes the English master would come in, and just nod politely. And never reported us. And the landlord knew we were under age, but turned a blind eye as long as we behaved. Then one day he told us we were welcome to come in on an evening as long as we were quiet and didn't draw attention to ourselves. A nice cool pint, followed by a second. Then back out into the cold afternoon air. Under the old railway bridge, its branch line long since torn up and overgrown with weeds and brambles. And straight ahead, the old school. Huge timbers propping up a gable end of the assembly hall. The school playing fields littered with interconnecting portable classrooms. Temporary homes for the pupils while the councillors decide whether to demolish the main building and start anew. Or to disperse the kids to other schools. Or to keep on patching up this crumbling edifice whose roofs leaked thirty years ago. And while they ruminate, and debate the issues in the council chambers, these portakabins gradually assume an air of permanence.

Down a narrow alley between the allotments, from which we used to steal rhubarb. And at the end, a long lane at whose streetlamps we used to fire stones from a catapult, and were often chased away. Only to hide among the allotments and emerge when the coast was clear. A thriving industrial estate of small units here now, on the site of the former woollen mill which burned down one night lighting up the November sky. I could see the glow from my attic bedroom skylight and watched for hours. Listening to the clanging bells of the fire engines, and hearing the distant breaking of glass, the crack of burning timber, and the rumble and thud of collapsing masonry. All caused by the spontaneous ignition of oily fleeces. Over seventy nightshift workers escaped. But two died.

On to the end and back on the main road. Nearing the centre now. Large, high-ceilinged houses on both sides, their front gardens buried under tarmac to provide parking for the staff of these small businesses which now occupy them. Solicitors, estate agents, insurance brokers, providers of financial services. Each with a hand in the others' pockets. A society of mutual back-scratchers. And here it is. Kelly and Kelly plc. Black BMW parked in front. Walk in to reception and ask the girl sitting at the desk, idly thumbing through a magazine.

"Good afternoon. Could I see Mrs Kelly, please?"

"Do you have an appointment?"

"Only with my Maker."

"Pardon?"

"No."

"I'm afraid she's with a client at the moment."

"May I wait?"

"Certainly. Is there anything I can help you with? I haven't been here long, but I've learnt quite a lot already. I'm sure I could answer your questions."

"I don't think so. Thank you."

"Try me."

"Very well. Perhaps you could tell me how many species of Lepidoptera there are in Britain."

"What's leopard...whatever you said?"

"Lepidoptera."

"Well, what is it?"

"Never mind. I'm sure Mrs Kelly will be able to help."

A side door opening and out comes a man carrying a briefcase. Behind him, Mrs Kelly, who shakes his hand and ushers him out as she catches sight of me. Her usual warm smile as she walks over and hugs me.

"Hello, Ray. How are you?"

"Fine, Elaine, love. You?"

"I'm fine. Working hard. Keeping the business afloat. But surviving."

"I'm pleased."

"What's happened to your face? Have you been in an accident?"

"I was attacked. At Christmas. Young lads with nothing better to do."

"Come through to the office. We'll talk. It's good to see you. You've lost weight."

"You too."

"I needed to. You don't."

"I'm on a hunger strike."

"And what are you protesting about?"

"The fact that I'm not eating enough."

Follow her through to the cramped office. A few filing cabinets, and a desk, littered with paper and files bursting open at the seams. Note her shapely legs beneath the smart sapphire blue business suit. New hairdo, cut shorter than of late. Takes years off her. I wonder if Duncan realises what he's given up.

"You don't change, Ray."

"I don't intend to. Not now."

"Still hurts, doesn't it?"

"Of course. But now it's just like...I don't know, like a gnawing sort of ache. Like when you're deprived of something you really came to rely on. And even knowing that it's going to happen doesn't help. You can make plans, and resign yourself to the inevitability of it all. But then when it's happened, you're still crushed. And stifled. The spark, the light. It's missing. And you just drift. And things happen. And you just let them. You don't feel able to take control. Because it really doesn't matter that much anyway. Because if you're happy, you are going to die. And if you're miserable, you're going to die. So, who cares?"

"That's a very cynical nihilistic view to take, Ray."

"So?"

"So, you should really think about what Lucy brought to your life. How happy she made you. And how she would have wanted you to continue to be happy. She married a man who was full of life and love. Do you really think she'd approve of your attitude to life now?"

"Probably. She said I'd to live my life however I wanted. She wouldn't be there to pull in the reins to curb my excesses."

"But she would have wanted you to be happy."

"I am. In a fashion. I'm carefree."

"Carefree is not the same as couldn't care less."

"Change the subject, Elaine. Lecture time is over."

"OK, Ray. What brings you back here? And how long are you staying?"

"Nostalgia, I suppose. Looking for some roots I can cling to. To stop me sliding downhill. And I don't know how long. A few days maybe. I've an appointment with my solicitor today, to tie up a few loose ends. Then there's nothing to keep me."

"And then where to? Back to Scarsby?"

"No. I've sold the house. And all its contents. All my worldly goods now fit neatly in a single holdall."

"Burnt all your bridges?"

"Yes."

"Oh, Ray. You poor man."

"I don't want your sympathy, Elaine."

"No. Of course. Have you...have you heard any word from Duncan?"

"Yes. I had a letter a couple of weeks ago."

"And how is he?"

"He's fine."

"Good. How does he like America?"

"He's in Tenerife."

"Tenerife? Good god! Mind you, why should I be surprised? I couldn't keep track of him when we were married and working together."

"It's his way, Elaine. How he is. I always envied him, you know."

"He always envied you. The perfect couple, he called you and Lucy. Not in any nasty sarcastic way. It was just pure admiration. Where Duncan and I always seemed to have to argue over any important decisions, you, either of you, just made them. With the full backing of the other. Duncan used to remind me that in fifteen years you and Lucy had never had an argument, whereas he and I couldn't last fifteen minutes in each other's company without the fur flying."

"But you loved each other."

"Yes. We did. And more than that, we needed each other as we raised the kids and matured, and came to realise what each of us really wanted from our lives. And eventually, we realised we didn't want each other."

"And what did you realise you want?"

"I have a career. A business."

"That's a living, Elaine. Not a life."

"I want a man I can rely on. Nothing more, nothing less. Someone to talk to. Someone to lean on. Someone to be there, when I need someone. Someone who is prepared to give as well as take. Can you understand that? Is it too much to ask?"

"I don't know, Elaine. I only know that failed marriages are more common that successful ones. But then again, yours would be regarded as successful considering its duration."

"You get used to people. You adapt. You compromise. You fight and argue without ever solving anything. And eventually, you just go along with it because it's easier than breaking it up. Then one day, you finally realise that enough is enough. And you call it a draw. Settle as amicably as possible. And throw yourself into something to kill the pain and occupy the time, and make you feel as if you've accomplished something on your own. Anything. Just to justify your decision to let go. And when you've done it you have to keep up the pretence. Of being successful and happy. While sweaty-palmed middle-aged men see you as single and successful and fair game. And they put business your way, in the hope that you'll pay commission by opening your legs and watching them dribble in their Y-fronts. Whereas Duncan would just take them out for a drink and a meal, and if they wanted more, he'd send a half-decent-looking whore to their hotel room. Usually a girl he'd vetted personally."

"Sounds like you miss him."

"Sometimes, yes. But most of the time, definitely not."

"What was it that attracted you to him in the first place?"

"He was a real charmer. Very attentive. Always happy and full of ideas. He made me laugh. And he made me feel special."

"He still loves you."

"I still love him. In a funny sort of way. At least life's never dull when he's around."

"I can't argue with that."

"So where are you staying?"

"Hotel. Near the station."

"Why don't you stay with me for a few days? There's room. And you'd be more comfortable."

"I have everything I need."

"But it's so expensive."

"Doesn't matter. Money is for spending. I've no-one to leave it to."

"Are you looking for a job?"

"No."

"Your money won't last forever, Ray."

"It'll last long enough."

"Long enough for what?"

"For what I want to do. What I have to do."

"You were never a quitter."

"Things change."

"Come and stay with me for a few days. Take time to think."

"I couldn't do that, Elaine."

"Hey, I'm offering you a bed. Not my bed."

"If you were, I couldn't accept. You're...you were Duncan's wife. I couldn't do that to him. However much I've wanted to over the years."

"You never said."

"No."

"Funny, I felt the same way about you."

"You never said."

"I would never have done anything to spoil your relationship with Lucy. Though I wish she'd felt the same."

"What do you mean?"

"Lucy wasn't an angel, Ray."

"I don't follow."

"I suppose you should know. You have a right to know. She had affairs, Ray. Several that I know of."

"I don't believe you."

"I'm sorry, but it's true."

"No. She wouldn't...Why?"

"She got bored, Ray. After you'd been together about six years. She talked to me about it. Said she needed some excitement. Her life was too orderly. Too predictable. And so, one night we went out on the town together. And both got ourselves laid. By two young lads. A sordid little episode. In the back of a car. One which I never repeated, however much Duncan cheated on me. But Lucy carried on seeing the lad for a few months before she broke it off and took up with a married man. Then it became a game for her, and there were others, lots of them. Some even charged for the privilege. And finally, when she became ill, she'd got it out of her system, and returned to acting the devoted wife. At least she was discreet, Ray."

"I had no idea. She never told me she was bored or anything. Jesus!"

"I'm sorry, Ray. I've only told you because you're acting as if Lucy's death is the end of the world. It doesn't have to be. You owe it to yourself, and to Lucy, to go on and enjoy your life. Nobody's perfect, Ray."

"I thought Lucy was."

"I'm sorry to disappoint. But angels don't exist. Just be grateful she didn't carry the child to full term."

"You mean it wasn't..."

"It wasn't yours, Ray. An accident."

Buzz on the intercom. The receptionist announcing the arrival of the next client.

"Ray. I'm sorry. I'll have to go."

"It's been nice seeing you again, Elaine."

"Take care, Ray. And if you change your mind, just turn up on the doorstep anytime. You're always welcome."

"Thanks, Elaine. Goodbye."

"Bye, Ray."

Tears in her eyes as we hug. Wiping them away and assuming her natural engaging smile as she goes out to greet her client. Gives my hand a warm comforting squeeze as I leave.

A drop of rain as I head down towards the city centre. Turning to sleet in the cold north-westerly. Snow forecast for high ground and blizzards in the highlands of Scotland. But here in the heart of the city it always seems to rain. Turn down the side road and enter the office of James W. Blegg, Solicitor and Commissioner for Oaths. Of which I've uttered a few, uncommissioned, in my time.

"Come in, Ray. Good to see you. What can I do for you today?"

"I just called in for a chat, Jim. And to check there's no unfinished business."

"No. Everything's in order. No loose ends. I have your Will and details of all your financial arrangements. The only thing I don't have is your permanent address."

"That's because I don't have one."

"And where are you staying?"

"Here and there."

"Hotels?"

"Mainly."

"And for how long?"

"As long as I feel like it. Or until the money runs out. If I stay anywhere more than a few days, I'll send you the address so you can keep track of my whereabouts."

"Why not settle here? You've still got friends here. I'm sure you could get a job. The area's become a magnet for the service industries. Call Centres springing up all over."

"I don't want a job. I had one once and didn't like it."

"Ray, take my advice. Take a long holiday. Recharge the batteries. Go somewhere nice and warm. And relax. Take stock. Give yourself a break."

"I've had a break, and I am relaxed."

"You're determined to go through with this, aren't you?"

"Yes."

"But why? You're still young. And healthy. Still full of life."

"Life's empty."

"Well, let me put it another way. Your life insurance policy won't pay out on suicide."

"Doesn't matter. There's enough money left to give me a decent send off, and to share between the people who've been good to me. Which reminds me. I haven't had an invoice from you for the changes to my Will."

"Forget it, Ray. Have this one on me. You've been a client, and a friend, of mine for what, twenty years or so. I owe you this, if it's the last time we do business."

"Thanks, Jim. I appreciate it. And all you've done for me in the past."

"My pleasure. Listen. I've no further clients today. Why don't I shut up shop, and take you for a beer?"

"Sounds like a good idea. Where do you fancy?"

"Well, I usually go to the wine bar down the road. It's where all the solicitors, estate agents, and the like, go. Useful for picking up bits of business. But to tell you the truth, I'd rather go somewhere a little more downmarket. What about the Cock? Good pint."

"Fine."

Wait while Jim phones his wife to tell her he'll be home late, and if she wants the car, he's leaving it at the office as he has to entertain an important client. Gives me a wink and a smile as he stresses the 'important'. And off we go. The sleet has now turned to a steady drizzle of cold rain and the wind blows straight in my face. It always has done. It's one of those phenomena which defies explanation. No matter which direction I take, the wind always blows in my face.

Through the doors into the Cock. Which is full of suits! What used to be one of the roughest pubs in town is now the 'in' place for the smart set. Where are the labourers and the brickies? The plasterers and the sparkies? The factory workers and the street-sweepers? Probably down at the wine bar. Looking for the upper-class totty which has taken over this place in a display of inverted snobbery. These lunatics have taken over the working man's asylum. An extensive range of fine ales, and they're all drinking halves! But the landlord will be happy. These lot don't fight every Friday night and wreck the place. Umbrellas and handbags at ten paces. Or else sue each other. Which is probably why Jim's brought me here. His pockets full of business cards. No legal aid for this lot. Top whack professional counsel on hand should anyone cast a slur on somebody's integrity. Daren't even fart in case someone brings a suit against me. For passive flatulence. Still, Jim was right. The beer is good. Obscure brews from around the country. I could taste these for a living. And that would be a living worth living. Savour this moment. Smooth dryness of the ale. Warm clean busy pub. Animated chatter from various groups of drinkers. Like Phil Spector's wall of sound. If you listen carefully, you can pick out individual noises, but the overall effect is one wave of sound. Rising and falling. Coming from different directions. At different pitches and volumes. And washing over me. Raising our voices to talk. About nothing in particular. Jim winding down after a hard day's litigation. Sorting out divorce proceedings, property conveyancing, and wills. Run-of-the-mill stuff. All in a day's work. And after a few drinks, taking me into his confidence. With spicy details of some of the divorce cases he's handling. The woman who won't make love to her husband unless he wears a black bin-liner, with holes cut out for his legs and his willy. And the trouble he's had with his neighbours for emptying their dustbins in the middle of the night and stealing their bin-liners when he felt horny. And the woman who caught her husband in bed with his brother and her father. And ran off to live with her sister-in-law. Tales of ménages a trois. And sometimes quatre. And once even sept. It's life, Jim. But not as I know it.

Jim knocking back the ale. Before turning his attention to whisky. A man of impeccably good taste. Prefers single Malt. And I join him.

"You know, Ray. There's only one drink more exquisite and satisfying than a single Malt."

"What's that, Jim?"

"A double Malt. The measures in here are far too small. A government conspiracy. Of high prices and tiny measures. To ensure that the wheels of the British judicial system don't come off the rails. Which, now and again, they do. But I am pleased to announce that throughout my career I have always acted in the best interests of my clients and maintained the highest of ethical standards."

"I don't doubt that for one second."

"I've built up a thriving business. I make loads of dosh. I'm well-respected.... So, why am I not happy?"

"Of course, you're happy. Who wouldn't be, in your position?"

"Sometimes I just want to pack it all in. Go somewhere. Do something different. Be someone different. Leave the wife to her show-jumping and skiing holidays. And the kids to their private school. And just live! I've spent all my working life studying, training, memorising and practising law. And all that time I've concentrated on making a living. But I haven't actually had a life. Just a living. Which is why, very, very occasionally, I get very, very, very drunk."

"And this is one of those occasions?"

"It is indeed. I feel the need to get extremely inebriated. And perhaps sing a mucky song and drop my trousers and fart on this lot. And then go on to a brothel and take a whore up the arse."

Both of us becoming somewhat the worse for drink. Jim returning from the Gents staggers into an insurance broker, spilling his half pint down the front of his suit jacket, and then shrugging off his complaints, telling him in his business he should know better and should have taken out insurance against such an event. And if he wishes to argue the toss, he'll take him back to the office, pull from a high shelf a dusty weighty tome of legal case studies, and beat him around the head with it. Then turning his attention to the broker's two female friends, young girls, who in all probability work for him, since he's too fat and boorish to command their attention otherwise.

"Why are you two lovelies with this clown? Look at him! Cheap shiny-arsed suit. Shirt buttons straining to keep a huge gut in check. Probably a tiny penis to match his IQ. Threadbare head, ill-disguised by courtesy of Rugs R Us. Why don't you leave this sad specimen and come with me and my good friend Ray to the casino?"

"I'd love to. But I'm sorry. Mr Stringer is our boss. We can't just leave him. He's giving us a lift home."

"Come with us. Have a drink. Play the tables. And afterwards have the ride of your life, all the way home if you wish."

"These young ladies are with me. And if you don't stop harassing them, I'll take you into the car park and give you a savage beating."

"You couldn't beat a drum. You fat bastard."

"Try me, you turd shunter."

Time to intervene. Reluctantly pulling Jim aside. And tell him quietly not to push his luck with this insurance broker who in his spare time is an amateur wrestler by the name of the 'Masked Mangler', whose speciality is tearing off his opponent's head and pushing it down his trunks.

"His trunks, or his opponent's?"

"His."

"In that case, I shall apologise most profusely. I have absolutely no desire to have my head placed anywhere near the vicinity of his sweaty groin. In case I find I enjoy it. So, we shall make our excuses and leave. Try our luck on the wheel of roulette."

Allow Jim to make his most gracious apologies, to both the fat man and his companions. And, honour intact, we walk down the road to the casino. Jim greeted by the doorman, who steps aside to allow us entry. Sign the book as Jim's guest. And follow him to the cashier, who pushes chips to the value of two hundred pounds towards him. Jim signs his chit, gives me half the chips and we push between two Chinese at the roulette table. Jim wary. Doesn't place a bet for three spins of the wheel. Watching the punters. Watching the wheel. Then eventually puts a single five-pound chip on numbers one to six. Eyes fixed on the ball rolling and bouncing wildly round the wheel, careering off the studs as the wheel slows. And finally settles in four. Jim ecstatic. Piling up the chips the croupier pushes towards him. And placing two chips on thirty-two and one on thirty-two-thirty-three. Incomprehensible animated chatter from the Chinese as the steel ball comes to rest in thirty-two. Jim does a lap of honour round the table as the croupier dispassionately shovels his winnings towards him. A small crowd gathering, rubbing his arm for luck. Jim flirting with a fortyish woman, saying if you want some real luck, try rubbing somewhere else. And his next bet successful, on one to twelve, when nine comes up. Jim arranging his mountain of chips into separate piles according to their value. The pit boss, who looks more like a pit bull, edging forward to keep an eye on proceedings. Several punters, sensing a winning streak, follow his bets, much to his annoyance, as he continues to win. So out of sheer perversity he refuses to place a bet for five consecutive spins. The crowd beginning to drift away as he places ten pounds worth of chips on zero. Within seconds, the two Chinese have both placed an equal amount on zero, and Jim watches with obvious satisfaction as the ball rolls into twenty-nine, which is covered by my solitary five-pound chip.

"Come on. Ray. Let's get something to eat. We'll play later, when the noodle-eaters have gone."

"Fine. As long as you let me pay. With my winnings from your stake money."

"Certainly."

Past the row of fruit machine players feeding in coin after coin. A machine vacant. Jim inserts a pound and presses the button. The reels spin and come to rest in sequence. Lights flash and an electronic jingle plays. And the machine clunks out fifty pounds into the tray beneath.

"My lucky night, it appears. Wait here, Ray. I must pay a call."

Sit at a table and order a coffee from this beautiful brunette in her long emerald green dress. Have a smoke. Jim talking to two young men, who follow him into the gents. The coffee arrives. Give the girl a fiver and a smile which says I'd love to give you more. She returns a smile which indicates not a chance you dirty old git. No sign yet of Jim. Better check he hasn't had a mishap. Push through the two doors into this large spotlessly clean tiled room. Jim bent forward by a washbasin, his back to me. Hope he's not puking. The two young men step forward to bar my way. As Jim turns to face me. A rolled-up tenner in his hand. Traces of white powder round his nostrils. And a thin line of cocaine on the pale green tiled surface by the sink.

"Hey, Ray. Come and join me in chemical heaven!"

"No thanks. Clean your face. We're leaving."

"Not just yet. I've started so I'll finish."

"Leave it, Jim. You don't need this."

"It raises my life above its humdrum level. I would recommend it to anyone who feels life has little in the way of excitement."

"Please yourself. It's your life. But don't ever again offer me advice on what to do with mine."

"Hang around, Ray. The night is still young. We're going to have a meal."

"Forget it. I'm going back to the hotel. Get real, Jim, and go home."

"Real? Real? This is real, Ray. This is the reality. The rest of it, the career, the respectability, that's all a facade. Like that huge mahogany desk in my office. You must have noticed it."

"Can hardly miss it. It takes up half your office."

"Exactly. But what is it exactly?"

"A huge mahogany desk that fills half your office?"

"Huge pieces of MDF. Cheap fibreboard, that's all. With the thinnest possible of mahogany veneers covering it. That's all it is. A facade. A sham. An illusion."

"But it looks the real thing. Imposing, and expensive."

"Precisely, Ray. But it's simply an illusion which must be maintained so that the reality can co-exist alongside and you can slide from one to the other. At will. Time after time. Until eventually the distinctions become blurred, and reality becomes the illusion and vice versa."

"I don't understand you."

"Choose your life, Ray. You are not one person. I know your respectable persona. Your veneer. But there must be another Ray, who has different needs, desires, as yet unexpressed, perhaps as yet unknown. Find yourself, Ray. Explore the reality you have submerged beneath The Great Illusion. Be a martyr. But don't die for your cause. Wear your veneer, but remember that's all it is. The real you lies elsewhere. Beyond your veneer-ial disease."

Collect my overcoat and exchange goodnights with this burly man on the door. Short walk to the hotel, hunched up against the cold. The streets empty and quiet, except for the distant sound of police sirens. Step round this broken glass and splashes of puke. Like pavement pizzas. And if Jim kills himself with his cocaine addiction, I wonder who will deal with my affairs. To whom does he bequeath his workload? Waste of a good man. Nobody, these days, seems happy with his lot. Except maybe Duncan, who refuses to allow adversity to pull him down and quench his indomitable spirit.

And back at the hotel where a sleepy-looking and unkempt night porter is manning the reception while flicking through a porn magazine, which he pushes hurriedly under the counter as I approach.

"Evening, sir."

"Good evening. Room one-four-two, please."

"There you are, sir."

"Thank you. And could you tell me where I can get something to eat, please."

"At this time? There's nowhere open at this time of night, sir."

"Pity. I'm starving."

"Would you like one of my sandwiches, sir? There's plenty. Sandwiches, pork pie, chocolate biscuits. The wife always puts up far too many for me. I usually end up throwing some of them away. So as not to offend her. Take a couple. Ham alright?"

"Fine. Thank you. Can I pay you for them? I insist."

"Well, in that case, give us a quid."

"I'll give you a fiver if I can have the pie and a chocolate biscuit as well."

"It's a deal. Here, take the whole bag."

"Thanks, but I can't leave you with nothing."

"That's all right, sir. I'll go down to the kitchen in an hour or so and raid the fridge."

A resourceful man. I admire that and wonder if he uses the same routine on all hungry guests. Supplement his meagre income with a little tax-free earning. Shows enterprise. The sort of thing Duncan would do. I've missed him. And briefly toyed with the idea of flying out to join him for a holiday. Get some sun on these thin white legs. But what use is a holiday to me?

I haven't done a stroke of work for months. One of the idle not-so-rich. Bored with this aimless life. A special day tomorrow. Time to move on.

CHAPTER 32

The taxi crunching to a halt on the gravel. Pay the fare and walk wearily towards The Carter's Rest. Much the same as I remember it, except a little dilapidated, and the sign by the car park has been crudely defaced, the C replaced by an F, by someone with a flatulence fixation and an adolescent sense of humour. Over the door, a sign bearing the legend "Diane Pullit. Licensed to sell by retail beers wines and spirits for consumption on or off the premises."

Up the gravel path, through the double doors and into the small lounge bar. Faint smell of polish and Brasso on the gleaming bar rail. A smiling face behind the pumps in this empty room.

"Good evening, love. What would you like?"

"Bitter, please. Pint."

The strong left arm pulling the foaming brown ale through the pump into a shining clean glass. Placing it carefully on the bar towel before me, froth spilling slightly down the side of the glass. And a huge head appearing on the bar at her side, flanked by two massive paws.

"Get down, Olaf! Sorry, love. Did he startle you?"

"A little."

"I'm sorry. He's harmless. Dead soft. The regulars love him. But he knows he shouldn't be behind the bar. Don't you, Olaf? Go on, now. There's a good boy."

Olaf trudging slowly round the bar in my direction. Breathe more easily now the huge beast flops at my feet with a heavy sigh. Opens his jaws and drops a skull on the floor.

"Don't worry love. It's a sheep. A sheep's head. The butcher lets him have one every week. He trots down to the village and sits outside the shop until the butcher takes pity on him and gives him a head in a carrier bag. I think he wants to get him away from the shop doorway really in case he frightens away the customers. But once he's got what he wants he carries it all the way home for me to cook for him. There you are, love. That's 1.70, please."

"Thank you. And do you have a room?"

"Yes, love. A single, is it?"

"Is room eleven vacant?"

"Yes, love. But that's a double. It's thirty-two pounds a night."

"That's fine. I'll take it."

"Would you like to see the room? If you'll just come with me, I'll show you round."

"Top floor, second door on the left, isn't it?"

"That's right. Stayed here before, have you?"

"Yes. A long time ago."

A long time ago. More than fifteen years. The taxi had driven up this driveway and deposited me and my new bride at this remote North Yorkshire inn. Where the landlord and landlady had made a fuss of us and insisted we stay in the "bridal suite", room eleven, at no extra charge. And flowers were placed on the table where we dined, and customers bought us drinks. And more drinks. And toasted our health and future. Until finally we said our goodnights and stumbled up to the room. Where Lucy was sick in the bathroom, and cried. And said sorry she'd spoiled everything. And I had consoled her, saying we had a lifetime left for making love. Fifteen years. A lifetime? And the next morning appearing sheepishly in the dining room to face the fried breakfast. Heads pounding, stomachs lurching as the sizzling sausages and bacon were heaped on to warm plates, then a scoop of beans and a runny fried egg. And fried bread and mushrooms to complete the cholesterol nightmare. And then a long bracing walk along the cliffs on that cool breezy April morning, carrying the hamper the landlady had prepared for us. Lucy laying out the red and white checked tablecloth. Sharing out the sandwiches and pouring the coffee as she poured out her hopes and dreams for our life together. Now cruelly ended.

"Another pint, love?"

"Sorry?"

"Ooh, you were miles away, weren't you? Would you like another drink?"

"Yes, please. And are you doing meals tonight?"

"Yes, love. Dining room opens at seven. That's when the barman comes in to take over in here. Then I can look after the kitchen and dining room. That is, if he comes in on time. He's not very reliable. And when I'm not watching him, he's helping himself to drinks and stealing from the till."

"Get rid of him."

"I'd love to. But it's hard to get staff out here. When my husband left me, he took the barmaid with him. Randy sod, he was. I was glad to see the back of him, but Barbara was a good barmaid. I asked her to stay, but she said she wanted to marry him and would I give him a divorce and could she have a reference. And so, I'm stuck with Mick. Unless you'd like the job. Have you ever worked behind a bar?"

"No."

"Well, I could teach you."

"Thanks, but I'm just passing through."

"Shame."

Followed by the faithful Olaf, I make my way through to the dining room where the few other diners watch quizzically as I insist that two places be set at my table. Ordering garlic mushrooms and prawn cocktail, sirloin steak and chips and a tuna fish salad. And a bottle of Muscadet which I pour into two glasses. Sipping alternately from each as I attack the food, slipping the odd chip to the slobbering hound at my feet. Then two coffees. Finally, a Grand Marnier and a Tia Maria. All the while gazing silently at the empty chair opposite.

Then back to the bar where I order another pint and have a laugh and joke with the regulars. Watching Mick take coins from the till for the fruit machine, cursing when he's lost it all.

"I'm a nudge short of the jackpot!"

"I agree entirely."

"What do you mean?"

"Wasting your money on a fruit machine. But then it's not your money, is it?"

"What's it to do with you?"

"Nothing. If you wish to steal from your employer, that's your business."

"Who's stealing? I look on it as a company perk. Do you know, I have to get a taxi here and back home again every night, just to work in this crappy place for a crappy wage. Costs me more than I earn. So, I have to rely on the perks. Diane doesn't mind. She needs me."

"How would you know what Diane needs?"

"Listen. I know how to run a bar. I know everybody who comes in here. I know what time they come in, what time they leave, and what they drink."

"So, Mick. What do I want?"

"Same again?"

"No."

"Well, what, then?"

"I thought you would know. But while you think about it, I'll have a small Malt."

"Coming up."

"Thanks."

Take a small sip, and feel the harsh burning sensation of cheap firewater.

"Mick, this isn't a Malt."

"Of course, it is. You watched me pour it."

"I did. But it's not a Malt. Now pour this down the sink and give me a decent malt whisky, and a full measure, before I ring Customs and Excise, Weights and Measures, Trading Standards, and anyone else whose number I can lay my hands on."

"Bloody tourists!"

Drinking steadily until closing time by which time Diane has finished in the kitchen, poured herself a drink and sat down beside me at the bar.

"I'm so glad you seem to be enjoying yourself. You looked so lost and alone in the dining room."

"I'm fine. I've quite enjoyed myself in the company of your indispensable barman."

"Mmmm. He's a bit full of himself."

"He's passing off blended whisky as malt. Unless it's your doing."

"No. Certainly not. He sets up behind the bar."

"Well, your malt whisky isn't."

"Isn't what?"

"Malt."

"You can tell the difference?"

"Certainly."

"Then I'll get rid of him."

"You do that."

"I will."

"Good."

"But then I'm left with the problem of replacing him."

"It's not a problem. Arsehole replacement will soon be as common as heart transplants."

"You've a healthy appetite for such a slim man. I like that. I like to see a man enjoying his food. Keeps a man's strength up. Never know when he may need it."

The bar emptying as the customers grudgingly accept that Diane is in no mood for a late session. Draining my glass, I pat the sleeping Olaf, say my goodnights and stagger to my room. Where I undress, hanging my clothes neatly in the wardrobe as years of Lucy had conditioned me. Pee away several pints, wash, clean my teeth and slide naked beneath the duvet of the double bed to seek the private world of dreams. Of happier days. Of Lucy. Of our life together. All of which ended the same way. With her death.

And in my fitful restless sleep, she comes to me again. I hear the door opening slowly and sense the presence in the room. Which approaches the bed and lies down snuggling against my back. Turning over to embrace Lucy. To touch her hair. To kiss her face. And feel instead the slobbering jowls of the snoring Olaf, who lets forth a long doggy fart and snuggles closer.

A nightdress-clad figure in the doorway groping for the light switch. Which flicks on to reveal my sleeping face being licked by Olaf's sandpaper tongue.

"Oh, Jesus! Olaf! Get down! Come here! You naughty dog!"

Olaf reluctantly climbing off the bed and padding slowly from the room.

"I'm ever so sorry, love. Jesus! What's that smell? I'll have to open the window."

Suddenly deprived of Olaf's warmth and feeling the cold breeze through the open window, I give a shiver. Diane noticing and sits on the edge of the bed.

"I'm sorry. You're cold now. Let me warm you up."

"I'm OK, thanks."

"I insist. It's the least I can do. There how's that?"

"That's nice. Thank you."

"Let me take my nightie off."

"OK."

"There, how's that?"

"Nice."

"Feel them."

"Mmmm."

"Do you like them?"

"Mmmm."

"I thought you would. I've always had good tits. I'm quite proud of them."

"And so you should be. They're lovely."

"Thank you. Do you mind if I touch it?"

"Feel free."

"Thanks. Oooh, it's big. God, I need this. Can I put it in?"

"Yes."

Diane straddling me, huge breasts dangling over my face. Gasping as I enter her, then riding furiously, finally collapsing on my chest with a sigh of relief.

"Wow! Sorry about the noise. I've always had noisy orgasms. It's sometimes embarrassing when the hotel's full. I get some funny looks at the breakfast table sometimes. Did I embarrass you?"

"No."

"Good. Can you do it again?"

"I don't think so. Not yet."

"I bet you can."

"I'll try."

"I'll help."

Pulling back the duvet. Her tongue tracing a trail of saliva down my chest, down my belly, to my bush. Where her mouth quickly breathes life into my limp penis. And slowly sucks the life back out of it.

And in the morning enjoying a full breakfast of thick rashers, sausages, eggs, tomatoes, mushrooms and fried bread. Served by a smiling Diane who hums little tunes as she works. Telling Olaf to take his skull and play in the beer-garden. Not to disturb her guest who needs his breakfast in peace to regain his strength. And Olaf trots obediently away. And Diane kissing me gently on the cheek and whispering 'would you like anything else?'

"Do you have to go?"

"Yes, Diane."

"Olaf has really taken to you. I can tell. I've never known him let go of his food for anyone but me. It's his way of telling you he likes you."

"Not many people show affection by dropping a half-eaten sheep's head at your feet."

"Dogs aren't as complex as humans. They either like someone or they don't. They don't go on looks or intelligence or prospects or personality or anything like that. They go on instinct. Feelings. They can suss someone immediately. The good or the bad. They're real judges of character. And Olaf thinks you're a good guy."

"And what do you think?"

"I go along with the expert. Seems to me you've had your share of unhappiness."

"I don't know. I'm not sure what constitutes a fair share."

"Me neither. But I get up each morning. Look forward to whatever it brings. Because I never know when someone like you might turn up on the doorstep."

"Someone like me could bring you sadness and misery. Break your heart."

"I doubt it. Olaf wouldn't let you."

"I have to go."

"I know. But not until you've paid your bill. And I won't give it to you. Until you give it to me. Just once more. Before opening time. Then you can help me move some barrels and crates in the cellar in return for lunch. Then, if you must, you can go on your way. Wherever it is you have to go."

"I have a date with destiny."

"In that case, you'll go with a full stomach. And in a state of sexual satisfaction."

In spite of myself, I can't help liking this woman. Who gives. Not takes away. Who demands nothing from me but a little passing warmth. She doesn't collect trophies, like Duncan does. She just brightens her life with casual embraces. Grazes, and moves on.

CHAPTER 33

Holdall in hand, I walk slowly down the road to the stile. Clamber over into the field. Seagulls banking and swooping overhead. And depositing white plop on my shoulder. The path meandering some five miles, rising gently until it comes to an abrupt halt at the cliff edge. From the holdall I take the red and white checked tablecloth and unfold it on the grass. Delving further to pull out two red plastic plates and a Tupperware box containing four ham salad and two cheese salad sandwiches. Prepared by Diane's loving hands. Sharing them equally between the two plates and placing a paper napkin by each. Pouring two cups of coffee from the thermos. Finally, opposite me on the tablecloth I place Lucy's urn. Enjoy my Last Supper.

And standing there at the cliff edge, the strong breeze at my back.

"Hey, mister!"

Turning to see three young boys striding towards me.

"Hey, mister!"

"What."

"Are you going to jump, mister?"

"That's none of your business. Get lost."

"Only if you are, can we stay and watch?"

"No. This is private and personal."

"Why do you want to jump, mister?"

"My wife's died."

"My mam died last year, but dad hasn't jumped."

"Go away."

"What's in the jar, mister?"

"My wife."

"Cor. Can we have a look?"

"No."

"Meanie. Well, what about them sandwiches? Have you done with them?"

"Yes. Help yourself."

"Ta."

Watching as they devour three sandwiches between them, the youngest wiping snot on his sleeve as he eats.

"Are you going to jump now, mister?"

"Not yet."

"When?"

"Tonight."

"What time?"

"Eleven."

"Aw. We have to be home by nine."

"Tough."

"We'll be back first thing in the morning."

"I won't be a pretty sight."

"No problem! We've seen a dead body before. Last year. A woman. Mark lifted her dress up to see what was underneath, and she'd shit herself."

"I'll bear that in mind."

"Thanks for the sandwiches. See you."

"'Bye."

I used to think my life was so complete. But since Lucy went, it's been full of thrills. And spills. Of semen mostly. This is the life that Duncan should have had. But it's not for me. All I ever wanted was a job, a home and a good woman. And now I have none of them. Not even the knowledge that my wife was faithful to me. As I had been to her. And what if I'd found out earlier in our relationship? Would our marriage have survived? Who knows? All the same, I'm glad I know now. She was human after all. And a little of the shine has rubbed off her halo.

Seated again, staring out to sea as darkness falls. A long tunnel of darkness, pierced by the regular sweep of light from the lighthouse up the coast. And in the distance, a return of light. Little more than a twinkle on the horizon, but a definite light all the same. My mind returning to thoughts of Lucy, for many years my light, but now so far away. Where is she? When I die, will we be re-united? Or will we be simply two separate piles of dust? Only one way to find out.

Rising to my feet, clasping the urn of Lucy the Angel Whore hard to my chest, and stepping forward to the cliff edge. Imagining how it will feel. The curious feeling of floating yet falling. Of peace. Of rest. Images flashing into my brain. Like flipping through a photo album. An ever-changing kaleidoscope of faces and places swirling and merging. A smile crosses my face as I visualise and recognise each one, then quickly flip to the next. Brief snapshots of our brief lives. Random glimpses of events and experiences which have meaning only to us. On this day which is the anniversary of our first meeting. Goodbye Duncan. Keep the pole raised and ready. Goodbye Plopper and don't do disrespectful things on Scamp's memorial sundial. Goodbye the E's. You were Everso kind. I hope you will keep Plopper in the manner in which he would like to become accustomed. Goodbye Julie. I hope you find happiness with your new man and your new teeth. Goodbye, you septic isle, you grey unpleasant land. Lucy, will you be waiting for me? I hope you have a drink ready for me when I arrive. I could use one. Lucy, I loved you. So much. And I forgive you. But why did you deceive me?

"Goodbye."

The urn flying through the air. Twisting. Tumbling. The lid flipping off and the ashes dispersing in the wind. As the urn disappears into the dark. Falling to meet the swelling waves with a distant dull splash. And sinking down, down. To be pulled and lashed by the strong current. Dashed against the cliffs by the tide. And finally gone. Here the illusion ends and reality begins.

Feel pressure at the back of my leg. And the warmth of breath. Turn to look down into the mournful eyes of the giant Olaf. Dogged by this malodorous canine, who playfully drops his sheep's skull at my feet and flicks his tail languidly. Pat the beast and feel the rasping tongue on my hand. A friend to ensure I don't die alone. Sit down on the dampening grass and pat his muscular shoulder while he gnaws at the skull, bone splintering from the pressure of powerful jaws. Open the bag and extract the malt. My constant companion. Twist out the cork and take a long pull. Feel the instant warmth. I haven't the guts to step off the edge into oblivion. I'd rather sit here all night and die of exposure. A less gruesome sight to greet the kids in the morning. Spare them the nightmares. I shall drink the bottle, and sleep. Never to awake. Leave this life of false dawns, treachery and dashed dreams. No one to mourn my passing. An unmarked grave after an inquest which nobody will attend. No note to indicate suicidal intentions. Death due to misadventure. Balance of mind possibly disturbed by recent events.

A trademark fart from Olaf breaking the silence. Disperses the smell with a lazy waft of the tail. Another pull of the whisky. All quiet save the grating sound of teeth against sheep bone. Feel the cold now but I'll sit on my coat rather than wear it. Can't stand the cold damp striking through the seat of my pants. Don't want to die suffering from piles. Swig the malt. Goodnight, furry friend. It's time you went home to your mistress. Which is what I probably should have done if only I hadn't closed my heart. But no matter. I feel at peace. Ready to accept the inevitable. No fear, breathing steadily and easily. Heart maintaining its rhythm. Light up a fag, take a drink. This would be extremely pleasant were it not so cold and dark. Shivering now. Take a deep breath and a deep drink. Olaf snoring. Chest rising and falling in long even movements.

One last long drink and time now to lay down and close my eyes. No second thoughts. No last-minute change of heart. And no Samaritans. Goodnight, Olaf. Sweet doggy dreams....

And dreams of being reunited with Lucy, and mum and dad, and Scruff. Happiness and gaiety. Laughter and love. And I hold Lucy in my arms and she says 'I'm sorry', and her beautiful face fades away in a mist and when it reappears she's Julie and I say 'I'm sorry' and her face fades and I'm holding someone whose face I can't see. However hard I try, her face is hidden from me. But she's warm and she loves me. I know. I just know. But I can't quite make out who she is. I know her, and yet I don't. And Scruff flinging himself upon me. Knocking me to the ground in his delight. Lying close against my chest, his hot breath on my cheek. Warm wet sandpaper licks on my nose. The warmth and weight of his body almost suffocating me. And I can hardly breathe. The immense weight on my chest holding me down. And the light exploding against my closed eyelids. Growing brighter and warmer. And a voice whispering 'come back' soft and low. Stay with this dream. Frightened to open my eyes in case it is only a dream. And frightened to open them in case it isn't. But I have to know. I have to know.

And as I open one eye I'm staring straight into the sleepy face of this canine. Not Scruff. Olaf! Lying on my chest.

Keeping me warm and alive. Stayed with me through my dark night. Licked my face. Kept me here. And now the sun is warm on my face. Push him gently aside. Stretch my aching limbs. My clothes damp and smelling of dog. And as I stand, I almost lose my balance through nausea and drunkenness. Put out a hand to steady myself. And feel Olaf's broad back between me and the cliff edge. He pushes forward so that I fall on my back. And resumes his position laid alongside me as I snuggle up to share the warmth of his body. Reach out my hand towards the discarded bottle not yet empty. And Olaf emits a low warning growl.

"OK, Olaf. Point taken. Go on now. It's time you went home."

CHAPTER 34

A rapping on the front door of the Carters' Rest. Diane busy hoovering and preparing for another long day, sighs and walks through the lounge to pull back the bolts and turn the key. Pulls open the door and smiles a tired but welcoming hello.

"I've brought your dog back. And I'd like to enquire about a job."

And so, I shall spend the rest of my days serving drinks to the most obnoxious of customers, and my nights sharing the warm bed of the warm Diane. I will be the genial host, with a smile and a joke for all. I will be the hard-working, conscientious landlord who will transform the sleepy hostelry into a thriving business. I will love life, and seize the day. And I will be The Great Raymondo, the Great Illusionist, who has finally made his beautiful assistant, the Lovely Lucy, disappear. Forever!

THE END.

Printed in Poland
by Amazon Fulfillment
Poland Sp. z o.o., Wrocław